Looking Through the Shadows
◊ Book 3 ◊

We Always Fight

Michelle Lee

BLUE FORGE PRESS
Port Orchard, Washington

For Stacy and Chad—
Without their help, this book wouldn't exist.

In honor of Risa and Dan—
Who jumped into this adventure with me.

Looking Through the Shadows
◦ Book 3 ◦

We Always Fight

Michelle Lee

The Early Years

Chapter 1

I shuffled my feet and hid in the overgrown shrub with prickly leaves. My dad would be so mad at me if they put a hole in my shirt. I'll never hear the end of how I won't learn the value of a dollar if I don't appreciate the things I have, and he'll make me buy my own, so I remember the lesson.

The thud of footsteps alerted me that they were closer; these older kids lived a couple of streets over on what my mom calls the wrong side of town. I'd been their target for a couple of months now. Small, scrawny, and bookish are my dad's words to describe me.

They were so close I could smell the stench of stale cigarettes and cheap beer. If they had just asked for my money, I would have given it to them. I wasn't stupid. I could see they were poor and needed to eat. Getting the shit kicked out of me for it wasn't the fun I wanted to have. I considered asking to join them, their gang.

I started to think that my parents, who never paid attention to me unless it was to criticize something, wouldn't notice. They'd notice. Then there were the thinly veiled comments about lowlife hoodlums that made black people look terrible that began popping up in their conversations.

"We ain't neva gonna eat this week!" one of the guys mumbled. I couldn't tell which one it was.

"Shut up! He's here somewhere," the other one snapped. "There's that skinny white chick we could always go for; she's always lookin' at us with those eyes like she wants to lick us."

I froze. Would these two seriously attack a girl? I moved to look, and one of the prickly leaves stabbed me in the eye. Oh, to hell with it. I'd rather get my ass kicked again than have some girl attacked. I rubbed at my eyelid and crawled out, the leaves jabbing me in the back and catching on my shirt.

"I'm right here, don't go hurting any girls." I stood up and faced them across the shrub. Skull and Trigger are what they called themselves. Thugs by necessity, I guessed. I didn't know their circumstances, but I did know that when they put a beat down on me and took my money, they always went and got food.

"Did yo' pussy ass just crawl out from that bush?" Trigger sneered coldly.

"If you're hungry, I can loot the food out of my parents' house and give it to you. You don't have to beat people up for it," I replied lamely. I hadn't recovered from the injuries from last week yet and braced myself for more.

"I don't want your pity," Skull moved closer, but instead of the hard shell I usually saw, there was a crack in it. He was *starving*.

"It's not pity. It's empathy. I've seen you apply for jobs. If I can help, I will. You don't need to beat it out of me," I tried reasoning again. "If it makes you feel better, go ahead; you already know I'm not strong enough to stop you."

"Got that right," Trigger advanced menacingly. Trigger's shoes had holes in them. I sized Trigger up, the older teen was taller than me, but his feet looked close to my size.

"Back off of the nerd. If he wants to give us food, I'm not gonna say no," Skull stopped him. "Your sister needs to eat, man."

"Go to the park down the street," I nodded in that direction. "I'm not sure if my dad is home or not. I'll bring the food to you."

"If you lyin', you won't walk for a week," Trigger threatened me.

I yanked my backpack up and pulled out my hidden stash of allowance from the pocket I had created inside it, all but invisible. "It's not much, but you should be able to get a pair of shoes," I handed Trigger the forty bucks. "I'll meet you at the park with food."

Skull narrowed his eyes at me and took the money that I held out when Trigger seemed like he would launch himself at me. "He's not puttin' you down. You can get shoes for you and your sister with this."

"Give me ten minutes," I called back over my shoulder, half expecting to be tackled and beaten. I kept walking and was mildly surprised when I made it safely home.

My parents were what people considered upper middle class. I can't say I was a big fan of the caste system. Skull and Trigger were victims of their circumstances and trying to survive. They went about it wrong, and I believed they wouldn't be as violent as they were now if they were in my position.

I don't blame them for not trusting me to come back; it's what they've come to expect from people. Poor and black equaled a lot of prejudice among many folks. It could be me in their position, except my parents weren't poor. At least not anymore.

Perception is a funny thing. I looked at my house through their eyes and saw grandeur. It wasn't really unless you lived in a crappy apartment and had no food to eat. Our two-story, four-bedroom house would seem like a paradise. The pristine white leather furniture that no one could sit on except my parent's esteemed company would look like a dream.

I ran around the house to make sure no one was home and quickly filled three bags with as much food as possible. My parents didn't do the shopping, they paid someone else to do it, and I doubted they'd notice it gone.

As an afterthought, I ran up the stairs to the end of the hall where their bedroom was and went to look in my dad's throwaway clothes pile. There were a couple of t-shirts he didn't like the color of, a sweatshirt, and a windbreaker, all of them in brand-new condition. I grabbed them all and beelined for the garage.

I hung the bags of food from the handlebars and opened the door, peering down the street to make sure I didn't see my dad's car coming. Seeing no one, I closed the garage door and jumped on my bike, pedaling as fast as possible to get to the park.

Skull and Trigger would stand out in that park, and I wanted to get there before someone called the cops on them for merely being there and breathing. I rolled into the parking lot and, not seeing them in the immediate area, steered my bike onto the little path that wound through. I was young but not stupid about the prejudice that still ran through our society, even if I hadn't experienced it.

I found them near the back at one of the picnic benches, slightly out of plain view. I hopped off my bike and grabbed the bags of food. Trigger eyed me warily but pounced and tore into an apple before I could blink.

"These might be a little big, but they were in my dad's throwaway pile," I told them and tossed the clothes down next to the bags of food.

"Why?" Skull asked me, his voice guarded.

"He didn't like the colors." I hung my head in shame at the waste. My dad liked to think I didn't know the value of a dollar, but I knew. I saw it every day in school. I saw it in the way poor people of every race got treated. It just seemed worse with black people.

"Not why about the clothes, why are you helping us?" Skull reworded his question.

"I could be where you are. I would hope someone would help me. It's not charity. It's kindness. It's not pity either. The way I see it, if you don't have to worry about where your next meal is coming from, it gives you time to try and better your circumstances instead of fighting simply to live." That was more words than I have ever shared with these two.

"You want us to be like you?" Trigger asked

around a mouthful of apple.

"No. I want you to be you, but not worried about surviving or making sure your sister survives. If you want to make this an equal trade, help me be stronger. Teach me how to fight back," I gestured to my body. "Help me not be a victim."

"You start hangin' with us, and yo' momma gonna be the one kickin' yo' ass," Trigger snarled, but the threat retreated from his voice.

"You get free time?" Skull shot a warning look at Trigger.

"As long as my homework and chores get finished, grades are up, and I'm not in their way, my parents don't pay attention to me."

"How old are you?" Skull asked while he was digging around in one of the bags.

"Fourteen. Does that matter?" My question came out snarkier than I intended, and Trigger raised his eyebrows at me. "What?"

"I thought you was younger," he responded and tossed the apple into the nearby trash bin with a perfect arc.

"How would this work?" Skull ignored Trigger. "I think they'd notice food missing every day."

"There's enough food here to last a couple of days," I told him. "You let me know when you need food, and I'll bring it. We can meet here or somewhere else. The days I bring you food, you give me a lesson or something."

"Cool," Skull decided. "First lesson, brace yourself." He stood up fast and shoved me. I fell right to the ground on my ass. "If you had braced yourself, that wouldn't have happened."

I stood up and brushed myself off, fighting back against the anger that flooded me. "How?"

"Like this," Skull moved one of his legs behind him. "If someone pushes me, I'm gonna shift my weight to the back leg, giving me momentum to push my body forward when I retaliate."

Simple physics; I should have figured that out. "You just stand like that all the time?"

"Nah, but I'll move a leg back if I think something could happen. I lose my edge if I'm down, so I do what I can to stay up. Start doin' pushups at home, strengthen your arms and your back," he told me, sitting back down.

"Next time, pick somewhere else for us to meet," Trigger added. "We gonna get busted if we walk from here with bags. Someone'll say we stole this shit."

"Yeah, I thought about that. Next time, just let me know where you want me to go." I looked around to see if we were getting watched. My family was the only black family in this neighborhood, and sadly, people watched us all the time. It made me feel like a museum oddity.

"Pushups, sit-ups, jumping jacks," Skull told me, standing up again and gathering up two of the bags. "Do those. We'll see you again in a couple of days. We'll be somewhere on your route home from school."

"Thanks," I moved to get back on my bike. "Go out through this little patch of woods. A small bike path will let out near a convenience store the next street over."

Trigger eyed me some more but kept his mouth

shut and followed Skull back into the park's forested area. I headed back home, wondering what kind of reception I'd get if I asked my mom to get me a weight set.

Chapter 2

The next day, I got my chance while my dad was griping about me not participating in any sports while having a dinner that he paid someone else to make. I wasn't a well-rounded enough son for him to be happy with; I was too much about learning and not enough physical. No college would ever want me because I wasn't active.

I knew that excuse was total shit, but it worked to my advantage. "Get me a weight set, and I'll start working on building muscle. Maybe by next year, I'll be strong enough to try out for the football team."

It was funny how quickly my dad shut his mouth after hearing me say that. He almost looked proud. His high school football career was something he often liked to throw in my face; without that, he believed he wouldn't have gotten into college. It was a strategic move on my part because my being smart wasn't enough for him to brag to people about at work.

My dad was one of those people that liked to hear themselves talk. He took me to a sporting goods store after dinner. He spent an hour telling me how strong he was and his fit physical condition helped him in everyday life; another shit excuse. My dad didn't do anything but work, from what I saw.

He wasn't physically in lousy condition, but he didn't do anything to maintain it. I was beyond caring. I only wanted to get stronger, learn how to keep from getting my ass kicked, and get the hell out of their house. Simple goals.

If trying out for football would get me there, then that's what I'd do. I wasn't planning on college, not anymore. I was looking for the quickest way out from under my parents' roof. Going to college would mean I'd either need to get a full-ride scholarship somewhere of my choosing, or I'd have to go somewhere my parents wanted me to go. I'd need to choose a field they thought appropriate for a young black man and listen to my dad hold it over my head for the rest of my life that he paid for my education.

I wasn't an unappreciative kid. I knew I had advantages that a lot of others didn't. I was just tired of paying for those advantages with pieces of my soul. I understood what's behind it, that they fought against racial and social currents to get where they are, and they didn't want me to feel that. I still felt them. They weren't bad people. They just let their success take over their lives. That's all that mattered to them anymore.

They looked at the downtrodden as a burden. I looked at those less fortunate than me as an opportunity. Unfortunately, some of them looked at me the same way. Loading my new weight set into my dad's shiny new BMW SUV highlighted that.

My dad spent more time with me that night,

helping me set up the bench and showing me the proper technique to using the set than he had in the past five years. It made me sad when I thought about it. I wanted to be successful, but not at the cost of my children if I ever had any.

After he finally left me alone, I started the workout regimen. I could only do three pushups, and I managed twenty-five sit-ups. That would be my benchmark, and I wrote them down in a journal with the date and the note saying goodbye to the old Darius.

I pushed myself hard in P.E. the next day, and by the time I was walking home, I was sore. I saw Skull standing in the shadow of the rundown gas station on the corner. I slowed down, unsure if I was supposed to approach him or not until he beckoned me over with his head.

I crossed the street, looking around for Trigger. The two were usually always together. "Trigger's sister is sick," Skull told me when I got close. "Food's low, and his mom is strung-out. Got anything to hold us over? We can probably make it stretch another couple of days. We've gotten good at that."

I shook my head sadly. "Yeah. Where do you want me to meet you?"

"Can you do the convenience store on the street behind yours?" he asked, his gaze going hard as a car slowed in front of the gas station.

I turned to look, and Skull shoved me back into the shadow he'd been standing in. The car was one of the old Caprice's that some bangers in the projects liked to drive around. Lowered and outfitted with speakers that make your bones vibrate from the thumping of the bass.

Skull stood in front of me until the car moved on, his posture rigid and tension coiled in his muscles. "You see that car again, and you find a way to get the fuck away. They ain't after nothin' but trouble. They won't beat you for your clothes; they'll just kill you. Now they seen you with me, they'll be looking."

Great. "Give me fifteen minutes, and I'll meet you at the convenience store. The Quickie, right?"

"Yeah. Watch at all times, kid." Skull shoved off from the wall and disappeared around the corner, his strides fast and quiet. I thought he moved like a dancer or a fighter.

I practically ran home, not caring if my dad was there or not. The house was empty, and I grabbed another three bags of food. I left a note that I grabbed some snacks and headed to a friend's place to help them study for a chemistry test and would be back before dinner.

There, that should explain a bit of missing food and my not being home. I'd figure out which friend it supposedly was later. Chances are they wouldn't ask. They never have before. I let the disappointment roll off me and realized I had too many bags to carry on my bike. I needed to keep my backpack with me to make my lie believable.

I ran back into the house, dug around my closet for a duffle bag, and then back down to the garage and loaded the food. It was as much of a workout as last night with the weight set. No big deal, I could do this. I got the bag balanced and moved while waiting for the garage door to close. Then, I took off.

Skull was right where he said he would be. I pulled the bags out of my duffle bag for him and watched as he visibly sagged in relief. We were standing in the shadows again, looking like hoodlums making a drug deal; instead, I provided them with life-sustaining food. The system was enough to make me lose hope. Because if anyone saw us, they'd assume it was drugs, not a skinny black kid giving food to a big even blacker kid.

"Will Trigger's sister be okay?" I asked Skull as he loaded the food into his bag.

"Hope so. Shay's a little younger than you, smart, and way too small for her age. I think fragile when I look at her," Skull said sadly. "Their momma uses drugs, but she works, so food stamps are only a small amount, and she buys what she wants with them. Uses her paycheck for her habit."

"Why doesn't Trigger report her?" I leaned my bike against my hip and turned to face the street, still nervous about the warning Skull had given me.

"Neighbors have. CPS came in and said they'd take both of them and put them in homes. Means Trigger'd get split from his sister. Not an option. Things be different over here on this side, kid," Skull's speech varied between proper and slang. The slang dropped when he let his guard down.

I realized it was different; I wasn't stupid. I didn't know Trigger and Skull's stories and how to apply my thought process to see if I could find a way to help. "She goes to school?" I wondered.

"Yeah, not sick, though." Skull set his bag down

behind his feet, and I noticed the spacing how he showed me.

"What about you and Trigger?"

"What about us?" Skull looked warily at me.

"Are you in school?" I pushed him.

"Nah, man, we gotta find money," Skull grumbled. "My mom works but spends it on herself. She don't care none that I'm hungry. I can't apply for help because I'm not an adult. There's no sense in me going into a foster home; I'll take care of myself."

"Beating kids up for money and food isn't taking care of yourself. I know you are doing what you have to do to survive, but I think that life is taking a toll on you. Why don't you get a GED, and at least that can help you find a job?" I thought out loud, absently kicking the store wall with my heel.

"Costs money," Skull moved and stopped my leg. "I probably couldn't pass anyway. I'm not dumb, but I don't know all the shit I need to know."

"I can help with that," I straightened up. "I'll get a GED book from the library, and we can use that as a guide. Most places only hire students who can prove they are in school and with their parent's permission or high school graduates. I know the test costs, but I'll save my allowance and help with that."

To my ears, it sounded like a good plan. It was actionable and attainable. I was a straight-A student and in all the advanced classes. I was actually on a course to graduate with my A.A. degree while I graduated high school if I stayed on track and stuck to my plan. I knew I could help him enough to get him to pass.

"Why, man? Why you wanna do all this for someone that kicked your ass?" Skull asked me again.

"You aren't so bad. I hardly have friends, you are helping me, and I plan to make tracks when I graduate. I help you, you help me, we both get better lives out of it," I plotted. "I mean, if you want to stay here and have this be your life, I guess that's your choice. I want more. I don't want to worry about whoever was in that car. I want to be someone that people look at and know they shouldn't mess with, but I wouldn't turn my back on them when they needed help."

Skull studied me in that detached way he had that made me feel like he would kill me or hug me. Either way, I just wanted him to do whatever he would do. There was a restless feeling in my soul that made me feel like the place I was at right now, at this moment, was a crossroads that would change things forever. I was ready for the first step.

"Trigger too?" Skull finally asked.

"If he wants," I shrugged. "I don't want my life decided for me by this," I gestured around me. "I make my own choices. That's what you guys gotta figure out."

"I can't tell if you're playin' me, or you serious?" Skull rocked back on his leg, then forward again.

"No games," I held out my hands in front of me, palms up. "It's win-win. You two get to try and move past this, and I get skills that will help me get to where I want to go."

"You're calculating," Skull decided. "I'm in. I'll talk to Trigger about it tonight. How soon you think you can teach us what we need to know to pass?"

"Depends on what you know already. I'll check out the book tomorrow. My dad got me a weight set because I told him I'd try out for football if I could gain some strength. He was all about that. I got it all set up and started a journal with what I was able to do to start, and I'm going to try to build on that," I told Skull.

"Yep, calculatin'. Add squats," Skull told me, picking up the bag of food, the slang coming back to his voice. "You're under my protection now. I ain't part of no gang shit, but that's why they stalkin' me. I turned 'em down and pissed 'em off. Gimme your phone," he held his hand out. "I know you got one."

"I don't, but I have a pager," I replied. "Phones are for the rich."

"Memorize my number, then; you need me, page me and add a three at the end of the number so I know it's you," Skull recited his number.

I turned to get back on my bike and head home when Skull's voice stopped me.

"Hey kid, think a gym would hire me after I pass the test to be a trainer?" he sounded almost hesitant.

"I don't see why they wouldn't," I answered. "Make something of me, and I'm your proof you know your stuff."

Skull chuckled and shook his head. "Challenge accepted."

I felt it in my bones. My life had just changed.

Chapter 3

We'd been at it two weeks when I started figuring out how to make this work better. I wasn't against lying to my parents because it was for something good. Studying with Trigger and Skull outside was starting to play games with all of us.

"You guys have nerd clothes?" I asked them suddenly.

" 'Scuse me?" Skull looked up from the book at that.

" 'Splain that," Trigger added with a snarl.

"Like regular jeans and a t-shirt, like I have on?" I clarified, trying to think fast.

"Why? We can't learn in these clothes?" Trigger's temper flared.

"That's not where I'm going with this. I'm trying to think of a better way so we aren't looking at every car that drives by us. It's distracting," I told them. "I'm figuring if you look like high school students, I can say I'm tutoring you, and we can do it inside my house. Where there is food and heat, and no cars are staring at us."

"What 'bout my sis?" Trigger demanded, his eyes

dark and sort of threatening.

"What about her? She can come. Makes it more believable, I think," I glanced over to where she was playing on the swings.

Skull was back to the detached look as he stared at me; I needed to learn how to do that look. It was intimidating as hell because I couldn't read his intentions. I tried to mimic him and must have failed because he started laughing.

"What are you doing?" he asked when he stopped.

"I was trying to copy that look you get," I looked down in frustration and shame.

"We'll work on it. We'll meet you here tomorrow lookin' like you," Skull promised, standing up. "You need to renew these books."

"I will," I gathered them and put them in my bag while Trigger called his sister.

"Think there's a chance we'll pass?" Skull tried for aloofness, but I heard the fear under it. He wanted this.

It hit me in the chest weird, this feeling of giving someone the courage to try more. "Yeah. You both are pretty smart."

"Coming from a fourteen-year-old, I'm not sure what to think of that," Trigger snorted.

"Stuff it, Trigger," Skull growled. "He's fourteen, but he's a hell of a lot smarter than either of us."

There was that strange feeling again. It was like I had power over these guys, and I wasn't sure I liked that. It could be why Trigger was acting so defensive. I hadn't lied to them; they *were* intelligent. "You're better than you think you are," was all I said.

"Bye, Darius." I felt tiny arms wrap around me from behind.

"See you tomorrow, Sprite," I told Shay with a smile. Trigger called her a Sprite because she was so small.

Sometimes she brought her homework too, and I helped her with that before going to play. She was eleven but looked about seven. Skull had been right, she appeared fragile, and I understood how Trigger wanted to take care of her.

Trigger grabbed her hand, and they started walking into the woods while Skull turned to look at me again, his detached look back. I stood there and stared back at him, unsure of where this was going.

"Better," he suddenly smiled. "Hide the emotions." I grinned and hopped on my bike to go back home.

When I walked in, my mom was looking at the mail in the kitchen. She glanced up, saw my backpack, and then looked back down. "Still studying with friends?"

"Yeah. My friends will come here after school if that's okay?" I played to the part that would matter to them. "It's easier than meeting at the park. I'm tutoring them, and they help me with workouts to get stronger. Tutoring looks good on school applications; I read."

"You are right. So do volunteering and sports. It sounds like you are planning for your future, baby." My mom gave me a small smile. I hated how her approval was necessary. I needed to get past that because validation was something that neither of my parents handed out willingly.

"So, you cool with them being here after school?" I asked, making sure. I knew she'd tell my dad. Their new kick was me being more social. It wasn't a lie I was telling them, but it wasn't the whole truth either; shades of gray.

"I think so. You are starting to come out of your shell," she said, pleased as if this was her doing; she could think whatever she wanted.

I resisted the urge to roll my eyes and shuffled off to drop my backpack in my bedroom and start a workout before dinner. From what I had been reading, the strength training needed to include cardio. I added squats to the rotation and then added jogging in place.

I wasn't coming out of my shell; I made things happen. I was forging my path out of here. I don't think my parents quite understood the lengths I would go to make it happen. At least on this route, I got to help people along the way.

Muscles burning and adrenaline coursing through my veins an hour later, I dropped into my chair at the kitchen table and shoveled food in my mouth like I had been starving. The entire dinner conversation revolved around my parents and their jobs. My mom was a tax attorney, and my dad was an executive at a marketing firm.

I excused myself and noticed that their conversation never faltered or paused to acknowledge me. Typical. I went and finished homework that was due the next week, showered, and crashed hard.

When I woke up, I scarfed breakfast down and

beelined for the school to renew the books I had checked out before classes started. That was the only thing that mattered to me today. Make sure I still had the books.

"Aren't you on the honor roll?" The librarian looked at me oddly.

"I am," I answered automatically.

"What are you doing with a GED book?" She stamped it and slid it back across to me. "You aren't dropping out, are you?"

"No," I said, surprised. "I'm helping some kids that fell between the system's cracks learn enough to take the test so they can get jobs."

"Oh," was her soft reply. "In that case, keep them both. You are the only one in twenty years of me being here that has checked those books out. I'll remove them from the system, and it will be our secret. It's a good thing you are doing, Darius."

I felt myself blush and stammered out thanks before rushing to get to class. More and more, I thought that I wanted to be a part of some sort of community outreach program. Like that was a goal for me to work towards accomplishing. I knew it wasn't anything my parents would see the value in me doing lifelong.

During P.E., the teacher noticed an improvement in me and suggested I try out for track. "Track?" I asked. "I'm working on building strength to try out for football."

"That's great; track can help with that, too. Running is a great exercise, and it will help your endurance. Just consider it." The teacher patted me on the back and continued making his rounds.

The teacher planted the seed, and after class, I went to find him. "What kind of commitment is needed?" I asked.

He told me the season duration, the practice lengths, and the gear I would need and sent me home with an information sheet to give my parents. I'd need a physical and their permission, naturally.

That wasn't my concern. My concern was how much time would it take away from me to help Skull and Trigger achieve their goals? I only thought it was a little strange that I valued their opinions more than my parents. I'd bring it up to Skull when I saw them.

Chapter 4

Two weeks later, I found myself on the track field, my t-shirts fit a little tighter and my energy a little more robust. Skull, Trigger, and Sprite were in the stands, all three studying from what I could tell. The librarian had given me a couple more books to use, and Trigger devoured them. I caught the looks some of the other team members sent their way. It made me try harder.

I'd told them I thought they were ready to take the test, but I only had enough money for one of them to do it so far. Skull thought Trigger should go first since he had a sister he was taking care of; I thought Skull should go first since he cared for both of them.

I made it through tryouts, and I was pleased I wasn't the worst. I fell somewhere on the lower side of average. I was eating a lot more food than usual, which my parents had noticed, but instead of ridiculing me for it, they just had the lady that did the shopping for them stock up on more.

I was starting to move like Skull. His training with me helped, and the running gave me endurance. Practices were exhausting, and I loved it. Something was freeing in running this way. The changes that it brought out in my body were helpful too.

When my first meet rolled around, I was more than shocked to find my dad sitting in the crowd next to Skull and Trigger, who were not in the plainclothes they typically wore to the house. I didn't see derision on my dad's face; instead, I saw pride.

It knocked me back a few steps as I stretched. That was new. I wanted to clutch on to it and hold it close, and I was afraid it wouldn't last. As much as I tried to steel myself against it, that look wormed its way through the carefully constructed defenses I'd built against my parents.

I shook it off and mentally prepared for the competition. Besides a science fair, this was my first time competing in anything, and my nerves became strung tight.

"Darius!" I turned to see Sprite leaning on the chain-link fence around the field. Her clothes were a bright dash of color against her upturned beaming face.

"Hi, Sprite!" I jogged over and gave her a quick hug.

"Kick some ass," she giggled and hugged me back.

"Go back and sit with your brother." I grinned, knowing I should call her out for the language. I couldn't; she was too cute. "I don't want you getting knocked around down here."

"I will," she promised. "Just wanted to wish you good luck."

"Thanks." I stood there and watched until she

climbed back up and sat next to Trigger. I saw him nod at me in gratitude.

"Cute cheerleader," a deep voice from behind me said.

I turned and saw one of the seniors stretching. "She's a good kid," I mumbled and moved away from him. He was one of the sprinters, and he was fast. Tall, wiry, and had a strength you would expect to see in a bodybuilder.

Something told me I needed to be wary of him, and my suspicions were confirmed when I saw him glancing up at Skull with anger. I didn't know everything Skull was involved with, but I knew he wasn't a bad guy. Skull had a band of followers that I heard talk about, people called them a gang, but he'd told me he was part of no crew. They might well be, for all I knew, but they weren't the same type that had been in that car.

Even when Skull and Trigger had been beating me up, neither of them had weapons, they never went too far, and they wanted to better themselves. That didn't mean I didn't believe they weren't dangerous. I knew they were. I knew they had to be to survive. I was sure of that.

Skull must have felt the weight of the stare. He leaned into Trigger and said something, which made Trigger snap his head up and stare at the guy, Warner, his shirt said, and then looked over at me. Skull got up and made his way down toward me.

Warner stiffened, and I moved to meet Skull at the fence. "Ignore him. He's got issues with me because his sister dated me, and I dumped her crazy ass."

I nodded mutely, not daring to look back. The air filled with tension, and I felt the presence of Warner. The heat coming off his body told me he was standing too close behind me.

"You got no place here," Warner growled at Skull.

"I ain't here for you." Skull schooled his look back to the detached one, and I saw the danger that lurked there. "This is my boy, and I'm here to support him. No more."

Warner said nothing else, and Skull bumped me with his fist and went back up the stands. I turned and saw he was indeed standing too close. Close enough that I could smell him. "He's bad news, Baker."

"No more than you are," I returned. "I'm tutoring those guys; they are trying to improve their lives."

"Be careful," he warned me and walked away.

I hadn't even known I'd been holding my breath until it whooshed out of me. What the hell? That seemed like way more than being protective of your sister. Skull would tell me if I needed to know or be concerned; I felt reasonably sure of that.

I threw all I had into the race I ran. The coach had decided I was a distance runner, so he had me running one of the longer ones. It just about killed me, but I came in second, hearing the loud cheers coming from the bleachers. That might have been the best feeling I'd ever had.

My dad took us out for dinner after the meet, which was nice. Only he talked about all his plans for me and my future the entire time and how he got to brag at work that his son would be a sports star. I didn't miss the sad looks that Skull and Trigger shot me as they started to understand my family life a little more.

It was a different kind of sad than their family experience was. My parents weren't bad people. I knew they loved me, provided for me, and wanted me to have a good life. They had an idea in their heads of who I should be, and it's not something I could ever measure up to or even wanted to try. I'm not the person they thought. I'm not the person they wanted me to be either.

Chapter 5

I looked up at the clock again, impatient to be out of school so I could see how Trigger did on his test. He had crazy sharp math skills, but his weakness was in the English part of the test. I was optimistic he would pass, however.

When the bell rang, I flew out the door and down the street where they usually met me. No one was there, and I waited for a good fifteen minutes pacing back and forth. Feeling dejected, I headed home with my head down, wondering where they were.

I didn't have to wonder long. As I approached my driveway, a body slammed into me from behind and heaved me up off the ground with a loud whoop. Happy that my ass wasn't about to get kicked, I madly grinned when I was dropped back to the ground and spun around.

Trigger looked happier than I had ever seen him before. "You passed?" I asked him.

"Man, I only missed like eight questions!" Trigger shouted and did a little dance.

Skull leaned against the mailboxes, smiling just as widely as Trigger was. "My man is going places," he declared.

"Brother for life, man," Trigger shoved me playfully. "Let's go work you out so I don't owe you so much."

We walked into the house to find a note from my mom telling me to order a pizza for myself for dinner, that both she and my dad would be out late. Using the money she'd left for me and coupons that came in the mail, we got a pizza for relatively cheap, and I saved the rest for Skull's test.

We worked out, fighting a bit more each time as they taught me moves that were more in line with street fighting than with any formal type, but in my eyes, it all counted. There was a growing bond between us that was something special.

Over the next month, it was the same routine, studying, helping Sprite with her homework, and working out. In between track practices and meets, that is. They were at every event to cheer me on, whether at home or away.

Trigger had landed a job and worked during the day while Sprite was in school so he could be with her after she was out. Things were slowly turning around for him, and it gave me a deep sense of satisfaction to see it happening. Trigger was growing up.

Skull would be taking the test in another week, and he received a tentative agreement to be hired at a gym provided he could prove he passed it. Summer and the end of the school year were rapidly creeping upon us.

Two more months, and I was a sophomore. Three more years, and I could get out of dodge. It meant I needed to buckle down, be able to play football, and ace every single one of my classes. My counselor's curriculum was intense, but I would get the credits needed to have my associate's degree come graduation time.

That would mean I could join the military and fast-track myself as an officer and be somewhere else, doing something others needed. That was my goal. I didn't know which branch appealed to me the most, but none would take me unless I got more in shape.

I shared my goals with Trigger and Skull. They disagreed with me joining the military, but they decided to help me get in good enough shape to hack the physical side. That was good enough for me.

We doubled down on the training sessions, and in track, I pushed myself even harder, and the changes became noticeable. Girls were starting to talk to me, another area I sadly lacked in. As much as I wanted to test those waters out, the distraction wouldn't help me.

I badly wanted the distraction. Girls were mysterious, scary, and beguiling. I wanted to experience all of it. My raging hormones wanted it even more than my brain did. My dad didn't help matters by encouraging it either. I heard nothing but how much he enjoyed one-upping his co-workers on the 'my kid did this' game.

That couldn't be what life was like; I held on to the belief that it held more than that. I liked that my life mattered to my parents now that I was amounting to something in their eyes. But I quickly realized that I valued the opinion of Skull and Trigger more.

My parent's validation was something I had always desired. Now that I had it, somewhat, it was making me sick. Skull and Trigger valued my intelligence and opinion, and they praised my goals even if they disagreed. They thanked me for helping them, and my growth made *them* feel validated.

My birthday was next month. I was counting down to eighteen. It was sad to be disillusioned with the world at fourteen, almost fifteen. I shrugged off the daydreaming and finished my homework as a motorcycle's sound roared into my driveway.

Trigger had bought it from someone moving out of his neighborhood and used it to get to and from work. It was great seeing him so happy and doing well. I couldn't wait to see what Skull would do.

I ran to let them in, and we got down to business with practice tests. Skull only had issues with some of the math, which Trigger helped him with; it was our routine in the evenings we had free until it was time for Skull to take the test.

My dad taught me about football, which was a good thing, considering I knew nothing about the sport. It felt a little odd to me, spending time with my dad when it was nothing he had ever really done before. Not like he was now.

It fueled my anger toward him more. Maybe anger wasn't the right word; indifference possibly. The same way he had treated me up to this point. I brushed it off as much as possible, and if forced, I would admit the time spent with him teaching me football was kind of fun.

The week passed in a blur, and suddenly, I found myself a bundle of nerves as I once again waited for the school bell to ring so I could find out how Skull did on his test. Except I didn't get to race home to find out, I had to go to track practice first.

I saw Skull, Trigger, and Sprite in the stands waiting for me halfway through. A crooked smile tilted my lips, and a girl on the team mistook it for a smile at her. She sidled up to me and complimented me on my form at the start.

I still wasn't used to the girls' attention, but it was another thing I found I liked, even if I was a completely awkward nerd in my responses. Trigger had been trying to teach me how to have game, but I don't think it worked.

Claudia was her name; I remembered in the next second. "Uh, thanks," I told her. "You're good too."

"I'm closer to the ground than you are," she replied with a smile.

I couldn't tell if she was flirting or complimenting me. I was way too scared to ask for clarification also. I shrugged because I didn't know what else to do other than spout off statistics about running physics. I didn't think that would win me points in the smooth category.

"You're cute," she gave me a flirtatious smile and pranced away.

What just happened? I pinched myself to see if I was dreaming or not. That was the first time a girl had ever told me I was cute. The sharp sting of pain on my arm assured me that it had been real. I think I floated through the rest of the practice.

When finished, I made my way across the field and saw Skull jumping over the fence, a face-splitting grin on his dark face.

"Man! You did it! You taught me enough to pass that bitch!" He wrapped his arms around me in a bear hug, thumping my back hard.

"Never doubted you. That gym going to hire you now?" I asked, grinning back.

"Yep!" Skull let out an exaggerated sigh. "Feels so good to know I'm gonna have money coming in."

I was happy for him. I grabbed my bag, and we left to celebrate, where the guys promptly started ribbing me hard about being called cute. Life was changing fast.

Chapter 6

Two years flew by like it was nothing. I made the football team and the basketball team. I stayed on the track team, discovered I had an affinity for chemistry, almost blew up the garage, and now I was about to take my driver's test.

I'd grown closer to my dad over the past couple of years, yet my mom remained distant. It bugged me more than I wanted to say, and it also made me work even harder for that distance to be bridged. Good and bad, both.

Even still, she was the one to take me to my driver's test. She looked nervous in the way she fidgeted with her hands. Like she was the one about to take the test. The written exam was simple, and I'd had zero issues with that and passed it with no answers missed.

I'd been practicing driving with both parents and in secret with Trigger and Skull on motorcycles. Man, those machines had gotten under my skin, and I wanted one. I hadn't figured out how to bring that up to my dad yet, and I knew that was where I would have to go with it. No way was my mom going to sign off on that.

When the instructor called my name, my mom

gave me a quick kiss on the cheek and pushed me off. She wasn't affectionate, and it threw me off stride, but I rolled with it. I was confident in my skills and knew this would be a breeze. I was right.

When I came back in with my passing grade, she hugged me, and I swear I saw her eyes all glassy looking. She didn't say anything other than calling me her baby. That alone almost made me cry. I held it together while the clerk took my picture, and on the way out of the licensing place, she held my hand.

"Mom, you okay?" I got the nerve up to ask her.

She handed me her car keys for us to drive home. "I am. Just proud of who you are becoming despite us being lousy at raising you."

I tripped over my feet as I helped her in the car. Nothing could have shocked me more than those words coming out of her mouth. "You are proud of me?"

"Get in, Darius," she smiled at me.

I raced around the car and hopped in the driver's seat, my heartbeat all erratic in my chest. "Mom?"

"Darius, the fact that you even had to ask me that tells me just how bad we have been," she put her hand on my arm. "Even still, you are turning out to be quite amazing. We are both extremely proud of you."

"Thanks, Mom." Why did she choose now to tell me this? Every awful thought I had about getting away from them flew through me at breakneck speed, making me feel like the worst son possible.

I started the car and drove us home. I figured at some point, Skull and Trigger would show up that night to see if I passed the test. We all knew I would, but those two had become my biggest supporters over the past couple of years, and they'd want to celebrate with me.

There was an unknown car in the driveway, and I pulled in next to it, wondering if Skull had gotten a car. My mom had turned in her car seat to look at me, and I didn't feel sixteen anymore; I felt about seven.

"Baby, your dad told me how truly awful we have been to you. He told me how much you have grown and how far you have come, all without us. He feels like he missed out on most of your life, and I do too," she told me softly, tears sliding down her face.

"You have." I couldn't help it. "Here's the thing, Mom. Neither of you started paying attention to me until I started playing sports. I don't know why that's so important to you guys, but I could have gotten some big scholarship or prize for something in my academics, and no one would have batted an eye."

"I'm sorry, Darius. I truly am. I didn't interfere with your schoolwork because you have always had it in hand. You are smart, baby. Super smart. We should have paid more attention to you. I hope it's not too late that we start now?" she asked me. Her face lined with hope, her voice that soft mother tone I'd wanted to hear for so long.

"No, Mom, it's not too late," my voice cracked.

"You aren't going to college, are you?" She reached over and cupped my cheek.

Her unexpected question caught me off guard. "What? Why would you think that?"

A slow, sad smile spread across her face. "Because, this transformation you have gone through, this muscle, the intelligence, the drive. It tells me you have something planned, and it isn't what we think."

"I want to join the military." I heaved a sigh at the admission.

"Why?" she whispered. There was a shocked expression on my mom's face and a significant pause.

"They pay for my schooling, great on-the-job training, travel, helping others," I ticked off. "There's a host of reasons why."

She nodded slowly, the sad look still on her face, and under it, I saw fear. "I understand. I can't say I like the thought of it, but I will say that it makes me even more proud of you. We'll keep it between us for now."

"Dad wouldn't be happy, would he?" I guessed.

She shook her head. "He's not one for that. It doesn't mean he isn't proud of you, but he will think you are wasting your life. Don't interrupt me, Darius," she said when I started to defend myself. "He's allowed his opinions. As a mother, it scares me that you will be in dangerous situations, potentially. I'm proud that you want to take a step and serve to better our country, even if it doesn't treat us as equals. You are right; there are many benefits to doing so as well. It's just something that carries risk. For now, keep doing what you are doing, and if you want to talk things over, I'm willing to listen."

"I want to make a difference," I told her quietly. "I think this is how I can do that. That is also why I'm doing the sports and everything I can get to graduate with my diploma and A.A. at the same time. The sports will help me get to a place where I can pass all the physicals, and the degree will help me if I can get into an officer's training program."

"You've put a lot of thought into this, haven't you?" she reached for my hand.

"I have. The past two years have been about doing everything to get to these goals. I haven't decided on which branch yet, but I think I am leading towards the Marines or the Navy," I replied. This conversation was surreal. I don't even remember when I had a meaningful discussion like this with my mom.

She sucked in a breath between her teeth, her big dark eyes wide. "Navy. Not the Marines."

"Why?" I'd been leaning towards the Marines.

"Feels safer," she shrugged. "I understand your reasons, and as your mom, I'll support you. I don't want to think about you being the first one sent into a dangerous situation. You always hear about the Army and the Marines on the front line."

That was precisely why I thought that, but I kept my mouth shut. "I'd consider the Navy," I answered instead, choosing the path of least arguments. "I'd considered the Air Force as well. I think flying a fighter would be fun."

"Can you forgive me, Darius?" My mom's lips trembled.

I nodded. "Does that mean you will make an effort to be a part of my life now?"

"If you'll let me," she squeezed my hand. "Instead of working this summer, why don't you join a club or something?"

Working got me money. "I applied for a counselor position in one of the youth day camps," I told her. "I thought working with underprivileged kids would be a good way to start helping others."

"You are a lot like your grandfather, Darius. He'd be so proud of you," she said and pulled her hand back. "Let's go in."

I liked how things were turning around with my parents, but there was something inside me, a deep instinct that told me not everything was as it should be. I was too afraid to ask questions and rock this boat. I didn't care if that made me pathetic, either.

I hopped out of the car and raced around to help my mom out, sliding my arm around her. She'd come from the deep south and had raised me to have manners. That was something I had been finding out a lot lately from the females I'd been hanging around with that was appreciated.

"Thank you, Darius," my mother said with a soft smile. Her accent was barely there anymore. It came out when she got overly worked up about something, which usually made me smile.

We walked into the house where I had expected to see Trigger or Skull based on the unknown car out front, but no one was there. My dad came out of the kitchen with a grin on his face. "Did you pass?"

"You know he did; stop with that." My mom playfully swatted at my dad.

"Look at you! All licensed, beefed up, strong and smart! Colleges will be fighting over you, son," my dad crowed. My mom frowned slightly and shook her head at me.

It wasn't a surprise. My dad has always been

upfront with what he saw my future being. Now that my mom knew it didn't align with his vision, I felt relieved. She hadn't tried to talk me out of it, which meant something to me.

I followed my parents back into the kitchen, where my dad handed me a box. "What's this?"

"Open it," my dad said, that big grin still on his face.

I pulled the lid open and saw a set of car keys. I pulled them out and looked at them. "My own set?"

"Your car," my dad corrected. "That car you parked next to is our gift to you."

"Seriously?" I dropped the keys; I was so stunned. "You got me a car?"

"We did," my mom answered. "You're going places, Darius. You need a way to get there."

I didn't even know what to say to that. I crushed my mom in a hug, then moved to my dad and did the same. "Thank you," I choked out. I snatched the keys back up and hauled ass for the front door, flinging it open and tearing out to the driveway.

It was a little Honda coupe, not super old either. Silver, with gray cloth interior and tinted windows. My very first car. I pulled on the door handle, and an alarm shattered the quiet street's air, making me jump.

"I had them add an alarm," my dad said from behind me. "The salesman said this is a popular car that gets stolen a lot. Figured it was better to be safe."

I fumbled around with the keys until I figured out how to silence the alarm and disarm it. "Dad, this is amazing," I said, still shocked.

"So are you, son. I should have told you a long time ago how proud we were of you. It took your friends saying how proud of you they were before it sunk in that your parents didn't even tell you that. Your mom and I decided that we'll pay the insurance as long as your grades stay up where they are. If you decide to get a job, you can save your paychecks for whatever you want to buy," he added.

"Then I'm going to save for a motorcycle," I announced and slid inside the car. I was happy it didn't stink like smoke. It was pretty clean and well maintained. Basic, no bells and whistles, but I also didn't expect my parents to buy me a car. It wasn't like I could complain.

"A dirt bike?" my dad asked me, sounding surprised.

"Nah, a street bike," I told him. "Dirt bikes are fun, but there aren't many trails around here."

"Would you rather me have gotten you that?" he shifted as if unsure about his gift.

"No, Dad. The car is amazing. Unbelievable, truthfully. I can take a girl on a date now," I grinned. Mentally I was trying to figure out which girl to ask out.

He laughed and crossed to the other side of the car. "Come on. Take me for a ride. Let's test her out."

Chapter 7

That summer was a summer of firsts for me: My first car, first job, first tattoo, first time drunk, first blow job, first girlfriend, first time having sex, first piercing, and not necessarily in that order. Those were the happy things. It was also the summer of my first real tragedy.

That something that I had seen in my mom back when I got my license came back up. Something wasn't right, but my parents were very cagey about what was going on. I heard the whispers that fell silent when I walked into the room. The carefully crafted masks they wore told me something terrible was up.

Apparently, they didn't want to tell me, so I did my thing. I worked at the camp during the day. I tutored kids, played with kids, and then had my sexual encounters behind some trees in the woods. Her name was Star, and she was a couple of years older than me and worked as another counselor. She taught me things.

In the evenings after work, when I wasn't learning the fine art of how to make a woman scream my name, I hung out with the guys. Trigger and Skull had gotten their own place, and Shay stayed with them most of the time. When Trigger's mom was sober, she stayed with their mom.

She was there the night I got drunk, which wasn't intentional. Trigger and Skull had been pumping me for information on Star, and one of their other friends handed me a drink. I didn't go there to drink. The longer I talked, the more drinks he gave me until I got smashed.

I stayed the night because I passed out cold on the floor. When I woke up, I found Shay curled up in front of me. I shot to my feet because no way was that acceptable. I was sixteen; I woke up hard all the time. She had grown up in the past two years and was no longer looking like a little girl. My dick didn't know who it was reacting to; it was just reacting.

I knew she had a crush on me, but that could not happen. Trigger would kill me, and she was like a little sister to me. Oh, Jesus, I hope that I wasn't the one that had pulled her to me. Shit. I needed to get out of here.

I checked my watch, scrawled a note that I had to get to work, and took off before anyone woke up. I flew home to shower and change and then headed for work. I was embarrassed and a little worried about Trigger.

"Phew! Dar, you been drinking?" Star asked as I walked up to her.

"I did last night; you can smell it? I showered," I lifted my arms and smelled my pits.

"Yeah, you can smell it. Go eat something," Star pushed me towards the snack area, where she laid out some bagels. "What the hell are you drinking for? That shit won't get you anywhere."

"It wasn't something I set out to do. I never drink.

That was my first time," I argued.

"Well, you can't be around the kids like that today. They'll for sure smell it, and some of them smell that enough at home. Take clean-up duty instead. I'll cover for you this one time, but you're gonna owe me," she winked, getting me hard instantly when she swung her hips.

Biting back a curse aimed at my crotch, I went outside and grabbed equipment to clean and sanitize. Maybe the sanitizer smell will cover the alcohol smell Star could smell. Luckily no one questioned why I wasn't working with the kids today, and I got everything spotlessly clean.

After the last kid left, Star led me into the lake and showed me how much fun swimming naked could be. Her ebony skin looked good wet. Hell, it looked good all the time. Anytime she offered up her lessons, my dick pointed the way.

Star was utterly different from the girls I was used to at school. At least as far as I could tell. She was wild and free; she told me exactly how to use the various parts of my body to do just what was needed to get her off. The girls at school all seemed more subdued. Not that I'd tried to sleep with any of them.

I wasn't under any illusions about what this was between Star and me either. She wasn't my girlfriend, and she wasn't interested in being my girlfriend; she just wanted sex. I was good with that; my body was good with that.

"I'm home," I called out when I walked into the house. "Going to shower!"

I didn't wait to hear any answers back. I just went straight to the bathroom and showered thoroughly, hoping that the smell of alcohol had worn off. My parents were proud of me, finally. I didn't need to give them a reason to change their minds.

When I came back downstairs, both my parents sat quietly at the kitchen table, looking morose. That was the only word I could think of to describe it. There was no smell of food either. "Did you guys eat dinner already?"

"No, son," my dad answered me.

"Want me to go grab something? Order a pizza?" I asked, leaning against the counter. I wasn't sure what to think of the scene in front of me. Maybe they'd been fighting. It happened on occasion, but not often.

"Sit down, baby. I need to talk to you," my mom requested. Her eyes were swollen and bloodshot.

I didn't want to. If I didn't sit down, my mom wouldn't tell me whatever had made her look that way. I didn't want to know. Scratch that, I did want to know, but I couldn't make myself move. Fear had me rooted right in the spot.

"It's okay, Darius. We'll deal with this as a family," my dad's voice was gentle but scratchy.

"Are you getting a divorce?" I blurted out.

"Why in God's name would you think that?" my dad asked, surprised.

"I don't know what to think!" I yelled out of fear.

My mom stood and grabbed my hand, tugging me over to the table. "Never let fear win, Darius. We don't always win, but we always fight."

Something in those words, in the tone she said

them, made my heart clench. "What are we fighting, Mom?"

"I've got cancer, baby. We are going to fight cancer. It started in my ovaries, and it's spreading. Today, the doctor told me that he would start me on chemotherapy first, try to slow it down before they do surgery on me," her quiet words fell like bombs.

"Fuck," I cursed, then winced. "Sorry, Mom."

"I said the same thing, son," my dad excused the foul language. "And a whole lot worse."

I took a deep breath and tried to keep my eyes from tearing up. "How can I help?"

"We might need your help taking your mom to appointments, or help around the house, things like that," my dad said, crestfallen. He looked defeated, and it terrified me. None of his usual arrogance was in sight.

"Okay, I can do that. We can work out a schedule, maybe keep it posted on the fridge or something so we can all see it," I suggested.

When I first met Skull, he'd called me calculating. I suppose I was that, but more than that, I was observant. I noticed things that a lot of people didn't. Small details. The way my mom clutched at her hands, the shift in her eye, the desperate fear that sat just behind her hazel eyes.

"They told us today that we will need to be very careful about germs," she caught me staring at her. "Do you mind meeting your friends at their place instead of coming here? That way, I can limit my exposure to things. I'll still work, but I'll take it day by day. Some of the other attorneys can drop things off for me here if going in is too much."

"Not a problem," I agreed immediately. I was also noticing there were many things they weren't saying. Namely about chances of survival as they'd talked about with grandpa when he had gotten sick. I wanted to ask.

She'd said, '*we don't always win, but we always fight.*' My grandpa had repeated those words all the time; God, I wanted to cry. I refused. We sat there in cumbersome silence; the air filled with sad tension. Unspoken words were hanging by a thread, and false bravery sat on their lips.

"How about we all go out to eat? You can't fight on an empty stomach." I stood up, and bent over to kiss my mom's cheek, something I hadn't done in years.

It hit me with startling clarity right then. When we'd gone for my driver's test, she'd known. That's why she had apologized. That's why she was making an effort. She was facing her mortality, trying to make things right.

The genuine possibility that my mom might not make it through this was life-altering. I wasn't hungry anymore. I didn't need them to tell me that they weren't either. I could see it all over their faces, and I wanted to run from the room, screaming. I needed air.

It was a selfish reaction too. I knew it. I should be sitting next to my mom, asking her what she wanted me to do to help her tonight. Instead, I let my feet carry me out the back door and down to the deck's edge, where I dropped like a rock.

I heard the soft pad of footsteps against the boards and knew my mom had followed me. She sat down next to me and leaned against my side. My hands were gripping my knees pretty hard, and I couldn't make myself pry them off to put an arm around her.

"Life goes on, Darius," her words floated on the air. "You continue to work, excel in school, and continue to make your plans. All this other stuff is just stuff put in your way to make you lose your step. I'm not throwing in the towel. I've got a lot to fight for; I want to see you make these things happen that you have mapped out. God knows I can't leave your dad alone. He wouldn't even know where the washing machine is."

"You don't need to try and make me feel better, Mom," I whispered harshly.

"I'm not, Darius. I'm reminding myself of the reasons. They are easy to lose sight of when you hear things like that. The more I remind myself, the bigger the fight inside me gets. I won't lie and say this will be easy because we all know it won't be. No one but God knows where this will go either. The fight in you is big, Darius. I might need to borrow it," she told me. "You get that from your grandpa."

I hung my head in shame for the way I was acting. "When do you start the treatment?"

"I go in for the port tomorrow," she said. "Darius, you *do* know that crying doesn't mean you are weak, right?"

No. I didn't know that. I was terrified that if I gave in to the emotions trying to suffocate me, I wouldn't make it back out alive. "I'm okay, Mom. Don't worry about me."

"Have you learned nothing about parents in your

last sixteen years?" she laughed lightly. "I'll always worry about you, Darius. It doesn't matter how big and strong you get, and it doesn't matter what age you are, I'll worry. I might not have been a stellar mom to you, but you are still my baby."

"I guess that means you have a lot of making up to do, so you better fight this shit and make sure you are around to worry about me then. I don't plan to take easy roads," I growled and bit my lip to try and stop the tears.

She saw them. She didn't make a fuss over them either. Instead, she started singing. Her voice was unwavering and beautiful in the church hymn. I swallowed a mouthful of tears and joined her, harmonizing with her, my deeper voice blending with her angelic soprano one.

When she switched to Amazing Grace, I broke down. She had sung this at my grandpa's funeral, and every time I heard this song, I thought of that day. I didn't want to associate a funeral with my mom.

"Sing with me, baby," she pushed at me. "It makes me so happy."

I did my best to stem the waterworks and finished the song with her. We both turned when we heard clapping and saw Skull and Trigger standing with my teary father. They picked a shitty time to show up.

My mom pushed herself to her feet and kissed me on the top of the head. "Thank you, Darius. That was beautiful."

I watched Skull and Trigger give my mom hugs, and then they made their way out to me. They dropped the same way I did and sat on either side of me.

"Your dad told us, man. I'm sorry," Skull started. "Shitty news."

"We won't drop by anymore, either," Trigger promised. "Is that why your mom's attitude suddenly changed?"

I loved the way Trigger pulled no punches with me. "I think so. Like she keeps saying they were, they weren't bad parents; they kept a distance."

"Tell us how we can help, and we'll do it. You've more than changed our lives. We've got you, brother," Skull smacked my back. Just like that, I didn't feel alone inside my head anymore.

Chapter 8

The rest of summer became a whirlwind of activity. I was lucky that the camp worked with me on my schedule for the days I needed to take my mom to an appointment. I caught moments with Star when I could, but it fizzled out, and we were okay with it.

Skull introduced me to his friend, a tattoo artist, and he helped me create a tattoo that embodied my friendship with Skull and Trigger. I can't say it was unique, but he drew a skull with a gun barrel going through its head, not getting shot, but like the skull was a part of the barrel, and it sat on an open book. Being shot out of the barrel was a bullet trailing the words: "Chase your dreams."

It wasn't fancy like some of Skull's artwork, but it summed us up nicely; at least, I thought it did. He inked it on my side over my rib cage. It hurt. Trigger thought that was hilarious. I also felt weirdly exhilarated after he completed it, too.

It wasn't long after that when football practice started up. My physique was shaping up nicely. I was starting to look cut, had broadened, and bulked up enough to be solid. I wasn't huge, and I didn't want to be.

Two weeks before my senior year started, one of the cheerleaders began flirting with me right after practice. I took a chance and asked her out. By the time school started, she was my girlfriend. Stephanie was the blond-haired, blue-eyed bombshell people always envied. She went by Steffie, and I wasn't sure what to do about her.

She was worlds different than Star was. Star hadn't been a girlfriend, but they would have been light-years apart even if she had been. Steffie was possessive and jealous, and it rubbed me a little in the wrong way. When she was normal, it was great. We had fun, and we laughed; there was chemistry.

Steffie was also very compassionate about the things in my family and with my mother. I loved that about her. Neither Trigger nor Skull liked her, which weighed down on me in the back of my mind. I valued their opinions, and they never pulled back on the truth with me.

My class schedule was heavy and stressful; add that to the appointments for my mom and football practice, and I felt the pressure. It built up fast. It made me withdraw from people, and for whatever messed-up reason, that made females want me more.

I never really understood the asshole draw. I appreciated a beautiful person just as much as anyone else, but if the attitude didn't match, they didn't hold my attention. Yet, I noticed that it was the opposite for females. The more I pushed them away, the harder they came at me.

That caused a lot of tension with Steffie. It didn't matter to her that I wasn't responding to it; she only focused on the fact they were always hovering. I'd been upfront about all my plans. I was in no way like some of the other guys on the football team. I wasn't about sleeping with as many people as I could. Steffie should know that.

I'd been upfront about the fact that I had a purely sexual relationship, that she was my first actual girlfriend, and that this was new for me. Even being a jerk thing was new for me. But when I walked out of football practice and found her leaning against my car waiting for me, the jerk reaction was the first one I had.

I did my best to keep my tone even, but it still sounded annoyed. "Steffie, I can't tonight. I need to get my mom from her appointment. Sorry, but I don't have time to sit here and talk tonight. I've also got several hours' worth of homework."

"You don't even have time for one little kiss?" she pouted, still not moving from against my door.

I leaned in, pecked her on the cheek, and picked her up to move her out of the way. She took it as an opportunity to wrap her legs around me. The simple fact that my dick didn't respond was enough to tell me this relationship wouldn't go anywhere. I should have felt awful about that, but I didn't.

"I'll see you tomorrow," I said, disengaging myself. "I don't want to be late."

"You have time for everybody else, but not me," she whined.

"Steffie, I went to classes and practice, and now I'm picking up my mom. Don't start this shit with me right now. You won't like the consequences," I snapped. I didn't even give her time to respond. I jumped in my car and slammed the door shut on whatever she was about to say.

I seriously began to appreciate the low drama way Star had been about everything and made a goal in my mind to search for only those types of females in the future. Once I was out of here, that was. Lately, I'd been having doubts about my plan with my mom being sick and our family now closer.

There was still something in the back of my mind that wanted it, though. I wanted to see the world. I wanted to help people in a meaningful way. I wanted to see something other than L.A. Sure, there were some great things here, but I selfishly wanted more.

I raced towards the hospital, hoping that my mom hadn't been sitting there waiting for me. My dad had a late meeting at work and had asked me to step in and grab her. He'd told us he would bring dinner home with him. I didn't mind.

So far, my mom was handling the chemotherapy well. At least, that is what the doctors said. I saw her wasting away, losing her hair, sick and weak. I hated it. I put on the happy face she needed to see, talked about the work I was doing in school and how practice was going, and sang with her when she needed her spirits raised.

I found one of the pickup spots close to the building and ran inside, returning to the cancer ward familiar now. The nurses greeted me with warm smiles and pointed to her inside the room. I took a moment to wash my hands and face and then went in to get her.

She was sitting in one of the recliner chairs, her eyes closed and a bright pink knit hat pulled down over her head. An open book lay on her lap, turned upside down so she didn't lose her page. I didn't know if she was asleep or just sitting there relaxing while she could.

I walked over as quietly as possible, picked up the book, slid her bookmark in, and placed it in her bag. She looked so small. She wasn't a large person, but her personality was so strong she appeared larger than life. Seeing her diminished by this was a blow to the gut.

"Hey, Mom," I whispered. "I'm here to bring you home."

A soft smile graced her lips, and her deep hazel eyes opened. "Hi, baby. How was school?"

I shifted my stance to help her stand. She hated the wheelchairs and insisted that she walk out of the hospital on her own. I kept my arm around her, matched our strides, and told her about my day and irritation with Steffie.

"She's a kid, Darius. So are you. Don't worry about tying yourself down to anyone just yet. You need to make so many mistakes first to understand what you truly want," she advised as we got to the car.

I helped her get in and ensured she was buckled up and crossed to get in. As I was sitting down, I noticed her observing me. "What?" I asked.

"Nothing, baby. Just looking at how handsome you are," she smiled.

I blushed and started the car. "You think I should break up with Steffie then?" I asked as we got underway.

"That wasn't what I was saying. Life is too short not to be happy. If you aren't happy, then yes, you should end it. If there's something between you two, then explore it but talk out the issues you are experiencing," she said, leaning her head back against the headrest.

"I don't think she's very receptive," I muttered. "I tried talking to her about backing off this jealousy stuff. I'm not even giving her a reason to act that way."

"Women are crazy, Darius. No doubt about that. She's probably insecure for some reason or just one of the people always jealous. Who knows. I was jealous of other women around your dad when I first met him. He didn't give me a reason to be either. I eventually realized it was my perception of myself that was making me that way," she said quietly.

Her admission kind of shocked me. "You don't come across as being insecure." My mom was always firmly rooted in the now, down-to-earth, and reliable. Confident.

"We all go through a journey to become the person we are today," she said quietly. "Being sick like this puts many things in perspective and shows me so much more than I ever knew. When I was young, I was always competing against others. I had to fight to get into college, I had to push hard to excel in my classes, and I had to demand attention. None of that was easy for a shy black girl from the south. You'd have thought it were eighteen-ninety-four the way some people acted."

I pulled into our driveway and swallowed a lump

in my throat. I didn't want to think about my mom being sick. It was indisputable that she was, but if I dwelled on it, I got pulled down into this mess of emotions inside me that were too strong for me to understand.

I didn't say anything because I didn't know how to respond. My parents had told me how rough things were for them growing up, and to their credit, I didn't experience any of what they did. At times, I got looks and judged on my skin color, but not what they experienced. I got out of the car and helped my mom inside. I set her up on the recliner and tucked a blanket around her.

I sat in the kitchen and did my homework to be close if she needed anything, and a couple of hours later, my dad finally got home. He smiled at me and immediately went to check on my mom. I heard the low murmur of voices and tried to stem the thought that either of us might have to deal with losing her too soon.

I closed up my books and headed to my room to call Skull. I was more and more reaching out to him to ease the mess inside me. He and Trigger stepped up in a way I hadn't really expected but quickly started to rely on as things progressed.

"Hey, man," I said when he answered.

"What's up?" his low voice sounded scratchy.

"I need help figuring out what to do about Steffie," I told him, settling on my bed.

"She gettin' crazy?" Skull guessed.

"Yep. Manipulative, too," I told Skull and filled him in on the day and her reactions.

"You don't need that shit. Dump the bitch," Skull said with a finality he didn't usually use.

"Just like that?" I couldn't say I didn't think the same way, but I also felt guilty.

"She chased you, she's all up in your business, trying to control you, and if she's insecure as your mama said, it's enough to derail your plans, Dar," Skull gentled his tone. "Don't lose sight of your goals for a piece of ass. There's all sorts of girls who would be happy with whatever time you could give them and not cause the grief she's tryin' to."

"Yeah, I guess," I hemmed. "Got a game on Thursday. We still on for the gym on Saturday?"

"All good with me, man. We'll be at that game too," Skull confirmed.

Chapter 9

I tried to do homework on the bus ride to the game, but it was so noisy and rowdy it was a lost cause. I shoved the chemistry book back in my bag and wished for the hundredth time I had driven myself.

The competitive side of it was fun. It wasn't what drove me, however. I enjoyed the physical aspect of the sports I was doing; seeing the progress and growth was satisfying. Winning felt good. Making the pass I couldn't make earlier in the week felt even better.

I hadn't broken up with Steffie yet, mainly because I hadn't had time. I also hadn't figured out how to do it without being an asshole. At halftime, I stuck to the locker room to avoid her, and one of the other guys noticed.

"What gives, Baker? You got a cheerleader out there waiting for you to show your face," he smirked, throwing a towel at me. His name was Mike, and he was a senior, like me.

"Man, chill with that," I snarled, throwing it back at him.

"She crazy?" he leaned up against the lockers.

I nodded. "Are they all like that?"

"Females?" Mike laughed. "Probably."

"Don't rat me out," I sighed.

"Nah. Steffie's one of those that only date black dudes. Take her to a party with your other friends, and she'll screw her way out of a relationship with you," Mike shrugged.

She hadn't even slept with me yet. She'd gone down on me and asked me to reciprocate, which I didn't mind. I could take her to a party at Skull's, there were plenty of other guys that would hit on her, and it might solve my problem without me having to dump her for no reason. It felt calculating, but oh well.

"Thanks. I might do that," I declared. I'd need to run it by Skull and Trigger. "Why are you hiding in here?"

Mike sat down on the bench across from me. "My dad is in the stands. If I go back out there, he will try to find a way to come down and tell me everything I did wrong. I don't want to hear it. How's your mom?"

"She's hanging in," I said, not meeting his eyes. They all knew and were supportive for people who were not my real friends. "You going to college?"

"No. I'm joining the Marines. At least for one tour. They'll pay for college, and it gives me time to figure out what the hell I want to do with my life," Mike sighed.

"I'm joining too. Probably not Marines. I'm leaning towards Navy because my mom thinks I should choose that one," I admitted for the first time to anyone other than Skull or Trigger.

"Talk to a recruiter now," Mike suggested. "They can guide you on options, give you info on the branch, things like that. Talk to each branch and find which one suits you best."

"Back to the field!" the coach's voice boomed into the locker room, making us both jump.

I grabbed my helmet and followed Mike back out, and we took our places along the bench with the rest of the team. I glanced up into the stands to see Skull and Trigger hovering around my mom. Trigger was wrapping a blanket around her. She leaned against my dad, and Skull was on her other side.

That was why these two men meant so much to me. I nodded in their direction and turned my attention back to the coach who was going over plays with us. With my mind back on the game, we got through it, won, thanks to Mike's touchdown, and filed into the locker room.

"Remember what I told you," Mike clapped me on the back, not elaborating more. Instead of returning to the bus, I cleaned up, went out to find my parents, and would ride home with them.

Instead, I found Skull and Trigger waiting for me. "She wasn't feeling good, so your dad took her home. We've got you," Trigger thumped me on the back, and we headed for the parking lot.

"Then get me out of here before anyone can find me," I said more snappily than I meant. Trigger pulled a beanie over my head, handed me his coat, and tipped my head to look at the ground.

"You don't look like you now," Trigger said lightly.

"Maybe, but she knows to look for you two," I mumbled, following them to Skull's car. I got in the back seat and slunk down as far as possible. Once they got in, I told them what Mike had said to me about Steffie.

"Shit, that ain't a problem," Trigger announced. "We got lots of boys that will hit on her just to claim they got a piece of cheerleader's ass."

"Spend some time with your mama, Dar," Skull told me quietly. "She got that surgery comin' up, and she worried 'bout it."

"Invite Steffie to the party on Saturday; we'll make sure you get rid of her," Trigger promised me. "Then, only worry about your mama."

"Keep the ages close to hers," I replied numbly. "We don't need cop trouble."

"You made sure we learned we ain't stupid," Trigger responded. "Won't be no trouble. Steffie only wants chocolate dick; we'll make sure she's got a pick of it that ain't yours."

Satisfied with that answer, I trusted them to have my back. "Think I should start talking to recruiters like Mike said?"

I saw Skull shrug. "Can't hurt none. If he's on that same path as you, take his advice. Talk to them all. I don't want you going; the world ain't right, man. But I'll support your decision whether I like it or not."

"The world won't ever be right. That doesn't mean I can't try to make it a little better for a few," I said as I glanced out the window at the street.

"You made it better for three people already," Skull pointed out but didn't push. "I don' want you to forget that, bro."

"Unlikely that I'd forget," I replied. "You assholes remind me all the time."

Trigger laughed. "You got the best shot out o' all of us, man. You gon' make us all proud."

They dropped me off, and I trudged inside, wondering if my mom was still awake or not. The unasked question got answered when I entered the eerily silent house. My dad was passed out on the couch, looking decades older than he was.

I crept down the hallway to drop my bag in my room and then peeked in to check on my mom. I thought she was asleep, but she whispered my name when I turned to go. I swiveled around. "How you feeling, Mom?"

"Tired, baby. How did the game end?" My mom's voice sounded raspy, so I moved to grab the glass of water next to her bed while she sat up.

"We won." I fluffed up some pillows behind her while she drank the water and then helped her lay back.

"Do you remember my poppa's words?" she murmured.

"We don't always win, but we always fight," I recited to her. "I know, Mom. We won this time. Are you ever going to tell me why he said that?"

"You want to know?" She seemed surprised by that.

"I do," I told her, reaching for her hand. It looked like the hand of a grandmother. The chemo hadn't been easy on my mom.

It hadn't changed her smile, though. My mom flashed her pearly white teeth at me. "Your grandpa marched in the civil rights marches down south. He was part of Mr. King's movement. My poppa wanted to change the world and make it a safe place for me. He'd come home from a march beaten sometimes, and he'd tell me, 'we don't always win, baby, but we always fight; because freedom, safety, and love should always be fought for.'"

I stroked the dry skin on her hands and reached for the lotion she kept next to her. "Grandpa was a protestor?" I asked as I rubbed the lotion into her hands, massaging gently.

"Not a protestor, baby. An activist. The hate and segregation never sat right with him the way it rolled off others. My poppa wasn't content to go along with things and not rock the boat. He once told me that his daddy told him that we weren't born equal; we had to earn it because our dark skin was a mark of shame. My poppa hated that; we had nothing to be ashamed of because of our brown skin. We bleed the same color. From the moment I understood, he'd say those words to me: We don't always win, baby, but we always fight. Not with our fists, but with our every action," my mom quoted, her voice fading.

"I'm proud that you think I'm like grandpa," I told her, tucking her blankets around her.

"So much like him," she murmured and drifted to sleep.

I silently walked out of her bedroom and went to wake my dad up to go to bed. "Dad," I shook him gently.

"Darius," his eyes dragged open. "How was the game?"

"We won. I just checked on mom, and she's asleep. Why don't you go to bed and get some rest?" I suggested. "I'll grab something to eat and make sure the house is locked up."

"Glad you won, son. I'll take you up on that offer. I'm beat." My dad heaved himself to his feet, gave me a half-hearted hug, and made his way to the bedroom.

I watched him go with mixed emotions. I wondered if joining the military was the right choice for me with the way things were going here. I thought about what my mom had told me about my grandpa and decided again that it was the right choice for me.

Chapter 10

When Saturday rolled around, I took Mike's advice and hit up all the recruiters to hear what they had to say. The Army recruiter sold an excellent line of bullshit but didn't make it sound very appealing to me. They had their points and offered a signing bonus; however, I wanted more than the Army.

The Air Force held a lot of draws. Being able to fly one of those planes sounded amazing to me, yet there was a part of me that knew it wasn't what I wanted in the bigger picture. The recruiter was less gung-ho than the Army one had been, and I wasn't sure how to take that. He was impressed with my schooling and wasn't going out of his way to sell it to me overall.

The Marine recruiter was aggressive. There was a part of me that liked that. Marines were where I had leaned before talking to my mom. Everyone knew them to be badass, and I think that's what I wanted. After seeing my grades, he offered a nice signing bonus, and his line of bullshit was similar to what the Army guys were.

The Navy recruiting office was farthest away, and when I got there, I was tired of listening to it all. I was exhausted, period. I walked into the office and saw a female and male recruiter, which surprised me since all the others had males. It was a nice change of pace.

So was the politeness. The other three weren't rude, but the recruiters had a pitch to sell, and they jumped right in without even asking what I hoped to get from it. These two smiled at me, and both stood to welcome me.

"I'm going to cut right to the chase," I told them, approaching the desks. "I've been to all the other recruiters today trying to figure out which way I wanted to go. I leaned towards the Marines, and the Navy was my second choice until I talked to my mom, who thinks I should choose you."

"I see," the male said, gesturing to a chair. "Take a seat."

I sat down. "I have to say, seeing that you have a female in here with you is a nice change. So I will tell you what I am looking for, and you can tell me if you think this is the place for me. First off, I want to make a difference. I've seen the equality issues in the system, which bothers me. I'm not just talking about black and white race issues, either. I want to travel. I like the discipline aspect of things, and I think I thrive in it. I'm on track to graduate with a four-point grade point average, and with my A.A. in science, at the same time. I like the competitive side of the sports I play, not necessarily competing with the other team, more competing with myself to see how much I can improve," I told them.

"And you don't want to go the college route?" the female asked.

"No. It's great, but I don't think it's for me. I am itching to be out of here. The part of college that bothers me is all the bullshit requirements they have. If I want to pursue a biochem degree or physics, I don't need to take English classes, humanities, or drama. I want the education I need, not all the other crap. I busted my ass throughout school to make sure my grades were on the top. I want a real education," I replied.

"If Navy was your second choice, why was it there?" the guy spoke up.

"Marines are always in the midst of things. I think for me, it's a great way to learn. I'm not typically as aggressive as they are, and that would be a good learning experience of stepping out of my comfort zone. Navy was on my list because there's a technical aspect calling to me. It's not just grunting and fighting. I'm not a great swimmer, but I like the thought of being out at sea. I realize that there are technical aspects to each of the other branches, too," I added as an afterthought.

"Did you bring transcripts with you?" The name on the uniform was Bridges. I wondered what her first name was.

"I did," I reached into my folder and pulled them out, along with a resume I'd made. I handed the papers over to Bridges and then looked back at the male. The name on his uniform was Rodriguez.

"This is impressive," Bridges admitted, handing them over to Rodriguez. "You mentioned biochem. Is that the field you are interested in?"

"One of them. I seem to have a knack for chemistry and physics. With that in mind, I thought a career in explosives might be interesting. The mechanics of things interest me. A little less so when the mechanics are vehicles or computers, but those also hold a certain appeal. I have a strong sense of observation, I see things differently than others, and it enables me to plot out a chain of reaction," I explained.

"Are you interested in special forces?" Rodriguez asked me, handing back my transcripts and resume.

"Maybe? I don't know. If I want specialized education, I know this is the way to get it. I don't have a problem going that route if that means special forces. I thought about joining an ROTC program, but I don't have time for that right now. My mother is sick, and between her appointments, sports, and school, it puts a strain on me for time," I admitted.

"You want to be an officer?" Bridges asked me. "It's not all it's cracked up to be."

I smiled at that. Judging from Bridges' uniform, she outranked Rodriguez. "Tell me, is this office set up like this to draw people like me in?"

"No, man," Rodriguez laughed. "It's honestly not. I can see how it looks that way, but the truth is, we have a rotating staff for this particular office, but our officers like to have one male and one female here. Ensign Bridges just happened to hit the rotation. We get females that come in looking for information, and if there is another woman in here for them to talk to on what it's like for a female, we stand a better chance of recruiting top females to join our ranks."

"I imagine that you understand being in the minority isn't always a good position to be in," Bridges said. "Instead of selling you the same lines that you've heard from all the others, we will send you home with a list of what the requirements are to join, expected physical requirements, and I'm going to throw the special forces list in there as well. Something tells me you would be a good candidate for that."

Rodriguez was also writing down something, and he handed the sheets over. "There's a signing bonus for us, too. You have to be a minimum of seventeen and graduate high school."

"Not eighteen?" I asked, surprised.

"No, seventeen will get you in and into boot camp," Bridges confirmed.

"Even if I will have only turned seventeen when I graduate?" My mom was right to suggest the Navy. The Marines still appealed to me, but the Navy looked a lot better. If the action were what I wanted, then special forces would be the route to go there.

"I am certain. I will double-check that for you, but you can always have a parent come in and sign a waiver," Bridges said. "You've still got a year left in high school. We can stay in touch if you are interested. Guide you a bit."

Not one of the other branches had offered that. "Deal. My mind is made-up. When I graduate, I'm yours."

"Then I'll tell you what, bring a parent back here with you, fill out the paperwork, have them sign. They can ask us any questions they'd like, we can go over anything, and I'll push through that bonus so you can enjoy it before you leave for boot camp," Bridges bargained.

Rodriguez gave me a twisted smile. "That's a good deal. A nice chunk of change to play with at sixteen. You can buy yourself a car."

"I've got a car. How do you think I got here? If I'm going to get money, I want a motorcycle," I told the man.

"Oh yeah? Street bike?" Rodriguez sat forward.

"Nah, think I want a big-boy bike," I told him.

"Harley?" Bridges laughed. "Good investment choice. Their value holds."

Her praise bolstered me. "Can you give me a card with hours, so I know when to come back?"

Rodriguez started writing again. "If you are looking for us, here's the rest of our schedule. Otherwise, the hours for anyone being here is on the flip side."

"Hopefully, we'll get to meet your mother," Bridges added kindly. "Best of luck to you in that, and my sincere hopes that she gets better."

"Keep straight, man. We'll see you soon," Rodriguez stood when I did and handed me the card.

I felt exhilarated when I walked out. I had a future, and knowing that felt good. Maybe this last year of high school wouldn't be a total bust. On the tail end of that thought was leaving my family, blood and non-blood.

It looked like it was time to include my dad in my plans. I wasn't sure if my mom would feel up to making the trip to the recruiting office.

Chapter 11

When I got to the party, Trigger and Skull dragged me away. "We need to talk to our boy 'bout his future," Trigger smirked at Steffie.

I doubted she heard him. She was eyeballing some guy across the room. From the rival high school across town, I think. I remember seeing him at a game. "Who's that?"

"Senior, under eighteen, a football player, an all-around player, you know what I mean? You played a game against him last week," Skull told me. "You talked to the recruiters today?"

Steffie's high-pitched giggle reached me, and I was concerned enough not to want her to get hurt. "He won't hurt her, right?"

"Nah, but he'll fuck her. That's all you need, bro," Trigger assured me. "We ain't gonna let the broad get hurt."

"Broad?" I snickered. "Your vocabulary is sad."

"Better than callin' her a ho." Trigger laughed and smacked my back.

Skull led me back to the bedroom, where he

closed the door against the party's noise. "Okay, spill it. Tell us the news."

I filled them in on the meetings. Trigger got quiet and contemplative, and Skull appraised me. "You chose the Navy, didn't you?" Skull guessed.

"I did." I told them the rest of the conversation, and they both agreed with my decision though they looked like they still wanted to argue against my joining. Thankfully they left it alone because I was having trouble thinking of not seeing them when I wanted.

"Let's go check on our operation free Dar," Trigger stood up suddenly.

Skull chuckled and stood. "Come on, soldier. Let's see what's happened out there."

I couldn't have predicted how right Mike would be. Steffie was in the corner with the guy, riding him in plain sight of everyone. Steffie threw her head back, and she was putting on a show. I was slightly irritated by how easily she did it and grateful to be rid of her.

"Hey, Steffie," I walked up to them. The guy didn't even slow down; he kept right on thrusting while she looked surprised to see me. "Consider this little act of yours the end of our relationship. Been nice knowin' you. Have fun, man," I nodded at the dude and walked off as he busted his nut.

"Ridiculously easy," Skull shook his head. "Gotta watch out for those, Dar."

Steffie came chasing after me a few minutes later. "Darius, you left me alone!"

Trigger shook his head and stepped between us. "Watch yourself, cheerleader. You got a room full of witnesses here. All he did was talk to us. He didn't plant you on that dick; you did that on your own."

I pulled my wallet out and handed her some money. "Catch a cab home."

Steffie threw a colossal tantrum in front of everyone, then tried to claim that she was drunk, and I got her that way. "Oh, hell no," Trigger stepped in again and smelled her. "You don't even smell like alcohol. James, you drunk, man?" Trigger called out to the satisfied-looking guy.

"Don't do that shit, bro. They'll throw me off the team," James called back. "Blondie came on to me."

Skull smirked at Steffie. "Would you like me to call you that ride? I mean, you've already taken one ride tonight. Is there more here you are lookin' at using? Not thinkin' any of my boys would be willin' now."

I had mixed feelings, and my upbringing demanded I see her home. "I'll catch you later, man. I'll take her home."

"Watch your back," Skull said in my ear. "She calculatin'."

"You said the same thing about me," I laughed.

"Yours is the smart type," Skull smiled. "Her's, not so much."

I understood what he was saying. "Time me. I'll call when I get home."

I led Steffie to the car, where she tried to throw herself at me, and I held her off. "Not happening. Put your seatbelt on, and shut up. I don't want to hear it."

Skull was right; I could see her scheming the whole way back to her house. She stormed out of the car, not even bothering to close the door. I reached over, pulled it shut, and sped home, calling Skull to let him know I was back.

"Got it all noted here if she tries to pull some shit," Skull told me.

"We'll see at school on Monday," I slumped against the wall.

The background noise diminished, and I guessed Skull returned to his room and closed the door. "Serious, man, watch out for those types. They pull some bad shit, and the brothers take the fall. That's why I got it all noted. That show she put on before you left was crazy."

"Should I tell my parents?" I asked him.

"I would. Cover yo' ass, man; that's the game," Skull advised.

"Great. Going to be some fun conversations here tomorrow," I mumbled. I hung up, went to my room, and worked out until I was exhausted.

My mom was awake and in the kitchen in the morning, making breakfast. "Sit down, baby. Your dad will be back in a minute. He ran to get some juice for me."

"Okay, Mom," I sat down. "I talked with recruiters yesterday. It's time to tell Dad."

"Let him eat first. He's having a rough time," my mom sighed.

That translated to: he was struggling with my mom's cancer. "Is there bad news?"

She answered without answering. "The surgery is scheduled for three weeks out."

I couldn't tell if that was a bad thing or not from

the tone she used. "I have something else to talk to you guys about, too," I told her instead of questioning the surgery.

"Oh?" my mom turned to look at me, her voice holding a question. "Is this a bad talk?"

"I hope not," I said immediately.

My mom finished frying up the potatoes she had cooked and set them on a warming plate in the oven when my dad returned. She was moving slowly, but it was more activity than I'd seen from her in a while.

"Good morning, son," my dad smiled faintly.

"Hey, Dad." I got up and set the table, seeing that breakfast was almost finished.

"Thank you, Darius," my mom told me as I grabbed the plates and glasses.

My dad grabbed the silverware, juice, and napkins and followed me. "How was the party?" he asked conversationally.

"That's one of the things I need to talk to you about this morning. Skull thought it would be a good idea," I started.

The statement alarmed my mom, but she kept her mouth closed and put the pans in the sink. My dad gave me a cautious glance and grabbed the food warming in the oven. She'd gone all out on breakfast and made a giant plateful of eggs, ham, potatoes, and toast.

"I figured you were growing so much you needed the food," my mom said as I eyed it all.

"It looks great," I told her, loading my plate up after they had taken theirs.

There was hardly any food on my mom's plate,

but she ate. She drank more juice than anything. Even my dad picked at his food, a sure sign that he had a lot on his mind. "Is your girlfriend pregnant?" he finally asked.

I choked on a potato. "What? No. I never even had sex with her," I fired off. "That's not what it's about; I mean, it is kind of, but not how you think." I finished my bite of food and then launched into the story of what happened.

"Your friend is right to keep a record of it all and witnesses," my dad agreed with Skull when I finished the tale. "It's not something we can't handle if she makes ridiculous accusations against you."

"Won't cops take her word over mine if she claims date rape or something?" I'd left out the part where her cheating on me was the outcome I'd been hoping for and why I took Steffie to the party in the first place. That could remain between my friends and me.

"Maybe," my mom said carefully. "If you didn't sleep with her, you shouldn't worry. I say that lightly because we know that the word of a young black man at a party like that, to begin with, will get dismissed. You have a list of witnesses and time frame, and since you called him from our phone, if anything comes of this, we have records to back up your statements."

That was my concern. I cleared my throat. "There's something else I want to talk to you about."

My dad looked up from his plate with curiosity. "You sound scared, son."

"I guess I am," I glanced at my mom, who kept her face remarkably blank. "I know you have my future mapped out in your minds, and so do I. It doesn't match yours."

My dad pushed his empty plate away and leaned back. "I'm listening."

"I want to join the Navy," I said bluntly. I outlined my discussions with each branch's recruiters, and then I jumped into why I wanted to join the military instead of attending school. It only was when I mentioned that being in the military would pay for college if I decided to go that route later that my dad's tension left his body.

"How long have you wanted this?" he finally asked.

"For about four years now. Helping Trigger and Skull study and pass their tests made it clear that I wanted to make a difference; I think this route will get me there and allow me to see other parts of the world," I told them. "I know I only need one parent to sign the form if that's even necessary, she didn't think it was, but I would feel better if you both came with me to ask them whatever questions you have to ease your mind about this choice."

I thought for sure my dad would argue. He was silent for a few minutes before he sighed. "It's what you truly want?"

"It is," I answered immediately. "I like the discipline of it, the challenge, and the opportunities."

My dad reached for my mom's hand. "If your mom is up for it, we can go talk to them next Saturday."

I was so relieved that it didn't turn into a fight, I almost embarrassed myself by crying. "Thank you," I said gratefully.

Chapter 12

Bridges stood when we entered, noted that both my parents were with me, and smiled brightly.

"Darius Baker, you came back. Does that mean you are going to sign?"

"I am," I nodded. "These are my parents. My father, Isaiah Baker, and my mother, Maisie Baker. Mom, Dad, this is Ensign Bridges, and Rodriguez, I don't know his rank."

"Pleasure to meet you both. Have a seat, and we can discuss what options Darius has, what things will look like for him, and you can ask us any questions you would like," Bridges gestured to the chairs in front of the desk.

"Can I get you anything to drink?" Rodriguez asked us.

"Do you happen to have any juice?" my mom asked him.

"Is orange juice okay?" Rodriguez offered. My mom nodded at him, and he went to get her a glass and returned promptly, setting it on the desk close to her, and he took a seat. "Darius told us that you weren't well. I hope that you are feeling better?"

"Thank you for asking; today is a good day." My mom smiled politely at him. "Do you mind if I start with a question?" She looked between Bridges and Rodriguez, awaiting a response.

"Please," Bridges granted.

"What's military life like for people of color?" My mom threw the blunt question right out there.

"I can answer that from a racial standpoint," Rodriguez offered. "I won't lie and say there aren't issues with it. I can vouch that some instructors and officers are good at squelching it. There will always be someone that doesn't like you because your skin is darker than theirs, and for me and my brown skin, I got slurs thrown at me that I should be out mowing lawns or growing marijuana. I even had a few gang insinuations. It often happened throughout boot camp because a diverse class of people entered the training. Those individuals usually reveal themselves pretty early on, and the officers and instructors make life hard for them."

"From a female standpoint, the same things happen," Bridges added. "Most of the people that go that route aren't the brightest of people. It happens with us as it does everywhere else. Most recruits don't seek resolution from their leaders, but we still notice, and it gets addressed. Sometimes, someone like that will make it into an officer position, and they make life awful. I've found that most enlisted and other ranks will speak up at that point, and we do our best to correct it."

"What happens after boot camp?" my dad asked. "And how long is it?"

"Boot camp is a total of eight weeks," Rodriguez

answered. "The first week is processing, then seven weeks of training; you're getting yelled at during the first week."

"Yelling is part of the processing?" My dad chuckled at that.

"I think it is for all branches," Bridges grinned personably.

"After boot camp, you head off to A School. The location of this will depend on the area of training you want to undertake. Some people head into boot camp thinking they know what they want, and at the completion, they have a different idea. A School can be up to two years," Rodriguez continued. "Darius expressed interest in biochem. Are you still leaning that way?"

"Biochem as it applies to warfare, I think," I answered.

"You'd probably remain in San Diego, then," Bridges answered. "If you go to special forces, you'd also remain here. If you are looking to travel to other bases, you might want to broaden your range of interest for skills."

"Wouldn't he travel if he got deployed?" My mom frowned.

"Without a doubt," Bridges agreed. "You don't often get a choice in that either. If I may make a suggestion, I would suggest A School in Virginia. Darius, your resume shows high intelligence, and Virginia trains for intelligence. If you choose to go special forces after that, you'd be that much better. You told me you are observant, a mark of special forces. But before joining that group, get some training under your belt and hone your instincts."

My dad looked impressed. "That's wise advice."

It gave me something to think about; special forces still had a spot in the back of my mind. I liked the thought of being specialized like that. "Can't you go special forces right after boot camp?"

"You can," Bridges confirmed. "You'd be going from boot camp to an even more intense version that many people don't make it through. If you go to A School and get adjusted, then go that route; I think there is a better chance of success. SEALs still have A School, and I'm not dissuading you from that route; just trying to help you understand. The length of time in A School depends on your field as well. We say two years on average, but it might not be that long."

"You say special forces; what does that mean?" My mom looked directly at Bridges this time, understanding she was the ranking officer.

"Most people consider special forces the SEALs. That is true, but there are different areas of that. If Darius's interest is to go that route, I'd suggest signing the contract saying you will go that route after your training. You still do A School, but signing that contract will give him different benefits," Bridges clarified.

My heart raced at that thought. A SEAL. "That's next-level crazy training, right?"

Rodriguez laughed. "Oh, man, you have no idea. That training is the ultimate challenge."

"I'm in," I declared immediately.

"Darius," my mom said quietly, her eyes wide.

"Are you sure?"

My dad swallowed whatever he was going to say and put his hand on my mom's leg. "If he wants to try, we should support that."

"If that's your choice, I'll put you in contact with someone from that program for further discussion, and they can be a guide for you through that process," Bridges said carefully. "Rodriguez gave you a sheet listing those requirements when you were here last."

"The processing time from start to SEAL is probably about two years, three if you add on some different A School," Rodriguez added quickly. "I agree with Bridges' advice about the school; however, if you go the SEAL training route, the schooling there is much more intense. You'll still need to go to Great Lakes for a time, but it's something you can discuss with someone from that program."

Bridges pulled out some papers and talked about the signing bonus, the length of service, physical requirements, keeping myself clean and on the right side of the law, and the testing that would need to happen for admittance to the program.

The thought thrilled me and scared me. SEALs were badass, and I'd need to step up the physicality of my preparation. My hands started to shake a little as the decision in my mind made itself up. Success, or failure, I was going to try for the SEALs.

Chapter 13

It took a month, and homecoming dance, before Steffie started squawking. At first, it was just rumors about why we broke up. By that point, I'd heard a mix of things and dismissed them all. It was after practice before the homecoming game that Mike pulled me aside.

"Hey, don't know if you heard or not, but Steffie is telling people you forced her to have sex with you," Mike advised quietly.

"Not true. I never slept with Steffie. Went down on her after she begged me to let her give me a blow job," I told him. "She fucked the quarterback from our first game at the party I went to in front of everyone. Rode him like she was performing in a rodeo, man."

"Figured it was something like that after we talked last time. Just wanted to give you a heads up if you get a call to the principal's office. They take those allegations seriously," Mike lowered his voice even more. "Got witnesses?"

"White and black," I confirmed. "Plus, I told my parents what happened because Steffie threw a fit in the middle of the party when she got caught riding his dick. Oh, and I took your advice about the recruiters. Signed with the Navy."

"Sweet. Not the Marines, then. Who knows, we may still run into each other," Mike replied. "You get a bonus?"

"Yep. Getting a Harley too. My dad will take me out to look at them this weekend and get me signed up for a class so I can get the endorsement on my license," I grinned.

"No shit? I would never have taken you for a biker type. That's cool," Mike grinned back. "How was your mom's surgery?"

"The surgery itself went fine, and they removed a lot of the tumors, but it still spread. She's still on chemo," I told him, my voice tinged with anger. "It's fucking awful."

"Man, I'm sorry to hear that. My aunt went through that too; it was rough," Mike said. Our smiles had disappeared with that talk, and we walked out to the parking lot together. "Hang in there, Darius."

Two days later, I got called into the principal's office to find my parents sitting there with a man I didn't know. The second I got the note from the teacher, I knew this was about Steffie. I hadn't expected to see my parents, though.

"Darius, take a seat." Principal McGowan waved a hand towards the chair between my parents.

I sat down, and my mom reached for my hand. Her skin started to look grayish, and it made me angry again. She was too young to be going through this. I stroked the back of her hand and kissed her cheek.

"It seems you were expecting this since your

parents told me that you informed them of the event that I called you to discuss. They brought a lawyer with them, and I'd like to say that I applaud your forward-thinking, and I'm ashamed that things like this happen," Principal McGowan started.

"Stephanie is claiming I raped her," I said bluntly. "We never had sex. The farthest we went was oral, and that was after her begging me to let her do it."

My dad made a coughing noise and then got it under control. "My son told us about the party, and I've contacted his friends and received the witness list, which I provided to the lawyer. If this girl's parents want to pursue this, they can take it up with him. My son did not do as she claimed, nor is he the father of that girl's pregnancy."

Whoa. "Wait, Steffie's claiming I got her pregnant?"

"The allegations made were that you forced her to a party, made her have unprotected sex with you in front of people, which resulted in pregnancy," the principal recited.

"Not one word of that is true." I exploded out of my chair, fury boiling through my veins.

"I know, Darius," Principal McGowan raised his eyebrows at my temper. "Sit down, please. Your record here at school shows you to be an excellent student and athlete. As the principal, I have to investigate the claim. They are demanding your expulsion, which I am hesitant to do, given the information provided."

"I don't want my son's name smeared through the mud because some bimbo has jungle fever. Darius has his future planned out, and it doesn't include this. My son hasn't broken any laws, and I will sue the school and that girl's family if he suffers because of this," my dad yelled.

I winced but agreed with him. "A simple paternity test would determine that I'm not the father," I said calmly.

"I agree, and upon that recommendation to Stephanie's parents, they feel victimized. I must warn you that this might result in the police becoming involved, though I am doing my best to keep that from happening and disrupting the school. I advise you to donate your saliva and blood to have this done, and your lawyer can make that happen," Principal McGowan sighed. "I'm sorry, Darius."

I was too. "Well, this is enough to keep me from dating anyone else. I would never have unprotected sex; it's just stupid."

Luckily, I didn't get suspended or kicked out, but the lawyer advised me to refrain from sexual activity. There weren't many women in my life other than my mom and Sprite. I wasn't sexual with either of those. I was content to take care of it myself until this blew over.

The school rumors were beyond crazy, and thankfully, word had spread about my witnesses, and the law never got involved. A part of me felt like that wouldn't have happened if I was white, yet I saw the same shit happening to white guys; it just got less attention. I had to admit that people were more willing to believe my guilt than the white guys. Whatever.

My attitude changed drastically after that. I was

never rude to females, but I shut down when they showed attention or interest. I didn't care if I became viewed as an asshole. I'd rather that than end up behind bars for a rape I didn't commit.

Skull and Trigger made the other quarterback appear at my school and confront Steffie. It turns out she hadn't even told him she was pregnant. He wasn't any happier than I was, and when she threw another fit in the cafeteria and claimed he raped her, she sealed her fate.

The episode was my first genuine glimpse into the racial divide that still existed despite years of fighting for equality. I was glad that Mike had warned me about it, too, and even happier that Trigger and Skull had the foresight into those situations to cover me the way they did. That one event could have changed my future forever.

Talk lingered at school, with only a few still casting questions about me. I stopped caring what they thought. I knew the truth; my parents and my friends did too. It would be enough for me. I threw myself into my studies and improved my physical condition.

I joined swimming because, out of everything, that was my weakest sport, and there was a swim challenge on one of the sheets that Rodriguez had given me. My dad kept pointing that out to me and offered to hire a coach to help with the swimming part.

I didn't want him to waste that money, so I suggested putting myself in lessons instead, in a class setting where I could observe the others. So it began. My schedule went from busy to insane.

Skull was sure that I had lost my mind, but he was

impressed with the level of dedication that I was throwing into it. At the parties I went to of his, I'd noticed that he kept me away from alcohol and made sure no one offered me any. Trigger bragged like crazy, he thought it was cool, yet he liked to say black people didn't swim.

"Yeah, they do. Remember Star? We had a few fun times in the lake," I reminded Trigger.

"Shit, a brother would swim for a fine piece of ass," Trigger conceded.

Bridges' advice also kept playing through my head like a broken record. Intelligence held an appeal for me as much as making and disarming bombs did. The projected explosion zones, the direction of the shrapnel, and how they could get created fascinated me. Jeez, I was starting to feel like a sociopath thinking about explosives.

Skull had made some new friends after he learned I was going to pick out a Harley. Bikers, and they talked to me about the finer points of things to look at when I went to pick out the bike, which my dad was taking me to look for tomorrow.

When Skull told me to go home, I didn't argue. I was tired and needed to get some quality sleep. I was excited to get a motorcycle. My signing bonus wouldn't come in until I finished enlistment, and my dad agreed to front the money. He said it was my college fund and told me I could keep the signing bonus, but I felt I should pay it back since I wasn't going to college.

When I settled into bed, my mind drifted to Skull and Trigger and how they had changed since beating me up. The two men took care of me, looked after me, and offered up support as I'd never experienced before. I still struggled with the thought of leaving them.

I used to think Trigger would shift to the more questionable ways, as my mother put it, and Skull would stick to the straight. It was the opposite, and it surprised me. I knew Skull had sent me home because he would make some sort of deal I would have questioned.

Trigger tutored kids having math problems as a side gig, which I thought was great. It did wonders for him to be able to help someone that was where he used to be. It did the kids good to see that they could overcome it too.

I rolled over and felt absurdly proud of both of them, even with the way Skull was leaning. As far as I could tell, he was peddling weed. I disagreed with it, but it wasn't heroin. I knew I was making excuses for the behavior, but Skull's heart wasn't evil. There was no question about that. Not even in my parent's minds.

Chapter 14

"Holy shit, bro, it's hotter than hell in here!" Trigger complained after my first swim meet.

"I know," I agreed. "Did you write down my times?"

"You know I did." Trigger shoved the notebook at me. "My sister lookin' at you. D'you know that?"

"Yeah. Won't happen, Trigger," I promised him.

"Good. Shay can do worse, but that's weird, man. I'd have to see if I could still kick yo' ass." Trigger thumped me on the back. "You fast enough to make those times on that sheet yet?"

"Nope," I scoffed. "Closer, but I need to tighten up the moves. I'm sloppy."

"You ain't sloppy, bro. You the only brother out there. And did you shave your legs?" Trigger shoved me.

"Helps with drag," I defended myself. "Man, that felt so weird asking my mom for a razor for my legs. I couldn't make myself shave my pits."

Trigger snorted as we walked out of the pool into the cooler air. "When you startin' the motorcycle thing?"

"I got the permit, and I know how to ride one, but my dad has me signed up for classes on Sundays and wants me to take the M1 test," I told Trigger.

"Can't wait to go for a ride wit' you," Trigger grinned as he got in my car.

"Me too, man." I dropped Trigger off, thanked him for suffering through the meet, and went home.

My dad was probably still at work, but I didn't hear any noise from my mom and wondered if she was asleep. I set my stuff down quietly in my room and snuck to her to peek in. She was sleeping as I had thought. I backed out of the room and made my way to the kitchen.

The amount of food I ate now was ridiculous. I burned far more calories than I ate, and while my physique was cut, there was a fine line I needed to balance, not to lose weight or muscle. I glanced at the time and hesitated to make myself a meal since my dad should be home soon.

I grabbed an apple and some cheese and sat at the table to start my homework when the air's unnaturalness wrapped around me. I ate my apple slowly and tried to figure out what it was. I put the core in the trash when I finished and walked around.

Intuition led me back to my parent's room, and fear coursed through me in powerful waves. I pushed the door open. "Mom?" I called out.

I hit the light switch when she didn't respond and watched her body. There was no movement. None at all. I waited a little more to make sure before I crept over to her bed with my heart in my throat. I laid my hand on her face, and feeling the cold skin, I yanked it back and howled out my anguish.

I raced to the phone and called 9-1-1 in a panic,

demanding they come and save my mom. I answered their questions as quickly as I could and hung up to call my dad. There was no answer at his office, and I called Skull, not knowing what else to do.

The second he answered, I burst into tears. "M-m-my mom," was all I was able to get out.

"On my way," Skull barked and hung up.

I went to sit on the porch, waiting for the ambulance, my dad, or Skull. It didn't matter. I knew she was gone. We weren't even there with her; she died alone, not hearing us tell her how much we loved her. My tears went from grief to anger and back so many times that I wasn't sure what I felt.

My dad beat the ambulance by a minute, and Skull and Trigger showed up a minute after the ambulance. They were in time to catch both my dad and me. Even before the sirens' sound registered in his head, my dad seemed to understand why I was on the porch.

He ran to me and wrapped his arms around me, and when the ambulance pulled up, his face crumpled, and the same howl that came out of me got pulled from him. Skull and Trigger dashed from the car and caught us. My dad went limp in my arms, taking me with him.

We numbly followed the medics into the house in time to hear them announce my mom's death. They let us say goodbye before taking her, and I swear my dad was about to join her on that gurney. My mom was my first experience with death that I understood and saw up close.

It wasn't something I handled well. Neither was my dad. Their marriage was one I'd classify as a goal to have. It might have taken them a while to understand I needed more from them emotionally than they gave me, but they were deeply in love.

My emotions veered wildly in all directions as I listened to my dad leave a message for their lawyer, informing him of my mom's passing. He called what I guessed was a funeral home taking care of whatever she wanted. After that, I stopped listening because I couldn't take it anymore.

I wanted to punch things and scream, something Skull seemed to understand and led me to my room and put me through a workout that left me weak, shaking, and still having crying fits. Trigger looked like he was about to join me in it too.

That night, the night of my mom's death, brought home how close I was to these two. They stayed the entire night and took care of my dad and me. Skull made up the guest room for my dad to sleep in because staying where my mom died was too hard for him.

Trigger made sure we both ate a little something; he hydrated us and was ready with condolences when my dad faltered. Skull watched me like a hawk, calling the school to tell them I would miss a few days due to my mother's death. They left nothing unturned.

Skull listened as I broke down repeatedly, talking about how I thought she was doing better. He told me about the things my mom had said to him and Trigger over the years at the events they were there to support me and sat together. She had seemed to be holding steady and fighting against the curse of the disease.

It helped me understand why Trigger was almost

as emotional as I was. My mom had given him a lot of advice, and Skull credited Trigger's turn around to my mom. It was true that Trigger and Shay had gotten close to my mom, but I hadn't realized it was to the extent that it was.

It gave me mixed feelings. My parents had been so distant with me for so long; hearing that my mom jumped into a mother figure role for two people she hardly knew hurt. The flip side was I was glad that she had been able to be a sounding board to someone that meant a lot to me.

When sleep finally came, it wasn't a peaceful one. I felt the intense aching loss and felt positive that the image of my mom lying dead in her bed would be with me for a very long time. A part of me was happy that my dad didn't have to see that or discover it, but I wished I hadn't either.

My mom hadn't been gone twenty-four hours, and the house felt different and haunted. I didn't want to be here, and several times that I woke up during the night, I had to fight the temptation to leave. I would have felt better sleeping in my car than across the hall from where my mom's life left her.

When the morning arrived, Trigger and Skull left for work, but they promised to check in on us later. My dad looked hollowed out, and I felt how he looked.

"Does it always feel like this?" I asked him.

"What, son?" My dad looked up from staring at the table.

"When someone dies. It's like someone beat me up and then did it some more after I fell," I tried to explain.

"If you love the person, it will always hurt, Darius. People say time heals the wounds, but I'm afraid I have to disagree. Some loss you don't get over," my dad told me. I didn't need to be a genius to understand that he was referring to himself in this instance.

"What do we do now?" I didn't know what else to say, and the silence hurt almost as much as my mom not being here did.

"We go on. It's what your mom wanted. Do you think your friends will be pallbearers?" His voice sounded robotic.

"You mean the people that carry the casket?" I asked.

"Yes, son." He went back to staring at the cold toast in front of him. "Your mom took a liking to them."

"I'm sure they will, Dad. I'll ask them later." I gave up on trying to talk to him.

"She knew it was coming, Darius. She told me not even two days ago. Maisie told me she was talking to her poppa," my dad's voice cracked. "Your grandpa came to take her home."

I shot to my feet, not wanting to hear this. I needed to run from the table, but all those manners they taught me kept my feet planted because I couldn't leave my dad alone when I knew he wasn't okay. He didn't even look this bad when his father died.

"It's okay, Darius. You can go," my dad told me. It was wrong, but I fled.

Chapter 15

Trigger and Skull stood with me in the suits my dad had bought us as we waited for the service to begin. The small Gospel Church my parents sometimes attended was full of people, most of whom I didn't know. It was a surreal feeling.

After the last people passed by my mom's coffin and filed into the church, my dad nodded to us, and we each took a position and carried what remained of my mother to the front. I was thankful the casket was closed now, and I felt ashamed that I had refused to look at her laid out in it.

I didn't want to remember her that way. It wasn't her. That was just her empty body; her soul was now wherever souls go when they leave here. Unlike my parents, I didn't have a firm belief in any faith. Regardless, it all felt like I was only going through the motions.

Trigger and Skull were somber. They sat with my dad and me in front of the church. The pastor talked about the person my mother was in life as if he knew her. We bowed our heads in prayer when he called for it, and we sang the achingly sad songs my mom loved to sing with me when she was sick.

That was when I lost the tenuous hold on my tears, singing Swing Low Sweet Chariot and Amazing Grace. My dad kept his hand on my back and shook like a leaf, and somehow, we made it through my mom's funeral.

The reception was at a hall down the street, and countless people my mom had worked with stopped by to offer their condolences, give us sad smiles and offered up words I didn't think they meant. It was starting to get to me, and Skull kept me sane by pulling me away every so often.

I passed out from emotional exhaustion when we got home, and the next day was a slew of people dropping off food. We had so many casseroles I didn't think we'd have to grocery shop for three months. We didn't even have space for it all in the fridge. My dad packed up over half of them, and we brought them to a shelter not far from us to feed the hungry.

"Go spend some time with your friends tonight, Darius," my dad told me, dropping like a stone onto the sofa. "I'm just going to sit here and be alone with my thoughts. I don't want you worrying about me."

It was odd that I felt like a grown-up right then. I went over and hugged my dad, kissed the top of his head as my parents had done to me, and left him sitting there alone as he wanted. I drove to Skull's and waited in the parking lot until he got home from work.

"There's a party tonight; you gonna stay for it?" Skull asked as we walked in. "Tattoo guy will be back."

That sparked a thought that stuck with me until the tattoo artist arrived. He set up a small station at the kitchen table for his stuff and looked at me. "You want another?"

"Yeah, can you do the words 'we always fight' down my side?" I asked. I talked it out with him, and he showed me different lettering he could freehand. We figured out the placement, and then the tattooist set up the portable table he brought with him in Skull's cramped kitchen.

Trigger showed up halfway through, looked me over for signs I wasn't okay, and grabbed a soda from the fridge. "How's your dad?" he asked me.

"Told me to leave so he could be alone with his thoughts." My answer came out clipped because the tattoo gun was over my ribs, and that shit didn't feel great.

"Time, man, time," Trigger shook his head sadly.

"It's making me think I shouldn't join," I admitted.

"Don't give up your dreams; your mom would hate that," Skull overheard us and stepped into the kitchen.

"You'd resent it too, and your dad would know. Shit like this ain't ever easy, but you gotta keep movin' even when it hurts," Trigger said wisely.

"I mean, for real, I want to tell you not to go, but I know it's what you want and need. My fears can't stand in your way and hold you back; yours shouldn't either. Your dad will be fine," Skull advised. Skull glanced at the words. "Thicken them up a little, so they are darker."

The tattooist grunted but did what Skull said. The needle was puncturing my skin, pushing the ink deep down to immortalize my grandpa's words that my mom told me to live by as she had. My side felt like a gaping wound that matched my heart when the guy finished.

He wrapped some saran wrap around me, and I pulled my shirt back on. I walked out of the kitchen to see the usual cast of characters that frequented Skull's parties. They all clapped me on the back and offered up their words of comfort.

It was starting to be too much again, and it became a choice of making a stupid decision and drinking or doing something else to numb the pain or leave. Trigger walked up behind me and handed me my keys.

"Go home, don't give in to those thoughts," he said into my ear and steered me to the door. "You're better than this, man." He hugged me tightly and then shoved me out the door. "I'll see you tomorrow."

I stayed home from school for the next three days. My mom had been gone for almost two weeks, and it wasn't getting easier to deal with the loss. The coach pulled me out of the next swim meet, partly because I was in no condition to compete and partly because he didn't want my scores too low for the team.

We went to see the lawyer instead because my mom had left a will, and my dad said we had to hear it. My attitude was salty because I didn't need a lawyer to remind me that my mom was dead. I already knew that. I tuned out the entire time and only refocused when my dad prodded me and handed me a letter.

"Mom left that for you." His melancholy voice stabbed another knife in my heart. "I have one too. We can go now."

I robotically stood and followed my dad out of the office and escaped to my room once we were at the house. It didn't feel like home without my mom here. I believed my dad felt the same way, even though we still lived here and had each other.

I flopped back on the bed and stared at the envelope clutched in my hand. My sixteen-year-old heart longed to open it to feel like my mom was talking to me, and my brain told me, hell no, you can't take that shit. I knew I'd read it because my curiosity would get the better of me.

Maybe not quite yet. I needed to do the homework that the teachers told me to do. I set it on the nightstand next to my bed, propped up against the glass of water sitting there. Falling behind now wasn't an option, and despite the fear of leaving my dad alone, I knew more than ever that I wanted out of here.

I pushed off the bed and turned on my computer, glancing at my weight bench with consideration. Nah, homework first, then the letter, then work out the emotions with weights. That was my plan.

I made it halfway through my homework before the weight of that letter sitting there became unbearable. Thoroughly irritated with myself, I saved my work and shut the computer down. The damn thing even felt heavy picking it up off the nightstand.

I held it in my hands again. This letter was more precious than any gold and more destructive than any bomb. If I were Superman, it would be kryptonite. Whatever it said, my mental state wouldn't get any better staring at it. I tore the envelope open gently and blinked rapidly at the shaky 'D' scrawled on the envelope.

Darius, My Son,

First, you must know that I love you with everything I have in me. I know I left you, but in my heart, I also know you are already grown-up, and there's nothing left for me to teach you or prepare you for whatever lies ahead.

I wasn't a great mother, and I'm sorry about that. I will try and tell you why I was so career-focused instead of giving you the nurturing you deserved. It's not an excuse I'm trying to make for my actions. I only want you to understand where you came from; our family descended from slavery.

You know I grew up poor, and you know I lived in Mississippi. I didn't see half the things my parents did, but what I saw and lived was enough to mark me. My momma worked two jobs, and my poppa did too. That only barely got us by. Black people were supposed to be free and equal, but we weren't. Not in Mississippi in that small town.

Being poor isn't a crime. Being poor and black was in some folk's eyes. My parents worked so hard for so little. They struggled every day, and I hardly saw them. My poppa was hard on me and pushed me to excel in school to be better than them. Other than doing the chores and babysitting or helping pick harvests, it was all I could do.

It wasn't easy, baby. So many other students hated

me because my skin was dark. It wasn't just us black folk that felt it. Other brown-skinned people did too. I learned early on in that place, and it didn't matter what I did. I wouldn't ever amount to what I knew I was.

My momma died early from the strain on her heart. She worked herself to death to make sure that I had clothes to wear, even if she had to be the one to sew them for me. I can't help but see the parallels here that I'm leaving you early too, but you have to know how much better than me you are, Darius.

Poppa always went to the marches. He always went to the protests, even if he had to leave a day early because poppa said he wanted me to have a future where I wouldn't be looked down on by anyone else. He organized drives to help people more impoverished than us, which was hard to imagine since we had nothing.

You are so like him, baby. You have that drive and passion for helping and making things better, and you are so bright, just like your grandpa. It matters to me that you know where you come from because he fought so hard to get me to where I was when I met your daddy.

I got scholarships from a negro fund and went to school outside Mississippi. I had to take buses for a week to get to California. In some places, employees forced me to wait overnight in the station because someone else felt another person was more important to be in my seat.

It wasn't like that everywhere, and the farther west I got, the more tolerable things were. Hatred is ugly, baby, and I don't want you to feel it. That feeling only grows and festers inside, eating away at the better stuff that makes you shine.

We Always Fight

I worked my tail off to get good grades. I held down two jobs waitressing to send money back to my poppa and get the things I needed. That's when I met your daddy. He was a sweet talker and a gentleman. His background was similar to mine. Only he wasn't from Mississippi. We dated all through college.

We married after I graduated law school, and I saw that things on the surface might look like they were better for people like us, but it was only that, a surface appearance. We had to fight our way up. Sometimes it was so disheartening to get passed over for something I worked for that I wanted to quit. Your daddy wouldn't let me.

We were putting in eighty-hour work weeks, and by the time I was pregnant with you, I was at a place where if I slowed down, it would have all been for nothing. I had to work three times as hard as anyone else to be recognized. Not even when you were born did they allow me to slow down.

I took you to the office with me. Because the moment they put you in my arms, I knew I didn't want you to live the way I did. There's a benefit to it, and I don't regret one thing in my life in Mississippi. It all shaped me to be strong, the way my poppa wanted me to be.

It was only sometime after I was here did I lose sight of the love my parents taught me. Not for your daddy. Our love was never a problem because we were each other's cheering section. Our focus was just on making sure you wouldn't ever live that way instead of sharing our struggles and what made us so driven.

I know the world has changed since then,

drastically in many ways, but some parts remain. That hate still lingers there, baby, and I know you understand. I saw that when you helped your friends, and they overcame what was holding them down. They did it because you believed in them.

I might not be with you, Darius, but I'm in your blood, I'm in your heart, and I'm in your memories. I'm going to be watching over you. I wish I could be there to see all the good things that will come, and I wish I could be there for all the bad that follows, only so you know you have a cheering section. There's always wrong, baby. It's everywhere. But don't let that stop you from shining that light that burns so brightly in you.

You go after your dreams, son. Nothing will stop you. It won't be easy because nothing worth having is ever easy. You won't always win, Darius, but you always fight. Your grandpa and I live on in you, and your daddy lives for you.

I know this is hard, baby. Please have patience with him. Get out of this house that will only make him stuck. Push him to stay in the present, and chase your dreams. Don't give them up. I'm so proud of you, Darius; you did all this without us. It's all you, baby.

Sing for me when you feel sad. Sing the hymns we sang together, and know I'm singing them with you. Keep shining your light on the evil, and have a little faith in your heart. It can carry you when everything else seems to let you down.

Your ancestors may have been slaves, but you aren't. They fought to survive, and you'll have to too. Knowing your path is hard for me because I want you safe *as your mother. I see now that life is still a war. I can feel it deep in my bones and my heart. I'll be leaving soon. My mind isn't always where it should be, and sometimes I'm back in the swamps of Mississippi, swatting the mosquitos away while I hang our laundry on the lines.*

Marry a nice girl and have some babies that you tell stories about your momma and her poppa and where they came from; we'll never be gone if you do that. I love you, baby. I should have told you that more often.

Love,

Mom

The writing was so shaky towards the end; it was almost unintelligible. There were also splotches on the paper that were probably tears. I gently folded it up, put the letter back in the envelope, and kissed it.

"I love you too, Mom," I whispered through my rush of tears.

There was no way I wanted to know what she had written to my father. I tucked the letter into my dresser drawer and vowed that it would come with me wherever I went. Wiping my eyes with my shirt, I sat down on the weight bench and threw my sorrow into working out.

Chapter 16

I received my motorcycle endorsement for my license and finished with all the school sports. I still did the swim club through the city and not the school. I was in the final two months of school; my seventeenth birthday would happen a week after graduation.

Swimming was still my weakest sport, but I had significantly improved my times and was adept enough to qualify based on the times on the sheets that Rodriguez had given me. At least the initial times listed for the SEALs. I was sure after getting in that those times would change.

I set my bag down in my bedroom, grabbed the books I needed, and returned to the kitchen, finding a note from my dad asking me not to leave until after he got home. It was fine with me. I hadn't made plans for tonight anyway. Tomorrow night was a party at Skull's that I was going to go to; tonight, I had figured I'd get all the needed homework done.

I had some big projects due for the college classes and wanted to stay ahead. Finals were in two weeks, and I tried to keep my perfect grade point average. I made a snack, set it on the table, and opened the books.

I lost myself in work and hadn't moved until my dad walked in and gave me a half-smile. As we tried to adjust to my mom's absence, things hadn't become more manageable. My dad had lost a lot of weight and was starting to look sick. The light-hearted banter we had been getting used to was gone, and the house was still unnaturally silent at times.

There wasn't tension between us. My dad still came to whatever events I had going on and asked about my life. His smile was gone now, and he was depressed most of the time. I didn't know how to help him get through it because I was in the same spot he was in, only I had school and sports to distract me.

"I brought home a pizza," my dad told me. "One of those we need to cook."

"Sounds good," I replied, standing to turn the oven on while he put his stuff down. "How was work?"

"Same shit. Some of the executives aren't happy with anything. They have their favorites and refuse to look at the bigger picture," he said glumly. "I'm going to change. I'll be back."

I watched him walk down the hallway to the extra room. He still slept in there, and I didn't think he'd move back into their bedroom. I turned and unwrapped the pizza, picking a piece of pepperoni off to eat it. When the oven chimed, I set the timer, put it in and leaned against the counter. It took my dad longer than usual to change clothes.

Shrugging, I pulled out some plates and set them on the table, shoving my books out of the way. When I heard him coming, I noticed how slowly he moved.

"Are you feeling okay, Dad?" I asked, worrying.

"Tired, son. My energy isn't where it used to be, and some days are harder than others. I'm not sick, so don't worry none about that," he tried to reassure me.

I let out the breath I'd been holding, grabbed my dad a soda, and handed it to him. "Did you want something else?"

"No, this is fine. Sit down, Darius. Relax." My dad popped open the can and took a gulp. "How's school?"

"Gearing up for finals. I have three projects due for the college-level courses next week. The week after that is finals. Finals for my regular classes, too. Lots of studying in my immediate future. I'll be glad when that is over; I don't think I realized how stressful that is," I admitted.

"You'd never know it to look at you, son. You've handled it all amazingly well," my dad praised me.

I wouldn't go that far. "Thanks, Dad."

Just as he was about to say something, the timer on the oven dinged. I motioned him to stay put, pulled the pizza out of the range, and brought it back to the table with the pizza cutter. I handed it to him to slice up and sat back down.

We ate in silence for a bit when I glanced back at my dad. His eyes were on me, but I don't think he was looking at me. He appeared lost in thought. His face relaxed into a sad frown. Whatever he was trying to work up the nerve to tell me, he struggled with it; I could see that much.

"Just spit it out, Dad. Tear the band-aid off," I said as gently as I could.

"That's about what it will feel like," he sighed. "I'm going to put the house up for sale."

I can't say I expected that, but it didn't surprise me as much as he probably thought it would. "Might be for the best," I agreed, shocking him. "I hate thinking about leaving here because it's where all my memories of Mom are, but at the same time, it feels haunted and different."

I saw the sheen of tears in my dad's eyes as he nodded. "It doesn't make sense to stay when you aren't here. It's too much for just me, and being somewhere fresh might help me move on."

I got the feeling there was more he hadn't said yet, and I gave him the time to figure out how to say it. "Should we have a garage sale?"

"We could do that," his faint voice was hard to hear. "I don't think I'll buy another house. Does that bother you?"

"What do you mean?" I wasn't quite following what he was saying.

"I think I'll just rent an apartment for a bit." He shot a guilty look at me. "There's been talk of opening a branch east of the Mississippi. I'm considering putting in for a transfer."

Now I was stunned silent. My dad never had anything good to say about living in the southeast. "Where?"

"They haven't decided yet. It could be northeast or southeast. They aren't sure. Does that bother you?" he asked, concerned.

"No. Maybe a little, but it shouldn't." I needed to

keep moving. "I'll be wherever the Navy stations me, and it's your life, so you should live where you think you will be best. Are you sure that's what you want?" I gathered our plates and brought them to the sink while he wrapped up the remaining pizza.

"I'm not sure about anything anymore, Darius. That's the problem. Nothing can fill the hole your mom's absence left in me, and a part of me feels like runnin'. Almost all my years here in California were with your mom. I'm not saying this to scare you, son, but I think if I stay here where she's everywhere, I might be joining her quicker than I thought," he slumped against the counter.

"Don't let worry over my feelings stop you from doing what's right for you, Dad. I'll be in the Navy for at least six years. After that, if I get out, I can go anywhere. You need to do what feels best for you because I don't want to lose you so soon after losing Mom. I see how it's affected you," I told him, busying myself with loading the dishwasher.

"It would be at least a year before they opened anything east of here." My dad put his hand on my shoulder. "Would you visit me?"

"Dad, why wouldn't I? You are my dad." The question made me want to cry.

"Not a very good one, son. I don't want to make any choices unless you agree with them. You're the only thing I've got left in this world, and if you want me here, that's where I'll stay," he said again.

"Dad, what I want is for you to be happy. I get that it doesn't seem like a possibility right now, but it might be in the future. If being here hurts too much, go where you need to go. Airplanes, motorcycles, cars, and trains can bring me to where you end up. Honestly, I agree with you about the house. It's hard being here," I hugged him briefly.

We spent the rest of the night talking about what he would bring with him to an apartment, which wasn't much. He could get rid of the furniture and everything else. All I needed to take with me were clothes and a few mementos I didn't want to lose.

We planned a day for a garage sale and started packing up things for the rest of the weekend. He said that he would put the house on the market after I graduated. He had me go with him to a couple of apartments, and we scoped them out.

Trigger offered to watch over him while I was gone, and Skull did too. We talked about it at his party. I met the girl that Trigger had started dating and spent some time relaxing with my brothers. The time seemed more significant now that things were closer to me leaving.

It felt that way with my dad, too, especially knowing he needed to leave as much as I did. We spent a lot of time remembering and telling stories as we packed up the things he wanted to keep and the stuff we would get rid of, and we started moving to a pile for the garage sale.

Nostalgia hit us hard a few times, and we had to stop when the grief hit. It was like that for the next two weeks. The countdown had started, and we both felt the pull of time. I wasn't going to be only saying goodbye to my friends and my dad; I'd be saying goodbye to my childhood home.

Trigger and Skull came over several nights, and they grilled dinner for us and peppered my dad with questions about when he and my mom dated. Memories that made him smile and cry both. They were helping him say goodbye, and I appreciated it more than I could verbalize.

Chapter 17

ollege class finals finished. Now I only had the high school finals left. In comparison, they would be a lot easier, and I was far less stressed about those than I had been for the college classes. My dad took us out for a nice steak dinner after the last of those finals, and we celebrated the A.A.S. degree that would get presented to me along with my high school diploma. Felt a little backward, but high school wasn't over yet, even though the other classes were.

Later, I went to my last party at Skull's before I left. He had them every other weekend, but I'd promised my dad that I would spend my last couple of weekends at home with him before I graduated and left. He was planning on having the guys over after my graduation for dinner.

Skull, Trigger, and I were sitting on Skull's balcony while the partiers inside did their thing. They'd said they wanted a moment with me without the others there to interrupt or be asses.

"I wouldn't be here right now if it weren't for you, man," Skull told me with a thump on the back. "I'd probably be dead, in a gang, or maybe on drugs. Who knows. Instead, I got a job, my GED, and my own damn place."

"Word. He got that right, bro. I talk like a thug, but man, it's because of you that Shay and me are alive. I'm so proud of you, nerd. I know I ain't say it enough, but it's true. Seein' all you've accomplished only makes me want to do more," Trigger added. "Nothin' but love, brother. That's what I got for you."

"You did it on your own. I didn't do the work for you. I just guided you. Give yourselves some credit," I told the guys again. "I wouldn't be this bulked-out beast that's gonna tackle the SEALs if it weren't for you two. The way I see it, the thanks and love go both ways."

"Beatin' you up was the best thing we did," Skull joked.

I laughed. "I'd probably still be hiding in those bushes if you hadn't threatened that girl."

"Nah, you ain't a pussy no more," Trigger grinned. "You dress better now too."

Skull was halfway out of his chair when the sound of gunshots registered with me. Trigger shoved me forward to get low as the slider behind us shattered into fragments and the night filled with terrified screams.

It felt like it lasted forever, and I honestly couldn't have said how long the gunfire went on. I only knew when it stopped. I'd never been so scared before. I glanced at Skull first and saw blood staining his shoulder and him leaning against the apartment.

Panic hit me, and I looked over at Trigger and almost screamed. I reached for him and saw the blood coming from his mouth, his breathing staggered, and I felt his pulse thin and racing too fast. "Oh, God. Trigger, man, say something," I pleaded.

He didn't; all I heard was a gurgling sound. I screamed for someone to call 9-1-1 and held him cradled in my lap; his hand clutched mine with fading strength until it went limp, and there was no more light in his eyes.

It was my second up-close brush with death, and instead of overwhelming depression, I became consumed with rage. I would have gladly broken the neck of whoever fired those shots that injured my two best friends, taking one's life.

Trigger's blood covered my hands, clothes, and skin. My heart hardened and broke, and I vowed revenge with every pissed-off tear that fell from my eyes. I only released Trigger when the medics came, their words announcing Trigger DOA ringing in my ears.

Only my concern for the state Skull was in kept me somewhat from losing my shit completely. Skull begged the medics to allow me to ride with him, and I followed numbly, watching as the white-covered gurney got loaded into a second ambulance.

Skull's blood-coated hand gripped mine as we sped through the streets to the hospital, and I promised to stay in that waiting room for him. The nurses allowed me to use their phone and call my dad, who came and held vigil with me as we waited to hear about Skull's status.

The police took my statement, doctors tried to treat me for shock, and I refused. They asked if I was on drugs, which pissed my dad off. I submitted a urine and blood test to prove that I wasn't. They made me do a breathalyzer to show I wasn't drinking. All the while, I was covered with my best friend's blood.

Somehow, we were to blame for someone driving up and shooting us for sitting on a balcony. Not even Skull or Trigger had been drinking. I was certain Trigger was clean and mostly confident that Skull was dead sober when that had happened. It was wrong and fueled the fury inside me to lethal levels.

When Shay came tearing into the hospital in a panic, that first little warning sign I was going to break happened. She threw herself at me, sobbing hysterically, and I set her down between my dad and me.

I saw the racial and class divide clearly for the first time in an up-close and personal way. Skull may have lived in a lower-income part of town, and he might be involved in some shady things, but in no way did that warrant the level of suspicion the cops were leveling our way.

My dad left a message for his lawyer and sat there with Shay and me until they said that Skull was in the recovery room and that the doctors had to do surgery on his shoulder. I wasn't going to leave that hospital until I saw him with my own eyes.

Media outlets started to show up and lobbed questions at me, getting in my face with cameras until a lone cop stepped in and threatened to arrest them for harassing minors. The tag on his uniform said Sanchez, and he moved us to a more private waiting area.

I wasn't aware that he was there to watch over me, that the other cop said I was suspicious. I didn't find that out until we got allowed to see Skull. Shay broke down in tears again, and a doctor had to sedate her. Skull groggily requested that they leave her in the room with him, and Sanchez pulled some strings to make it happen.

Then the cop came clean about why he was there and threw question after question at Skull. He could only answer half of them through the pain medication they had him on, and my dad stepped in and said to save it for when the lawyer got there.

It became the longest night of my life. Having Trigger die in my arms solidified my need to make it through SEAL training and become someone that wouldn't get messed with and demanded respect. It might have been idealistic, but it was all I had.

Three other people had gotten shot that night. None of the others had severe injuries or required surgery like Skull. If Trigger hadn't shoved me down, I probably would have received my own wound or bled out with him. Five people were injured, and we had no idea why.

Shay couldn't find her mother to tell her and wailed that she was probably out wasted somewhere or selling herself for money for her next hit. When Skull woke up again, he had her climb on the bed next to him, and he promised to take care of her.

My dad vowed to help Skull with a lawyer, and almost half a day later, he left the hospital with me in tow. Sanchez cleared the way for us through the media that camped out and promised me he would look out for Skull.

"It wasn't my call to question you, kid. I'm sorry you had to go through that and that you lost a friend. I've been through it too, and it's senseless. I will ask you how the living situation is for Shay?" Sanchez asked as he escorted us to my dad's car.

"Her mom's a junkie, and her brother took care of her," I snapped. I didn't give a shit if he thought I had an attitude. "That shit they pulled was because we are black, right?"

Sanchez didn't answer, but the guilty look on his face spoke volumes. "There's gang activity in that neighborhood. Not all gangs are black, and there are Latino ones nearby. If you had looked like me, you would have gotten the same treatment. I'm not condoning it, just explaining."

My dad hustled me away from the cop and pushed me into the car. "Stop talking, son. It won't help," he hissed at me. He thanked Sanchez for the escort and took me to get my car.

I found bullet holes and immediately decided to sell the car with the house or donate it. I wanted nothing that reminded me of the bullets that took my friend from me. I longed to set the thing on fire and watch it burn to nothing.

Jesus, this was a mind fuck, and I didn't want to be on this ride. On the tail of my mother dying, one of my best friends gets murdered. Then the rest of us get accused of criminal acts. I drove home feeling shell-shocked, following my dad, thankfully, or I might have kept driving since I wasn't seeing where I was going.

Saying I went on auto-pilot wouldn't be correct. I was aware I was making moves, that my brain was calculating, planning, coping, adjusting, and grieving. I just wasn't aware of what came of any of it. I parked the car and let my dad lead me into the house and to the bathroom, where he instructed me to leave my god-awful clothes outside the door so he could get rid of them.

"The car, too, Dad," I said quietly. "Today, I became someone else."

Chapter 18

Two days before graduation, there was a knock on my front door. Since Skull was here with me, I wasn't sure who it could be. My dad was still at work. Fearing more media, I shot Skull a look to stay put and flung the door open with a lot of attitude behind it.

Standing there was Rodriguez, looking a little surprised. "Baker, I saw in the papers what you are going through. Can I come in?"

Rodriguez wasn't my enemy and didn't deserve my ire. He wore fatigues, probably the same size as me, but he had more of an edge than I did. I couldn't shake the attitude rolling off me, but I stepped out of the way to allow him in. The place was full of boxes and scant furniture. We'd sold or donated everything else.

"Moving?" he looked around.

"My dad doesn't want to stay here after I join. My mom passed," I informed Rodriguez.

"That's a lot to deal with, Baker," his face fell. "I'm sorry. With your path taking you to the SEALs, I only wanted to stop by to wish you luck and hope to find you staying on the straight side of things after that shit that went down."

"Barely," I admitted. "It changed me. I want to destroy everything now."

"I've been there, brother," Rodriguez nodded sadly. "Channel it into something productive, or it will take you apart."

"Nothing takes this man apart," Skull walked out then. "Nothing and no one. You got me, homey?"

"The SEALs program's design is to take you apart, break you down, and make you weak," Rodriguez didn't bat an eye at the implied threat. "It's only when you know your weaknesses and how to conquer them and use them to achieve your goals will it make you who you want to be," Rodriguez replied, looking only at me. "Don't let this add to that weight. Channel it, Baker."

I nodded my understanding. "You back in the recruiting office?"

"No, I had a day off, and I'm shipping out tomorrow. I took the opportunity to come out here and check on you because I've seen the papers. You've got what it takes to get through this, Baker, I've never believed in a fresh young recruit the way I do you, and I don't want to see this deter you. Let it be your fuel," Rodriguez offered again, flicking his eyes at Skull. "Be the support he needs."

Before Skull could get pissed, I stepped closer to him. "He always has been, from the start. Where are they sending you?"

"Persian Gulf. Maybe we'll cross paths again, Baker. Things like this have a way of shaping you but remember you are in charge of what that shape turns out to be, no one else. Two of my friends didn't make it through the program, and they were tough sons of bitches. It's okay if they break you, don't stay that way. Use it as a platform," Rodriguez advised. "Take care of yourself."

"You too, man. Stay safe out there," I stuck my hand out to shake his, and he yanked me in to thump me on the back in a one-armed hug.

"Sorry that you have gone through this, and my condolences on your mother." Rodriguez nodded at Skull. "My condolences to you as well."

"You seriously care, don't you?" Skull shifted uncomfortably.

"I do. Baker left a big impression on me. He's starting from a much better place than I did, and he has the drive." Rodriguez saluted me and turned to go back out the door.

"Thanks, Rodriguez," I called after him. I closed the door quietly and looked around the living room. "Might as well put these muscles to work."

Skull carried things with his uninjured arm, and we loaded up my dad's SUV to bring stuff to his new apartment. My graduation day was the day my childhood home was on the market. We'd take a load, unpack and get the place set up, return to the house and do it over again. Four trips later, the apartment was mostly set up except for beds.

"You know how Trigger's mom made a scene at the funeral?" Skull asked suddenly.

"Yeah?" I looked at him warily.

"She ain't been sober since," Skull breathed out.

"The lawyer your dad hired for me kept me from being charged with anything, even though I did nothin' wrong. We was just sittin' there. But I'm worried Shay's gonna end up in the system. They got eyes on her now."

"What's your plan?" I asked as we sat in the backyard on the deck since the patio furniture was still there.

"Don't know. Shay's been staying wit' me," Skull's slang was fading in and out. He was struggling as much as I was with the whole thing.

"Ask the lawyer if you can petition for guardianship," I suggested.

"I did. Lawyer's not sure I can get it." Skull adjusted his sling and sighed angrily. "Trigger's prolly rollin' in his grave worryin' 'bout her."

"Start the process whether the lawyer thinks you can win it or not," I told him. "It's better than doing nothing."

"I gotta move too," Skull shook his head to clear his thoughts. "As your dad said, the place has too many memories now."

I could see that. When my dad got home, we talked more, and he told Skull he'd think about it and explore the options. He agreed with Skull that Shay needed to be away from the toxicity of the environment that their mother presented.

Rodriguez's words were floating in my mind while the two of them talked. He was right; I needed to channel this anger and shape it how I wanted it to be, not a product of a society already filled with hate. Sadness weighed on me at the thought.

What would Trigger want me to do? I wondered. He'd like me to overcome it all and make it matter. That was who he had been becoming, someone that wanted to make a difference the same way I did.

Two days later, at my graduation, I still hadn't figured it out. I was the class valedictorian and had to make a speech that I hadn't written because there was too much in my head to get that far. I was getting a diploma and a degree, and I had lettered in track and football. My mom and Trigger weren't here to see it. In the audience was my dad, Skull, Shay, and to my complete surprise, the cop Sanchez.

They called me to the stage to make a speech, and I dragged my feet as much as possible. I stared blankly at the sea of excited and expectant faces looking back at me, waiting for my words of wisdom or something.

I cleared my throat. "I stand here before a group of students that have accomplished their first hurdle in life; high school. It's not easy, given how society is turning out to be. Some are born with gifts, whether they have a privilege or not. Some are born with privilege, and it doesn't matter what they do in high school or after. Some fall through the cracks and learn to survive. Those people aren't seated among you today unless they are in the audience."

I saw Skull nod at me. "I know this much; whatever you put into it is what you'll get out of it. For everything. Life, work, relationships, school, sports. I had the honor of getting beat up by two of the best men I have ever known. Instead of making myself a victim of bullying or circumstance, I turned the tables on it and showed them how to allow themselves to make things different. I think this is the message I want to impart to all of you. You can turn the table on anything, and you can help others doing it. That's how we change the world, one life at a time. Adversity is an opportunity to change and grow."

A few heads bobbed among the seated students, the ones who had to fight for their place to be seated there. "The only thing that defines you is yourself; your actions, behavior, and how you get through roadblocks put in front of you. A Navy man told me a few days ago that life shapes you, and it's true. In the last few months, I lost two extremely vital people to sickness and murder. Even though life shapes you, you choose what shape it will take. High school gave us barely enough knowledge to survive what's coming for us; it's a starting point. Those deaths taught me that. You have your futures ahead of you, which might be hard. We don't know. But fight for it, fight for yourself, and fight for those you love. The world isn't a kind place, but that doesn't mean you don't have to be a kind person. Make the choices that will move you closer to the shape you want. Fellow students, congratulations on making it over this first hurdle. Here's to the future," I said and tipped my cap at them. I stepped away from the microphone to a burst of applause.

A few football players stood and chanted my name as I took my seat. The principal took the stage and thanked me. "Some of you might not know this, but Darius also joins the military after graduation. I'd like us all to send him off with good thoughts and prayers for safety and success."

Slightly embarrassed, I smiled my thanks to the shouts and cheers of the people around me. I patiently waited while they went through the names. I stood in line while the students in front of me received their diplomas. When it was my turn, I received two and another short speech praising my academic achievements. I faced the audience, hearing my cheering section be louder than anyone else present.

"For Trigger," I mouthed to Skull, held the two papers high, and marched back to my seat with tears in my eyes. I'd done it. I had accomplished my first set of serious goals with blinding success and heartbreak.

After the ceremony, I learned my dad had invited Sanchez to see that his son wasn't a worthless kid who would amount to nothing but another life that ended up on the street. Those were his words, and Skull flinched.

"Son, I'm not referring to you," my dad put a hand on Skull's uninjured shoulder. "That statement is aimed at the people who took your friend's life."

"My other reason for showing up, other than to see you take some pretty big steps," Sanchez smiled kindly at me, "was to inform you that we have a lead on the people that shot at you."

These words had Skull paying close attention. "Who are they?"

"I'll bring them to justice. I promise you that," Sanchez gave Skull a stern look. "Don't get involved. Darius doesn't need another casualty added to his list."

The statement had the desired effect of calming Skull, but Shay was chomping at the bit. "Who are they?"

she repeated Skull's question.

"A local gang. It turns out that one of the sisters of this group was at your party," Sanchez told us without naming names.

And then I knew. The only new face was Trigger's girl. I saw that Skull had made the same connection. It came to me that Sanchez also warned Skull to stand back and not go after justice independently.

I couldn't tell whether he would heed the warning or not. Later that night, Skull answered a call that delivered more news. It wasn't good, but maybe for the best. Shay's mom was found dead from an overdose. My dad decided to take her under his care and set the lawyer to work to see if he could become Shay's legal guardian.

Skull was a little relieved knowing that Shay wouldn't be sent into the system and end up in an equally dangerous place, but he was also disappointed that he wouldn't get to take care of her. In my opinion, it gave Skull a chance to find a new place to live, a little breathing room for her to get his life back under control.

A week later, I stood before my house and said a final goodbye. My heart drummed painfully in my chest to the echoes in my memory of my mom and me singing. Two hours later, I left for boot camp with fire in my veins.

Skull would be okay. He and my dad were watching over each other and Shay. It was harder than saying goodbye to the house, but I knew I'd see them again. I wouldn't be the same person I was now, and I shouldn't be.

In the Navy

Chapter 19

The physical part of boot camp wasn't so hard. The constant yelling and talking down was especially difficult since I joined with a chip on my shoulder. After all, my best friend had died bleeding out in my arms from senseless violence and then getting treated like a criminal because I'm black.

I barely managed to keep my mouth shut because Rodriguez had warned me about this. Thankfully, I wasn't getting singled out more than anyone else. A few drill instructors knew I was going to BUDS training after this, and they rode me hard on some of the physical activities, which I didn't mind.

Up early and start. I can't say the eight weeks went fast, but they didn't crawl by either. I lost some weight, but my muscle tone also changed. I didn't have much weight to lose, so I ate a little more when we got our meals.

The females in our basic training were badass, even though there were not many. I only saw one flinch when they were getting yelled at, and she came across as softer than the others. The woman still put the work in, always made the times, and I just got the sense she was here because it was the option that worked best for her life.

The mentor assigned to me kept track of my progress the same way I was. I kept the journal I'd started several years ago to track my fitness, spot weaknesses, and where I needed to improve.

That first week during the meals, our class would talk about the areas they were interested in joining and what they looked forward to the most. When it came to my turn, and I told them I was heading to BUDs/SEAL training, they got quiet and started to treat me a little differently.

After that, they separated themselves from me; usually, the women in our class sat with me. Which I was okay with; I scored a few minor hookups that way and got to test if Star's lessons had stuck. It seems like they did. One of the women even taught me some new things. I wasn't having an awful time.

For as hard as people say basic training is, it's not. It's the same stuff I put myself through at home, minus the yelling. Even that starts to fade to background noise after a few weeks. I knew it was only a shadow of what I had coming toward me, but I looked forward to it.

I'd aced all the tests they'd given me, and my mentor had suggestions on what areas he thought I would excel in. Some I agreed with; I still felt that explosives would be my goal. I liked the challenge it presented and the intel gathering and surveillance.

I called my dad after basic training finished. I gave him all my updates, and he filled me in on the situation with Skull and Shay. Both were living with him for the time being, and Skull was applying for guardianship. My dad was doing everything he could to help ensure that Skull got it. Shay maintained her grades, but my dad said she'd lost the spark she used to have.

Understandable, in my eyes. Death had changed me too. I had one day between the end of basic training and the start of BUDs A school. Since I didn't need to travel, I took the opportunity to ride and get my head clear.

I had two months of preparation training and three weeks of introduction to BUDs. My mentor had told me that these three weeks of the introduction would show me what life would be like during training. My last times in all the physical exercise qualified me without a doubt. I beat the officers' times that had been on the list.

I took that to mean many more people in my face trying to get me to snap, which was why I decided to take the ride. Not only did I feel like it connected me with Trigger's spirit, but it also made me get outside of my head and pay attention to the pricks around me that weren't looking for me.

When I returned, I moved my stuff to the new barracks and ran into the woman from basic training. Rachel was her name, and she flirted with me a bit and offered a one-time fuck that I took. We parted with Rachel giving me a kiss on the cheek and a pat on the ass. There was no shame in admitting that Rachel owned me for that hour.

I smiled as I walked back to the barracks. There was no shortage of sex on base if you knew where to look. Since no women were in the BUDs training, I figured that would change slightly, but I didn't need to get laid as much as some other guys did.

I nodded to the guys that arrived in the barracks and sized them up. A couple of them looked like they wouldn't get far, but I couldn't say that for certainty since they passed the physical tests to get to this point. One guy was so big he looked like he ate people for breakfast.

Whatever. I didn't have to like any of these guys. I had to work with them, train, and live with them. The only guy who didn't introduce himself to me and the others was the smallest, and he looked to be Asian of some sort. This man was the one I knew I needed to watch out for; size isn't indicative of skill, and he exuded danger.

We were going to get woken up early and shoved into some endurance training right off the bat. My mentor had given me a little insight into what would happen. I supposed he felt a bit sorry for me since I was the youngest here by at least a year.

I was ready. I was even awake before the drill instructor screamed into his bullhorn. The big guy and the little one got prepared moments later while the rest struggled. I knew then that those two would make it through the program. I'd set my mind that I would.

By the end of that first eight weeks, I was a beast, and people noticed me. I paced myself, never showing just how far I could go without losing the times I had posted on my exams. As we headed into the next two months, we were assigned a boat crew, and the big guy, whom we called Moose, and the little guy, we called Mouse, were both assigned to my team.

We now completed our runs in boots and pants, and under the heat of the California sun, it wasn't fun. From what I could see, we were the top three recruits in the class's entirety, and the instructors wanted us where they could see how we worked together. Moose was laid-back, whereas Mouse had that same chip on his shoulder that I did. There wasn't a lot of socializing, yet we meshed.

Ocean swims were my least favorite part, mainly because sharks and the thought of sharks scared the shit out of me, but that worked in my favor because I swam faster to make sure I didn't get eaten. Little by little, my body was adapting to the extreme activity level we were going through.

Then came Hell Week. Physically I handled it okay, I was exhausted and running on empty for most of it, but the mental stress pushed me farther than I'd ever gone before. The little sleep I got, which wasn't more than three hours probably, I'd have nightmares of Trigger. I assumed it was because of how weakened my mental state was, which even traumatized me. It also fueled my need to succeed.

By the end of that week, I was ready to tear the instructors' heads off and hand-feed them to the sharks; I think Mouse and Moose were, too. It was the most intense thing I'd gone through yet, and a handful of times, my brain told me to ring that damn bell. The instructors had carved that chip right off my shoulder and shoved it down my throat.

I didn't quit, and I'm proud of myself for getting through it. I knew it wouldn't get easier from here on out, it was only going to get more challenging, but the instructors wouldn't break me; I refused to succumb. Charting was interesting, and when we got to combat diving, I struggled a little more because of the fish. I hadn't seen a shark yet but encountered a whale and almost shit my wetsuit.

Whenever it came to demolitions and explosives, my skills outmatched anyone else's, even some of the instructors. I was on their radar after that. Land warfare was a piece of cake for me. Parachuting was fun, and the advanced training and cold weather training weren't so bad. My eighteenth birthday passed, and Moose offered to get a hooker for me.

I laughed and told him I didn't need help in that area. When it came time for individual training, my mentor suggested the same thing the instructors had, surveillance, advanced demolition, and some field medic training. I agreed to the field medic part because of Trigger.

When we made it through the training, got our tridents, and got assigned squads, I heard talk about adding me to a particular team. Then the shit hit the fan. A few months after turning nineteen, terrorists attacked us on our home soil. It was devastating, heartbreaking, and terrifying. Each time the news replayed the towers in New York falling, I wanted to get sick.

All military branches kicked into high gear, and those of us available and ready got deployed. I was allowed one week before the Navy sent me overseas for nine months, and a few people told me to make peace with whoever was left in my life because shit was about to get real.

My dad was worried, and Skull was furious. Shay was sixteen now, and Skull decided to move north out of California. There was a biker club that he had met some people from that he wanted to join. Skull had secured himself a position with a gym and gotten Shay enrolled in school. The day before I deployed, he left for Washington state.

My dad was getting ready to move east to Chicago. I helped him pack, and we had another goodbye when the movers came the same day Skull left. He gave me an e-mail address and physical address to write to him, and he'd gotten a cellular phone for which he provided the phone number on the chance that I could make calls.

To my eyes, my dad was still firmly in the grieving process, and it wasn't something I thought he would ever get over. I hoped that Chicago would be suitable for him, and I promised to visit on my next leave. We shared a teary goodbye, and I headed back to base to mentally prepare for war.

Seeing the destruction caused by the towers falling in New York was an excellent motivator to kick ass. The squad I'd gotten assigned was the same as Mouse. Moose had gotten transferred to one on a ship, and he'd left while I was on leave. I don't think any of us were ready for what we got sent into, land or sea.

Chapter 20

Command sent my assigned squad on a few missions to remove isolated terrorist cells. I thought California was hot. I was wrong; we were in Hell. Weighed down by heavy gear under the beating desert sun, it felt like my blood was turning to tar inside my body.

The gathering of the intel, planning the attack, and mapping it out weren't so bad. Pulling the trigger at someone was a different type of hell; you trained for it, but nothing could prepare you. At least I didn't feel prepared. I did it because it was either do it myself or die while they took the opening I left.

These fuckers were using kids and women. It made me sick. The stench of death, that heavy gunpowder smell mixed with the piss, shit, and blood, was putrefying. I was deliriously happy when the commander pulled me out of close combat and had me assemble some explosives to take out the buildings in a covert destroy mission. Killing from a distance was more comfortable for me.

Explaining how the charge would detonate, the debris field, and what we could expect for damage was nothing. It didn't bother me that I knew my creation would take lives. Well, it did, but not like staring at the eyes of the person you were about to shoot dead did.

I had to admit that I was a little jealous of Moose being on a boat on the water. I excelled at land warfare, and I wasn't surprised that it was how they used me. Mouse's small size allowed him to get in places easier than some of us bigger dudes, and he often took my bombs and placed them.

I wouldn't say we were friends, but we respected each other and had each other's six. We were out there doing the shit no one else was doing, which made my ego a little bigger. I had become the badass I set out to be.

I can't say that I ever thought it would come to fruition in Iraq, but whatever, I was a lethal machine. My skills were earning me attention in several areas, and our squad got requests all the time for us to clear the way for ground troops.

When we were allowed, I'd use the communications tent and send emails to my dad, letting him know I was fine, and I'd write one to Skull to check on him. I received replies from my dad far more than I did Skull, but I was happy when I got one.

I was on that first tour in Iraq for an entire year, not nine months. I had many more encounters with death than I expected, and it never got easier, not even when I was the one dealing it out.

I felt weird going back to the states for a visit with my dad. It wasn't my home, nor anywhere I'd ever been. I took an opportunity and flew out to Washington to see

Skull, and that felt more comfortable to me, probably because it was Skull and Shay and maybe the west coast. I didn't know. The desert had fucked me all up.

"Damn, Dar, you've changed," was the first thing out of Skull's mouth after we had a brother hug.

"War does that, Skull. Thanks for sending emails back. It's nice to know no one's forgotten me over there. That shit is intense, bro," I settled onto his couch. He had a small house in a city called Tacoma.

"Feels shitty to tell you that things are going good for me when you get bathed in blood." Skull offered me a beer, and I accepted.

"Still contributing to a minor, I see," I laughed.

"Only in age. You doing shit grown-ass men over here ain't eva' done." The slang came back thick in his voice.

"I'm still me, Skull," I replied. It felt like a lie.

"No, Dar, you aren't," he went back to talking without slang. It was as if he couldn't figure out how to act around me. "You're different, man. You got this feel to you that screams come near me, and I'll fucking kill you and not blink twice."

I visibly flinched. "Sorry. Fallout from being over there, I guess. People coming at you don't mean anything good over there. I'd never hurt you, Skull."

"I know. Tell me about your team," Skull requested and relaxed and sat back in his chair.

I told him about training and Moose and Mouse. I told him about my squad and how Mouse was the only one I felt somewhat attached to out of all of them. I gave him brief descriptions of things I'd seen, missions we'd gone on, and some of the scary close-calls we've had.

Skull's expression shuttered closed, and he looked worried for me. "How about you come to a party at the club with me tonight? You'll get laid. There's these ho's that hang 'round for that purpose only. Just use protection," Skull offered with a careful grin.

I shrugged. Getting laid wouldn't be so bad. "I need to stay clean, so no alcohol and no laced drinks," I warned Skull.

"Got your back." Skull stood and showed me the bedroom I could use while visiting. "Shay's in school, but she'll be back in a couple of hours."

"A lot's changed in a year," I said, looking around and dropping my bag.

"Yeah, it has." Skull's answer was quiet and reverent. He shook it off quickly. "I'm number two in the club. Rose through the ranks pretty fast after they saw my fighting skills. They taught me to ride better, shoot, and some tricks they don't show you in the Navy."

"Ah, my friend," I smiled at the challenge in his voice. "In this case, the student has become the teacher."

Skull guffawed and thumped me on the back. "Got a setup in the garage. We can battle for old time's sake."

"Deal." I stripped off my shirt, and Skull gave me a once-over, noticing the scars.

"I ain't asking, cuz it will piss me off." He turned, and I followed him to the garage, where he had a mini-ring setup. "Pads?"

"To be safe," I warned him. Something weird was

happening inside me, and I rolled my shoulders to loosen up.

Skull tossed pads at me and then some gloves. He geared up while I did the same and shoved a mouthguard in before I put the gloves on. Skull was a hell of a fighter, but I wasn't the same kid he taught to throw a punch.

I dropped him the first two rounds with minimal effort. It spurred him to try moves I hadn't seen him take, but he still couldn't get one over on me. I started to show him some of the techniques, and he caught on quickly enough.

After I dropped him again, he let out a yell that transported me overseas instantly, and I wasn't standing in a garage boxing ring anymore. I was in the middle of sand with crazy fuckers holding machine guns and grenades.

Some honed instinct took over, and I fought to save my life. I didn't have any weapons or gear and couldn't figure out why. Only the cold barrel of a gun to my forehead stopped my movement, and Skull's worried voice broke through the suicidal screams of the insurgents.

"What the fuck, man? Where'd you go?" The gun barrel moved a fraction of an inch, and I disarmed him, unloaded the gun, and threw it off to the side.

I dropped to my knees and covered my head, trying to make sense of what happened. My body was shaking, and I became covered in a cold sweat. I jerked away when Skull touched me, and he moved to sit in front of me. His vision helped remind me I wasn't in that war zone. It was the first clue that I was more affected by the war than I thought.

"Fuck, man. You've got PTSD. I didn't think that shit was real. You back here now? Or you gonna try to kill me again?" Skull asked softly.

"Sorry," I managed to get out through gritted teeth. I worked on controlling my breath, feeling it go in and out, and hearing the air's sound as I exhaled.

"What set you off?" Skull asked, trying to understand.

"I don't know. I think it was your yell. All of a sudden, I wasn't here. I was in sand and had no weapons to defend myself against an insurgent attack," I confessed. Jesus, I was shaking badly.

"Yeah, Darius, you are a scary-ass motherfucker. I ain't ever seen you fight like that, and there is no way I could have stopped you, man. I seriously thought you was about to kill my ass. That's why I pulled the gun," he explained. "That move almost had me shitting my pants. I ain't neva' want to pull a trigger on you."

The reality of Skull's statements pressed on me. "PTSD?" I echoed like a fool.

"I been hearing about it on the news. Some of the guys coming back from over there have it pretty bad. Lots of vets in this area come home pretty injured or missing body parts," Skull explained. "Easy to believe they are exaggeratin' until you see it."

"It's the first time something like that has ever happened to me," I lifted my head off the ground and sat up.

"Bet your black ass I'm gonna be learnin' all I can about it now. That shit ain't claiming you, man. You mean way too much for me to let that happen. I'm gonna learn how to help you get through that. I'll get Shay to help me," Skull promised. "You're my brother, Darius. I got you."

A year of blood and death and Skull's words were what it took to make me break down. Saying he was alarmed was like saying a nine-point earthquake made the mirrors shake. I did my best to get it under control, only to get set off again when Shay came in.

It felt like my Mom was speaking through her when she started singing Amazing Grace to me. Skull joined in, and finally, I did too.

"We'll take care of you, Darius," Shay promised.

Skull took me to his party that night, introduced me to his club, which was truthfully a gang, and I didn't care. I had my first three-way in one of the rooms in the back of the clubhouse. The club president and Skull declared the place to be my room and off-limits to anyone other than me.

Several bikers came up to give me thanks and praise me for what I was doing for the country, while in the back of my mind, I was thinking that my fighting for our freedom allowed him to break the laws I was trying to protect.

Whatever. These guys accepted me, watched out for me, and genuinely liked me. They were impressed as hell that the bruises Skull sported were from me, and only one person in the room glanced at me with worry, and that was Skull. Always watching over me to make sure I was okay.

Chapter 21

In the Hamrin mountains of Iraq, we met up with Moose again. It was my third time over here. I guess they pulled several SEAL teams in on this one. Skull wanted me to get out, but it wasn't time yet. That was something I instinctively knew, just as he knew being here had undeniably altered me.

One team held themselves away from the rest of us, and I couldn't figure out why. No question that these men were seasoned and hard asses, but three people stood out from that group. If you saw one, you saw the other two. And it seemed like this team was in charge of all of us.

It made me think of Trigger and Skull so much that I had to fight back homesickness when I saw those three guys. They moved like they were in each other's heads. When they requested the explosives, I answered the call, listened to the Master Chief, and prepared to deliver. He demanded that kind of response, even if it wasn't a verbal command.

I crafted the bomb with precision. I sketched out how the detonation would work and where the most substantially hit areas would be. Those men had told me what they wanted to accomplish, and with me wanting to get out of these mountains, I gave them that and a little extra. I told them where to place it. I told them the collateral damage to the existing landscape we weren't targeting and how the projectiles I'd added would get blown in the direction they assumed the targets clustered.

The SEAL that was going to plant the bomb was impressed, and the Master Chief looked thoughtful while the third in their little clique watched over us with his rifle pointed out with deadly efficiency.

Moose's team would be the first in after the explosion, followed by my squad. The lead team would be coming in from a separate entrance, and we hoped to pin the terrorists between us. The rumors told was there were several bombs hidden in this area that these guys planned to use to take out ground troops that patrolled through here. We were to take those bombs out of commission and any terrorists around to use them.

When plans were in place, the guy who took control of my explosive stood and shook my hand. "This is excellent work, Baker. I'm Caleb Grayson; my guys call me Ghost. We don't use our real names out there; too many psychos listening."

I shook his hand and left to rejoin my team for some quick shut-eye before entering the elaborate tunnels, our watches set and gear ready to go. Thank God for shadows out here. It was a desert, but the rocks provided some excellent cover.

Our intel said these guys came out right when the sun set and planted IEDs in the road under darkness. We planned to go in about an hour before the sun set. We'd gotten used to sleeping in the blazing heat and direct sunlight whenever we could catch rest.

We knew of two caravans due through the road we were above the next day. We were trying to clear the way so they didn't get taken out. IEDs were a bitch that these guys had down pat. Dirty bombs. Now they were up against me, and I wanted to do everything I could to make sure none of our guys went home in pieces.

I was awake before my watch told me I needed to be, and I waited patiently. I created a few extra explosives and hadn't attached the detonators to them yet. I would plant them as we went into the tunnels and detonate them after we were out.

SEALs were precise. It didn't take me long to notice that the lead team's sniper had kept watch over us. I glanced at my watch and saw them take off to get into position while we took up ours. They had an extra twenty minutes to arrive at their location. I set up the explosives to cause maximum damage when I blew them and pointed them out to our teams, so no one accidentally tripped them and sealed us in the damn tunnel.

On the mark, we moved like shadows. Blending into the darker places inside and held our position until we heard the bomb explode. I couldn't help the smile that spread across my face as the chaotic screams reached our ears. Panicked terrorists began fleeing toward us, and we took them out. A secondary explosion sounded, and I turned to see what it was.

Moose came flying out of the dark and slammed

me into the wall with an expulsion of air that didn't sound normal, and I saw lifeless eyes staring back at me. Shit. I motioned for the guys behind me to move out and dragged Moose with us.

A third and louder explosion went off, shaking the walls of the rock we were under, and it seemed that we should be a bit faster to get out from under something that could bury us alive. Mouse grabbed hold of Moose with me, and we made tracks in time to hear the largest explosion yet, and rock started to crumble.

We made our way to the rendezvous point and waited for signs from the lead time while communications called for transport for the fallen. I waited until all our units were out of the tunnel before detonating the bombs that would bring the cave down on the terrorists inside if they were still alive. None of us knew what had happened in that tunnel, except for maybe Moose, who wasn't talking.

The medic worked like crazy to stabilize some of the injuries. I took up the post as a guard and waited and watched. A few minutes later, I saw the lead team Master Chief come out and signal me that they weren't alone.

I motioned Mouse, and we took up position laying down protective fire and the sounds of barking guns filled the air while the lead team made it to us, and the sniper joined in. We were strangers, but we worked like a well-oiled machine until there was no one left coming after us.

Ghost made his way over to me. "Man, I've got to hand it to you. That explosive was genius. You predicted it down to the nth degree. Brilliant. Took out all of the weapons we found. If you haven't earned a call name yet, you just did. Well done, Boomer."

"Boomer?" The sniper grunted a laugh.

"Yeah, Boomer." Ghost grinned at me. "You make things go boom."

"Boomer it is," I laughed and accepted it. "What were the other explosions?"

"I caught sight of some of their bombs and triggered them with a few well-placed bullets," the sniper told me. "The idiots ran just how you said they would and left them exposed."

"It was a successful mission," the leader declared coldly.

"We lost some men," I told him, my hackles rising.

"Sorry to hear that," his face changed marginally. "It was still successful in taking out the insurgents that would have taken out several conveys."

He had a point, but it was hard to accept that loss was acceptable. I let it go because that guy didn't seem like one I wanted to piss off. It was easy to see he'd been in longer than me and seen worse than I did.

We jumped on one of the waiting MH-60 Blackhawks and began lifting off to head back to base; only we left a survivor down there somewhere that took out one of the helicopters. A burst of red caught my eye, and my brain was slow to recognize the rapidly growing smoke tail streaking towards the other bird that held the rest of my squad. Some prick had an RPG. A fireball lit the sky in a blinding display as the tail rotor separated in a shower of flame. The Blackhawk swirled out of control in a crazy death spin, crashing into the ground in an explosion of molten fire and bodies. I could feel the searing heat and smell the fuel burning.

Half my team had been on that bird. I howled out my rage, ready to spring out of the helicopter, and the bark of a gun beside me startled me back into my place. The sniper gave me a sad look. "I got him. RPG from the cluster of rocks we were near."

It did little to ease my mind. "Did any of ours make it through that?" I asked hopefully as the sniper panned around, looking through his scope for a sign of survivors. I knew his answer.

"I don't see any. I'm sorry, Boomer. They got the fuel tank." He relaxed his posture and moved his gun to rest across his lap.

Ghost put a hand on my shoulder and squeezed, and the leader squatted in front of me. "Would you be interested in joining our team? I can put in a request." He spoke directly into my ear.

With my heart aching, I could only nod. "Darius Baker," I told him. Anguish blossomed bright in my chest at the astonishing loss I'd witnessed.

Ghost sat next to me. "Damien's our Master Chief, and we call him Demon. I'm Ghost, as I told you earlier, and this is Jake Foxwood, Foxy," he introduced the sniper. "Welcome to the black."

"The black?" I shouted to get heard.

Ghost handed me some ear protection and turned on the earphones. "You have SEAL teams, and then there's us. We are the elite of the elite. We don't exist."

Guess I got what I wanted then. I was part of the

biggest badasses over here now. I'd only had to lose half my team to get there, and a guy I started with that might have been a friend but was definitely a brother. It wasn't how I wanted to achieve that status, but I learned that war didn't often deliver good news. I closed my eyes and leaned against the side of the chopper and wondered how long it would take for me to get transferred to this squad.

When we landed, I was whisked off for debrief, visited by a general who handed me reassignment papers. There was no stalling here; keep moving and stay alive.

That was the answer to my question; these guys had some pull. I grabbed my gear and sought out my new team. They were a somber group; I introduced myself and crashed. The emotional toll of watching my team die was heavy, and sleep was what I needed. Moose and Mouse, more brother's gone.

Chapter 22

My new squad was on a break from missions, and they put me through some extra intense training that overshadowed all the rest of the training I'd gone through. These men weren't joking that they were elite. I kept up, but barely.

Ghost was my favorite of them all. He was a genuine and all-around nice guy with a soft heart. Until we were in the field, and then he was deadlier than anyone else I'd ever encountered. Foxy was hands down the best shot I had ever seen, and Demon a close-combat legend. I'd never seen fighting like that before.

Each of my skills improved after training with these guys for a month. Ghost worked with me on getting in and out of places, and I taught them more about explosives and the precise science behind them while we all shared surveillance knowledge. Their last explosives expert had caught some shrapnel from a dirty bomb that left the rest of the team on edge.

The medic was quick-witted and magic with his fieldwork in patching people up. The communications guy seemed like he could pull a signal from the grains of sand we were sitting on in any location. They called the medic Bandy, short for band-aid, and the communications guy was Hacker.

From what I could tell, Ghost, Foxy, and Demon sometimes got called out without the rest of us, but most of the time, Bandy, Hacker, and I would go along on some of the missions. Then there were times that sixteen of us went out.

I'd thought the shit I'd seen up to that point in this war was insane and sickening. The places I went with this squad put it all to shame. Human depravity was rampant in these places. The vilest things were everyday occurrences, and I wondered how these men were still sane.

Ghost got letters several times a week. His family must write to him daily for them to come in like that. But the ones he got from his sister had us all in stitches or tears. Ghost idolized his sister, and it became evident that Foxy was in love with her, too.

It was true that being a part of this team was more demanding than anything else, but the rewards of this close-knit feeling were better than the other squad I had been a part of, hands down. Demon went out of his way to keep us together and safe. Often, he was putting himself at risk to do so. I admired the hell out of him.

Ghost felt like a brother, like what Trigger had been to me. It wasn't anything I could put a price on, and I would protect it to my dying breath. Foxy and Demon felt the same way about Ghost. The entire team did. It was my first time experiencing this kind of magnetism; Ghost was the center of this squad.

I got along with them all. Demon held himself

back from me, but he respected me and my knowledge, and he never once pulled rank on me or questioned my intuition regarding surveillance or explosives. He didn't make me feel like I couldn't step in when I saw something wrong, and he listened to each of us on the team.

This type of relationship in my team was what I had been searching for when joining the Navy. Something that emulated what I had with Skull and Trigger. I'm certainly the third wheel of their group, but Ghost includes me, ensuring I never felt left out. The nature of our missions kept us needing that closeness.

Our assignments were nasty with a capital N. The plus side was learning to overcome my fear of pulling the trigger on someone. I can't say that was something to be proud of in the grand scheme of things, but it's saved our bacon more than once.

We were on our way back from a remote part of Iraq and sleeping under a convoy. We hitched a ride back to base. Well, most of the crew was sleeping under it. Demon, Foxy, and Ghost were under the lone tree in the area and were not sleeping. Each was touching the other in some form, but they were also carefully watching over us while making themselves the easy targets to give the rest some breathing room. If Trigger and Skull had been with me, that would be us. I envied the friendship and longed to be part of it. More so than I already was.

Ghost had asked me about my family before we left for this assignment, and he'd listened attentively to me talking about my parents, Skull, and Trigger in an attempt to get to know me better.

Ghost even cried with me when I talked about my mom dying and Trigger getting killed. He was an anomaly out here that I wasn't used to seeing. Genuine, raw, open, and sensitive. So many of the soldiers I'd encountered had been jaded and bitter, and I can't say I wasn't one of those.

Ghost was just different. Down to earth and kind when we were back at camp between assignments and only training. Out in the field, it was rare that anything got by him. If anyone ever asked, I'd say Ghost made a better leader than Demon. More would follow Ghost too.

We each had our strengths. Foxy was hands down the best with a gun and could back it up with actions and awards. Demon, I'd never seen fighting like that before. In hand-to-hand combat, that man was unmatched. Except Ghost was a damn close second to Demon on that, and with training, I think he could surpass Demon. Ghost had this way of moving that made it seem effortless, and he's been able to get in and out of places that stumped others. That's how he earned his name.

Bandy should have been a doctor, and he said if he makes it out of this place alive, he might go to medical school and make that happen. Hacker hasn't met a piece of electronics that he couldn't make sing for him. This small team within the squad was the definition of top-notch. I was lucky to be included.

The rest of the squad were no slouches. We had a tactical driver that made Indy racers look like turtles. We had two divers born to be in the water, and even more impressive, one of them was able to scale rock walls like he was a lizard, carrying gear.

When we hitched rides with the convoy's going by, they eyed us with speculation. Demon was a huge man and was intimidating when he had his war face in place. Ghost was scarier than Demon in that mode, but when he smiled, the guys around him would ease up. Then there was Foxy, perhaps the most intimidating of us all, and he wasn't even aware of it. Danger leaked out of that man's pores on assignment. Foxy seemed to shine in that millisecond between life and death, reaction, and retaliation.

Yet, he was also the most playful and humorous of the group. He didn't reside in the dark places of his mind like his friends did. It was a puzzle, and I was trying to find where I fit. I was between the three of them and Bandy and Hacker. I didn't quite mesh with either, but all accepted me.

The other notable thing was that no one in our squad treated me differently for being black. It amazed me because I don't think they looked at my skin color once, made reference to it, or even joked about it. I didn't get blamed when shit hit the fan or if we got spotted on reconnaissance. I was just Boomer.

I glanced back at the tree. Ghost and Demon were worried about Foxy. He'd made the tough decision to end a kid's life to save all of ours. Not a choice I would have wanted to make, and the bomb that had gone off had been all sorts of messed up. It was created with no skill and left unstable components after detonation. Once the bullets stopped flying and we made sure Ghost was okay, I had to move in and detonate them to ensure nothing else caught us off-guard.

Seventeen bodies littered that camp, and the kid's pieces that the bomb left. It was gruesome and smelled putrid. It cemented Foxy's position as the scariest motherfucker around too. Also, he was one of the best people to have on your side because he'd do everything he could to keep you safe.

I wasn't surprised when he broke down and started to shake after he confirmed everyone was dead. What surprised me was how he pulled himself back together to keep watch over us and make sure none of these crazy assholes surfaced and took shots at us.

I knew that was why Demon and Ghost flanked him now. They were trying to give him a safe place to come to peace with it. I believed that you couldn't. Not on the scale we were performing on and not in this place. The terms here were kill or be killed.

The medic had a camera that he carried with him to send scenery (that made me laugh) pictures to his family. I borrowed it, got a picture of the three men, and asked him to give me the print. I rolled from under the vehicle and approached. Demon eyed me warily, but Ghost patted the ground next to him.

"Pull up some shade, bro," he called out.

I plopped down next to him. "When shit got so bad in my head, my mom would ask me to sing with her. Her favorite was Amazing Grace. I know your hurtin' Foxy; I would be too. I'm not asking you to believe in God, but let me sing it for you. There ain't no god to be found in this shit, but today, you were our grace."

"Sing it," he told me. Foxy sat up, and the anguish in his eyes was fierce.

Demon looked at the convoy and saw that people had taken up watch positions, so he relaxed a little. I started to sing, and Ghost picked up the song with me in a lower and quieter tone. It wasn't harmonized like when my mom and I sang, but the effort was there, and it helped Foxy release some of that bad mojo that was building inside him.

Foxy might have been the best looking out of all of us, but that man couldn't sing to save his soul. He even tried to join in at the end and butchered it. Something that made all of us laugh, and he finally smiled. By no means did that mean Foxy felt okay now; he only wasn't stuck in that dark void that lives inside us all where our death-tally card was filling fast.

"You must have been one of those choir girls," Foxy tried to joke as we headed back towards the convoy.

"Boomer probably did those choir girls," Ghost joined in.

"Can't say I ever went that route," I told them. "Too afraid of those girls' daddies."

"Thanks for doing that for me," Foxy put his hand on my shoulder.

"I'll sing whenever you want if you promise not to join in," I ribbed him.

"Put that in writing, Foxy," Demon grinned. "You should never sing."

"Assholes," Foxy mumbled. "I bet Frankie would like my singing."

I hooted out a laugh as Ghost shoved Foxy right into me. Maybe I was more of the group than I thought I was. They accepted me willingly enough when I tried to be a part of them.

"You're willing to torture poor Ghost's sister like that? Man, that's cruel. I could at least sing her to sleep after a date with you, so she has good dreams that don't include banshee's wailing," I added.

Ghost glared at me. "Frankie would eat every one of you up and spit you out. That girl goes through men more than we go through underwear."

"That's because we never change them," Demon laughed.

"Don't disparage the love of my life," Foxy elbowed Demon.

The comment earned Foxy a solid punch to the gut, leaving him gasping for air and laughing simultaneously. Demon bent over and threw the coughing Foxy over his shoulder to dump him in the vehicle. I swear that man has taken more hits over Frankie than anyone else.

"You know that's all kidding, right?" Ghost asked me.

"Which part? The punching or Foxy being in love with your sister?" I asked for clarification.

"Oh, I know he loves her. It doesn't bother me. She'd be perfect for him. She'd whip him so fast we wouldn't know what happened," Ghost grinned and climbed in the truck. "That's our secret."

Chapter 23

entered a tent where Demon and Foxy had set up a makeshift ring for training. To my complete shock, I found Demon there alone. He was shadowboxing, and his face was ravaged-looking. Whatever he was fighting was in his head. I apologized for intruding and turned to go.

"You don't have to go, Boomer," Demon called out. "If you came here to work out, hop in the ring. I can put you through the paces."

"No doubt about that," I scoffed. "Not sure I can keep up with you."

"You do fine. Give yourself some credit. You wouldn't be on this team if you couldn't hold your own." Demon gulped water from his bottle.

I shrugged, climbed in the ring, pulled my shirt off, and wrapped my hands. "Don't beat my ass into the ground," I said with a smile.

"I'd never do that to my team," Demon gave me a half-smile. "What's the meaning of those tats?" Traces of whatever had been on his mind when I walked in were still evident.

I tapped the one of Skull and Trigger. "Symbolizes

my friends and me," I explained a little about how we became friends and ended with Trigger dying in my arms. "I'd like not to repeat that experience if possible."

"It's the worst." Demon once again floored me by opening up. "Some days, I don't think I'll make it out of here alive; some days, I don't want to. Then I look at you guys and tell myself I have to make sure you do. This place is like spreading cancer that's slowly killing me."

I didn't know what to say to him. I tapped the other tattoo. "That one is for my mom." I launched into the story about my family's slavery origins, right on through to my grandpa and all he did and how my mom told me the story of him saying it to her. "After she died, it seemed a good way to remember her and not let her down."

There was no doubt that Demon was in a dark place mentally. His eyes were full of shadows that I didn't typically see. It was worrisome to a degree but more understandable than anything else. I've seen some of the things that put those shadows there.

"Come on, Master Chief Ocasta. Kick my ass," I challenged him. "Whatever is in you trying to pull you down, don't got shit on you." I took a considerable risk to my safety by stepping into him and shoving him a little.

I grew more concerned that he didn't react to the provocation, and his eyes were slightly unfocused. Something had a fierce grip on my Master Chief, and I didn't know what to do to get him out. I shoved him again, and he only stepped backward.

"Fuck this! Demon! Get your head back here. We

always fight!" I snarled at him, raising my voice. This time when I shoved him, I tripped him. "We always fight!"

Demon snapped out of it and shot to his feet, his body vibrating with the need to destroy. He'd snap my neck if he fought me in this state. I danced away from him and waited a moment.

"I only did that to bring you back," I told him softly. "The sentiment stands, Demon. We always fight. Bleed it off so you don't obliterate me."

"Does it ever get you, Boomer?" Demon's softly spoken question felt like a sucker punch.

"All the time. Seeing my team go down with that helicopter made me feel like jumping out the door. Pulling my dead friend out of those tunnels was something I could have done without," I replied.

"I worry I might become desensitized to death, and I don't want that to happen. Everyone's life means something; if I lose sight of that, I don't think there will be hope for me. I don't even know how to survive not being in the military. How stupid is that shit? I've never had a normal life that wasn't lived on some base," Demon growled.

"I think your boys will help you adjust," I answered honestly. "I don't imagine that you'll settle somewhere without them close by."

"Where will you go?" He looked up from his clenched fists and met my eyes.

"Most likely, I'll go where my friend Skull lives. He's part of some motorcycle club that he's enjoying. Since I like to ride, it makes sense to me," I shrugged again.

"Motorcycle club? Foxy and I both ride," he pondered that information.

"Well, if you want to go that route, I'll put in a good word for you. Now, come on. Shake this off and kick my ass," I taunted the lethal man.

Demon chuckled, but we sparred, and he taught me a few more moves and worked with me on my close-combat skills. It was beneficial for both of us, and when we finished, I felt a little closer to Demon than I had since joining them.

I understood now that the distance he kept was because of the things he was fighting in his head. I saw his fears over anything happening to one of his team. And it was why he risked so much to keep it from happening.

We parted ways. I went to the shower, and Demon went running. How he could run in this heat was beyond me. I cleaned up, grabbed a little food, and went to find the others. Foxy and Ghost were reading another letter that Ghost's sister had sent.

I sat down to listen and laughed with the rest when she described some of the people she was working with at a hospital. Ghost passed around a picture that she had sent of some exceptionally green place, which made us all envious since all we saw was brown. Dirt, sand, brown mountains, it was monotonous.

Demon stomped in about an hour later. "Let's hit the town tonight, get some food that isn't what we exist on. Ghost, maybe we can find something in the market to send your mom and sister."

It was usually Foxy suggesting that we head out,

and it caught the rest of the team off-guard. To cover the surprise, I jumped in. "Change of scenery would be nice. Tired of looking at all your asses."

Foxy grinned at that. "So you noticed my ass? Think it would win over Frankie, or should I tighten it up some more?"

Ghost stood and punched him in the gut. "You *are* an ass."

"No, I'm a Scorpio, and they are the perfect sign for Libra's," Foxy went on.

"Dude, do you ever learn when to shut up?" Bandy called out.

"No, he doesn't," Ghost answered and shoved him. "Get moving."

"Seriously, I read an article about it," Foxy kept going.

I think I was the only one who saw the slight smile on Ghost's lips as he shook his head. I followed behind, trying not to laugh. Ghost and Demon became a little more rigid as we left the base's relative safety and headed out.

I was alert, but not like they were. Despite Foxy still rambling about the pairing of his sign with Ghost's sister, I could see he was observing everything too. Hacker was driving, and Bandy sat in the back with me. Demon was in the passenger seat, and Ghost and Foxy were in the middle by design. That way, Ghost could continue to punch Foxy.

"Don't make me squeeze your balls until you can't walk," Ghost warned Foxy as we parked. "I need to find something today to make Frankie proud and declaring you her perfect match isn't it."

Demon chuckled as he got out and looked around. I found myself watching him more after the way I saw him earlier. There was still tension in him, but he was in control. "How's that Army girl, Foxy?" Demon asked, relieving Ghost a bit.

"Feisty," Foxy answered with a grin. "It won't go anywhere because our signs don't mesh, but she's great at relieving some pent-up energy. She says I have a devil tongue because she swears it's forked."

Hacker belted out a laugh at the look on Ghost's face. "There go any chances you have with Frankie," he chortled.

"I can't help it if I'm talented with the ladies," Foxy shrugged.

Ghost dropped back next to me. "Honestly, Frankie's probably perfect for him the way she goes through men. If you repeat that, I'll kick your ass."

"Secret's safe with me, man," I promised, biting back a smile. I told him a little about how I found Demon earlier, falling farther behind the others for some privacy.

"Demon's been struggling," Ghost agreed. "He's a lot like me, or I'm like him, whichever way you want to look at it. This stuff we see, we do. It feels like it takes a piece of my soul. Every day I'm here, I feel like it's changing who I am, and it's not a good way to feel. I say that because who it's making me is someone I'm not sure I like. Demon feels the same way."

"I gotta call bullshit, bro. You three are the best damn men I've ever met in this place. You have morals and ethics, and you're loyal and real. You care. Look around us. How many can you say feel that way?" I asked.

"I hear you. Still doesn't stop me from wondering if we'll ever get out of here, and if we do, who will we be, and can we go back to living life like we didn't murder a bunch of assholes?" Ghost asked, his tone cold.

The killing part is what I agreed with in his statement. How do you return and find a job that doesn't involve throwing yourself to the ground when you hear what sounds like gunfire? How do you look at some asshole you know is hurting people and not kill them when it's all we do here? Theoretically, that is. I didn't think I'd go home and start killing assholes, but I'd feel tempted.

I had questions about going home, but I knew I wanted to. Not everyone over here is doing what we do, but for damn sure, our team is, and I bet if I asked Demon, Foxy, or Ghost how many people they've killed, they could list them all. I know I could.

Ghost heard the small cry at the same time I did, and he let out a low whistle that I didn't think the others would notice. I was wrong because Demon was at his side in a second, his body tensed and ready to fight.

"Something down that way," Ghost whispered and pointed to a narrow street between buildings.

I immediately went into surveillance mode and looked for mounted cameras, posted guards, and law enforcement. I cataloged everything I saw. Ghost was doing the same thing, and Foxy faced out, watching our backs.

"Boomer, go with him," Demon instructed me.

"We'll keep watch."

Hacker, Bandy, Foxy, and Demon each stepped onto the street and split themselves on either side, leaning against the buildings. Hacker pulled out a pack of cigarettes that I know he didn't smoke and lit one, passing it between them as if they were catching up and sharing.

Ghost motioned me, and we slid into the shadows. I wasn't sure what we were looking for, but I'd heard the same small cry he had. We heard it again about halfway through the street. Ghost paused, and I took the opportunity to scope everything I could.

"No surveillance," I told him after a minute.

"Probably why these assholes think they can get away with raping a small boy," Ghost growled.

I felt sick. I still hadn't seen what Ghost had seen until he moved. Three men to one little kid. "Fuck," I whispered. My brain took in every disgusting detail, and I stayed close to Ghost's six as we made our way over to them.

The one facing us would have seen us had his head not been thrown back while he was fucking a child's face. That singular act pushed me over the edge, and I motioned to Ghost that I'd take that one. The boy couldn't have been more than eleven.

I was acutely aware that we could get thrown out of the military and have charges pressed against us for interfering. I didn't care. If our government was willing to turn its cheek to this shit, what the hell was I over here fighting for if not to help?

I snuck behind the guy and broke the man's neck

with an ease that I refused to acknowledge. When he went limp, I tossed his body to the ground, yanked the kid off the ground, and pushed him to safety behind me.

Ghost had dropped one, the one not actively raping the boy, and broke the other guy's neck like me. I strategically placed the body to make it look like that guy did this while Ghost grabbed the boy and called out to Bandy.

Fuck. I'd just murdered someone. I raced over to a garbage can and puked my guts up. I'm not sure Frankie would be proud of us for this, but we did save a boy. Demon came to stand behind me and glanced back at the bodies.

"Bandy's checking him over. We need to get out of here," Demon told me unnecessarily. "Ghost has never killed outside of battle before."

"You think I have?" I snapped.

"No, Boomer. I'm only saying that means he's probably close to how you found me earlier. These motherfuckers deserved it. You did the world a favor." Demon patted me on the back while I hurled again.

We walked back to the street, and Hacker handed me the pack. I lit up like I'd been smoking my entire life. I didn't care that the shit would make me sick later; that cigarette became the focal point that kept me from losing control. Each nasty inhale and exhale that filled my mouth with the tobacco taste didn't remove the stench of excrement I had caused. Jesus, I was fucked.

The boy directed us to where he lived with hand signals, the language barrier preventing us from understanding his words, holding Bandy's hand the entire time. He was sobbing, scared, and probably hurt in ways we couldn't see. But we got him home safely, and that is something that I am sure Ghost's sister would have been proud of him for at least.

Chapter 24

We're goin' where?" I asked, stunned.

"Gulf of Aden," Demon repeated.

"We get to see the water!" Ghost whooped and did a little dance.

"Do you remember how to swim in something other than sand?" Foxy grinned, despite the reason we were going.

Demon rolled his eyes, crossed his arms, and gave us a stern look. "This is the entire team going. We need the divers, drivers, explosives, and everything else we've got going for us. Listen up, team."

Demon pulled out a map and spread it across the table. He pointed between Yemen and Somalia. "This is where we are heading, and this is a heavily pirated area. Command has reason to believe that a ship is headed this way with smuggled weapons that will dock in Yemen and get transported through Saudi Arabia into Iraq. Our job is to board this ship, see if there are weapons, disable it, and see if we can find any intel on where this originated. That means interrogation," Demon nodded at the two that had special skills in interrogating terrorists.

I hadn't seen them in action yet, but I'd heard

stories. Still, in that order, I found Foxy, Ghost, and Demon the scariest on our team. "Any idea what the ship looks like, or are we just going to be boarding all of them?" I asked.

"That's one way to extend our time on the water," Ghost smirked at me.

"Gotta be honest, guys, sharks scare the shit out of me," I added sheepishly.

"Boomer, I'll keep the sharks off you," this statement got a laugh out of our very serious leader. "Now, we do have pictures of two suspected vessels. One is larger and carries agricultural goods, making it a more obvious choice. However, this smaller one would likely not be suspected, and I believe it would be this one."

Demon set two aerial views down of the boats. My mind kicked into gear as I looked at the vessels. "Can we get specs on these two?" I looked up at Demon.

In return, he gave me a cold smile. "I knew you'd ask me that. That's why you are the best, Boomer."

Demon pulled out two sheets listing the structural information on the boats. I studied them carefully, grabbed the pencil from the table, and started to do some calculations. While I was doing that, Demon went back to the map.

"Open sea, they both are coming in this direction. We'll be on a pleasure boat outfitted for assault on approach and drop anchor about 2 miles from where we expect to encounter the targets. If we can catch the vessels out here, there is no overly huge chance for collateral damage. Keep in mind that this also makes us a target for pirates. We need to not draw attention to ourselves that way, but if they come upon us, we can take them out," Demon's voice got a little steelier.

"What about evac?" Foxy asked, studying the map.

"Sub," Demon answered. "Our assault will be amphibious. While Speedy will be doing most of the driving, we will have an intelligence op who will leave with the boat once we enter the water. A sub will be picking us up once we have confirmation of the weapons. The agent will be calling in the coordinates, and we'll have friendlies under us. So if we have to sink the ship, we need time to make tracks."

I looked up from my calculations at that. "Sinking it only leaves the weapons within reach. Do we have a map of the seafloor for that area?"

"That was my concern, too," Ghost said. "Why send us out here to stop the weapons from entering the area if we are going to leave them to get salvaged?"

"I asked the same thing. The Navy would send in a recovery team if we had to sink it. Our goal is to take the weapons into our possession, but these waters are tricky, and our only option might be to sink them. If we do, here is the best place to do that," Demon pointed out an area on the map.

"That's the deepest part?" I looked closer.

"Deepest with the most technical aspect that command doesn't believe these guys have the capabilities to launch a recovery for," Demon specified. "If it's shallower water, they could potentially retrieve the weapons. Barring the location, if things go FUBAR, we obliterate the boat. Blow it so that nothing remains."

I looked back at the specs and started calculating again. Cursing, I wrote out an extensive list of supplies I'd need and handed it to Demon. "To start. How much time do I have?"

"Two days," Demon met each of our eyes. "Tell us what you think, Boomer."

I went over the points of weakness on the smaller boat that would be good to plant a charge to stop the vessel without sinking it. I then showed them the places that would slowly sink the ship and the areas that would drop it fast. I did the same with the other boat and told them I needed the materials ASAP to make these. Underwater charges could be tricky, and I required precision.

"What about total annihilation?" Ghost asked me, curious.

"Plant them all along here," I pointed to the spec. "We get the fuck out as quickly as we can and have the sub back off a bit. Not under us. I don't think the sub should be under us at all; no sense in rocking the submarine's ride, even if the concussion won't damage the submarine. I'm not sure a sub is a good way to evac either. If we make either of these vessels puzzle pieces with nothing left of the cargo, I believe we will need to plant charges inside the hull and outside. That list I gave you, Demon, will allow for both types of charges. We need incendiary inside and damage outside to blow the structure in." I sketched out what I was referring to and saw the light dawning on Foxy's face.

"I get it. We must plant charges around the

engine room if we scuttle it with little trace."

"Would blowing it underwater cause less of a show?" Ghost asked me.

"Most likely, but there are more opportunities for that to go sideways without trial runs. We won't know how heavy the vessel is, the weather, the currents, and the water temperature. There are variables that we don't have that all affect what the charge will do," I explained.

I went over the explanations for the math I had done to get the desired results. I further elaborated on how each of the variables would affect the charge and the damage it did. Demon paid close attention, and I saw him figure out the situation.

"Go big, then," he finally said. "We can't leave those weapons in their hands."

I shrugged, figuring that was what his decision would be. "At least the concussion wave will keep the sharks away."

Hacker laughed and smacked the table. "Way to think positive, man!"

"Five-minute delay timers," Demon added, giving each of us another look. "No dawdling to look at the scenery."

"Jesus, Demon. Have you ever dawdled when one of Boomer's creations is at play?" Ghost smirked.

"Add sensors to the list; we don't have to use timers on the ones outside the hull if they have sensors. When the inside charges blow, it will trigger the outside ones," I told him.

"We need to cover all eventualities. I'll add them, but ensure we are covered," Demon stated. We spent a little more time going over ingress and egress, which Ghost took over.

I spent the next day and a half making intricate explosives that were small enough to carry on our bodies with enough power to stop a moving boat and incinerate it to nothing. Paranoia about instability was high in my mind, and even though this crew knew how to handle explosives, I still talked the guys to death about it.

I could only work with the projected weather, currents, average temperature, and water temperature of the past few days and the speeds the boats were traveling. It was enough to drill down what I was doing, but sometimes even a few degrees made a difference in the outcome.

Ghost helped me, and he told me about his sister and her life while we worked. He talked about his mom's cooking and how he and his dad fought like crazy when he was younger. Some of the crazy shit he pulled off in those days made me think of Trigger.

I told him more about Trigger, and we commiserated on what it was like to deal with significant losses like that at a young age. What struck me as odd was that we were both still young and talked like we'd lived several lifetimes.

I guess, in a way, we had. War changes you; being in this place does too. Ghost and I had committed unsanctioned murder together, which also left its mark. Was that one life we saved worth what it had cost me in my soul? A large part of me said it was. My mother's voice was in the back of my head, telling me that all life was precious.

I shook my head and voiced my thoughts to Ghost. I bared it all, knowing we were heading into another life-threatening situation, and if I died, I wanted someone to know who I was.

"All life is precious, Boomer. Your mom had that right. It cost me too, and what we did was on the darker side of gray; those men were firmly in the black. This place has pockets of poison, and when I saw that happening, my first thought was, what if that happened at home to my sister, and someone walked by, saw it, and kept walking. I know I put Frankie into all the scenarios I logically understand won't happen at home, but that kid didn't deserve that," Ghost sighed. "It wasn't consensual. That was pure pedophilia."

"There is no right answer, Ghost. Not here. I hear you guys crying in your sleep, and there are nights I do that, too. How did we evolve to this as a race? Where in the history of humans did things like this become acceptable?" I wondered aloud.

"Demon says God doesn't exist. Only the Devil. I want to think it isn't true, but it's hard to argue. Demon and I have darkness in us that Foxy doesn't have. It might stem from different things, but it's there. You can see it in the aftermath in his eyes. I try to shut down, but it shows. For some of the people here, we are the monsters, not them, and that's a sobering thought," Ghost said and stood.

Demon poked his head inside the tent. "Pack your swim trunks, boys; it's time to play in the water. Get sleep while you can."

Chapter 25

"Holy shit," Ghost exclaimed while Foxy blew a low whistle. "That's what you call a pleasure boat?"

"It's a pleasure boat," Demon said over his shoulder with a childlike grin. "We'll get pleasure from being on it."

"That's a fucking yacht," Hacker said in awe.

"Outfitted for SEALs," a guy on the boat popped up and said with a smirk. "Welcome, gentlemen."

We boarded the yacht, and my eyes took in the careful placement of mock furniture that I knew hid some impressive weaponry. Speedy headed directly to the cabin to check out the equipment, and Hacker started setting up his communications for our team.

Ghost grabbed our bags full of explosives and took them below where they'd be out of sight. I roamed the deck while Demon conversed softly with the intelligence guy. C.I.A., I assumed. Ghost came back out and joined me.

"Man, did you see that pilot?" he asked me as I peeked at one of the hidden mounted guns.

"Hard not to. She flew the plane," I ribbed him.

"She was hot."

"I almost asked her to put it on autopilot and join me in the bathroom," Ghost grinned.

"You sure know how to treat a lady," I laughed.

"The sight of blue water is about as close to sex as I can get right now. Smell that?" Ghost breathed in deep.

"Fish and seaweed?" I smirked, knowing that wasn't what he meant.

Ghost playfully shoved me. "Demon, we got a few minutes before anchors up?"

"Yeah. Go ahead," Demon smiled casually.

Ghost needed no other prompting; he started stripping out of his clothes on deck and headed to the bow. He climbed up on the railing after scoping out the area and let out a war cry before he swan-dived right into the water.

Foxy came up behind me and pushed me like he would toss me in, but instead, he stripped and cannonballed right off after Ghost. I would look like a giant pussy if my black ass didn't jump in that water after those men.

Figuring it was too shallow for sharks, I shed my clothes and joined them. Speedy, Bandy, and Hacker weren't far behind me. The water was surprisingly warm, and I must admit it felt much better than sand on my face.

Ten minutes of splashing around like kids later, Demon came barreling over the boat's side in an impressive somersault between Foxy and me. With a surprised shout that I barely got out, I got pulled under the surface, thinking I was about to get eaten by jaws.

I broke the surface to see Ghost cracking up and laughing. "Not a shark, man. Just a demon fucking with you."

When we all climbed the ladder to get back on deck, it hit me that I had a family with these men. I'd realized it before, but these rare moments when we got to relax drove it home. We were back to business all too quickly, and Hacker and I sat at the vessel's stern. Foxy and Ghost weren't too far from us on either side. Speedy and Buster were on the bow pretending to drink beer.

Demon and the C.I.A. guy were in the cabin going over more intel while Bandy learned the yacht's controls as a backup to Speedy. The rest of our team was below decks, assembling gear, checking out the engine room, and getting our diver propulsion vehicles, D.P.V., ready for action.

Hacker and I caught sight of a smaller craft that trailed us, and we observed it for patterns that said it was following us. We often went out with smaller squads for specialized assignments, but we worked together like a well-oiled machine. Our comms were in our ears, and we were on duty.

I radioed the location to the rest of the team and noticed the subtle shift in demeanor. Bandy veered us off the path a few degrees to make it look like we were heading somewhere else, and the smaller craft fell back.

Every hour we changed positions and who we were paired with, sharing information and doing our best to look relaxed. Demon was positive that someone was watching us. When we reached the point where we would see the first vessel come into sight, we stopped. High-power binoculars were scanning the horizons for the boats.

"Change of plans," Demon started when we gathered in the cabin. "Six guys are staying on the boat. We've garnered some attention from suspected pirates. Same reason those weapons can't get into their hands, this boat can't either."

We reviewed the different scenarios, and the six staying positioned themselves in view like they were party boys chilling on their yacht. Within reach of each of them were several weapons. The rest of us stayed out of sight until the comms in our ears came alive.

"First target in sight," came the warning.

We strapped our gear on silently and entered the water from the chamber hidden below the waterline. Demon was communicating with the sub on coordinates, and we used the D.P.V. to approach. With the vessel in sight now, Ghost and Foxy boarded the ship operating a grappling hook, disabled the crew with non-lethal methods, and the rest of us joined them while we searched for weapons. As Demon expected, it wasn't this vessel, and we disembarked as quietly as we boarded. The Captain never knew we were there.

We returned to our boat and played the waiting game some more. A couple of hours later, our second chance arrived, the sub communicated the vessel was in range, and we repeated our process. Ghost and Foxy scaled up the side with another well-placed grappling hook.

Our comms clicked madly only moments after

Ghost and Foxy were aboard, signaling they met resistance. Our guys had spotted weapons. Demon and our interrogators were in motion and ascending to assist. We moved faster this time and in sync. Hacker, Bandy, Buster, and I quickly planted charges on the outside of the boat and joined Demon on deck when given the clear. Our interrogation specialists were hard at work, and Foxy had taken a position with a rifle and watched from a high point. They hadn't found an overly large crew, but all were armed to the teeth.

Demon communicated with the sub and the C.I.A. guy while the rest went to seek out what hid below us; gunfire met me. A path of fire sliced across my arm as we took cover.

"Al Qaeda," Demons voice sounded in our ears. The warning came a little late.

"Fuck," I muttered and aimed. "Flesh wound, Bandy, I'm fine," I told him as he checked my arm. "We gotta get these charges planted."

"Shit! How many of these fucks are down here?" Buster growled. "Go low," he told me.

I dropped and shot out the feet while Buster went high, and we covered Bandy's forward movement to push them back. The confined space wasn't to our advantage, but their lack of skill was. Their return fire was wild and random, wasting their ammunition while we fired carefully to kill.

A ricochet caught Buster in the leg, and he went down. Bandy jumped in to get him as patched up as possible, and we pressed on until there was no more firing. Demon joined us as we searched the boat as efficiently as possible, looking for more hidden surprises that wanted to kill us.

"Motherfuckers!" I screamed after opening the door to a berth. A bloodstained mattress greeted me, two bound dead young girls and one that looked barely alive and scared to death of me.

Bandy ran in at my scream, glanced her over, and sadly shook his head at me. "She won't make it. We have to leave her, Boomer."

Demon yanked me out, looked, decided to blow the boat to nothing, and pushed me farther down to the engine room. "Plant the charges. We have to leave the girl. There is no way she will make it swimming, and it puts the entire team at risk. We are the only ones out here right now; this is our chance."

I was pissed. I did as told, but I argued with Demon the entire time. It wasn't right. We were killing the girl. It made me sick, and I wanted to beat the shit out of Demon for making me do this. Ghost found us and informed me that he'd planted the charges amidst the weapons.

"Boomer!" Demon roared at me. "Head in the game. She won't last the evac, and I'm not putting any of you at risk. I get that it fucking sucks, but her life isn't worth more than yours, or anyone else's on this boat. Do you think a call like that makes me happy?"

No, I didn't. I knew why Demon made it, but it still pissed me off and wasn't right. The girl could die on this boat and not know what was happening or die in the water, where we would all have to watch her painfully drown. Which level of Hell was a better option?

I finished my work with thoughts of Demon flying through my head. It didn't matter what I did. This kid was in Hell no matter what. I wasn't angry at Demon; I held no animosity towards him. I respected him and knew we'd butt heads more than today. He was the soldier everyone aspired to, and no one wanted to be. It wasn't his fault; it was these people and this place.

I set the timer for the charges, and we dove in unison off the boat; the cover of night wouldn't be above us for much longer, which meant more boat traffic. Demon already notified the sub to be out of the impact zone, and we pushed our diver propulsion vehicles to the max to get us as far away as possible.

The fortunate turn was that the waters around us were clear and not murky; there were no other boats, and the tide was with us. Unfortunately, Buster and I were bleeding in the water, calling all the sharks in the area, or so my mind told me. Time was ticking down, and I felt like we were too close to that boat.

The concussion of the first blast left me dizzy, and when the secondary detonation hit, I felt like I lost all sense of direction and couldn't see my teammate's beacons around me. I knew the water flow had moved me off course, but I couldn't tell how far.

My ears were ringing, and my vision blurred. A third shockwave clinched it, and I stopped the D.P.V. to try and get my bearings. My earpiece crackled. "Boomer? Where are you?"

"I don't know, man. The explosions disoriented me. I got knocked off course," I replied. "I stopped moving."

"I'll find you," Demon's gruff voice gave me a sense of relief.

It didn't take him long, and soon the looming shape of the sub came into view. I followed Damien to the dive chamber and entered, waiting until the water got pumped out before I pulled my mask off and lightly shook my head, feeling my equilibrium was not what it should be. My ears were still ringing something fierce.

"Med bay," Demon instructed me, his eyes critical of me. "Bandy's waiting for you."

I wasn't going to argue. I was suddenly too tired of everything and felt like I could barely move. I trudged after Demon, forcing one foot in front of the other, and dropped on the chair that he shoved under me.

Bandy shone a light in my eyes, making me flinch, tugged on one of my ears that hurt like a son of a bitch, shoved some cotton in it, and started stitching up my arm. It was a flesh wound, but it was a deep one. He dimmed the lights when he finished and told me to lay in the dark.

Depression hit hard once Bandy was gone. I figured that was the reason for my sudden lethargy. I'd just killed a little girl, one that had obviously gotten raped and probably kidnapped. A part of me wanted to kill all the motherfuckers; a child's life should be treasured. All life should be respected.

Chapter 26

A scream woke me out of a dead sleep. The door burst open, and I rolled to the other side of the bed and flattened myself to the floor, wondering where my gun was. The light flashed on, blinding me temporarily, but I didn't hear the sound of the flashbang, and I saw a face in front of mine, which had me reeling backward.

"Son! It's me, your dad," my dad said kindly. "You were having a nightmare."

I blinked slowly, trying to recalibrate my brain. I was at my dad's place in Chicago. My breathing started to slow down, and I slumped forward. "The screaming I heard was me?" I asked softly.

"Yes, Darius. Want to talk?" I looked up to see him sitting on the floor in front of me, his legs crossed and a patient look on his face.

"You don't want to hear that shit, Dad. No one does. It's ugly, it hurts, and I think it's permanently messed me up," I admitted. "Sorry for waking you up."

"I'm not. It's hard to see you like this, but I'm also the proudest dad in the world, son. You've made it places that many have tried and failed. I can't pretend to understand what you have to do, and judging from what I hear you saying in your sleep, I don't want to. It doesn't detract from the fact that you are making a difference, son, in a big way. How many people can say that?" My dad tried to console me.

"All of us over there can say that, and I think the price we are paying is too high," I muttered darkly. "That place is taking pieces of our soul that we won't ever get back. I'm not the same person I was when I went in, Dad."

"No, son. You are a man now. A damn fine one, if you ask me. Come on, get back in bed," my dad pushed himself to his feet, his knees protesting and cracking with the movement.

I shot to my feet to help him stand. "Lay down with me, Dad. Maybe it will keep the nightmares away."

He lay beside me on the bed after turning the light off. The look on his face had me fighting a rush of tears that pooled. He appeared elated that I needed him. I made a mental note to remind him of that more often.

"Sing with me, Darius. Let's sing your mom's favorite song," he suggested.

I started with the first few words of Amazing Grace, and my dad joined in. My dad wasn't there when I woke up, and I checked the time. It was well after nine, and he was probably at work. Who knew that was what I needed to get me through the night?

I sighed, took a shower, and went to grab something to eat. I faltered, seeing my dad sitting at the kitchen table, reading over some paperwork. "I thought you'd be at work?"

"I took time off while you were here so we could spend time together. I don't see you often, and no, that isn't a guilt trip. I know why you are gone, and I took the time to maximize mine with you. I meant what I said, Darius. I'm so proud of you," my dad repeated.

"I love you, Dad." I blinked back the stinging tears and grabbed a yogurt from the fridge and a banana. "Show me your city today," I suggested.

"Sure," he agreed happily. That's what he did. He showed me where he worked and the sights to see in Chicago, introduced me to their pizza, took me to a show, and paraded me in front of his co-workers one night. It was a perfect way to spend my time with him. We reconnected.

I flew to Seattle for a few days after leaving my dad's and spent some time with Skull. I met a woman who showed me how appreciative she was of my service to our country, and I was happy to see my dick still worked, even if the nightmares came back.

It scared the shit out of Skull the first night that he heard them. "You still have those?" he asked the following day.

"Don't think they'll go away, Skull. You should hear the others; it's worse than mine," I snapped, then felt guilty. "Sorry. Those places over there have a way of killing who you are."

"Get laid again tonight; at least I'll send you back satisfied. You get any while you're over there?" Skull asked curiously.

"Sometimes. Not often. My mindset is not the

same when I'm over there. I know I'm in enemy territory, and that one wrong move will end my life. Not trying to die with my dick out," I tried to explain. I didn't want to tell him any more than I wanted to tell my dad.

"I get it, man. You don't need to explain. The few emails I've gotten tell me what you don't say. I can hear you, but it's not really you. Don't think I don't know what hate feels like, Darius. Look at me. I'm well acquainted with it, my color, and my choices. It's part of the territory," Skull replied curtly.

"I know." If there was anyone I could tell about this shit overseas, it was Skull. So I gave in and did. I told him all the gruesome details of our boat mission, and he cried with me. I told him more about the squad and that I'd told Demon to consider joining when he decided to leave.

"This Demon, he's a fighter?" Skull looked interested.

"Best I've ever seen. Demon could put you down with no trouble," I said with a respectful tone. "I want to hate the man, but I can't. Demon's good. Inside and outside. He's got some dark shit in him that he's struggling with, probably more so than the rest of us, but he has our backs."

"At least you have a good crew looking out for you. That makes me feel a bit better about sending your ass back out there," Skull clapped me on the back. "Let's go find you a new flavor to sample tonight."

That's what we did. Skull introduced me to a saucy young thing that showed me some dance moves. We spent hours dancing, and by the night's end, I was a decent dancer. Skull thought it was hilarious, but not once that night did I think about the people I killed or those who wanted to kill me.

I flew back to California, and we were there for a month doing some extra training on surveillance and intelligence. Ghost looked better than he had, and so did Foxy. Demon was still tight around the eyes and stuck close to the other two.

It became the cycle repeated over the three years I had left. I figured I would re-up. As awful as it was over there, I wanted to remain a part of this team; they were a family of sorts. We'd deploy for a year, come back to the states for three months, and then deploy again.

The leave we had right before I needed to re-up, I rode my bike from Tacoma to San Diego. I wanted to stop in and visit my mom's grave before we left again. Skull came with me, and we had ourselves a little road trip. He'd get my bike back up to his place for me.

The squad had a rough year. Foxy was close to a mental break, and Ghost had started talking to a Chaplain while stationed overseas. A few of the other squads did that too. I wasn't sure what to do about the things inside me, and I tended to follow in Demon's footsteps and keep it bottled up.

When I looked at Demon and Ghost, I could see the darkness inside them, and I didn't feel like I was at the point they were. I knew there was a fine line in that mental place, and it wouldn't take much for me to be right in the thick of it with them, but I still sang Amazing Grace to my mom when I felt like it was getting unbearable. It seemed to do the trick and help ease the strain.

Sometimes Ghost would hear me and join me for the few verses he knew. He'd talk more about his sister Frankie, and his mom, ask my opinions on the guy she was dating and vent about how she picked assholes all the time.

We all loved hearing Frankie's letters to him, especially Foxy. It was familiar and pleasant. It was hilarious when an Army girl he'd been sleeping with punched him in the dick for declaring his love for Frankie. I swear, Demon about swallowed his tongue.

Ghost's family would even send care packages to us that brightened our weeks. Those were the moments that being over in this hellhole was tolerable. I'd stopped telling Skull the things that got to me. He wouldn't understand because he's never been there.

Skull still took care of me on leave when I visited him. Nightmares would often wake me up, or small things that others wouldn't notice, like a tone of voice, or body language, would trigger a memory of some type of hell we survived, and Skull would have to talk me down.

He'd stopped asking me what happened after the talk we'd had the one time. All Skull had said was I'd changed, and he couldn't tell if it was for the better or worse. I took it with a grain of salt because I knew I was different. There wasn't any way you wouldn't be after fighting in this war.

We were heading to England next to take part in a joint mission. It was a welcome change of scenery when we arrived, but the mission felt sketchy and dangerous. In my mind, they were all starting to blend and bleed into each other. Hidden compounds, endless tunnels, and caves. Recon in places where no logical human would want to live. Blistering hot sun, dry sand, nomadic tribes, insurgent camps. They were all the same.

The enjoyable part was getting to sit in a pub, drink a beer, and watch Ghost get hit on by a cross-dresser with Foxy looking on in jealousy. It was a scene that would carry me through some heavy times. Ghost was known for fast hook-ups. He'd meet a hot woman who was all about a man in uniform, they'd head off to the bathroom, and ten minutes later, he'd come out with a grin and satisfied look.

I wouldn't have let it go that far with an obvious guy, and how they didn't see it was beyond me. So I told Demon, and he played into it. Short of Foxy getting punched in the dick, that had to have been the most comical thing we'd witnessed. The cross-dresser had rubbed Ghost's hand over his crotch and loudly declared that Ghost wasn't ready for him yet.

I snorted beer through my nose. Later, I also ended up in a fight because some clown from the joint task force was talking shit about Demon and his skills as a Master Chief. That shit wasn't going to fly with me. I'd take the reprimand. The people lost on that assignment weren't our fault or the fault of Demon's leadership.

The soldier had even gone so far as to say Demon's name was because he must have sold his soul to the devil to get into a Master Chief position. Fuck that. If he'd seen the shit Demon brought us through, his mouth wouldn't have ever opened. So I closed it for him.

"Those bridges you set fire to lead back to me,

asshole," I snapped before leaving. "You're on the wrong fucking side of those bridges. Better hope you don't need us one day."

Chapter 27

"You've gotten harder, Boomer," Ghost walked up to me and sat.

"What's that supposed to mean?" I looked over at him.

"Don't let this place take away the soft parts of your heart," Ghost clarified.

"Might be too late for that talk," I huffed, exasperated with the conversation.

"Bullshit. I saw you cry when I read Frankie's letter. There's still humanity left in there. I have no shame in saying she's the reason I hold tightly to mine. Yeah, I've killed way too many people for it not to affect and change me, but I haven't stopped caring. I still wonder what the family members feel and how many lives I've ruined with that one trigger pull or fatal knife wound. I think about children they might have had and how they have to grow up without that person now. It's what separates us from mercenaries," Ghost's tone faded into melancholic sadness.

"Why you still here?" I asked him. "Why not go home to Frankie?"

"Because my place is alongside Demon and Foxy.

I've known that for years. Frankie doesn't need me watching over her shoulder and telling her to pick different men. She's got her mind and will live her life how she thinks she should. Who am I to tell her otherwise? She's done a damn good job at making something of herself. Demon needs me, and I need them," Ghost gave me a guarded look.

I went back to watching the Air Force pilot that captured my attention the same way she had caught Ghosts. I didn't care if it made me a stalker, but I had gotten a vague smile and nothing to indicate she would be interested in getting to know me when I approached her.

So I watched her when her plane brought her here. She was working out, and the heat of the day, combined with the warmth of her body, made the hair at the nape of her neck curl into little tendrils. For some reason, I found that sexy as hell. She'd pulled her dark hair into a knot, and her muscled frame was rippling with exertion in that sports bra and spandex shorts. Her face was in shadow, but I could see the outline of her full lips.

"Why do you stay, Boomer?" Ghost pressed me.

I shrugged. I'd asked myself the same question repeatedly. "Haven't figured out that answer yet, man. Maybe it's you, and maybe it's the feeling of closeness of our squad. It's for damn sure not this place. Part of me thinks if I go and live with my friend, I'm gonna fall into the habits he's into, and they aren't exactly in line with the reasons we are here putting ourselves through hell."

"We *are* family. I'll give you that. I'm only concerned that you will lose that part of you that is essential to who you are. I saw it happen with Buster, and I think if he didn't get out when he did, he would have become someone dangerous to himself. From the moment I met you, I knew there was something special about you, Boomer. You are smart, like Frankie; you care, like Foxy. You have shadows, like Demon and me. Don't let the shadows win," Ghost said with a sigh.

"Are the shadows winning in you?" I threw back at him.

"Sometimes. I get those moments when we are out in the middle of a shitstorm, and bullets fly everywhere. I feel tempted to stand up and beg them to shoot me because the depravity of it all sucks the life out of me, and I look around me at you guys, fighting to keep each other alive, and think, what the fuck am I thinking that way for when you guys are counting on me to help? I see it in Demon, I see how he puts himself at risk to keep us alive, and I wonder if he cares if he lives or dies. I care, I don't want to die, I don't think. Other times I think I already have," Ghost spilled his secrets.

That was a feeling I could relate to down deep. "Yeah, I hear you. I think I died with my friend Trigger when he got killed. But you know, Ghost. If you die, you are leaving them anyway. Demon does what he does to ensure that doesn't happen and that you go home to your family."

"I know, Boomer. I think Demon forgets that he's my family too. So are you. Seeing you like this makes me think you are too close to that point of no return. God only knows Demon, and I have toed that line too many times. Tell me what you need, man. I'll do it," Ghost said.

"I don't know anymore. That's the truth, Ghost. I know if you left, Demon and Foxy would follow you. We all look up to Demon because he's the perfect soldier. We all want to be like him, at least the new recruits do. The rest of us want to be like you. I'd lose my will to be here if the three of you left; I can tell you that," I admitted.

"Foxy's ready to line the streets with porn, have a hot dog festival and beat down the first person that protests. Foxy is who I wish I were more like; he can still find his sense of humor, compassion, and iron will that will kick some serious ass," Ghost gave a wry smile. "Instead, I'm more like Demon."

"What makes you think you and Demon have no softness left inside you? Yeah, you got the shadows you speak of; we can all see them. If Demon didn't care, half of us would be dead. If you didn't care, you'd have left. Why you so worried about me? Your sister sees the real you and is still proud of you. There's more good than there's bad, Ghost. I know this shit hits hard, and you see Frankie's face on many of these people. I get that. I see Trigger's face on some of them," I pushed, wondering what brought on this talk.

I hadn't been aware I was putting off any vibe. Yeah, I was sitting alone and staring at the distance to where the pilot was working out. We'd gotten back from another recon mission, and I wanted space. I'd had a few rough nights on the task, but nothing that would warrant this conversation. That's when it hit me that he needed to talk; this was Ghost reaching out in a manner that didn't flat out say he needed help.

I studied his face for signs of a bad state of mind. "Do you ever wonder if we'll get judged when we die for the shit that happens over here?" Ghost finally asked.

"All the fucking time," I answered. "My mom was a big believer in doing good, fighting for what's right, standing up for those that can't do it on their own, and believing in diversity. I have to wonder what she thinks about all this. Everything we see defies those things, and we must do some nasty shit to survive."

"Think she'd be disappointed?" Ghost turned to look at me with that question.

"Sometimes. It's not the way her dad taught her to fight back against injustice. He still got his ass handed to him more than once for the non-violent approach. Is there a right way? We can't change how these people think; why are we trying?" I jumped into the conversation with both feet. "Same way that we can't change the way racist people at home think."

That startled Ghost. "People profiled you at home?"

"I was. Not to the same degree as others, but it happened. You can't say we aren't doing the same thing to these people. For fuck's sake, we flinch when kids approach us, and I'm not saying it's wrong because it appears to be valid over here. But they hate us. No matter our color, we're Americans or Westerners, and they hate us all because of that. We're over here to kill them in their eyes," I said, heating up to the topic.

"We aren't here to kill them," Ghost protested, but not strongly.

"In their eyes, we are. That's what they see when

they look at us. Just like when some cops look at me, they immediately think 'criminal.' Doesn't matter if it's not true; we can't overcome our own prejudices, much less make the ones here who hate us understand we are here to help them restore balance to their country." I gestured around us, "We're walking around armed to the teeth and ready to fire on the first person approaching us."

Ghost pondered it and fell silent, thinking. "I'm circling away from here because we live this shit daily. I don't think it ever occurred to me that you would face the same thing back home. I can visually see you're black, but I don't think of you as black. You're just Boomer or Darius. Not black Boomer, or black Darius."

"You are one of the few then," I leaned back on my elbows. The Air Force lady finished her workout, and I felt a little letdown. "Most people see the color of my skin first. If they described me, they'd say the black guy over there, not the hazel-eyed guy with short dark hair. It's no different for Latino people or Asians. The color of our skin automatically differentiates us."

"Do you believe that's because they see you differently or that it's just the easiest way to separate you in a crowd? I'd probably say the black guy too, and I'm not racist in the slightest," Ghost replied.

"No, I don't believe that it's always someone calling me out for being black. But in a crowd of black people, and you had to point me out, you couldn't say the black guy. You'd have to look beyond the color of my skin. See the difference?" I pointed out.

"I do," Ghost fell silent again. "Was your family

targeted? I know you told me about your friend's death and what happened after that."

"They were." I told Ghost about my mom's letter and the few things she'd verbally said to me over the years. I told him about my grandpa's general disposition and how he was generally known for being outspoken but kind.

"He'd educate people? On how to look past the skin color?" Ghost had a faint smile on his face. "It's kind of incredible to think I'm talking with a relative of someone who was in all those civil rights marches. The deep south drastically differs from where I grew up in the Pacific Northwest."

"Like separate countries, man," I chuckled at that. "We're the same; we just tan differently."

Ghost laughed. "Not quite the same. My family history doesn't include segregation, racism, or slavery. I get what you are saying; generally, that's how I treat people. Makes me angry that you've lived that. I'd stand with you, Boomer. You're my brother."

"Same, man. Now, you really don't see that what people did to black people at home is what we are doing here?" I circled back to the original topic. "I think that's part of what bothers me so much. They are doing the same thing to us, but we are the invaders and the danger from their perspective."

"I know, you're right. It doesn't make what these people are doing to their people right. They are stealing people to fight for them and promising them paradise and that they are born to be sacrifices for ridding the world of infidels," Ghost dropped his head. "I know,

Boomer. You don't have to tell me. We can't change how they think."

"It's not right, Ghost. I know that, too. I imagine this is how the Vietnam vets felt while fighting that war. For that matter, it's how soldiers probably felt in all the foreign wars. There are days that I can see we are giving voice to the people here who want Al Qaeda gone; they want a peaceful life." I paused to look at him. "Then, there are days where I believe we are the devils they think we are."

"The price of freedom is our sanity," Ghost whispered.

Chapter 28

I've watched this building for twelve hours and still seen no signs of life. It didn't mean there weren't any; it only indicated if there were people in there, they had as much patience as I did, and they had the cover of the hollowed-out building. There were parts of it we couldn't see.

A series of clicks sounded in my ear, signaling that we would move in. It wasn't an agreed-upon decision, and I signaled back my negative response. I knew it would bring Demon to me. I had probably thirty seconds to figure out a good reason why. I had nothing other than intuition.

As I'd predicted, Demon showed up at my side, his voice the barest of sounds in the too still air. "Do you see anything?"

I shook my head and tapped my head and my heart; he'd know what it meant. He frowned and sent the signal back to hold steady. He sat with me and watched it from my viewpoint. It wasn't just the view; it was everything combined. We knew there was life in this village, despite the destruction. Yet we had seen no sign of it anywhere, from how the air hung motionless around us to the dulled sound of silence.

It wasn't right. It screamed ambush. We had the high ground, we should have been able to see more than we could, but the village's destruction looked staged. The fallen wall on a building created a perfect place to hide underneath in the dark shadows it made. It was like that for all the facilities. They weren't rubble, it was fallen walls, and roofs, strategically collapsed.

After a few minutes, Demon shook his head. "Trap?" he asked me quietly, and I nodded. I pointed out some of the places I'd been watching and saw as he took in the same nooks and crannies I had. His jaw ticking was the only movement in Demon's body.

I knew he was running through situations in his mind and waited patiently. It felt like we crawled up the devil's asshole, it was so hot, but I'd rather be sweating than dead. Our intel hadn't told us how many people lived here, just that people did. We'd been hoping to get an idea with today's surveillance.

"Intel could be wrong," Demon finally whispered. We didn't dare talk too loud; it would carry with how silent it was around us.

Something about the situation just felt off. It could be wrong, and it wouldn't be the first time. I could see that Demon felt it too, and he shifted to look in a different direction. I waited to see if he'd notice the footprints. They were faint but visible, and it wasn't a military boot.

They led into a half-crumbled building that looked like it used to be a store of some sort. I wrote out the words staged destruction on the sandy ground, tapped

Demon, and pointed. From our angle, we couldn't see more than that, and I guessed that the store was still functional.

He read it and then glanced around as if looking at it from that perspective. He nodded and sent a series of clicks telling us to fall back to our hidden spot. We returned to what we were calling camp, which was out of sight of the small village nestled in the hills behind it.

"I agree with Boomer," Demon started, still talking in a barely perceptible tone. "It looks staged."

"Perfect set up for an ambush," I added unnecessarily. "The air is too still. Not even animals made a sound."

"Think they knew we were up there?" Foxy looked at Demon.

"Possibly," Demon sighed and shook his head. "I think if we look for a different vantage point, we might be better off, but it also puts us at risk of being seen."

"What about sending just me?" Ghost volunteered.

"No," I said automatically, realizing I stepped out of place. "Sorry, Demon."

"I want to hear why." Demon gave me a calculating look.

"If it's a trap, he'd be walking into it alone, same reason I didn't suggest just tossing a flashbang down and letting it go off. We'd draw attention and let them know that we are indeed here. Where would you put him in that mess if you had a high-value target? They know we'll come for him. Look at how little they value life. If one of us get seen, or we let them know in some way, they'll only kill him or one of us," I blurted out. I'd had twelve hours to sit there and think.

"Did you see the footprints?" Demon asked me.

I smiled then. "Wondered if you'd see those. Yeah. I think that place is functional. Whoever set up this staging did it in a way that speaks of some intelligence."

"Wait until dark," Foxy suggested. "My guess is if they move around, it will be then because they'll feel safer. It gives us a better opportunity to be unseen unless these assholes have night vision. It's a possibility, but it's our safest bet."

"As a group, tight formation," Ghost agreed. "We can't discount Boomer's intuition. He tops all of us in surveillance."

"I agree with Boomer completely," Demon told us. "From where he sat, the whole village feels eerie and unnatural."

"I had the best view of the village, and Foxy wouldn't be able to cover any of us if we went into those buildings. Think of one of those haunted funhouses with the nooks, crannies, and crevices the creepy clowns hide inside. The debris covers the angles," I tried to describe.

"The aerial shots didn't show any of that," Foxy mused.

"It's a flat image. There's no dimension," Hacker put in. "It was taken directly overhead with the sun behind it, so it didn't even cast shadows."

"We go at night," Demon decided. "Sleep. We need to be sharp if we are walking into a trap."

One of the many invaluable lessons I learned as a SEAL was sleeping anywhere. We had to huddle together, which wasn't anything new. We were under cover of a camouflage net that looked like the local shrubbery in these parts.

"Foxy, I swear if you fart, I'm going to rub your pillow all over my sweaty ass when we get back," Ghost threatened. It was the lighthearted moment we needed as we settled in for some rest.

Demon woke us as dusk was settling in, and we prepared. Hacker radioed back that we would infiltrate the village and would advise when we needed evacuation.

We took a more circuitous route than we did when we surveyed. Foxy had been right. There was movement now, but it was very little and hurried. There were five buildings that people were coming out of or going into; that's what the footprints said. Those would be the ending buildings. We methodically searched and cleared the others silently and tediously until we got to those five.

That storefront where the footprints had been was one of them. So we had five buildings to check that we had confirmed there were people inside. Splitting up would be the fastest option, but it didn't feel right. When Demon made that call, I signaled no, but he overrode me and stuck to his choice.

Hacker and I went into the first building. Silently we stalked the muffled sounds we heard, viewing it all with the green glow of night vision. We had to time this carefully, and when the clicks came that the first two teams were in place, we moved a little faster until we saw where the people gathered. It wasn't possible to do this in close combat; it would be a gunfight. The positioning wasn't correct.

I saw no sign of the hostage; thankfully, there was no sign of women or children either. The back wall hid a cache of weapons of grenades, machine guns, swords, and knives. There could be more people, but Hacker radioed that we were in place. He tapped me and pointed to the light in the room, indicating he would take it out. I shrugged because the flashbang I threw would do that.

I counted twelve. Not the best odds. However, I had gotten a lot better under Foxy's tutelage on shooting and could take more than a few before they could get to their weapons. I pulled one of the flashbangs from my pocket and showed Hacker. It wouldn't be subtle.

He perceptively nodded, and we waited for the go countdown. Hacker moved behind a wall for cover, and when the time came, I tossed it, ducked and rolled backward, and took cover. Incessant gunfire started ringing out from the village. The air was no longer still. If there was a hostage here, I had to think he had to be dead by now.

Hacker and I crept forward and dispatched the people who survived the blast while temporarily blinded. Then we set a charge to blow the weapons and got the hell out. Insouciant screams pierced the air as if they were taunting us with their indifference to us kicking their asses.

Hacker pulled me down behind a wall as bullets pinged off the rocks around us. I looked back, saw the shooter's position, and pointed him out to Hacker. We both aimed and let loose. One of us got him, and I didn't care who.

We would have to clear all these secondary buildings that looked empty, and I didn't want to do it until our team was back together. Too much separation wouldn't be practical in this case. Bandy and Cowboy came stumbling out of the structure they had been in, and we darted over to join them.

Bandy kneeled and fixed up Cowboy, who'd taken a slug in the arm. "We cleared it," Bandy told me while he worked. "Nine of them, no sign of the hostage."

Once Cowboy gave us the nod that he was ready, we stood and moved as a unit to the next building. Two more team members came out, and we kept moving towards where we knew Demon, Foxy, and Ghost were.

"Taking heavy fire," Demon's voice broke the silence of the comms. "Hostage not here. Foxy down."

We jolted into action and made our way to where Demon had gone in. Ghost and Demon would level this village if they lost Foxy. I'd help. We advanced and pinned the terrorists between us, taking them out slowly and with methodical precision.

The cloying stench of death was overwhelming on top of the putrid smell of human waste. Whoever these guys were, they didn't even have the sense to shit outside where it wouldn't stink up where they were hiding.

Bandy brought Foxy around with some smelling salts and looked at the gash on the back of his head. Demon told us someone had clubbed him. Then he came to the same conclusion I had; there might not be a hostage, and this op was probably a trap from the start.

We split up again to search the buildings, and that was my mistake for not arguing. We couldn't risk leaving a hostage behind, so we began to clear each of the secondary structures we had thought weren't viable hiding places. By the fourth one, we assumed that the village was empty. There'd been forty-one dead between us.

I'd entered one of the last structures left and saw several odd things. Before they could register, I'd gotten clubbed the way Jake had. I met the ground, but I didn't stay out. I came to with a muffled shout and found four men holding me down while a fifth was chattering away in Arabic, pointing a gun at my face.

As strong as I was, I couldn't beat back five terrorists while I was pinned down and on my back. The guy speaking moved and stood on my throat and laughed with a twisted look on his face. I seriously didn't want this to be the last thing I saw before I died.

My vision was blurring. My lungs were beginning to starve for oxygen when one of the guys threw a punch at my head. It wasn't enough that the embodiment of evil was standing on my chest, blabbing about who knows what while his other foot crushed my windpipe.

It was a game to him. When I blacked out, he removed his foot, and when I came to, he put it back on. I felt the blade of a knife slice into my triceps, and I bucked, knocking the asshole off-balance and allowing me to shout.

It didn't sound loud to me through the wheezing

sound I was making, but it was enough to get Ghost and Demon's attention. I saw Demon barrel into the tormentor through hazy eyes while Ghost kicked the shit out of the others, and Hacker dragged me to safety.

I heard the sound of five gunshots and knew the terrorists were dead. There was also a shocking shout with Hacker bolting into the structure while Bandy looked me over. To my surprise, the guys came out with a bleeding, banged-up older white man that looked like a limp bag of bones. Foxy was awake with his head bandaged and peering through his scope, watching to make sure no one snuck up on us. There'd been a hostage after all.

Hacker called in for evacuation, requested medical services, and Demon ordered an airstrike to wipe this staged hidey-hole off the map. Three of us took damage on this assignment and on a team of utter badasses that said something. We'd gotten the hostage, but I didn't know if he was alive or not. I didn't argue with Demon.

Chapter 29

I couldn't breathe; there was a foot on my throat. Sweat dripped off my body, my vision was black, and I could hear the sick laughter of the bastard trying to kill me. I tried to roll, but I couldn't move. I was being held down, knees on my limbs. The rhythmic pinging of bullets was starting to sound like music.

My heart was racing so fast that it felt like I was in the middle of a heart attack, adrenaline shooting through my veins, propelling me to move. The blades of thousands of knives pierced my skin, and finally, I could scream and hope that someone would be able to hear and help me. When I felt hands touch me, I could move, and I rolled away, dropped to the ground, and wondered where my night vision goggles went and if the terrorists had stolen them.

"Boomer!" I heard and tried to focus my eyes. "It's me, Ghost!"

"I can't see! I lost my goggles!" I screamed, hoping he could hear me over the sound of the bullets. My hands frantically fumbled around on the gritty floor for the lost goggles.

"Shit!" Demon's voice penetrated, and then I was

doused with cold water. My eyes opened, and I saw my squad gathered around me. I could still smell the blood and sour smell of the un-showered terrorists. Yet, I was not there. I was in my tent.

"Nightmare, Boomer," Ghost reached his hand out. I let him pull me up and sat me down on my bunk. "Do you have them often?"

I tried to clear it from my head and felt like I was in a fog. "Not like you, but yeah," I admitted, accepted the cup of water Foxy handed me, and gulped it down. "Does that happen to you? You can't move?"

Demon sat next to me. "It's happened to me. Were you being held down?" the Master Chief guessed.

I nodded. Shame washed through me as I realized I woke everyone. I dropped my head into my hands and tried to slow my heartbeat down to normal. My arms were shaking. No, that was wrong; my whole body was shaking.

"It's fucked up, but we all get them. Sometimes the nightmares are bad like yours was, others we don't wake anyone up but ourselves, and we have to remind ourselves where we are," Demon went on.

"Demon, Foxy's looking a little wild-eyed. Take him. I'll stay here with Boomer," Ghost said. One of the other guys got Ghost's blankets and brought them back, where he stretched out on the floor. "Lay down, Boomer. I have to force myself to remember it was just a nightmare, and then I can usually fall back asleep. You've got to sleep some, or those fuckers win. The nightmares drain you of energy."

That was no lie. I could still feel the knives

stabbing me, even though I could see my skin and see nothing was touching me. I lay back. "It's so real."

"Yeah, I know, man. Those nightmares fuck you up. I once threw Frankie across my room when she tried to wake me up. I cried the rest of the night after that. It's PTSD, Darius; we've all got it. I don't think you can escape this place without it. That one had a good grip on you," Ghost said, sounding as tired as I felt.

"I could smell them again," I whispered. "I felt the knives in my skin. When gunfire sounds like music, I should know it's not real, but I couldn't move. They were holding me down again. It happened so fast in real life, but they play out slow in these nightmares, and it fucks with me."

"I saw. It's unnerving to see, and I feel worse for Frankie now." I heard Ghost shuffling around.

"You can move up here next to me. We can squish," I offered sheepishly.

Ghost let out a weak chuckle. "Your shoulders are too wide for that."

I moved, grabbed my blanket and pillow, and stretched out next to him on the floor. "I don't care if people think I'm a pussy. That shit was real, and they were going to kill me. I'd rather sleep knowing that someone friendly is next to me."

"I get it," Ghost replied, his tone sad.

Hacker moved and got down on the floor with us. "They fucking suck. I haven't had one that bad, but there are times that I wake up, and I don't know where I am, and I swear someone had a knife at my throat and a bomb strapped to my chest."

"Well, for damn sure, we aren't letting any of these fuckers take you from us, Boomer," Ghost finally said. "Can't say seeing someone standing on your throat was a good vision. You've looked better."

The quiet laugh that bubbled up was what I needed to break free from the reins the nightmare had on me. "I probably looked better underwater, swimming as fast as I could not to get eaten by a shark."

Ghost and Hacker both laughed. "Man, I wasn't afraid of sharks until you said that," Hacker added. "When we got back in the water, I waited for Jaws to come up and bite my damn leg off. Don't think I've ever swum that fast before."

I didn't care if he was only saying it to make me feel better; it was the banter bringing us back to the moment and not stuck in our memories of awful shit. "Foxy?"

"Demon's got him. He'll be okay," Ghost reassured me. "Remember, we always fight."

Even if we don't always win, I thought. We all succumbed to the exhaustion and fell back asleep. This time I knew I was in a nightmare and was able to push past it. It didn't make for good sleep, but it was better than staying awake for the rest of the night.

We debriefed in the morning and learned we were moving to Afghanistan. I wondered what new sights would greet us there. I felt like we've already seen all the world's worst. We'd been in so many places where we were sure death would come for us.

We grabbed our trunks and caught the transport, the female Air Force pilot again flying us, and this time

Ghost made sure to talk to her. Nothing more than cracking a few jokes to make her smile, but it still made me jealous. Ridiculous. Like I had a chance to start a romance here in these pits of hell?

Something about her drew me in; she was like an irresistible drug. I mean, I'd noticed the way her hair curls when she sweats. I can't say those details ever came up for me before. I shrugged it off and closed my eyes for the rest of the flight, her lips forming a smile floating in my mind.

When we landed and took in the new area we would be calling home for a while, I saw it was just as depressing as the last place. The pilot was under the plane, checking something. I veered off and walked up to her.

"Hey, my name is Darius. Thanks for carting us around," I offered my hand.

"Amelia, and you're welcome. I've carted this crew around before." She smiled, and I swear my tongue was sweating. Her eyes were luminous pools of cashmere.

"Want to get a meal next time you come through?" I asked, sounding as pathetic as I felt.

"Maybe. I never know where I'll end up," Amelia smiled again, this time in apology. "Hard to make plans in these places."

Amelia had a point, and I tried not to take it personally. "Be safe," I saluted her and rejoined my squad.

"Did you just get shot down?" Foxy gave me a crooked grin.

"No, not really. Brushed-off without the shoot down. The woman said she doesn't know her schedule," I relayed.

"That's true. Could have been a flat-out hell no, so I'd say you still have a chance. She's cute, but she's no Frankie," Foxy said a little louder.

"Man, he's gonna beat your ass if you keep that up," I elbowed him.

"It keeps him sane. I can take his beatings," Foxy called out again. "Ghost likes touching me."

I genuinely laughed when I saw the look on Ghost's face. "Bromance is alive and well."

Ghost reached in his pack, pulled out the hat his sister had sent, and settled it on his head. The cap read bromance, and Ghost blew a kiss at Foxy, who, in turn, pretended to catch it and plaster it on his face.

Demon was cracking up right until the base commander walked up, and we all snapped into a salute and calmed down immediately.

"At ease. The specialist team, I presume?" the commander's lips twitched at Ghost's hat.

"Yes, sir," Damien answered. "Master Chief Ocasta and my team. Our commander is back at the airstrip."

"Get settled," he handed Demon a paper. "Bunk assignments. Meet back here," he pointed to something on the sheet, "in an hour. We need to send you out."

"Yes, sir," Demon responded, and we saluted again. He turned to us. "Looks like four per tent. Two are next to each other, and the other two are a couple of tents away. Split how you want."

Ghost came up to me. "Why don't you stay in ours? I'd feel better if we were close enough to help with the nightmares."

"I don't have to blow kisses to Foxy, do I?" I turned to look at Foxy.

"Chocolate kisses could be good," he quipped in response.

"You guys have problems," Demon laughed. "Boomer, offer's open. That was a potent nightmare."

"No rest for the wicked—they already gonna send us out?" I nodded my acceptance and followed. Hacker and Bandy took the tent next to ours."

"Sounds like it," Demon slid into the Master Chief persona as we each checked our go-bags for anything we needed to add to them.

Chapter 30

I can't say this place looked any different than the last one. Even the assignments were more of the same. We got maps, showed a route we could take, and told us it would be on foot and what we were looking for; that answer was always more Al Qaeda, only they wanted one alive this time.

If we removed all threats, there was a chance we'd get a helo evac. We'd have to return on foot if we didn't clear the supposed camp. We received warnings that the insurgents here were much more fanatical than we'd seen elsewhere. Translated, they were bat-shit crazy, more of the same.

Demon told us this was going to be our home for a while. I saw that we wouldn't be traveling outside Afghanistan for an extended time through what he said.

I emailed Skull and my dad, telling them I'd moved and was now in Afghanistan, gave generic news, and talked a bit about the joking between Ghost and Foxy. We never used names in letters or emails, or phone calls. We always referred to the others by their nicknames.

I had an email from Buster that I shared with the guys, and we responded as one. His words sounded happy, but there was an undertone that Demon caught on to the same way I did. Buster was struggling with adjusting.

I had another burst of fear skitter through me that I would be facing the same thing. We all would; home was a different world than here. It might as well be separate planets. I sent our responses and gave up my computer time, and went to mentally prepare for whatever shit we were about to walk into again.

A few of the squads looked at us in curiosity. I knew we had reputations. When Demon ran us through drills, we got dubious looks as if they couldn't believe what we were doing. It was intense, but those drills kept us alive and sharp. If you asked me, they could use a bit of it, and maybe their losses wouldn't be so bad.

This routine was what it looked like for us for the next three years. Our bright days were the ones Ghost got letters from his sister and sent care packages. We got leave when things got too much for more than one of us—and Demon went to battle that we would end up casualties if we didn't get it and said they'd lose their precious mercenaries. He'd seriously called us mercenaries.

Some of these missions they sent us on were so twisted and fucked seven ways from Sunday. I saw the Air Force pilot a lot more frequently, she gave me shy smiles, but I noticed that her eyes drifted to Ghost more often than not. I didn't begrudge him for it. We each needed to find whatever we could to get through the shit.

It still disappointed me that I wasn't her choice,

yet I couldn't deny that Ghost had an insane draw with the women. He was also a lot more outgoing than I was. I didn't go without; I hooked up when I could. I had two years left to serve, and I wasn't coming back after it was up.

I could readily admit that I was disillusioned and broken inside, and I didn't think it was safe to reside in that mental place. Hell, I didn't even know I would survive another two years of this. On each mission we'd gone on, one of us had returned injured. IEDs were a way of life and not a good one.

Dirty bombs contained kitchen cutlery in some of the structures we'd gotten sent in. It's not pretty getting a chunk torn out of your arm by a kitchen fork. Fuck, I wanted out now. There wasn't a hope in me that my life would be normal, and I'd already emailed Skull that I wanted in his club.

I mentioned the club again to Demon, who was more than interested, which gave me an odd sense of comfort. More than the riding part of it, I needed the feel of a family around me. With as many members as they had, it would be closest to what I had here. I knew I needed that.

Foxy wasn't interested, but I felt he was ready to be done too. Ghost for sure. Some days he looked hollowed out and empty. Seeing how he lit up when he got letters from home made me smile. It was followed by a look of anguish and intense sadness that I wished I could ease for him.

Ghost was such a salt-of-the-earth type person, as my dad would say, and each conversation I had with him brought me closer to him, as close as I was with Skull and had been with Trigger. I think he was worse off than me, perhaps not quite as far gone as Demon was. However, Demon managed to pull it together and rein it in every time we left the base. I don't know how, but I was thankful for that ability of his.

I was sitting outside again and saw Ghost sauntering off. Amelia, the Air Force pilot, had landed not too long ago, and my guess was he was heading off to see her. Intuition told me the squad would be leaving base soon, even though we hadn't gotten any word to that effect yet.

The squad had intense interrogation training earlier this week, followed by a more stringent physical training regimen that Demon put us through. There were women here, but they were scarce. Despite that, I needed to burn off some energy and didn't feel like looking for an available woman, which wasn't a lot. I felt the need to hit something.

I got up and went to seek out any squad member not actively engaged in something and ended up with Foxy, who was looking a little desolate.

"What's up, Boomer?" Foxy looked up as I walked in.

"Need to burn off some energy. Interested in a run or something?" I hesitated before asking.

"You want to run in this heat?" he sounded surprised. Then he shrugged. "Why not? Give me a minute to change."

Foxy set something down, and I saw it was one of the pictures Ghost's sister had sent. The man had it bad for her. "Feeling okay, Foxy?" I chanced, asking him.

"Yeah. Little bit out of it today, but sleep was rough last night. Why?" he asked, lacing up his shoes.

"The expression on your face," I answered him, stretching lightly.

"The need to see something other than sand is pulling at me," Foxy admitted. "I already read the book Frankie sent, so staring at the picture was my only avenue."

I knew it was more than that, but I wasn't going to push him. We all felt the same way. Ghost was right that Foxy channeled it better than the rest of us. Foxy gave me a concerned look as I fidgeted while he stretched.

"Boomer, you are more introspective than most of us; I'd say very similar to Ghost and Demon. Something on your mind?" Foxy correctly guessed.

He followed me out to the worn path that wove around the base. "Wondering who I have become," I told him as we broke into a run.

Foxy groaned. "Man, you want to talk and run while we are in this heat? You are just as sadistic as Demon."

I chuckled. "You're used to it. Don't give me shit."

"You are who you've always been, Boomer," Foxy huffed out.

"Bullshit," I challenged him. "This place has changed you as much as it has the rest of us."

"It hasn't changed who I am at the deepest levels. My core beliefs are the same. Other things, you're right, they are different, and I'm still trying to figure them out.

You aren't alone in that," Foxy finally agreed.

"I don't even know what my core beliefs are anymore," I said on an exhale. "I won't figure it out here, either."

"You want out?" Foxy slowed and stared at me.

"Don't you?" I pushed back.

He nodded. "I think all three of us are ready not to be here. Don't worry about what you'll do when you get home. You need to decompress first."

"I'm gonna join Skull in his motorcycle club. Maybe some good hard riding will wash this shit from my head," I muttered.

Foxy pressed his lips into a thin line but didn't contradict me. I understood that Skull's club might not be on the side of right, but what we were doing wasn't either. I know it was in the name of war, but Demon calling us mercenaries had stuck with me.

"You don't need to join a club to ride," Foxy pointed out as he picked up the pace again.

"Aside from you guys, he's the closest thing to a brother I got. I need that," my throat thickened up a little. "I can't fight this shit in my head alone, man. I'm not like you."

"No, you're like Demon and Ghost. What's right for one isn't what's right for all, but you need to do what you feel is right. Ghost is trying to get help; Demon only bottles it up. I just don't want to see you on the wrong side of things after all we've dealt with in this shithole," Foxy replied.

"What are you going to do?" I asked as we rounded a corner.

"Figured I'd join the police," Foxy answered. "I still want to help. I want to help where I can see a difference in the people living around me. I don't know if we are helping here, but it certainly isn't helping anyone at home what we are doing here. Maybe in the bigger picture of national security, I guess. I don't know anymore."

I thought about it, and the police force had little appeal to me. I could be useful on a bomb squad, but I didn't want to be in any more gunfights or life-threatening situations. I also thought that I wouldn't be able to live happily with my dad, and that thought hurt.

"Don't worry about it today," Foxy said, seeing me struggle with my thoughts. "These places have taught me to value the day you live in; no guarantees on anything more."

"That's not exactly helpful," I growled.

"No, but it's true. Even at home, it's true. Race you to mess hall," Foxy grinned and broke into a sprint.

Foxy was right; none of us had a guaranteed a tomorrow. But that didn't mean I would let him beat me in a challenge either. As much as I hated the thought, since I had been so meticulous in planning my path here, I was not planning my future.

Chapter 31

We were gathered in the command war room, having another assignment laid out before us. Intelligence ops were spreading their precious information like it was sweet nectar, and we should be thanking them for allowing us to hear it. Too many times, it hadn't panned out and cost us something. Like a team member.

It was safe to say I was cynical and jaded, and something felt wrong about this assignment. I wasn't the only one that thought it either. Demon was on the fence and not happy. Ghost frowned almost the whole time. Hacker asked more questions than usual, and Foxy was oddly silent.

Intel rumored high-level targets lived in a tunnel network that a passing-by squad had spotted. Drone footage showed children playing, and night vision showed several places where heat signatures registered. It could be nothing more than one of the nomadic tribes that lived in the mountains.

It could also be a training camp. They were leaning towards a training camp. They wanted surveillance that gave them room for us to act. That meant sixteen of us against god only knows how many armed people, trained and untrained. I felt sick to my stomach. It was eerily similar to when I had lost my first squad.

When I felt eyes on me, I looked up to meet Demon's gaze. The look I read in his eyes told me he understood my unspoken body language. I was going to be an integral part of this assignment if we discovered a training camp. They'd made it clear they wanted us to kill if it was a camp.

Kids. I would have to kill more kids, and it didn't sit right with me. I knew they were training to kill us or anyone that didn't agree with their train of thought; even still, it was kids. Fucking place sucked all that was good in me out and spat it out into this killer I'd become.

I paid attention when they showed aerial photos of the area. There wasn't a lot to build off of, and I said so and gave them an idea of what I thought should get used. I suggested an airstrike that left us out of it altogether. The agents didn't feel the same way. They wanted our boots on the ground and a bomb planted in the tunnel.

"Look, I am not siding with that because it puts us in danger," I finally said, exasperated. "The blast radius of what you are looking for extends past here." I pointed to the map. "We'd need to be within this area to trigger the explosive and ensure it goes off. If it doesn't, or if someone gets to the explosive and disarms it before I blow the charge, those guys are now in possession of a deadly weapon that can get used against us."

"You asked for our expertise," Demon

interrupted. "Yet, the top explosives guy we have is here telling you his expert opinion, and you aren't listening to him. Are you sending us in there to get killed? If that's the case, I'd like to know upfront."

As many times as we butted heads on decisions over the years, I had never been so grateful to have Demon's support. "The math doesn't lie, gentlemen," I replied drily, tired of the charades. I wrote out the mathematical formulas and showed the projected blast area and collateral damage areas using different colored inks and their photos. "Anything inside this radius, using these materials and your suggestions, would not give us time to clear the area. Are you sending us in with vehicles or on foot?"

"Clandestine means on foot," one of the intelligence operatives snapped.

"Watch your tone," the base commander replied coldly. "These men have survived worse shit than you could have possibly seen. It won't work if they tell you that it won't work. Based on the scanty information provided, I'm not sacrificing the best the Navy has. If you want them on this assignment and want it to succeed, it will get done how they see fit, not you, unless you are planning on joining them."

"You can't refuse," one of the other agents supplied. "This comes straight from the president."

Demon smacked his hands on the table, making them jump. "We'll do your damn dirty work, but we'll do it in a way that ensures I won't lose my team because some cabinet member with his head up his ass doesn't care if we live or die. Got it?"

It was rare to see Demon lose it like that, and he radiated a level of danger that had even the base commander arching his eyebrows and backing up. Ghost moved and put a hand on Demon's arm. "Our Master Chief is correct. You sought us out for a reason. You should listen," Ghost said with a calm none of us felt.

"The specifics of how you carry out your assignment is up to you," the one I assumed was the senior agent ground out between clenched teeth. "Accomplish the objectives."

"We always have," Demon's tone set my teeth on edge. The man was about to snap.

"Run us through the logistics," Hacker broke in, hoping to ease the room's tension.

"There is a convoy that will be running back and forth on this road here," the agent pulled out another map. "There is a four-day window between the convoy reaching the base and the return. It's a tight window, but it should be doable."

"How far from the road is the location?" I asked, looking at the map. Calling it a tight window was a bit understated if it was a significant distance, especially carrying gear. "Is the convoy our only method of evacuation?"

"No," the base commander insisted. "I'll make sure of that."

"No one is allowed to know you've even deployed," the agent spit out, turning red.

"Kind of hard to keep sixteen men a secret on a convoy," Foxy growled. "Especially since you expect us to disappear from the convoy. I think that would get noticed. Common sense."

Demon and I snorted simultaneously and began to wonder how these agents got through their training to make it where they were. Their lack of intelligence for an intelligence operative was astonishing.

The agent in charge shifted again. "We will defer to your expertise. Obviously, you will be seen by other troops as you move. This intel is the first credible lead we've had on this particular camp. If we can stop them, the child abductions will drastically slow. I am aware we don't need to tell you how to carry out the assignment," he shot a look at the one who was talking before. "Simply a reminder that this is as black as they come."

"Understood," Demon barked. He pulled the map towards him and then proceeded to tell the agents how he saw it getting handled with minimal exposure and risk. As he talked, we crowded around the map, and I saw several places where we'd be at risk.

I tapped the map when Demon paused to look at me. "If it was us, these spots here are where I would pick to hide."

"It looks right over the road we'd be on." Demon agreed, and Ghost looked thoughtful.

"High IED risk," Foxy replied. "Snipers could also be here and here."

We didn't typically have others listening in while we planned our course of action, but we had no choice. Only the agent in charge looked impressed with our planning and trying to cover all eventualities.

"One last thing," the agent in charge said before we packed up. "If we are right about this camp, they should be receiving a new truckload of recruits within the next couple of days. That's what the chatter we've picked up has been about."

Shit. That meant these guys would be on high alert. I didn't like this one little bit. Foxy looked damn uncomfortable too. The rest of the squad fell silent as they contemplated that information, and Demon and Ghost were the only two that looked resigned.

The person this war had shaped me into didn't trust anyone outside my squad. I wouldn't say I liked the look or feel of these agents, and they were gambling with our lives. Demon gathered up the maps, and the base commander dismissed us.

"We've got thirty-six hours," Demon told us. "Make them count. Sleep, eat, and create," he said the last to me. "Whatever help you need, ask. They make this sound routine, but it doesn't have its feel. Those agents called it surveillance, yet they also asked us to obliterate the place off the map when an airstrike would be easier and more effective. It doesn't add up. I don't care what the chatter says; there are a lot of holes in this. I'm betting it's political, the way this is getting rushed."

The squad agreed with Demon's assessment wholeheartedly. I went to send emails to Skull and my dad before I started making any devices. Like I knew Ghost was writing a letter to his sister, I wanted to let at least the two people worried about me know how much I cared for them.

Hacker, Bandy, and Demon joined me two hours later in making our charges. The mood was somber, and none spoke other than directions and questions on what we were making. I don't know why they didn't want to send a plane to blow the place sky-high; nothing made sense about this. One other thing this war taught me: I hated politics.

Chapter 32

It wasn't dusk yet, but we set out to keep the timetable where we needed it to pass the point where they stopped to stretch and rest between switching drivers. It took a bit of finagling on Demon's part to get us placed how he wanted us on the convoy. Our game faces were on, and no one approached us for idle talk.

That was when we'd break away since we'd have a tiny bit of cover to use to blend into the background. The bad part was it took us right through that chokepoint that had bothered us all in the afternoon light. In other words, visible without any equipment.

Drones had flown overhead and reported that the route was clear no less than an hour ago, but it did little to ease the worry in my mind. I was in the front truck; the driver was an Army guy, a Marine on the gun. Hacker was behind me, and I was in the passenger seat.

Demon, Foxy, and Ghost were behind me in the second truck. The rest of the squad watched our six in the last two trucks. We all had our comms in and were in touch. I called a halt to the driver, spotting what looked like our first IED of the trip. I had the driver radio for the rest to back up, and we waited while the trucks maneuvered.

The Marine on the gun aimed and shot at where I pointed, and sure enough, the ground blew as we took cover. A couple of Army guys came and filled in the hole to pass over it once I looked around. The blast's size should have detonated anything close to it, and I didn't see signs of disturbed ground anywhere else.

The driver felt shaken, but we carried on, and he quickly followed my lead. The drive was quiet for about four and a half hours. Ghost radioed that he thought he had seen something moving at two o'clock, and Hacker started spotting.

Foxy then communicated that he thought he had seen something flash in the mountains at ten o'clock. I didn't dare look away from the road and trying to spot anomalies in the ground. But in' my sweeps with the binoculars, I extended out a bit.

Our senses were on alert now. We were approaching that chokepoint, and like I'd told Demon if someone was going to ambush us, this was the place to do it. To my right was nothing but dunes, with a steep drop-off to the sand below. Not something the trucks could navigate. To my left were the mountains we were supposed to be crawling through later.

Seven miles up this stretch of road, the ground evened out, and we could flee into the sand with the vehicles if we needed to. Not here. The road was too narrow to avoid much of anything. I wanted to demand that we drive faster, but I knew it could cost us our lives.

"Ghost is right; something is out there," Hacker said in my ear. "I caught a glimpse of something moving before it disappeared. Could be an animal, though my gut is saying it was a person."

"Why would a person be out here? The closest village is thirty miles away," the driver grumbled, afraid to take his eyes off the road.

I briefly wondered if that delivery of recruits happened and if one escaped? I wished I could ask Demon, but too many ears were not part of this assignment in the vehicle.

"Foxy's got eyes on something in the mountain. He's got the gun pointed," Hacker relayed. "His body language is tense. Something's up."

"Both sides," I said aloud. I activated my comms to call for a halt when Ghost beat me to it.

"All halt," Ghost yelled into the comms.

I spotted something in the ground ahead at the exact moment and called it out. Hacker cursed and shoved his door open, and I automatically followed suit. Ghost and Demon were out of the vehicles looking out at the dunes.

"Ghost is on the move!" Hacker shouted at me.

Demon yelled through the comms that it was a trap and to stop running. I saw the woman then. I'd keep running too. A pregnant lady was running through the dunes towards us, obviously in distress, and her clothes were blood-soaked.

Demon screamed at Ghost to stop through the comms again, and I dove for him. Ghost was the fastest runner out of all of us, and he easily evaded me. He stopped about seventy feet away from the truck we'd been in ahead of us. He helped her lay down when it struck me that the woman's belly wasn't the shape it should be for a pregnant lady.

I saw the bomb the moment Ghost moved her dress. Two seconds later, it blew with a cacophonous sound like we were standing right over the top of it. In that split second, all I could think was that bomb was clumsily thrown together to have that blast zone.

The next second was agony as my brain caught up to what my eyes had seen. My body went flying through the air from the concussion, and I slammed into Hacker, and we both hit the truck hard, my arms and legs flailing around trying to find purchase.

My ears rang so loud it took me a second to realize that I had heard gunfire. The smell of blood, burnt flesh, gunpowder, scorched earth, and a million other things I didn't have time to think about slammed into me.

I slung my rifle over my shoulder as I got to my feet and used the truck's hood to aim where I saw bursts of gunfire stemming; Hacker took up position next to me. The booms from grenades and the incessant firing of the large .50 caliber mounted guns shook the vehicles.

We'd all been right. I didn't have time to ponder on that. We had weaker positions, and they held the high ground. I heard wailing coming from around me and knew we were up shit creek. We had injuries. I couldn't dwell on Ghost yet. My brain was still processing that I saw someone I considered a brother incinerated and shredded to pieces before my eyes.

A second blast tore through the air, and too late, I remembered the anomaly I'd seen; another IED. More shrapnel flew through the air and struck several of us as the concussion lifted us off our feet and tossed us backward. This time, upending the vehicle that I'd been leaning against for firing because it had been closer than I thought it was.

I lost all sounds of the machine guns barking under the ringing in my ears. When I could get to my feet, I saw Demon down and panicked. I ran right into the line of fire and dragged him out. Bandy was hauling out Foxy. All around me, people were dropping.

I ran to Bandy when I saw him falter and took a hit. Excruciating pain lit my body on fire as I dropped Foxy and fell next to him. A second slug hit me in time for me to register that Hacker was dead. The smoke filling the air gave us a little cover, which might have been the only thing that saved us. Twenty minutes of pure hell was what it took to tear us apart.

In between bouts of consciousness, I saw Demon trying to find pieces of Ghost, and I wanted to die. In all of our scenarios, this wasn't one of them. I felt the morphine enter my bloodstream and heard someone screaming for evac. I gave in to the blackness.

The next thing I knew: I was waking up in a hospital, with some nurse looking over my chart and checking the machines. I surrendered to the dark again and relived everything in my sleep. I woke again to feel the sting of a needle in my arm and someone speaking softly. This time I didn't dream.

I woke up crying. I couldn't go back, not after that. Nothing remained of Ghost, Hacker was gone, and I had no idea what had happened to Foxy or Demon. The squad wasn't the squad without Hacker or Ghost. I wanted no part of it anymore. If that made me a failure, I was okay with it.

I gladly floated back into the dark recesses of my mind having no concept of how long I'd been here, and when I woke up this time, General Allen was in my room, along with Foxy and Demon and all the assistants that came along with the general. Neither of my teammates looked to be in any better shape than I was, but I was beyond relieved to see they were alive.

The look on Demon's face told me he wished he wasn't; I could relate to that. Devastated wasn't a strong enough word for what I was feeling. A wave of pain shot through me when I shifted and made me heave, which only made it worse.

"Stay still, son," General Allen put a hand on me. I never understood what interest the general had taken in me, and I didn't care. Right now, I didn't want his hand on me.

"Leave him alone," Demon replied, his voice strained. "You didn't see that shit, General."

I swallowed thickly, and tears stung my eyes. "What happened? Demon, Foxy, are you okay?"

"Nope," Demon answered, and I heard the anguish in his voice. He didn't elaborate, and I didn't push because I wasn't sure I could deal with it. I knew the signs he was exhibiting.

Foxy's eyes were glazed and empty, and I closed mine to avoid falling into the hole. "How long have we been here?"

"Three days, son," General Allen answered. "I'm here in an official capacity and to personally check on you men. Brass wants to make sure you remember there's a gag order on this. Caleb Grayson's family has received notification that he was killed in action, and his remains cannot be recovered.

I heard Demon's ragged breathing, and a nurse rushed in and sedated him. Foxy was still eerily silent. "What's wrong with me?"

Foxy let out a sound of derision. "You're over here in this shithole of a war that has cost us way too much. That's what's wrong with you."

General Allen blanched. "Baker, your collarbone took a direct hit and shattered a part of it, and a bullet nicked your lung, clean through. That's why it's hard for you to breathe, and the oxygen is in your nose. Leave it there. You'll all get offered an honorable discharge. Baker, the doctors don't think you'll regain enough strength in those muscles to pass a rigorous physical."

That was bullshit, and I knew it. I could heal it up and pass anything the Navy threw my way. The problem was I didn't want to. It was unnecessary if General Allen said that so I could save face and take the easy way out. I wanted out. I didn't give a shit what anyone thought of that decision. Underneath this abject and agonizing grief was volatile anger.

"I'm so sorry," General Allen sagged a little. "Caleb Grayson was an exceptional man and soldier. I know my words do little to ease the pain of a loss like that, and I'm not saying it to be trite. I admired Grayson, as I do all of you."

"Hacker?" I asked.

"Shrapnel," Foxy answered. "Bandy couldn't help;

an artery severed."

"Fuck. He had kids," I whispered, unable to scream, and the tears came again. "I want the discharge," I shouted as loudly as possible. An out-of-the-norm reaction, and Foxy knew it.

General Allen pursed his lips but nodded. "Understood." When he left, I looked back at Foxy and winced at my neck's movement now that the pain meds were wearing off.

"Shrapnel," Foxy answered my unasked question. "Took a chunk of my leg, and I was bleeding out. Demon was bleeding out; shrapnel shredded his vest and embedded in his side. You seriously gonna take the out?"

"I can't do it anymore, Foxy. That part of me died with Ghost," I admitted, more fucking tears clogged my throat. "I'm done. I want to go home to my dad."

"I think significant parts of all of us died with him," Foxy closed his empty eyes. "Ghost was trying to help."

That was the shittiest part. I closed my eyes again and let the tears fall; I was over this place. As much as I could be wearing the permanent scars this war had gifted me.

After the Military

Chapter 33

A scream tore through my throat, waking me from a dead sleep, and I threw myself off the bed and rolled under it, frantically searching for my rifle. Dust filled my nose, causing me to sneeze, and then my eyes adjusted to the darkness, and my brain caught up.

The thudding bass of music wasn't artillery shells or gunfire. Sweat dripped off my face, and I rolled out from under the bed, thunking my head on the floor. How much longer were these nightmares going to last? I'd been out a year, and it felt like they hadn't eased up.

I pushed to my feet warily and wondered if Skull was here. I checked my watch and frowned; it was only two, so probably not yet. I got dressed in ripped jeans and a t-shirt and headed out of the back into the clubhouse's bar section.

One of the newer guys was posing around for the chick he'd brought in with him, and my lip curled into a sneer upon seeing it was one of the bar rats I'd turned down numerous times. I only took up offers when a woman looked clean and was at the lowest I could get and needed the contact.

Otherwise, I steered clear. I wanted something

more in-depth. I wasn't sure I had a right to want that, given the things I've done, but it still hung in the back of my mind every time I got hit on. Sometimes, I swear it turned into Caleb's voice, asking me what the hell I was doing with my life, and I had no sufficient answer. It was strange how I now thought of them with their real names and not the nicknames I had gotten so used to using.

They released me with an honorable discharge, and I immediately went home to my dad. I wasn't in my right mind, and I scared him more than once with how fucked up I was. Skull had been bugging me to come to Washington and join him, and finally, my dad pushed me out the door, hoping I'd find a direction.

I wouldn't call joining a motorcycle club a direction. Not a good one anyway. I'd figured that Skull was into some shady shit, but nothing prepared me for the whole of it. Damien, Jake, and Caleb's voices often played through my mind chastising me. More Jake and Caleb than Damien.

He ran an illegal fight ring, which wasn't all that bad, but they were brutal, and more than one person has walked away with a permanent injury, which I disagreed with; he ran drugs but never did them. Skull didn't get involved with trafficking, or I probably would have kicked his ass myself, but I think he had some prostitutes on the payroll. His most recent thing was guns.

Skull begged me to come on board and join the club, and with my state of mind as far gone as it was, I latched on to his need and blindly stepped in. I refused to fight, wouldn't run drugs, and wasn't touching weapons. The most I did was gather information for him and run a security detail. I didn't need a gun to be deadly.

I walked behind the bar, filled a clean glass with some soda, and downed it in two gulps trying to clear my mind. The computer nerd Skull hired sat in the corner with his laptop, scowling at the screen.

That reminded me to check my email to see if Jake or Damien had written to me. They checked in every so often to let me know they were still kicking. I extended the offer of joining to Damien and told him about the fights. He was interested, but they'd re-upped.

It caused me some guilt. I felt like I'd abandoned the guys, and I guessed I had. Caleb's death had been the last straw for me. I'd tried to find his sister over here, but it never amounted to anything, and I wasn't sure she'd want to be looking at my face as a reminder of what she'd lost.

"Hey! Make me a drink!" the new guy shouted at me. Tim was his name. He talked a big game, and I doubted he could back it up. Regardless, I wasn't there to serve him, and I wasn't about to start.

I flipped Tim off, refilled my glass, and sat on the customer side of the bar. Some days my shoulder felt like it was still injured, and other days it was as if it had never happened. At least until I took my shirt off and saw the scars.

I'd predicted it right, though. I'd healed up and had full functionality within the year. I think the days the pain surfaced were when the psychological bullshit from the war tormented me. It was like my body thought I was reliving that day. Fuck, I'd relived it enough times in my head already.

Skull had to slap me the first time I saw a pregnant lady walk into the bar. I lost my mind, and cool as a cucumber, he struck my face until I focused on him, and he dragged me back to the room he'd designated mine and made me talk.

I couldn't tell him everything, the gag order was in place, and I'd gotten reminded repeatedly to keep my mouth shut. But I told him about Caleb, the man he was, the Ghost he was, and how losing him fucked all of us up. I didn't tell him about the pregnant lady that wasn't really pregnant.

I needed some quiet. The music was getting to me, and Tim got in my face as I stood. "What the fuck? You ain't doin' shit. You coulda made me a drink! I'm entertainin' a lady! Fuck! I ain't good enough for you or sometin'? You only suck black dick?"

I closed my eyes and counted to ten before giving in to the urge to bash his head against the bar. "Your arms work. Make your own drink," I told him. "I don't answer to you."

"Nah, that's right. You the boss's bitch," Tim smirked, shoving me.

Under no circumstances was I in the mood for this. Nor was I about to back down. When Tim shoved me again, I didn't move. I'd only fought twice since I'd gotten discharged, and both times were after severe flashbacks that made me believe I was back there, fighting for my life.

Tim had me close to forgetting why I didn't fight. He was trying to pin me against the bar, and it wasn't working. I wasn't sure if this guy was already drunk or stoned, but he crossed several lines. One of them was touching me.

He took it a step too far when he patted my face and called me a good boy. I pivoted and drove him into the wall behind me and held him up by the throat with my hand. "Don't. Touch. Me. Ever."

Tim's face turned a reddish-purple, spit formed at the corners of his mouth, and his legs were futilely kicking out. He grasped my arm with both hands and tried to pry mine from around his neck.

"What the fuck is going on?" Skull roared.

I glanced over and dropped Tim. "I'll let Tim tell you."

Skull's eyes pierced the extremely pissed-off man. "Your boy fucking choked me out," Tim snarled.

"If that was the case, you'd be dead. What'd you do, Tim?" Skull yanked him to his feet and shoved his back into a stool.

"Why you assume it's me?" Tim shouted.

"Boomer doesn't get physical unless he's pushed into it," Skull growled.

"Fucking stupid name, Boomer. We all know he's your pet dog," Tim snarled, spittle spraying Skull in the face.

I shook my head and rolled my eyes—stupid move. Almost the rest of the club supported me, save for a few who didn't understand. Skull was ridiculously protective of me like I was of him.

"Consider yourself failed. I don't want you in my club. It would have taken him minimal effort if Boomer wanted to hurt you. The man was a SEAL, served in the war, and came home injured. You need to learn respect, Tim," Skull replied, his voice dripping with venom.

It was probably the look on Skull's face that made the idiot shut up. It certainly wasn't because I was a government-trained mercenary. Tim's eyes shot daggers at me as he shrugged out of Skull's grip and stomped off like a child.

"Sorry, man, he pushed my buttons," I apologized, not quite contritely.

"Don't do that, Dar. The fact that you had him in a grip like that told me all I needed to know. I can ask the ho' if I want specifics," Skull nodded to the woman sitting there gawking. "You had another flashback?"

"Yeah. I need to ride. You need me tonight for anything?" I asked before making my exit.

"Nope. Why don't you take a couple of days and go visit your mom and Trigger?" Skull suggested. There was something in his tone that caught my ear. That same tone he got when he used to send me away from the parties because he was about to do something I would find questionable.

I rolled my neck and listened to it pop in the sudden quiet because Skull killed the music. "I can do that. You sure?"

"Wouldn't have suggested it if I wasn't," Skull's voice softened. "Maybe you should talk to a counselor."

"Considering it. This shit isn't fun. I rolled under the bed," I confessed and sat next to Skull at the bar. I hung my head for a few moments, stretching the back of my neck. "Jesus, Skull, I could taste the smoke like it was coating my tongue."

"I want to ask you what happened, but something tells me I'd be having nightmares of my own," Skull looked sympathetic. "I can't say I understand what you went through. I only see how it's changed you, which is plenty scary for me. You have more honor and courage in your curly, sissy, pretty-boy eyelashes than all of us put together," he elbowed me gently and gave me the crooked smile I remembered from my childhood.

"That was a creative insult," I cracked a weak smile. "You really think I'm pretty?"

Skull barked out a laugh. "There he is. Go, ride. Clear your head. If Tim harasses you, kick his ass. He ain't welcome back here."

"He said I only like black dick," I informed Skull with a smile.

"Hell, naw, he didn't?" Skull looked at me, shocked. "He played a race card? Fucking moron. If I see him again, I'll smack him with my black dick." He moved and guided me to the door. "You aren't a killer, Dar."

I was. We both knew it. I tried to remember each kill I made, and it was too many. It sent me down a dark hole, and I know that wherever Caleb was, he looked down on me that night, shaking his head because I drowned those sorrows. I drank so much that I blacked out, and someone carried me to my room.

Chapter 34

Three years later, I ran into Tim. He was still a cocky motherfucker, and a racist one to boot. I didn't hesitate; I let my fist fly when he opened his mouth. I wasn't proud of it, and I only broke his nose. That was my justification. I'd wanted to do worse.

"Skull, man, guess who I saw," I called out, walking into the clubhouse.

"Who?" he looked up from the papers in front of him on the bar.

"Tim. I got some of his blood if you want it," I showed him my fist.

"You hit him?" Skull raised his eyebrows and gave me a considering look. "You okay?"

"Fine. Just didn't want to hear Tim's shit. I only wanted some damn cookies," I set the package down on the counter.

"He started shit at the grocery store?" Skull burst into laughter.

"Parking lot, but yeah," I tore open the package and stuffed a cookie in my mouth. "Got news for you.

Demon said he would do some fighting when he got here. He's leaving. Gotta say I was surprised. If you think you can't fuck with me, no one should fuck with him. Demon made it clear; you are getting Demon, not Damien. There's an important distinction there, Skull. Demon's in a dark place and probably one of the most lethal men alive."

"Dangerous?" Skull went quiet and studied me.

"Very. Demon's also got a good heart, and he's not a bad person. The war fucked him up, and the things we did and saw are no joke. He was in a lot longer than I was. I don't know how to warn you of him, but tread carefully. I don't want to get pitted against you two. Demon saved my ass more than once," I told him, my jaw ticking.

"Clue me in. I'm not sure I understand what you are saying," Skull worded his statement carefully.

"Demon won't patch in, and he won't do shady shit. Don't ask him. He'll fight, and he'll win, but there's a line with him that shouldn't get crossed, and I don't know where it is now," I fumbled with my words, unsure how to convey the essence of Damien.

"Demon's like you?" Skull paraphrased.

"No, man. There's no one like him. Foxy is joining the police and will keep a close eye on Demon, but those are two men that no one should ever be against." I thumped my chest for emphasis. "I love them both, Skull, as I do you. Expect an extreme version of how I was when you saw me after I came back. That's how he was when I left. I butted heads with Demon a lot, but he's a brother."

"Will Demon turn on us?" Skull finally asked.

"No. Respect him, and he will respect you. Treat him like shit, and you can expect him to stop it," I explained poorly. "Demon didn't tolerate people talking down to us. He backed us, and even when we disagreed, he didn't berate us. Our lives were more important to him than his, yet he took no shit when questioned."

"Why the hell does he want to fight illegally then?" Skull shook his head, not understanding.

"It's how he escapes the shit in his head." I fully remembered our times working out. "Demon knows what the club's about; fighting is all he'll do. Demon said he would open a garage and work on bikes."

"The man can turn wrenches?" Skull completely forgot about the papers in front of him. "When did he find time to learn that?"

"Beats me, but he kept his bike in tip-top shape, and Foxy only allows Demon to work on his bike. The man's got more layers to him than anyone I know," I shrugged. "I would have been strangled to death by an insane asshole terrorist if it wasn't for him. The fucker was standing on my throat. Demon tackled the bastard. Five men and Demon and Ghost took them out by themselves."

Skull's eyes were intense, and his dark skin turned slightly lighter. "That's not the worst of it either, is it?" Skull dropped his voice.

"No. But Demon came for me. We walked into an ambush. They were holding me down, Skull. One man on each of my limbs and the other standing on my throat. He'd wait until I passed out, then got off, only to repeat the process. I only got one second to make a noise, and Demon heard. I was positive I would die, and he came for me," I bared my soul to Skull. "I will never forget that."

Skull swallowed and took a slow and deep breath. "Me neither. Demon's got my everlasting gratitude for making sure you came home. He can be an asshole. I don't care."

I chuckled darkly. "I'm sure Demon will be. He's earned it. They both have. Foxy was the sniper, and Demon was our Master Chief. Ghost was our ace in the hole." It was weird to slip right back into the nicknames when I talked about them to Skull.

Skull looked at me sadly. "I hate that you lost him, Dar. I know what losing Trigger did to us. It's not a huge stretch to imagine the void left by someone that saw you through ugly shit. I'm not ashamed to say that I cried like a baby when I heard you were seriously injured and then again when you said you were coming back. You don't gotta tell me stuff, man. I'll listen, but don't feel like you have to. I think you should talk to *someone* because it's a lot of bad juju you got locked inside you. Speaking of juju, I heard you singing. Does it still help?"

I nodded in answer. The words to Amazing Grace would always be bittersweet, but the song could ground me when I was alone. "Foxy, Demon, and Ghost sang it with me once. Not long after I joined their squad, they're family, Skull."

"Understood," Skull's gaze slid past me to the door opening behind me. "No more," he warned, telling me not to talk about them. He trusted the other club members, but not with me or the things I was dealing with other than telling them not to fuck with me and take care of their brother who fought in the war.

So it began, the preparation for Demon to join the mix; that is who he would be to them, not Damien. Skull had me briefly explain who he was and conveyed that Demon was in the same mental place I struggled with daily. Most of them got it, but a few concerned me.

A few months later, it was an emotional reaction when he connected with me to introduce him. Demon had demons, for sure, and they showed if you knew him. He started the fights, and after the first one, Skull was stunned and speechless. I had to call Jake to come and get Demon because he wasn't in the right headspace.

Demon opened his garage and instantly had all the club's business. Some of them thought they didn't have to pay, and Skull tried to set them straight, but I think they went around him. Demon's attitude towards them got progressively worse as time went on.

Skull banked a ton of money off Demon's fights, but there was a shift in how they happened that didn't sit right with me, and from the expression on Demon's face, he didn't like it either. It's like they were forcing the fighters into a deathmatch, and no matter what kind of pressure these other people applied to Demon, he wouldn't cave. He never inflicted permanent damage.

Demon's world was insular, and I was okay with that. We didn't engage too much, and I think I reminded him of being over there, which he was trying to fight from remembering. I foresaw him pulling back with what I knew of Demon, and I warned Skull it would happen.

The fights weren't Skull's biggest moneymaker,

but they were close to the top. Skull liked the reputation that Demon gave him of having the toughest motherfucker alive on his team. It pushed our club to the top of the dominance chain.

More than once, Demon asked me to back away from the club, but the thought of leaving the safety the clubhouse gave me made me sick. That killer I was overseas was just under the surface. Without the club's backup, I wasn't sure I'd be able to fight it back if something triggered me.

When Demon said that to me, I reminded him about a counselor I talked to a couple of years ago. Demon insisted he was fine and had things under control. Yet I could see he didn't. He didn't like that either.

It had an adverse effect on me when I saw him like that too, and I began to wonder if we were setting each other off. I started to avoid him to see if Skull noticed a difference in his attitude and when Skull came back and told me that Demon said he wanted out, I was not as shocked as I should have been. He followed it up with rumors that had trickled down to him about one of the other clubs having beef with us about Demon.

It gave me mixed feelings. On some level, it felt like I was losing Demon again and couldn't measure up to Demon's standards. Then, when Skull said Demon had found a woman, which was why he was leaving, I hit an all-time low. How did Demon manage to get what I'd been searching for fruitlessly?

I felt inadequate once more like I'd never been able to measure up to him, and I didn't care that I shouldn't be trying because we were two different people. I ran into him coming out of a store. I didn't miss how he moved to stand in front of the female with him. Did he think I was a threat to her?

I had a snarky conversation with him when she stepped out from behind Demon, and something in my brain clicked, and her words drove me into the deepest parts of my mind that I'd locked up. The attitude coming off this little lady reminded me so much of Caleb.

When she said he was her brother, I damn near lost my mind. I tried to play the tough guy, but all I wanted to do was beg at her feet to love me as her brother did. I finally knelt at her feet and praised Caleb. It was all I could do before either of them saw me cry. It was then that I realized Demon was becoming Damien.

I took off and raced back to the clubhouse to tell Skull that Caleb's sister was the woman, and if anyone touched her, I'd return to being a soldier. Skull understood the implied threat and had me follow him to his office so the others wouldn't hear.

"You think these rumors are shit, then?" Skull cut straight to the point.

"Yep. No way in hell would Damien switch sides, not with Frankie in the picture. He wants out because he found a way to beat the bullshit trying to take him down," I said, sure that was what had prompted this. "I don't know why the rumors are there, but if someone's got a beef with Damien, it's because they couldn't beat him or because of something that happened over in the Middle East."

"I told him I wanted three fights. I told him that because I thought it would give me a chance to see who was behind the rumors. Think he'll do it?" Skull sat back in his chair and gave me a penetrating look.

"I told him to give you two," I replied honestly. "Don't fuck this up for him. Damien's got a chance to be happy and earned that more than anyone else I know."

"If you want me to figure this out, we can't let him know I don't believe the rumors. I've already called him about it, and was an asshole. I even threatened him," Skull sighed heavily. "Do what you are so good at doing, Darius, and get me the information."

I cringed. "You threatened Damien?" Why the hell would he do that?

"I did. I had people around me. You know I wouldn't go after him. I'm not stupid," Skull promised.

I had to wonder. Threatening Damien would not get him the desired results. "Let's avoid that route in the future. I've seen what a pissed-off Demon can do."

I woke up every night with a nightmare, in a cold sweat on the floor, the smell of scorched flesh and earth filling my nose. The chain of events that got set off was something I wasn't ready for; I could feel it looming like that mission that took Caleb. It felt wrong. Sometimes I screamed. Others I lay there and cried.

It got back to Skull, and he started staying at the clubhouse to watch over me, and all I could do was throw myself into finding out what the hell was happening and why Damien was getting targeted. I saw Damien out with Frankie, which didn't sit right with me either.

I was happy for him; he looked like love smacked him in the face with a brick when he looked at Frankie. In my mind, she should be with Jake. I'd shake it off and continue to watch from a distance.

Skull notified me ahead of time that he was calling in Demon for a fight. I went to scope out the warehouse to see if a trap was set and put up a few surveillance cameras that no one but Damien would notice. There wasn't much else I could do.

Chapter 35

"Fucking hell, Skull!" I shouted to my best friend. "Damien's triggered, that kid got immobilized, and I'm about to lose my fucking mind! They brought guns!"

My hair was semi-mohawk style, had been for the past couple of years, and if there had been hair to pull on either side of my head, I would have pulled it.

Skull put a hand on my arm as I paced a five-foot section in front of the clubhouse bar. "Yeah, they had guns, and your boy took them all down. I'll admit, I've never seen anything like that, and I will concede that he is every bit as lethal as you declared him to be. But you got a video of it; we can look at the crowd now and see if we can narrow down who is behind this shit."

Skull played the right card to get me to focus on that task, and that's what I did. I dove through everything, used all my contacts, and finally got a hold of Damien to meet and talk with me. He had us meet at Jake's house, and Frankie looked like hell.

We discussed my conclusions, and Damien said he would try to get me the information on who was on the missions with us. I was sure that the person behind all this was a vet. Damien didn't like the thought more than I did, but he agreed.

After watching Frankie get sick, I left and did my best to find a trail to follow. To my surprise, Damien delivered on that list of names. "We always fight," I'd told Damien when we talked.

He grunted in response, but I knew he got my message. He laid low and stayed out of sight until he surfaced out of the blue. I saw his bike at the hospital and figured he was picking up Frankie. I hung back out of his sight but followed because there was no way I would let something happen to Caleb's sister.

I couldn't have stopped it even if I had been right next to him. I watched another brother, my Master Chief, and a person who saved my life more than I could count get murdered. I saw Jake, knew that he had witnessed the entire thing, and did my best to get through the crowd to him.

Shit. Damien was dying in Jake's arms. Flashbacks of Trigger assaulted me with every scream and sob from Jake. I furiously texted Skull what was happening and tried to get through to Jake. "I've got him. Go take care of Frankie," I told Jake.

I'd been right all those years ago; Jake was far more deadly than Damien was. He was about to tumble down that void that Caleb and Damien had been so close to falling into themselves. I would have promised him anything, and I promised I would not leave our brother alone. Not for one second.

This murder had changed my life the way Trigger's had, the same way that helicopter crash did. Skull hovered around me so much that I wanted to snap. I couldn't think. I did everything I knew to try and keep Jake on this side of things. I lost my shit the same as he did when I learned that Frankie was pregnant with Damien's baby.

We were in dark days, Jake and me. They'd brought me into their close group over in Afghanistan, and now it was only the two of us left. I needed to find this asshole. I craved justice for Damien and Frankie. I broke down like a baby at the funeral.

I gave them space after that because we all needed it. The loss was significant, and I relied on Skull more than ever to keep me from being stupid. Jake brought me back into the fold and shared information that he'd learned from his Chief and told me he quit the force, and as a final bomb, he and Frankie had gotten married.

The only thing that felt right was that. I was envious, but not of Frankie; she felt like a sister to me. We grew close, and when I learned of her project about showing the faces of PTSD, something in me clicked. I started to let her in and let the shit out.

She took photos of me for the book, and I told her my story. There was not an ounce of judgment in her, and she cried with me. Jake asked me to be part of the birthing team, and I jumped on the opportunity. I was a part of their family.

Skull watched and pulled away from me a little, business-wise. He pushed me at Jake and Frankie more often than he took me from them, and when we got word that the shooter was in custody, it was like the bottom fell out from under all of us.

Damien's baby was being born, Frankie was about to die, and Jake gave me his adopted child to watch over while I tried to hold on to a semblance of control. I looked at the baby boy cradled in my arms and promised Damien I would protect little Damien with my life. I swore I could feel Caleb and Damien with me too. I felt like I was dreaming.

We got through the trial, Frankie delivering a speech that Damien and Caleb would have stood and applauded, even with tears streaming down her face. Skull watched over all of us, making us practically untouchable.

When Frankie's book got published, we sat there in the audience of her interview, and I proudly watched as she stood her ground when the jerk of a host tried to imply that she lived her life wrong. I saw Caleb in her. I saw Damien's touch, and I saw the love.

It reminded me of what I was missing out on in my life. Then, life threw another curveball at me as we were preparing to leave to take a celebratory birthday shot for Caleb. Frankie opened the door, and all I could do was stare and cycle through my brain the list of people I knew because I was positive I knew this person.

I had to move fast to catch Frankie as she passed out, and I hollered for Jake as I now stared at a mini-Caleb. My gaze switched back to the woman. "I know you," I blurted out.

Jake came running and pulled the squirming baby from Frankie's arms, and we got her situated on the couch with Jake while he stared at the woman the same way I was. Then, I knew. It was the pilot that had captured my attention.

Amelia was here and had a kid who looked like Caleb's doppelganger. When she said her name, I about fell over. I was right. Pieces started falling into place as she spoke to Frankie and Jake after Frankie decided to stun Jake with another unsuspected pregnancy.

I looked back at Franco, Caleb's son, and I almost cried along with Frankie. When she insinuated that she brought Franco here so that he had a family to look after him because Amelia didn't expect to survive the recurrence of cancer she was battling, every protective instinct in me woke up. My life snapped into focus.

Amelia wasn't escaping me this time. I needed to figure out how to get her to see I was worthy of her love. I sounded like a sap in my head, but she was the only woman who ever made me feel like I wanted to chase after her.

I made my intentions clear after she decided to join us for our celebration at the beach. I asked her endless questions since she was a captive audience for the drive, and what she hesitated to answer, Franco filled in with his innocent chatter.

Franco became enamored with his aunt, and Jake looked like he was in shock. I reached for Amelia's hand. "Take this as you want, but I feel like Caleb and Damien had a hand in this," I told her softly.

"Maybe. Darius, you can't possibly want to date me. I don't even know that I'll survive this. That's not fair to you," Amelia stated bluntly.

"You will," I decided. "I feel it here." I thumped

my chest like an ape. "My mom died of cancer. Hers started in her ovaries and then spread before they could stop it. I'm gonna take care of you, Amelia."

"Was Frankie serious about me living in her house?" Amelia glanced at Frankie, who was talking animatedly with Franco.

"You better believe it. Frankie won't take no for an answer either. Frankie is a woman that makes things happen," I smiled a crooked smile.

Amelia chewed on her lip, her skin pale, and her eyes round and filled with a dim hope. "I'll need to return to get my stuff and break the lease on my apartment."

"I'll go with you. Franco can stay with Frankie and Jake," I suggested quietly. "You aren't alone anymore, Amelia. Trust me, that woman will drill that into your head until you want to pop a cork in her mouth to make her stop talking."

"I heard that," Frankie called out.

"Of course, she heard that," I rolled my eyes. It got a small laugh out of Amelia that warmed my cold heart. I got the sense she hadn't laughed much in the past few years.

"I'd like to ask you to a dinner date tonight," Amelia looked at me, and my heart stopped beating for a moment. "Interested?"

I croaked out a yes that made Jake burst into laughter. "I've never seen that man tongue-tied before. Do more of that," Jake told Amelia as he juggled Damien back into his arms.

"Watch it, baby maker, the one brewing will be like you," I smirked at Jake.

"I don't doubt it," he laughed. "Thank God these kids have a SEAL for an uncle. At least I'll know when I drop them off that you can handle them."

"I'll help you babysit!" Franco slid into the booth next to me.

I couldn't help but grin at the Caleb clone. "You will? That's cool. It might take an entire army to watch DC there," I pointed at baby Damien. "He's as stubborn as his daddy was."

Franco looked at the baby with a soft expression. "Damien isn't stubborn; he's just teaching us a better way."

Floored, Jake and me stared at Franco. The boy didn't even realize that he sounded just like his dad. Frankie saved both of us from breaking down in tears by announcing that it was nap time and asked Franco to help her.

"Let's get Uncle Jake to take us back to the hotel. Maybe this unruly baby will listen to you, Franco. You seem to have a good read on him," Frankie stood and held out her hand. She winked at me, "Better up your game."

Amelia snorted and covered her mouth to try and hide her laugh. Damn, Frankie wasn't wrong.

Chapter 36

Jake offered to have Franco stay with them while I went back with Amelia to move her here. I knew she struggled with everything since she went from being a single mom alone, fighting a disease trying to kill her, to having a family offering her everything.

I slid my arm around her shoulders, squeezing her gently, and got shoved out of the way by Frankie. She gathered Amelia in her arms and shooed us out of the room. I let Jake pull me away while Frankie worked her magic.

"Go slow, Darius. Amelia's got a lot on her plate with the cancer fight," Jake warned.

"You don't think I know that?" I countered. "I watched my mom fight it and lose."

"I'm sorry," Jake frowned. "I forgot about that. Does it trigger you?"

"A little," I admitted. "If I think about it too deeply, I start to worry that I'll find Amelia like I found my mom. It's a different trigger than you think it is, though. It was traumatizing, but it wasn't violent. It's more of a thing that makes me realize my mom won't ever be able to meet my wife or you guys or know how hard I tried, despite joining the club."

"About that," Jake leaned against the counter and held his hand up when I was about to interrupt. "You are fully patched in, yet, you don't participate in any of it, do you?"

I'd grown close with Jake over the past year, and other than telling me to pull back from the club, he hasn't ever asked me for details on anything. I'm aware Demon thought I was in deep with them, and he wasn't wrong in that assumption, but I was in deep because they kept me from losing my mind.

"I don't," I finally admitted reluctantly. "I do security for Skull, mostly. I know what you all think, and it doesn't bother me that you do. I fit the mold."

Jake shook his head at me. "You don't, Darius. You play the part well, but it's not you. If you want to start something with Amelia, pull back. That's all I was going to say. Doesn't mean you don't remain friends with them. Just don't be a part of it."

I huffed out an irritated breath. It wasn't anything I hadn't told myself over the past twenty-four hours. "I know, man. I've gotta talk to Skull. He's my oldest friend. He's kept me alive as much as Caleb, Damien, and you have. I know what you all think of him too, but I'll tell you this: he sends me away when he's up to shady shit. He always has."

"I'm not judging, Darius. I only want you to remember that there are young eyes on you now," Jake said bluntly, and the words reverberated through me.

I hadn't thought about it quite in those terms,

probably because Damien was still a baby. Franco wasn't. I nodded. "I'll talk to him soon. I want to get Amelia moved up here and settled in first. That's the trigger, Jake. The need to take care of her like I took care of my mom."

"I get it. We've got pieces of our brothers back now, and I don't want them to lose you to some stupid shit. I won't say anything more than that, I promise." Jake righted himself as Franco walked into the kitchen, struggling to carry Damien.

I grabbed him from Franco and tossed him in the air a bit, loving how he squealed and smiled. "While I'm gone, kid, make sure you have the biggest blowouts in history all over your uncle daddy."

Jake guffawed, and Franco gave me a confused look. "Ignore him, Franco. Darius will get his due when he's babysitting two of them at the same time."

I barely resisted the urge to flip him off and instead tickled the baby. DC had Damien's eyes all the way. He looked like his dad too, but he was bright like Frankie. This kid wasn't going to be a walk in the park when he grew up.

"Keep 'em on their toes, DC." I handed him over to Jake and hugged Franco. "The one you really need to babysit is your Uncle Jake," I stage-whispered to Franco and grinned at Jake over his shoulder. "He's trouble."

Franco gave Jake a sly look and laughed. "Nah, he's fun. Take care of my mom, please." Franco's face turned serious and worried.

"Promise," I vowed. "We'll be back soon and get her settled into treatment, and she'll be good as new."

A skeptical look on the boy's face told me he'd had a very blunt talk with his mom about this subject. Franco didn't argue with me. He simply nodded somberly with sad eyes and climbed onto the counter stool.

Jake frowned again but rooted in the cupboard for a snack and slid it across the countertop while DC giggled and kicked his pudgy legs like he was trying to cheer up Franco. Babies were magic in that way.

Jake motioned me to go, and Frankie stopped talking when she saw me walk in. That woman knew all my dirty secrets, and I knew she saw right through my need to help Amelia. "Be good, Darius," Frankie whispered and kissed my cheek, giving me a fierce hug.

"I'm not kidnapping her," I snipped, trying to ease the strain on their faces. "Not yet. I'll wait until I cross state lines for that. Give me a little credit."

Amelia laughed, the worry lines vanishing from her forehead. "Frankie did tell me to make you pack my stuff up shirtless. She said it would be worth it."

I heard Jake laughing in the kitchen. I shook my head. "I'm the one that needs to be good? Go grow a baby and stop harassing me. You better hope this kid doesn't inherit its parent's cavalier ways." I laughed at the abrupt stopping of Jake's laughter.

Frankie blinked slowly, then laughed. "Well played."

I led Amelia outside and helped her get settled on my bike. "I've never ridden with someone on this bike before," I said carelessly, not once thinking that would make her nervous.

"Maybe we should have Jake drop us off then?"

Amelia suggested timidly.

"Why?" I looked over at her after getting my helmet on. "Oh. This bike; I've ridden with people on other bikes. You are safe, Amelia," I rushed out after realizing what I said. "If you are still nervous, we can have Jake take us."

"Are we riding the bike to the airport?" she turned those luminescent gray eyes on me.

"No, I was going to have my friend Skull drop us off," I answered. "I need to grab some clothes, even if you have me pack your stuff up shirtless."

"It's okay. We can take the bike." Amelia gave me an embarrassed smile.

"Tell me if you aren't up for it. I'm fine leaving the bike here. Jake will take care of it. If you are scared or don't feel good, whatever, it's okay, Amelia. The bike isn't our only option," I assured her.

"Is it a long ride?" her voice came out hesitant.

"Not by my standards. It's about twenty minutes," I answered, patiently waiting for Amelia's decision.

"That's okay. I'm only a little cold," Amelia finally admitted.

"Easily solved. Wait here." I ran back inside and asked Frankie to borrow her riding jacket. She surrendered it without question, and I returned to Amelia and settled it over her shoulders. My gloves would be too big for her, but they would work, and I handed them to Amelia.

"Thank you," she smiled gratefully.

I put my finger under her chin and raised it a little.

"Never be afraid to tell me if you aren't comfortable. I'll get a car when we get back, so you don't have to worry about riding on a bike."

Amelia protested. "Darius, you don't need to put yourself in debt for me."

"Hush," I smiled and got on the bike. "Wrap your arms around me and hold on tight."

Amelia hadn't been big when I met her for the first time, but she was muscled. She felt diminutive now after fighting cancer for so long. Despite that, she still had a strength that you could feel, and I liked those arms around me.

Jesus, I needed to calm down. My brain was already plotting my entire future with her, and she'd only given me a slight hint that she was interested in me. I got us to the clubhouse in record time without doing anything stupid and got it parked in the shed.

I helped Amelia off. "I apologize upfront; this isn't the best place to bring a lady."

"What makes you think I'm a lady?" Amelia scoffed. "I was a pilot in the Air Force. Half the guys that worked with me thought I was gay."

"Right. Well, men are notorious idiots." I honestly had no idea how to respond to that.

Amelia followed me into the club through the back door that led to Skull's office and the few rooms back here. I unlocked my door and practically dragged her in to keep some of the assholes from seeing her.

I snatched my duffel bag out of the closet, threw a week's worth of clothes into it, grabbed my toiletries, and stuffed them in. As an afterthought, I put my sneakers in the bag. I pulled them back out and took my boots off, and switched what I was wearing. I didn't need boots to pack up Amelia's apartment or drive a truck back here.

Nothing personal of mine was in the room except the letter from my mom and a few overseas photos. I opened my dresser drawer and gently placed those in the pocket of my duffle bag.

Amelia watched it all with a half-smile on her face. When we'd first met her, I thought she was Hispanic of some sort, and now I didn't see that as much. Her hair was dark and, at the moment, very thin. Her eyes were a soft gray framed by dark lashes, and she had plump lips that women usually paid a lot of money to achieve. Cancer had made her face gaunter than I remembered, but she was still beautiful.

I grabbed the beanie on my dresser and pulled it down over her head. "Let's go find our ride," I held my hand out to her, and she tentatively took hold of it.

Skull was in his office waiting for us, and his eyes immediately went to Amelia. "You must be Amelia. I go by Skull, or prez, as some here like to call me. My name, however, is Jamal. Very few people know that, and since you are important to Darius, you are important to me."

"Nice to meet you, Skull. Darius might get tired of me, but your secret is safe." Amelia held out her hand and gave him a lopsided smile.

Skull let out a gentle laugh. "Oh, you don't know him very well if you think that. Dar doesn't do anything halfway. Come on, let's get you to the airport on time."

Chapter 37

I don't remember seeing Skull while you were overseas." Amelia turned to face me once the jet leveled out.

"Skull didn't serve. He's a childhood friend. Of the squad you saw us most with, only Jake and I remain," I lowered my voice so it didn't carry.

"What can you tell me about Caleb?" Amelia gnawed on her lower lip like she didn't want to ask.

"What do you want to know?" I countered.

"He's Franco's father, but I feel like I never knew him. Caleb mostly talked about Frankie and his team. I didn't even know you all called him Ghost. Never anything personal. I don't know that you can call what we did dating, but I do recall one point where I thought if the circumstances were different, I could fall in love with him," Amelia spouted off truths.

"You weren't in love with Caleb?" I don't know why that surprised me the way it did, but I had assumed she was in love with him.

"No," she let out a small laugh. "You learn not to get attached while you are over there. We had sex, Caleb gave me a tiny amount of information, and I think we used each other for comfort more than anything. Human contact, you know?"

"But you turned me down," I replied stupidly.

"Ah, well, yes." Amelia reached for my hand. "You, I could see myself getting attached too quickly, and I shied away from that as much as possible."

"You turned me down because you were attracted to me?" I knew I sounded like an idiot. If that was a line, it was an effective one.

"Essentially, yes. I was attracted to Caleb, too, don't get me wrong. I also knew it wouldn't go anywhere because of where we were. That's what I needed. I worried about him, but more as a friend than someone I wanted to wake up to every day. I know that sounds cold, but we both knew the score going into it. Franco was a shock, and I put feelers out to try and figure out where he'd gotten sent so I could notify him," Amelia was quick to answer. "Finally, I heard that he'd died on a mission. I tried to find the others hoping to get word to his family, but all I hit were dead ends."

"So did the guys. They looked for Frankie too," I replied automatically. My brain was processing the information poorly. "I swear, I'm not dumb. I'm just processing."

"You thought I wasn't interested?" Amelia guessed. I could only nod. "I can see why, but it's not the truth. You had a quiet intensity that I felt drawn toward like a magnet. We were in a shit situation over there. Not quite as much for me since I mostly did troop transport, though I had a few hairy moments. Getting you guys safely back and forth between places was my job, and if

I'd gotten involved with anyone more than I did, my concentration wouldn't have been what I needed it to be."

"Tell me about you," I requested instead of asking any of the ridiculous questions that didn't matter.

"Air Force pilot, single mom, cancer fighter, unemployed because airlines don't want to hire a pilot fighting for their lives. I had Franco about two months after they discovered cancer. Luckily, I'd gotten the medical discharge after I was four months pregnant, so the timing worked out well. Once I went into remission, I got hired to fly cargo. When it came back, I took charter jobs mostly because I needed a paycheck. Cancer wiped out all my savings," Amelia said in a rush.

"What about your family?" I asked bluntly.

"I was adopted as a baby. My birth mother abandoned me in a hospital parking lot. My adopted parents were older, and they died within a year of each other. It was kind of sweet because my dad had always said he couldn't live without my mom, but devastating at the same time." Amelia shrugged. "I may have a blood family somewhere, but none of the genealogy things I've done have pointed the way to finding them."

"Frankie will make damn sure you know you have a family now," I replied gruffly.

"Tell me about you, Darius," Amelia patted the back of my hand. "You are a man of mystery."

"Hardly," I barked out a sad laugh. I bared my soul to this woman for the rest of the flight. I answered her questions and laid out all the complicated shit that had made me who I am. I talked about my mom and Trigger. I told her about the flashbacks and how Skull had gotten me through them. I spoke about Damien, Caleb, Jake, and finally, Frankie.

"Frankie is like a hurricane," Amelia smiled softly. "Not in a bad way. She hits like a force, but instead of leaving destruction, she makes sense of the chaos and puts things together. I was so worried she wouldn't want anything to do with Franco."

"Frankie would move a mountain for people she loves," I shook my head and sighed. "She took me in and gave me a purpose. Despite the ties to some not-so-good things."

"I thought the pictures she took of you for the book were astounding. That intensity I saw all those years ago was staring right back at me. Darius, not everyone sees the not-so-good things or the color of your skin. Frankie saw past all that and captured the heart of you. Guarded, deep, intelligent, and reflective." Amelia gave me another of those soft smiles.

"When you smile like that, my tongue sticks to the roof of my mouth," I blurted out. Trigger would be ashamed of my lack of game. Skull probably would have smacked me on the back of my head.

She grinned. "Buckle up; the plane is starting to descend."

I did as she said and tried to come to terms with the fact that I had just told this woman my life's story. The only other person who came close to knowing this much about me was Frankie, and that is because I felt like I was talking to Caleb.

I looked over at Amelia. "Is it my turn to ask for a

date? Or is that off the table now, thanks to my verbal vomit?"

"Is this a case of conversation remorse?" Amelia cocked her head to the side and studied my face.

"No. Not really. If we are going to truly date, those are all things you need to know about me. Frankie's told me a bit about waking up with Damien in the throes of bad flashbacks. Jake's had them too. As I bluntly told you, me too. I can't imagine being on the other side of it. Skull tells me it's awful," I boldly spoke the truth.

"I had a few, but I never saw the things you did. I saw the aftermath, the bodies getting loaded, and whatnot. I know I have loadmasters for that, but I like to check myself and make sure the loadmaster isn't overwhelmed. Don't feel ashamed for it, Darius. It tells me you have humanity. Not that flying to my place to help me pack it up and move doesn't, but you could just be doing that to get in my pants," Amelia winked at me playfully.

My tongue wasn't glued to the roof of my mouth anymore; I damn near swallowed it. Amelia laughed at my expression, then fell silent and turned to look out the window as we descended closer to Las Vegas.

I wasn't sure what had made her turn reticent, but Amelia was allowed her space. It's not like she didn't have heavy shit on her plate. She essentially went from Franco as her support group to a larger group of adults. It was a difficult transition, as I well knew.

Once we were on the ground, I turned my phone back on, looked up truck rental places, and put a hold on one using my card. She had made a significant argument about Caleb's money getting turned over. I figured Amelia would argue with it, so I didn't ask.

I kept my hand on her lower back as we disembarked and went into the concourse. Neither of us had baggage to claim, so I followed the passenger pick-up signs and waved a cab over. Amelia didn't protest, and I glanced at her to see her expression still somber and reluctant.

I gave the driver the truck rental place's address, and she stirred at that but didn't argue. I picked the truck up, and she gave me directions to her apartment, which wasn't in Las Vegas, so we had to drive a bit, which I didn't mind.

A little over an hour, we arrived at her place while the office was still open, and she went in to break the lease. I followed behind her as she told the manager that she had to move because she was getting cancer treatment in Washington. Amelia didn't give a sob story, nor did she break down into hysterics; she was calm and somewhat rigid in her stance.

The manager reduced the fee for breaking the lease but wouldn't waive it. Amelia thanked her, signed the paperwork, and stiffly headed back outside. She pointed to her building and told me the unit number, and I moved the truck while she walked and checked the mail.

Exhaustion lined Amelia's face now, and the toll it was taking on her was evident. I dropped my bag next to the couch. The apartment was small and wouldn't take any time to pack up, even if I was doing it alone.

Amelia moved and dropped into the chair across from the couch, and her head drooped forward. "I'm telling you this because I know you'll understand. I've stared at my mortality enough to know that big changes like this scare the hell out of me. Not for myself, but for Franco. There's more than a decent chance I won't make it through this, Darius."

I knelt before her but kept my hands to myself out of respect for personal boundaries. "Fuck what the doctors say, Amelia. You got lots of fight left in you, and if you don't, you have me to lean on. And trust me, I got lots of fight in me. What I don't have, Frankie does."

Amelia raised her eyes from her lap and stared into mine. "Has anyone ever told you that you look like Tommy Vext?"

It took my brain a minute to catch up, and then I belted out a full laugh. "Frankie did. How about that date?"

She smiled then. "Feed me, Boomer. Then we can go get boxes."

"You got it, Wings," I waggled my eyebrows at her.

Chapter 38

Four days later, we were on the road back home. Amelia still hadn't let me in on what the sudden worried looks she would send my way were about, and I wanted to ask; instead, I held my tongue. I hadn't even kissed the woman yet and wanted to dive into her mind.

We drove straight up Nevada to go through Idaho and cut back over. About six hours in, Amelia asked me to stop at the little town we were approaching; she wasn't feeling good. She had taken treatment the day before and had her records transferred to the facility Frankie had gotten her into for cancer.

Sweat bathed Amelia's face, but she was shivering uncontrollably. I remembered this from when my mother went through it, and I handed her the beanie to put on while I changed lanes to exit. I saw a gas station ahead and figured I'd top off while we were here.

Amelia was hopping out of the truck before I got around, and she sagged the moment her feet hit the ground. I ran to her before her knees struck the pavement and straightened up to help her inside.

"Is this man bothering you?" a gruff voice said

from the gas pumps' other side.

Startled, we craned our necks to see some cowboy-dressed man glaring at me. It was nothing new to me; I'd encountered it on many motorcycle rides I took that brought me through small towns.

Amelia glared at him. "Why would you think that? Because he has tattoos?"

Bless this woman, but I knew it wasn't because of the tattoos. It was my skin color and the fact that she looked sick and white. I hadn't gotten around to asking her nationality as it didn't matter to me, but I knew she wasn't white, even if she looked like it.

"Let it go, and ignore him," I whispered in Amelia's ear.

"No, I'm not going to let it go. I'm sick, and this man is helping me. Why the hell would you think he's bothering me? You just saw me get out of the same vehicle as him," Amelia insisted with her body trembling.

"You could be gettin' held against your will," the cowboy sneered at me.

I was ready to punch him. Amelia needed to get inside, though. "It's my skin color that has his panties in a bunch. According to people like him, someone like me isn't supposed to be with someone like you."

Amelia flinched as if she'd gotten slapped. "Are you fucking serious?" her voice got that tone that women could pull off with no trouble, the one that said shut your mouth this instant and don't you dare talk back. "Racist piece of trash, don't speak to us. The audacity of some people floors me," Amelia said to me. "I'm sorry you had to hear that, Darius."

I silently cheered her on, hoping the truck was intact when we returned. We left the guy spluttering his insults behind us and got inside the convenience store, where Amelia showed her medical bracelet that she hadn't taken off yet and asked to use the restroom.

The kid behind the counter didn't hesitate and handed her the key. Once she was safely inside, I went back to prepay for some gas and waited, thanking the kid for assistance. "Do you have cameras out there?"

"Yeah," the kid replied cautiously. "Why?"

"Can you take a peek and make sure the truck is intact? The other guy that was pumping gas was harassing us, and I'd rather not have to take time to get a new truck when she's sick like that," I answered.

The kid looked confused but checked the camera and said things looked okay. "Do I need to call the cops?"

"What for? He didn't assault us, just ran his mouth. I'll check over the truck when we get back out there." I went and grabbed a couple of cold bottles of water and some sports drinks to keep Amelia from dehydrating and paid for them while I waited.

I had my back to the door, so I didn't see the asshole approaching. The kid's eyes widened, and the swinging door slammed hard into the glass wall. Instinctively, I ducked as a fist came flying at my head. "Go ahead and call the cops now, kid," I called out as I kicked the legs out from under the guy.

I did nothing other than dodge his blows and knock him down to keep him away from me and the poor kid behind the counter who was calling the cops. The asshole wasn't a fighter, and it wasn't hard to deflect his attacks. I wasn't suspecting the kid of pulling a shotgun either.

I'd stared down the barrel of a gun one too many times, and I fought those memories hard when my eyes met the cold steel. A barrage of sensations was building to a crescendo in my head, and it took everything I had in me not to react.

"Darius?" Amelia's bewildered voice came from the doorway. "What the hell is happening?"

"I'm saving your life, broad," the asshole screamed.

I saw the realization hit Amelia's face as she began to understand what happened and that I was triggered. She calmly walked up and pushed the barrel down, then wrapped her arms around me. My heart raced, my hands shook, and the smell of smoke still filled my nose.

"Talk," Amelia held her phone to my ear.

"Darius?" Frankie's voice penetrated. "Breathe. Whatever's happening there isn't what you think. You are moving Amelia here so we can fight her cancer. Listen, Darius. DC is laughing; he recognizes your name."

I took a shaky breath in and felt my vision start to return to normal at the sound of DC's giggles. "Frankie, we might need legal advice if this town is like the asshole that just tried to assault me," I managed to get out.

I heard Jake cussing in the background, and then he took the phone from Frankie. "Boomer, do not give in to the flashbacks. Do not give in to harassment. Stay in the moment and with Amelia. Give the phone back to her, please."

I pushed the phone back to Amelia, keeping my eyes on the gun's barrel and the guy who ruined my day. Amelia was speaking quietly and holding on to me. It didn't take long for the cops to arrive, and the kid told him precisely what happened.

One of the cops looked me over in a way that set my teeth on edge until he asked, "You served?"

"I hope you are asking that regarding the military and not prison time," Amelia snapped, leaning heavily against me.

"Yes, ma'am, I am," the cop gentled his tone.

"We both did," I answered, sliding my arm underneath Amelia's to support her better.

"Then I'm glad that neither of you killed this guy for acting that way towards a veteran who served his country in hell," the cop glared at the cuffed man.

I chuckled then. "You too?"

"Yeah, but you look like special forces, and that wasn't me. Marine," he offered up.

"SEAL," Amelia pointed to me, then herself. "I was a pilot in the Air Force."

"Respect," the cop held his fist out to me, and I bumped it. "Not all people in this town are racist. I hope this doesn't give you that feeling. You two are free to go. Hope you feel better, ma'am."

Amelia looked stunned by the dismissal, and she shot another nasty look at the cuffed man. I grabbed our drinks and thanked the cop, leading her back to the truck, where I filled it up. I didn't bother to go back for the change. I just wanted to put the place in my rearview mirror.

I handed Amelia the drinks and got back on the road. Amelia was texting and finally put her phone away.

"I sent a message to Frankie that they let us go. I wasn't sure what would happen, to be honest," she replied, opening a sports drink. "That situation just put everything you told me into perspective for me."

"I was lucky. It was far between occurrences of that type, but still disappointing and frustrating that shit like that still happens," I huffed out, my nerves finally calming. "What gave away that I was triggered?"

"The gun," her voice went timid again as if she were afraid to talk about it with me.

"Amelia, speak openly. I look like an asshole, but I promise I won't be one to you intentionally," I reminded her.

When I looked at her again, the side of her lips quirked up. "I don't think you look like an asshole. You look like a biker, and I admit that Frankie was right; shirtless is the way for you to be. Wow, are you blushing?"

Flattered and a bit flummoxed, I only nodded and hoped she went on. Amelia brought out these responses in me that I was unused to feeling. Truthfully, I'd never felt them for any of the women I'd gone out with; the closest it came was Frankie, which wasn't romantic. Even though I liked to tease Jake that it was, we all knew she was like a sister to me.

"You haven't touched a gun since you discharged, have you?" Amelia broke the silence.

"I have. Skull insists I carry one when I do security runs for him or ride with him. I've only pulled it once when he got threatened, putting me in a dark spot. I don't like them and have stared down my fair share of barrels. You are correct; that triggered me," I replied with a barely discernible voice above the engine sounds.

"Frankie sort of clued me in to what responses look like in you if something brings those feelings up. She told me that keeping you busy helps push it down, but we were in a convenience store. There wasn't a lot I could do there to keep you busy; hugging you and calling Frankie were the only things I could think of, Darius." Amelia fidgeted nervously.

"I'm not upset with you," I frowned, seeing her worried face. "Hey, Amelia, you did good. You kept me on this side of it."

Amelia's body was shaking again, and I pulled the truck over to the shoulder, got her wrapped up, and wedged a pillow between her head and the door. Moments later, she fell asleep.

"Keep her alive, Mom. This one is a keeper," I whispered as I got back on the road.

Chapter 39

It took us an extra day to get home because Amelia was sick. Instead of dropping her at Frankie's house, where she and Franco would stay until they found a place they liked, I took her directly to where they lived now, and Frankie whisked her off for her appointment at the treatment center with Franco tagging along.

Jake and DC came with me to unload the truck of furniture into Frankie's garage, and we got the beds set up. We moved Frankie's old bed into the guest room, where I'd use it if I needed to stay over and help with anything.

Jake placed a few of her photos around the place to make it feel more like home to her, and we put her kitchen stuff away and unpacked what we could. Jake walked me through the security setup, got me included in the notifications, and then returned the truck and went back to his house.

When Frankie came back, it was just with Franco, and I felt a terrifying moment of panic that sent Franco rushing over to me. "She's okay, Darius. They wanted to watch her tonight," Franco hugged me.

Jake raised his eyebrows in a silent question, and I

didn't know what to do. "For a nine-year-old, you are a smart kid," I told him. "Want to come and help me pick out a car? I can only fit one of you on my bike, and if we wanted to go anywhere, that could be difficult."

"For real?" Franco looked excited. "You'd let me help pick it out?"

"Sure. I want to get something you like, too," I squatted down a bit. "What do you think?"

"Let's go!" Franco bounced in place.

"We gotta beg your uncle for a ride," I shrugged helplessly. Frankie was frowning at me with that look that told me she would do something I didn't like. "No, Frankie. I've been living rent-free for a while now and getting paid. I've got plenty."

Jake smothered a laugh as her shoulders deflated. "How'd you know what I was going to say?"

"'Cuz it's that look you get that tells me I'm not going to like whatever is about to come out of your mouth. That was the only thing it could be with what I was talking about," I told her.

"Come on," Jake pulled his keys out. "I'll drop you off. That means you have to find something, or you're walking."

I shooed Franco out the door with Jake and turned to Frankie. "What did they say? Truth."

"She's fragile, and what she has is very aggressive. It's possible they can beat it, but it won't be easy. Amelia was severely dehydrated; despite her drinking a lot. They are monitoring her to make sure her body hydrates. You can go pick her up tomorrow," Frankie hugged me. "We'll beat this, Darius."

"And if we don't?" I hated myself for asking the question. My fists clenched, and I wanted to hit something.

Frankie took my hand and massaged it open. "Then we love her through it and make sure she knows what your mom looks like so she can meet her, and then we send Damien and Caleb to go find her."

I blinked back tears. "I think I love Amelia, Frankie."

"I know you do, tough guy," Frankie smiled back at me. "Now go buy a car like a good soccer daddy."

I chuckled, kissed the top of her head, and went out to Jake's truck. Franco gave me a worried look. "Nothing to worry about, kid. Your aunt was only giving me a hard time. What do you think we should get?"

"A truck like this!" Franco replied with enthusiasm.

"I have a truck already. I was thinking of something a little easier for your mom to get in and out of. It might be hard for her on some days to step up. My truck sits a little higher than this one," I told Franco. "DC tried to be born in it."

"It was only a scare, Franco. You should have heard Darius whining about getting his seats dirty," Jake laughed at that.

Franco giggled. "Okay, let's look at cars. Will you guys teach me how to ride a motorcycle?"

"You bet," I answered quickly. "After getting a car, we can look at dirt bikes that are more your size. That's what I started on."

"Where is your truck?" Jake asked.

"Skull's house. He's got it parked in his garage for me," I told Jake as he brought us into the city. "Suggestions?"

"Personally, I'd look for a crossover type. Those sit a bit higher than sedans. That way, it's not a concern if it's hard to sink into or get out. Make doesn't matter unless you have a preference." Jake pulled into a lot and stopped. "The entire street is dealerships. If you can't find something, you are hopeless," he teased me. "Keep him in line, Franco."

"Thanks for the ride, Uncle Jake!" Franco hopped out and slammed the door, patiently waiting for me to get out.

"What he said," I thumped him with my fist. "Thanks for everything, Jake."

We began our search for the perfect vehicle. Franco loved the test drives. Probably because I drove like a madman when I could. That came crashing down when Franco asked about my mom. I was trying to make it fun for him and keep our minds off the bad stuff.

"Auntie Frankie said your mom died when you were a teenager," Franco threw out there as we walked to the next dealership.

"She did. I know cancer is scary, and I know how you feel watching your mom go through it, but we are all here to make sure she has everything she needs to fight this. I promise you that, little man. I'm all in," I tried to reassure Franco and not talk down to him.

"Auntie Frankie said she's going to turn you into a nursemaid," Franco gave me a sidelong look.

"She'll try," I laughed. "I'll do my best to make

sure both of you are taken care of all the time," I promised again. "That means I'm going to have to learn how to cook. That's what's super scary."

"Uncle Jake said I better like macaroni and cheese," Franco giggled again.

"He's right, that I can make pretty easily. I mean, it comes in a box. It would be hard to mess that up," I directed Franco into the next lot.

His eyes landed on a new Jeep model, and he beelined for it. It fell in the crossover category, and I looked around for a salesperson. It didn't take long for a female the approximate size of Amelia to come out.

I whistled to get Franco's attention, and he met me in the middle of walking up to the salesperson. "Can I ask you for a really strange favor?" I started before she could throw pitches at me. "Can you follow Franco to the vehicle he was looking at and get in and out of it? You are about the same size as his mom, and I want to see if it will be too low or too high for her."

Franco beamed Caleb's smile at the woman, and my heart tripped all over itself as I followed and watched. He was Caleb's mini-me. Franco asked the woman to get in and out about six times, and thankfully she went along with it. It was about the same as the Kia we looked at last, but this one looked slicker, and it had caught Franco's excitement.

It looked like they had a good assortment of colors too. We looked around a little more, and Franco's eyes kept sliding to the model he initially looked at, so I asked for a test drive. There were two more dealerships to look at, but this Jeep was a contender.

I circled the area this time, looking for a bank branch and finally spotting it. I drove us back to the dealership. "Give me out the door cash sale bottom line price," I told the saleslady. Her face registered surprise, and she quickly covered it. "Go write up whatever you are going to write up, price it for the most loaded model you have on the lot, and that's where we'll start. Franco and I will look at the colors you've got."

Flustered, the woman scurried away to do as I asked while we perused the colors. "Whatcha think?" Franco asked me as we stood in front of a dark-gray-colored one.

"Why do you like this color?" I asked him, admiring the choice.

"It's better than black, and I like the red one too, but I think this color matches all of us better," Franco replied carefully.

I checked the sticker on the window, saw it was almost fully loaded, and nodded to myself. "Good call. Want to keep looking, or should we get this one?"

"I can't tell if you are serious or not," Franco glanced at me.

"Totally serious, little man," I vowed. "Out of all the places we've gone, this is the only one you got excited about." I glanced at my watch. There was about an hour left until the bank closed.

"I like this one," Franco replied timidly.

I handed him my phone as we walked to find the woman so I could close the deal. "Done deal, then. Let's find the lady, get the price, and make a quick trip to the bank. Sound good? We can grab some dinner too. Oh wait, call Frankie and ask if she wants us to pick something up?"

She came running up to us as we stood there. "Did you find a color?"

"The slate-gray one out there," I told her. "If you can give me a deal, I'll retake a test drive to the bank to get a cashier's check."

Again with a flustered look, she led me to her desk, worked out a reasonable price, and handed over the keys to the one we test drove earlier, so I didn't add miles to the new one, which made me laugh. She let us go and arranged to have it detailed while I was getting the money.

"We're buying it, little man. What did Frankie say?" I asked, waiting for him to buckle up.

"She said to bring back tacos," Franco grinned. That's what we did.

Chapter 40

After a couple of months, we fell into a routine. Amelia asked me to stay with them when the doctors told her there was no change, and she grew desperate. Frankie taught me to cook, and Franco and I would experiment with recipes.

There were times he was so like Caleb that it threw me into a tailspin. I'm not sure what it looked like physically, but Franco seemed to understand what those little attacks looked like, and he would ask me to tell him stories about his dad, like Frankie used to do.

Amelia enrolled Franco in school, and I'd help with his homework. I still hadn't kissed the woman who'd stolen my heart, but there was no question about me falling hard. Everyone knew it too.

With Franco in school today, and Amelia on an even keel and sleeping, I decided it was time for me to talk with Skull. I snuck into Amelia's room to check on her before I left, sitting on the edge of the bed and brushing the hair from her face.

Her color looked better, and I ran my hand over her forehead to check for an elevated temperature, but her skin was cool to the touch. I had a brief flashback of finding my mother, and I stared hard at Amelia's chest to make sure it was rising and falling.

"Are you ogling me?" Amelia's voice came out weak, but there was humor there.

"Hi, beautiful. I was checking on you before I went to talk to Skull. Sometimes you are so still it reminds me of finding my mother, so I watch to make sure you are breathing," I explained.

"I know, Darius," she reached for my hand. "I just wanted you to smile. What are you going to talk to Skull about?"

"Me pulling out of the club. I think it's time," I sighed dramatically. "It will get Frankie off my back."

"What will you do instead?" Amelia rolled to her side to look at me.

"When I met Skull and Trigger, I wanted to make a difference. The military was the place I was supposed to make that happen. I don't know what we did improved any lives there or here, and I've been a little lost all these years. Now that you're here, I find those old longings stirring. I was thinking of enrolling in school to become a social worker," I told her, feeling braver than I had before I walked in.

Amelia gave me one of those patented smiles that made my tongue glue itself to the roof of my mouth. "Why haven't you kissed me?"

I almost fell off the bed. Of everything that woman could have said to me, that wasn't what I expected. "I didn't know you wanted me to," I croaked.

"I asked you to move in here. That should have been your first clue. You haven't pressured me or made any advances either. Why? I can see on your face that you have feelings for me. Is it because I'm sick and you are scared to get involved? Or is it something uglier, like you can't make yourself want me because I'm disfigured under my clothes?" Amelia bluntly threw the questions at me.

For a few painfully silent minutes, all I could do was blink rapidly and try to process the thoughts that flooded through me. "I've never seriously dated anyone," I managed to get out. The look on Amelia's face had me throwing caution to the wind.

I dipped my head and kissed her. The lip balm she was using tasted like strawberries, and Amelia herself tasted like dark, passionate nights, which made no sense to my cluttered brain, but that was all I could think of as I drowned myself in her lips. I was sure I looked pathetic and like a love-sick puppy when I pulled away.

"Finally," Amelia grinned and slumped back on the bed. "I've wanted you to do that for months. Invite Skull over for dinner. You can talk to him after Franco goes to bed."

After that kiss, I would have done anything she asked me to. I yanked out my phone and sent Skull a text extending the invitation. I set the phone on the nightstand next to the bed and stared back at Amelia, who watched me. She shifted and patted the bed.

I lay next to her on my side. "Do you honestly believe that I would find you disfigured?"

"No," she answered softly. "It's a fear I've had since the first surgery. I don't believe you feel that way. I threw that in more to voice the fear inside me than to accuse you of thinking something like that."

"Boobs don't make a woman a woman or define your attractiveness. For me, it was the way you moved. You walked like you belonged on that plane and that it was there to serve you. Confident, strong, and with this undeniable grace," I confessed.

"Why haven't you made a move then?" she boldly moved my arm and rested her head on it so I was holding her.

"I figured you had enough on your plate without adding a screwed up, problematic, questionable man to your life. I wanted you to know I was all-in. I can think of several reasons, and they all sound stupid now." I moved my arm a little and brought her closer.

"You were going to wait, then? Until when? What if this doesn't go away?" Amelia prodded me.

I wasn't sure where she was heading, and honesty was the best route. "That's not as easy to answer. Would I have waited until you got better? Probably not. I was waiting until this extreme sickness relented a little. If it doesn't go away, then we take it a day at a time. My interest hasn't waned."

"I forgive you," Amelia replied with a teasing smile. "Stop waiting. Life is short enough. Kiss me often, hug me always, and feel free to take your shirt off. Maybe your pants too, but not when Franco is around."

"I love how bold you are," I breathed out. I reached down and pulled my shirt off to show Amelia I was more than willing. "I'm gonna ask a rude question now," I warned her.

"Feel free," she answered while running her

hands up my chest.

"What's your ethnicity?" I blurted out, fighting the need to stop her hands before I did something she wasn't ready for yet.

Amelia's hands stilled on her own. "That's the rude question?" She let out a small laugh. "Not rude, but from what the DNA kits I've done have said, I have some Latino, African American, and plain old European in a small percentage, the way I figure it is that one parent was Latino, the other black. Franco got all his dad and none of me. Even their attitudes are similar, and Franco never got to meet him. It's eerie sometimes. But I was raised by white parents in a white neighborhood, and I think people see me as white. I never experienced what you did."

"He's got you in him. I can see it in his intelligence. Caleb was smart, too, don't get me wrong. There are still times I can hear you coming out of that kid's mouth," I smiled to show it wasn't a bad thing.

My phone buzzed on the nightstand, and I glanced at it. "Skull said he couldn't come for dinner, but he can come by around seven and allow me to feed him dessert."

"Fair enough. If you help me, we can make a cake," Amelia suggested. "Now back to the dating thing, don't waste time. If you want to date me, do it. That means kissing and touching and singing to me."

"You want me to sing to you?" I couldn't help it; I laughed.

"I heard you singing to Franco," Amelia said and rested her head on my chest when I lay back.

"Did I wake you up with it?" I twined my fingers in her hair and reveled in the level of closeness I felt with this woman.

"No. When I'm that sick, I don't sleep deeply. I'm up and down too much. I call it drifting. I'm aware of what's happening around me even though it looks like I'm asleep," Amelia told me while running her fingers over my nipple.

Things were going to become evident in about two seconds. I tried to shift the lower part of my body away, but she only moved closer. I sighed and tried to distract myself. "Franco was worried, and I told him that when my mom felt bad when she was sick, she had me sing with her. So he asked me to sing with him."

"Amazing Grace, you said, right? That's the song your mom liked?" Amelia remembered.

My heart warmed. "That was Mom's favorite. She liked Swing Low Sweet Chariot too, but we only sang that one at her funeral. She liked the hymn Go Tell It On The Mountain too. Also, Wade in the Water. She said her daddy sang that one to her."

"Isn't that an Underground Railroad song?" Amelia shifted more, and she was half-laying on me.

"You know what you're doing to me, right?" I tilted my head to look at her.

"Not yet, I don't. I know what I'm hoping for." Amelia's eyes glinted with humor and heat. "We've been dating for over two months, even if it was chaste dating, and you didn't know that's what it was. It's been so long since I've felt a man," her voice trailed off as she moved again and settled over me.

I couldn't have hidden my body's reaction if I wanted to. I wrapped my arms around Amelia and held her, trying to calm myself down. "Isn't Franco due home soon?" I thought to ask before I gave in.

"Yes," Amelia moaned into my chest. "But damn, just let me feel this a bit longer." She slid her knees down the outsides of my hips, and all I felt was her heat.

"I think you're killing me," I whispered into her hair but refused to let her go.

"Do you think if you sing Wade into the Water, the grim reaper will lose the scent of me and not be able to track me down and take me?" Amelia asked wryly. "Not trying to be macabre, honestly, but maybe when I have those bad moments, you can sing that to me to remind me to fight."

"I'll sing you whatever you want," I promised.

"This tattoo was for your mom, wasn't it?" Amelia's fingers traveled up my side.

"Sure was. My mom told me that phrase after she announced her cancer. 'We don't always win, Darius, but we always fight,' she told me. It got me through some tough spots after she died. Win or lose; I'm right here fighting with you and for you, got that?" I said it gruffer than intended.

"Oh, I know. Will you help me shave my head after we make the cake? If this follows the same patterns as last time, this more intense round of chemo will make it start falling out in clumps, and that part scares Franco a little bit," Amelia responded quietly.

I wanted to cry. Instead, I held Amelia tighter. "Does it make me a pussy if I say I love you?"

Amelia let out a delighted laugh. "No, Darius. I already knew that. You'd only be a pussy if you didn't admit it."

Chapter 41

Skull showed up a little after seven. He dropped the hardass exterior he usually displayed to everyone else, and the person he was with me when we were alone came back out. He talked with Franco for over an hour about riding dirt bikes. He spoke about Trigger when he got his bike, and that's when they found out they loved being on motorcycles.

Franco was captivated. "Darius said he would get me one!"

Amelia gave me a look, and I felt like a deer in headlights. "I would have talked to you first," was all I could think to say. It made Skull laugh. "I'll go get the cake," I sighed, shuffling off before getting into any more trouble.

"Mom sent me in to help you," Franco bounded in after me.

"What do you want to carry? The cake or the plates?" I offered him a choice.

"The ice cream," Franco crowed. "I know there's some in here."

I grinned and let him root around for it. "Your dad would be so proud of you, Franco." The words slipped out without warning.

"He would?" Franco turned to look at me.

"Hundred percent, no lie," I crossed my heart. Franco beamed and resumed getting the ice cream. I stacked some plates and silverware, grabbed the cake, and followed Franco.

We ate cake, and I watched the scene from a mental distance, and it kept striking me how much I wanted this to last. I craved laying down roots with Amelia. I had an overwhelming desire to be the person I wanted to be when I was a kid, to make Amelia proud of me.

Franco cleared the table and went to get ready for bed, as Amelia told him. I stood up to wash the dishes. "I'll be there in a minute, Franco," I called out.

It wasn't just singing he requested of me; he liked the prayers too. Something else that made my heart swell with more emotion than I knew what to do with; my mom would love it. It felt like she was extending her love through me to Franco.

I dropped a kiss on Amelia's beanie-covered head as I walked back to Franco's room. He was in bed with the covers pulled back, waiting for me. It never failed to make my heart stutter to see a young Caleb staring back at me.

"I did something right in my life to get to have you a part of it, Franco. What's it gonna be tonight, a song, a prayer, both?" I sat on the floor next to the bed and leaned against the wall.

"Both," Franco answered immediately. "I like Amazing Grace. It makes me feel good when I sing it with you."

I nodded and started to sing quietly, and he joined in. We got through the song, Franco, with a sweet smile on his face that made me think of Frankie. "Want to start the prayer, or do you want me to?"

"You started the song. I'll do the prayer," Franco replied eagerly. "Dear God, please take care of my mom and help her get better and stronger so we can be a real family. Watch over Auntie Frankie so Uncle Jake doesn't drive her crazy. Help Darius sleep well, so he doesn't forget we will get a dirt bike. Remind Uncle Skull that he's loved. Thank you for my life. Amen."

I bit the inside of my cheek. I wasn't sure if I felt like laughing or crying. "Dear God, thank you for bringing these people into my life to remind me of my path. Watch over Jake, so Frankie doesn't push him into insanity. Take care of Skull, and remind my brothers up there with you that I miss them and think of them every day. Last, heal Amelia so I can plant roots. Amen."

"What does that mean, Darius? Planting roots?" Franco slid under his covers.

"It means I don't want to leave you ever," I told him, tucking the covers around him and kissing his forehead. "Sleep well, little man."

I turned and saw Skull and Amelia standing in the doorway. Skull's face was unreadable, but I knew it meant he hid the emotions he didn't want Amelia to see. Amelia's face was soft, serene, and filled with something I didn't want to hope for yet.

She passed me on her way to say goodnight to Franco, and I led Skull back out. It was a clear night, and

I'd rather be outside for this talk if Franco woke up or took a while to fall asleep. I opened the slider and motioned him out.

We settled in the chairs by the firepit, but I didn't light it. "Wait." I stood back up and went to get Amelia's blankets from the closet. I knew she'd get cold out here. I set them on the chair on the other side of me and slid them closer.

Skull watched with an amused smile. "I'm happy for you, Dar. She's gonna beat this. I refuse to believe anything else. Before you start with why you called me here, let me guess. You want to pull back?"

I sighed because it was hard to hear. Skull sounded wistful but not angry. "I do. I can't have any of that stuff touch them, Skull. That kid healed a hole in my heart that I was scared to talk about with anyone. Amelia, I don't know how to say it, but I've never felt this way about any female. I want to go to school and become a social worker."

"I can't say I want you gone because you are my brother, but you don't belong in that life. You never have. Some might pitch a fit, but we'll announce it as a retirement. They know she's your woman, and they know she's sick. You'll always be under my protection. Just promise not to forget me; go on rides with me," Skull told me, his tone a little sad.

"Jamal, this man won't ever forget you. You are a part of him," Amelia announced, walking out. "Darius isn't leaving you; he's leaving the club. He might still need your help in making moves on a woman."

Skull burst out laughing. "Dar, you lost

your game?"

I scowled at him. "It matters now."

"He's still got it," Amelia giggled. "He just won't let it free. Anyway, I'm not picking on him. I want to point out that you matter to that little boy in there, this bigger one here, and even to me. You are part of our little family."

I can't say I've ever seen Skull look as floored as that, and it made me chuckle. "What she said. Nothing between us changes, man. I know you keep me away from the bad shit. This move only makes it so that you aren't shielding me, and they have nothing to gripe to you about."

"I was hopin' you'd get to this sooner than you did, and you won't get any arguments from me on it. I know what losin' Demon did to you, just as I know what losin' Trigger did. If you still are waking up at night, and that boy knows, do somethin'. Talk. Don't let it eat at you like it did, Demon," Skull lectured me with a grave tone.

"I'm working on that," I admitted softly.

"Now, next topic, your dad called me," Skull sat forward. "He's retiring and wondered if you'd oppose him moving here."

I frowned heavily. "Why wouldn't my dad have asked me that?"

"He doesn't want to burden you, Dar. He knows you're taking care of your woman. He misses you. Hell, he even said he misses me," Skull laid it out for me.

"My dad wouldn't lie about that." I heard the guilt in my voice. It'd been about three weeks since I last talked to him. "I'll call him. Maybe you should think about retiring, Skull. He's gonna see it if he moves here."

"I'll deal with that when he's here, if he comes," Skull ground out. "It's not like I have something to fall back on."

"Bullshit," Amelia piped up. "Aren't you the one that taught Darius how to work out, build muscle, and fight?"

"Open a gym. Help the other little versions of me's out there running around like you did me." I bit back the grin forming on my face.

"What parent in their right mind is gonna send their kid to someone like me?" Skull threw back at me with a huff.

"Why wouldn't they?" Amelia stepped in again. "Because you have tattoos? Because you are black with tattoos and ride a bike? Most people that society praises are covered with tattoos and have a sketchy past. Sports stars, actors, politicians, musicians. It's not like these people know your past, and your past doesn't determine your future."

People didn't challenge Skull like that, and I found it funny that he had nothing to say. He would have argued with me. I simply gave him a pointed look because he knew Amelia was right. When Shay moved out and got her own place and started dating, Skull freaked out. It took him a while to adjust. Change wasn't easy.

I got it because she was a link to Trigger, the same way Franco was a link to Caleb, and DC a link to Damien. "Your only limits are yourself," I finally broke the silence.

"I got time to figure it out. Just make sure you call

your dad. Next club meeting, we'll retire you," Skull stood and stretched. He surreptitiously checked his watch and gave me a considering look. "Up for one more ride?"

I glanced at Amelia. "What kind of ride?"

"Nope. Never mind. I don't want you there," he reconsidered quickly.

I pursed my lips but didn't push. It wasn't a leisure ride Skull was talking about this time. "Watch your back, bro. I'll summon your damn ghost and torture you if you bite it."

"Don't plan on it, Dar," Skull smiled sadly and headed out. He didn't need me walking him, and I let it go.

Chapter 42

My vision went black, and I was getting held down. I could feel the enemy on my left. I smelled smoke, and panic was creeping in fast. I couldn't move. Shit! Was I paralyzed? I could feel the foot pressing down on my throat. No, that wasn't right, nightmare, wake up, I told myself.

I couldn't. I couldn't get enough air to move; I remained pinned down. I could feel beads of sweat dripping down the sides of my face. Wait, I wasn't sweating; tears fell. I felt locked in my mind and aware that I was locked. My body wouldn't respond, and my voice didn't work.

The black faded, yet I knew I was still trapped in a fucked-up nightmare that wouldn't quit, memories mixing with fear and creating a hellscape. The foot on my throat belonged to my mom. I could see her lips moving, but my ears filled with the sound of gunfire and screams. Chaos incarnate ensued.

Nothing made sense. It was different scenes blending into one horrific shithole of a vision. I saw Damien beating the hell out of Trigger and Caleb pointing a gun at my mother with Amelia crying in the corner of a mud hut with Franco wearing a bomb. The smell of a burning helicopter filled in the empty spaces. Wrong, it was all wrong. When Hacker appeared and shot Skull in the head, my paralysis broke, and I rolled.

I hit the floor hard, and I couldn't remember where I was. I heard Amelia call my name, and I kept moving. I didn't know how to escape the twisted collage that had just happened. I bolted. Down the hall, out to the backyard, where I collapsed on the ground.

The cold seeped into my body, the blades of grass tickled my face, and the rich smell of dewy earth filled my nostrils. Roots, plant roots, I chanted in my head. It switched to repeating, not real, until the images weren't so sharp in my mind.

I didn't even move when the skies opened up. My body felt boneless in the face of what played out in my mind. Thousands, maybe millions, of raindrops fell in a violent rush, flooding the ground with their fury. Fury that I felt. Thousands of individual tears from the sky, the many becoming one giant puddle, solitary in its place in the low spot on the ground, hiding its real depth from shallow eyes.

That one nightmare showed me just how deep the trauma went. You'd never know how deep it was until your foot hit it. Comparing it to the pool of water in front of my eyes was all I could do. I got lost in the splattering raindrops as the puddle absorbed them.

"Soldier! On your feet!" Amelia's voice broke through the white noise.

I jolted; Amelia shouldn't be out here. She could catch a cold. She was between treatments right now, and this could set her back.

"Baker!" Amelia screamed. "Did you hear me? On your feet!"

"Mom?" A sleepy-eyed Franco joined the mix, and shame washed through me.

"Go help Darius, baby," Amelia whispered to him. "He had a horrible nightmare."

Franco was ten now. A ten-year-old shouldn't be rescuing a grown-ass man. The level of panic that flooded my veins should have adrenaline pumping through my body, making me stronger than usual. Instead, I felt not strong enough to stand.

My brain flashed between Caleb and Franco's images as the boy stepped out of the house and walked toward me. His sweet voice was ringing out with the opening verse of Amazing Grace. I was immensely grateful for the rain on my face that hid my tears.

I rolled to my back and struggled to sit up, Franco reaching his arm out to help me. I crossed my legs, pulled him into my lap, and hugged the singing kid tightly. Franco was affectionate and didn't protest; he just continued to sing.

When I finally found my voice, it came out raspy, but I joined him for the last verses. Our voices faded into the rain, and I rested my forehead on the top of his head. "Thank you, Franco. I gotta tell you, little man, you are the best, and I love you with all my heart."

Franco moved so he could see me better, patted my face, and smiled. "I know. I love you too, Darius. Let's go inside."

Regaining enough strength, I stood holding him in

my arms and carried him like a sack into the house, setting him down. "Go change into warm clothes, and I'll be in." Franco nodded and went to wait for me.

"Darius," Amelia whispered, concerned.

"You too. Go to bed, get warm. I'll be in soon. I need to text Skull to ease my mind." I leaned in to brush my lips over hers.

Her eyes raked over my face but gave me a terse nod, and I heard her check on Franco. I grabbed my phone from the counter and toggled it on.

Tell me you are okay. Had the worst nightmare ever; I texted Skull and waited for his response.

Sitting on ice, I'm so chill. Need me? Skull texted back a minute later.

No. Just wanted to make sure. Thanks. I responded and set my phone down, took a deep breath and exhaled slowly.

My phone buzzed again. *Then talk to Amelia. It's time;* Skull wrote back.

He was right. It was time when Frankie had her baby and let me name her. My niece, little Izzy. I told myself to pull it together, grabbed a bottle of water, and went to say goodnight for the second time to Franco.

"Are you better now, Darius?" Franco asked from his dark bedroom.

"After that, how could I not be?" I sat on the edge of his bed. "I'm sorry if that scared you or woke you up."

"Were you thinking about the war?" His innocent voice knifed through me.

"Sort of; it was all mixed up this time, and I'll say that I think it can't get worse than that. Maybe now that it got out, things will get better. Think that's possible?" I asked him.

"Mom says anything is possible, so I think so," Franco shifted, his voice getting sleepy.

"Love you, little man. Go back to sleep. I'll make us pancakes for breakfast," I kissed his forehead.

"Chocolate chips," Franco requested, drifting off. "Love you."

I waited a minute before heading back to the scene of my destruction. Amelia had turned on one of the lamps to its dimmest setting. I closed the door behind me, leaving it unlocked. "Let me change," I spoke softly. "I don't want you to get cold."

I'd been sleeping in Amelia's room for the past four months after Izzy was born, though I still hadn't had sex with her, partly because she had a bad bout of being sick, which was the last thing she needed. I grabbed a pair of shorts and stripped off my wet clothes, sliding the shorts on and toweling them dry.

"Just leave them in the hamper," Amelia called out.

I wrung as much water out of them as I could, and dropped them in, brushed my teeth again. I knew it was a delay tactic. Amelia knew it too. Amelia didn't call me out on it, though; the saint of a woman just waited patiently.

I opened the water, swallowed a couple of ibuprofens, and sucked it up to face the love of my life. Franco had asked me to marry his mom, which was overwhelming because I wanted nothing more than to do that. He'd even gone with me to pick out a ring, and we had it hidden in his room.

I slid between the sheets, and Amelia sighed. "I'm going to tell you if you want to hear it," I offered meekly.

"I do," she held her hand out to me, and it was icy. I held it between mine to warm it up and did the same with the other as I gave her every fucked-up detail of what happened in my mind. I went over the event that kept popping up where I was getting pinned. I bore every disgusting mark on my soul.

We sat there in silence after I finished. When I started to think it was too much for Amelia to deal with, she slid closer to me and rested against my arm. I shifted to put it around her, breathed in her scent, and cherished the way she felt pressed into me.

"Darius, I think that was as bad as it's going to get. Maybe this was the nightmare that threw it at you to make you face it, air it, and move on. I don't know, it could happen again, and if it does, you know you can get through it. That was a lot to process, and you weren't weak in the face of it. Your body went right from adrenaline to shock. Your mind was telling you to fight, and we all know there is not one chance in hell you will raise a hand against any of us that you saw in that nightmare." Amelia stroked her hand over my abs.

"It's as good an explanation as any," I agreed softly. "I feel like someone carved out my insides, let a bear gnaw on them, and then tried to put them back in. Sending Franco out could have been dangerous."

"Nah, I know at the deepest level of me that you would never hurt him," Amelia sounded so sure of herself. "You were seeing Caleb?"

"Yeah." I lay my cheek on her head and closed my

eyes. "Part of me thought it was one of those vision dreams people talk about, and I needed to make sure Skull was okay."

"He is, right?" Amelia's hand drifted a little, and I tensed.

"Yeah." My voice dropped. I fought the instinct to halt Amelia's hand. If she wanted me, I wasn't going to stop her. I probably needed her more than she wanted me.

"You just let me in. Did you know that?" Amelia sat up, leaving my side cold.

"I do. Do you wish I hadn't?" I couldn't get a good read on her face.

"Hell no. I'm glad you did. It gives me the confidence to do this." Amelia reached down and pulled the sweatshirt she slept in off. "No one has ever seen me like this except the doctors."

Amelia's scars were there for me to experience. Careful of her port, I reached out and lightly ran my fingers down the puckered flesh. "Were you worried I would find it ugly?" My voice was whisper-soft.

Yes, they were harsh, and I wished she hadn't had to go through all of this. Those scars were a testament to this woman's strength, and I found them beautiful. I touched all of them. I kissed them, and I rested my head against her chest.

"Yeah, I was worried," she finally responded. "For nothing, apparently."

"We've all got scars," I told her. "There's not any part of you I don't love. You are the first woman to whom I've said those words, and I don't know if I ever told you that."

Amelia bit her lip, and her eyes penetrated mine. She pushed me back, and I let her do what she wanted. I'd give this woman anything she wanted. "Take these off," Amelia tugged at the waistband of my shorts.

It might have been the fastest I've ever shed clothes. I trembled and uncontrollably shook as Amelia explored and touched me everywhere. Jesus, this was going to be how I died. She brought me right to the brink of no return, and I shifted to push her back.

"If you want this to be our first time, it isn't going to be one-sided. God didn't build me that way. I told myself to let you do whatever you want, and I will, but tell me what you want, Amelia." My voice was so rough and gravelly; it sounded guttural.

Amelia pulled off the rest of her clothes. "I want everything, Darius. I want you powerless and falling apart and you to do the same to me. I want us to get there together. Give and take, go ahead and worship me as you want, and then prepare yourself because I'll do the same and tear you to pieces, and you'll love it."

"Fuck," I groaned when she lay back and opened herself. "You're beautiful." Amelia was right. I worshiped her until she held a pillow over her face to muffle her cries. When she pushed me away, I tried to will myself to last longer than I felt I could.

No one ever promised or tore me to pieces the way Amelia did, and I loved every second of it. "I love you, Darius," Amelia purred and took me right over the edge.

Chapter 43

I put the phone down and looked over at the hospital bed that Amelia lay in, looking tiny. Her eyes were closed, and I hoped that meant she was sleeping and not just fighting pain. It had been seven months since we breached that last line between us.

This is the worst she has looked and been throughout that time. To say I was terrified was an understatement. How much more could her body take? When Damien died, and Frankie was hurt, Jake was inconsolable, and I hate that I understood it now.

At least the staff here had brought in cots for Franco and me. We'd spent the last two nights here with Amelia. We sang quietly to her when she woke up in pain from her body fighting. I moved silently and lowered the railing on her bed, and scooted the cot closer so I could be next to her.

Nurses made their rounds through, checking her vitals, giving me encouraging smiles, and asking if I needed anything. I hated the smell of the place. I wanted Amelia to get well enough to come home. I'd clean every hour if I had to, but I wanted not to be here and staring sickness in the face.

"Who called?" Amelia's faint voice drew my eyes.

"Dad," I answered. She'd started calling him that. "He wanted to check on you and see if you were well enough to come to the retirement party."

"You better still be going. Don't you dare not go because I'm in here. Franco wants to meet him, and you should be there. It's a big deal for him," Amelia's eyes picked up some fire with her voice rising in volume.

"Wings, I don't want to go without you," I replied solemnly.

"Boomer, I'm not dying. I like having you around; you aren't on the other side. Go, be there for Dad and bring Franco; it will mean so much to him. Frankie will come to check on me. If they release me, I'll go home with her until you are back," Amelia said forcefully.

"Amelia," I whispered, looking for the words to voice my fear of leaving her.

"Darius, hon, I know you're scared. I'm not checking out. You won't come back and find me gone. Call Dad and tell him you and Franco will be there. He'll get to meet me when he moves here, and I plan on being better by then," Amelia softened her voice.

"You understand what the thought of leaving you is doing to me?" I closed my eyes to try and control my breathing.

"I do. I know it will hurt, and I have every confidence that you can do it because you know it's the right thing to do," Amelia reached her hand out and caressed my face.

"Promise me we aren't going to have the preparations for my funeral talk. I don't want to leave thinking that thought is in your head." I opened my eyes and saw the spark in hers.

"I promise," she made a cross over her heart. "Want me to pinky swear too? I meant it, Darius. I want more time with you. I want what you are afraid to ask me."

I let out a small scoff. "Not afraid. This room is hardly the place."

A small smile played on her lips. "There you are. Make the call. I want to hear it."

I reached for my phone, chuckling. "Women are evil creatures." I dialed the number and put it on speakerphone, setting the phone between us.

"Darius? Is everything okay?" my dad answered, sounding worried.

"Hi, Dad," Amelia mustered some strength in her voice. "Everything is fine."

"Hi, angel girl, it's good to hear your voice. You getting out of there?" I could hear the relief in my dad's voice at hearing Amelia.

"Hopefully soon," Amelia told him. "Darius has something to tell you."

I chuckled again. "Franco and I will be there for your party."

The smile on Amelia's face was worth it. She muted the phone for a second. "Told you. He's crying, Darius," Amelia informed me quickly and unmuted the phone. "I'll be there in spirit, Dad."

"We'll see you in a few days, Dad. Should we get a hotel, or do you have room for us?" I watched Amelia's face while I waited for a response.

"I'd love it if you stayed here," my dad replied with a teary voice.

"Great, consider it done. We'll help you pack too," I offered. "See you soon, Dad."

We hung up, and Amelia smiled again. "You did good. I'm so proud of you."

I leaned forward and kissed her tenderly. "I'm not sure I can say no to you."

"Whipped already, I love it," Amelia smirked and kissed me this time.

"I used to tease Jake about being whipped, and he would tell me it wasn't as bad as I thought. I hate it when he's right," I sighed. "He should be here soon with Franco."

"He's going to be so excited to go," Amelia shifted and winced. She grabbed my phone from where it lay and called Frankie. "Hey, you are on nurse duty. I convinced him to go," she declared when Frankie answered.

It wasn't on speakerphone, so I couldn't hear what Frankie was saying, and all Amelia was doing was listening and agreeing. I got a few side glances from Amelia and didn't know what was happening. She didn't look worried, so I didn't.

Amelia returned my phone a few minutes later, right before Jake and Franco walked in with a toddling DC. I grinned and sat up, catching his eye. Innocent giggles filled the room as the baby ran towards me, and I grabbed him, throwing him up in the air.

"Unca!" DC crowed.

"Yeah, great, get him all wound up," Jake

grumbled good-naturedly. "How's today looking, Amelia?"

"No change. That's not good or bad, means I'm holding steady," Amelia told him, hugging Franco. "Just hung up with Frankie. She will sit with me this weekend unless they let me go. In that case, I'll be crashing with you."

"You're going?" Jake glanced over at me. "Good."

"Hear that, DC? Your uncle daddy is poking at a bear," I told the laughing, squirming boy. I set him on the cot, and he scooted over to cuddle Amelia.

Jake rolled his eyes and grabbed the baby before he could pull on the IVs in Amelia's arms. "No, DC, we don't touch those. When do you leave?"

Franco looked up at me with a forlorn expression. "Can I ride with you to the airport?"

"You have to. You're coming with me," I sat down next to Franco. "We leave Friday after school."

Franco glanced back at his mom, then at me cautiously. "Auntie Frankie will be with Mom?"

"That's what she said," I held his backpack steady while he pulled out his homework.

"Okay," Franco let a small smile out.

"Wait until he grows into Caleb's cockiness," Jake warned. "I probably just jinxed myself with DC by saying that."

Amelia laughed, "Sure did. Add in Frankie's mischievousness too."

"Daddy's doomed," Jake told DC. "Keep up the good work, Amelia. We'll get out of your hair."

After they left, Franco looked back at me, "How

are we getting to the airport? Isn't Uncle Jake taking us?"

"No, Skull will." I wanted to stay here tonight and knew that I needed to go home with Franco. He couldn't spend every night at Jake and Frankie's. "When we go home tonight, pack a bag of clothes you want to wear."

Franco sat on the edge next to Amelia and talked about his homework, what he learned in school, and the upcoming projects they would be doing. He voiced his fears of not doing well enough because he didn't understand science too much.

"Darius can help you," Amelia stroked his hair. "He's probably smarter than the both of us combined when it comes to that stuff."

"Phew," Franco sighed happily.

My throat clenched, sealing up my airways. I wanted this so badly; these two had become my world. It scared the hell out of me and made me feel more alive.

Chapter 44

As the plane started to descend into Chicago, my heart raced again. I wanted to punch something or destroy it. I despised being this far away from Amelia. I felt like screaming out a war cry but didn't want to get banned from flying either.

"Are you okay?" Franco asked, looking away from the window to me.

"Yeah, little man. I just don't like being this far away from your mom. It's driving me crazy," I told him, hoping the blunt truth wouldn't scare him.

"She'll be okay. She promised, and Auntie Frankie is with her," Franco assured me.

I couldn't help but smile. "I'm glad you are with me, Franco. You make my life better."

He beamed at me. "Have you been here?" he turned back to look out the window.

"Yep. I came to visit my dad a lot. I like home better, yet Chicago has some cool things too. I'll take you to see the lake before we go," I promised him.

"The big one?" Franco asked excitedly.

"The biggest. Lake Michigan." I grinned at his enthusiasm.

"Is that it?" Franco moved, and I looked out the window at the water.

"Sure is. Pretty, isn't it?" I leaned back in the seat and wished that Amelia was with us for the millionth time.

"It looks like the ocean," Franco's voice held deep awe. He stared for a few minutes and then fell silent as the apprehension and excitement of a new place settled over him. When we were able to deboard, he clutched my hand.

I flung our bags over my shoulder and called my dad with my other hand. "We're heading to the passenger pick-up, no bags to claim."

I led Franco through the terminal, and we eventually made it to the passenger pick-up area, and I stepped to the curb. Franco hugged my side, suddenly shy, not letting my hand go. I didn't care; it made me feel like a hero that he trusted me this much.

I saw my dad's vehicle and smiled. Still, with the BMW crossover, some things never change. I pointed him out to Franco, whose eyes got a little wider. I waited patiently for my dad to make his way to us and stop the car. He flung the door open and ran at me.

"Darius!" He threw his arms around me and thumped my back. He felt smaller to me, and I hugged him back with my free arm. He let go after a minute, then composed himself and turned to Franco. "You are perfect, Franco. It's a pleasure to meet you."

To my surprise, Franco let go of my hand and hugged my dad as powerfully as my dad had hugged me. "Can I call you Grandpa?" he asked my dad.

My dad's breath caught, and his eyes shone with tears. "If that's what you want to call me, it would be a huge honor to me."

"You're my first grandpa," Franco turned shy again and reached for my hand.

My dad looked at me. "I can't tell you what this means to me. Come on, let's go."

I got Franco situated in the backseat with our bags and climbed in the front. "We'll want to see Lake Michigan one of the days we are here," I informed my dad.

"Of course, Franco has to see that," my dad agreed readily. "Have you started school yet?"

"Two weeks," I answered, taking in the city again as we drove back to his place. Some of it looked more worn down than it had last time I was here. Chicago reminded me a lot of Seattle. I wasn't crazy about either of them.

"We'll need to take him to have a Chicago deep-dish pizza, too," my dad said, looking in the rearview mirror. "You like pizza, right?"

"Heck yeah, I do," Franco crowed. "Darius told me I had to eat vegetables, too."

"Darius has more discipline than either of us," my dad chuckled.

It all hit me then, we were already a family, and my dad was coming to join us. The happy thought immediately followed with the darker one: Damien had gotten everything he wanted and was killed and couldn't enjoy it.

I reached for my phone again and texted Amelia,

telling her we had landed and were on the way to my dad's place, and I missed her. My dad wasn't the only emotional one. Amelia said she missed me too and was proud of me.

I shoved the phone back into my pocket before I called her and cried. I hadn't had a nightmare since the bad one that sent me outside where Franco had to rescue me. I was a little worried being away from her would bring it back. It was nothing more than stupid pride that didn't want my dad to see me that way.

He'd seen the flashbacks, and that was bad enough. "Do you have boxes and everything already at the house?"

"I do," my dad glanced at me. "Have faith, son."

"Darius sings Wade in the Water to my mom when she's feeling bad, and he sings Amazing Grace with me when I go to sleep. Sometimes we sing other songs too, and he raps for me too," Franco giggled.

My dad looked at me again and smiled. "I knew someday you'd be here in this place. Your heart is too good for you not to be."

I became overwhelmed with emotion again and turned, staring out the window at the streets passing by in a blur. Indistinct faces were rushing around with purpose, and bodies were sitting still, begging for money. It was seamless and never-ending.

My mind wandered to all the people I've lost, everything I stood to lose, and finally to everything I had. It was an eye-opening thought that what I had should have been what I thought of first because everyone I've lost is already gone.

I'd spent so much time worrying and wondering what Caleb would think about me being with Amelia, and it was time wasted. The cold truth is Caleb wasn't here. He didn't have time to start a relationship with Amelia, even though he created life with her.

I don't know why it took seeing strangers on the street in a city I didn't live in to understand that I can't put my life on hold for reasons that there is no way we could predict the outcome of or wonder about hurting the feelings of someone no longer with us. Franco had been right to start to push me.

As intelligent as I was, I was still an idiot. I shook my head with disgust and sighed, causing my dad and Franco to stop talking and look at me. "Ignore me. I'm in my head, lost," I failed to come up with any other reason for my dramatics than that.

Honestly, Caleb would be happy that I was taking care of his kid. He'd be glad I was starting school too. Why was I thinking all this now? I kept still but berated myself silently.

"Those thoughts might be worth more than a penny," my dad broke the silence.

"I'm fine." I was happy to see we were minutes from my dad's house. Packing would give me a distraction, at least. "Where's the party tomorrow?"

"The president of the company's house. I can't wait for him to meet you, Darius, and now Franco. They've all heard so much about you and seen your pictures. Thank you for being here," my dad repeated.

"I'm happy I'm here, Dad. I think Skull will want to have a party for you when you get there, too. He wanted to come with but couldn't get out of his obligations." It was a slight lie. He did have set meetings, but he could have rescheduled them.

He was working on extracting himself from the club, and I wasn't going to pressure him to stop doing that. They'd had enough issues with his treatment of me, and with him following my footsteps, I didn't want fallout to land on him.

When my dad parked the car in the driveway, Franco shot like a bullet out of the door, flung mine open, and hugged me like he was afraid I would float off. "Do I need to sing?" his tiny voice asked.

I glanced at my dad, who looked worried and shook my head. "No, little man, I'm good. I promise it wasn't thoughts about the war." I squeezed him tight. "I was wondering why I've been so stupid and haven't asked your mom to marry me yet."

"For real?" Franco looked up, hopefully.

"For real," I promised. "I'm going to propose to Amelia after this round of chemo is over. We have about six months to plan something super cool."

"That's still a long time away!" Franco pouted but followed me as I grabbed the bags from the back.

"That means I get to be there for it," my dad interrupted. "I think that's pretty cool."

Franco's face transformed instantly. "Yeah! We can do something really fun!"

Crisis averted; attention diverted. "You want to bunk with me, or do you want one of us to sleep on the couch?" I offered Franco.

"I'll stay with you." Franco stayed on my heels as I

carried the bags down the hallway to the room my dad pointed out.

The rest of the night we spent catching up on everything. Franco talked my dad's ear off; it was as if they were long-lost friends finally reunited. It did my heart good to see it. Franco fell asleep quickly, and I snuck out to call Amelia.

"How are you feeling?" I asked after she answered.

"Better, they are going to release me tomorrow. Call Frankie after you hang up with me," Amelia demanded, her voice light.

"Okay, I will. You should see Franco and my dad together. It's like they've known each other all their lives. Franco asked if he could call him grandpa," I relayed as I settled into a living room chair.

"He's such a sweet boy." Amelia sighed, "That kid is going to go far in life. He isn't doing badly away from me, is he?"

"I think he was at first. He held my hand for a long time. Then he was attached to my dad." I got up, needing to move, and started to pack things from the living room in one of the open boxes.

"I wish I was there." It was the first time since she told me to come here that she sounded disappointed and wistful, and it hurt.

"Fuck, I do too. It feels like I've been gone weeks," I admitted with a wry grin.

"I'll welcome you back properly if you behave," Amelia flirted.

I groaned. "You're gonna kill me, Wings."

"I can promise an explosion, Boomer," Amelia fired back.

We talked for about an hour until she got too sleepy, and then I went to bed. I expected nightmares and only got dreams of having a family instead.

Chapter 45

The appearance of a Middle Eastern man rushing towards us was almost enough to make me engage, and a split-second later made me painfully realize that I was typecasting, and it was wrong. I blinked and intentionally slowed my breathing down. For four seconds inhale, hold for four seconds; exhale for another four seconds, and have lungs empty for four seconds. Repeat.

"Isaiah! You have company!" The man reached us and hugged my father.

"Stan!" My father bellowed. "I do! Meet my son Darius and my grandson Franco."

"Well, it's a pleasure to meet you, Franco," Stan held out his hand, and I fought the ridiculous urge to slap it away. I was mildly annoyed with my dad for not telling me and even angrier at myself for caring. Stan turned to me. "Darius, it's an honor. Thank you for your service to our country. I'm in the presence of a real-life hero," Stan saluted me and held out his hand.

I could practically hear Damien and Caleb shouting in my ear to man-up and shake the guy's hand. I held out my hand without saluting back. "Thank you, sir. It's a pleasure to meet you."

"Darius, I feel like I've watched you grow up; your father has talked about you so much. In the forty years I've known him, he has shown me what I should be like as a father. You should be proud of him," Stan told me sincerely, and I started to relax.

"He's pretty great," I agreed and felt Franco slide his hand into mine. "I hope I can impart at least a portion of that to Franco."

My dad was beaming, and he and Stan took us to the other people gathered and introduced us. I only remembered a handful of names though what stuck were the glowing remarks about my dad, his ethics, generosity, humor, and love of his family.

It was a side of my dad that I didn't get to see. Outside of me, these people were his family. They stood by him when I was injured, got him through hard times, and celebrated with him when I came home. I was immensely thankful to them for taking care of him.

Stan called everyone's attention, and the room fell silent. "We are here to wish Isaiah well in his retirement. He's worked very hard for it, and it's certainly our loss. However, it would be extremely insensitive of us to have him feel guilty for following his heart and moving closer to his family. Isaiah won some of our biggest and most lucrative accounts because of his family. He's leaving us in a better position than we've ever been, helped introduce the people taking over to our clients, and ensured all parties were comfortable. Isaiah is an incredible man, and I can say that he has enriched my life many times over."

There was a round of applause that had my dad looking somewhat bashful. He murmured his thanks to the group. I put my hand on his shoulder, and Franco moved to take his other hand.

"Isaiah, meeting your family today was an honor and privilege. We are in the presence of a real-life hero, folks. Remember those stressed-out meetings where we'd get a news alert about something happening overseas? Here is why. He's standing among us today, alive, healthy, decorated, and proud of his father. I'm not trying to put you on the spot Darius; you are famous in our group. Isaiah, thank you for your forty years with our company, friendship, intelligence, winning charisma, and sharing so much of yourself and your family with us from the bottom of my heart. We wish you the best that retirement has to offer and all the happiness one heart can hold," Stan wrapped up his speech and moved to hand my dad a gift.

Glad to have the attention back on my dad and not me, I gave him space to open it and stood a few steps away. He pulled out a framed photo of the group and a bundle of gift cards to places that were national chains. Nothing spectacular, and the picture was touching and made him smile fondly at it. Last, he pulled out a plaque made with crystal and wood.

This plaque was the culmination of my dad's years of hard work, neglect for the first part of my childhood, and the result of making his dream come true. He was more touched by the people who came, bestowed the honor upon him, and genuine emotions that he would be missed for more than his work alone. The gifts were unnecessary.

The party wound up a few hours later, and we left to get a late dinner of pizza that my dad had promised Franco. Many stories were told of my childhood when I was working out, right after I had met Skull and Trigger. My dad even talked about Trigger.

I was glad that we had come. It was nice to see that my dad's years of work paid off in more than just a paycheck and a see you later. My dad had real friends and a vested interest in their success. I loved it.

I snapped a couple of pictures while they were talking and sent them to Amelia. My phone was silent, so it didn't interrupt their conversation, and I told her about the party. Then I got in trouble for not calling Frankie. Damn. I can't believe I forgot to do that.

"Be right back," I told Franco and my dad as I slid out of the booth. I walked outside the restaurant and called Frankie.

"It's about damn time!" Frankie yelled in my ear. "You were supposed to call me yesterday!"

"Sorry, I fell asleep and forgot all about it. Something wrong?" I asked, worried.

"No. Wanted to tell you in six months, you will be an uncle again," Frankie answered excitedly.

"Damn, woman! You are fertile! Tell Jake to get off you and do something else with his time," I retorted.

"You can't blame him. I jump him all the time," Frankie laughed. I could hear Jake in the background, agreeing and laughing when Frankie relayed my message.

"Congrats, Frankie. Know the sex yet?" I

wondered. Izzy was a little jewel in my eyes, though I wasn't sure I could take the stress of another female. I was already plotting how to follow her on dates and cyber-stalk her to make sure she was safe from predators.

"We are going to have this one be a surprise too. I think it's a boy. Jake thinks it's a girl," Frankie informed me.

"We all know you are always right," I replied automatically with a smile. "Never argue with Frankie. Are you happy?"

"Ecstatic," she answered softly. "Are you going to do right by your woman?" Frankie sharply turned the conversation.

"I am. I'll probably wait until this rugrat is born now. Give me time to plan something extraordinary. I have the ring, Frankie. I wasn't ever not going to ask her to marry me. I think I only needed to get some things right in my head first," I glanced through the windows to Franco and my dad still talking. "Wait until you see these two together."

"Our family is growing, Darius," Frankie's voice had that soft, whimsical tone that she got when happiness filled her. "Amelia is doing good. Her cell counts are right where they should be. Imaging showed that the spread has reduced. The chemo is awful, but it's working."

I slumped against the window. "It's receding?"

"It is. See? If you had just been on it when she told you to call me, I would have had all this good news to you yesterday," Frankie teased me.

"Hey! *You* could have called me," I defended myself.

"I know, but it's so much more fun to torture you. Is your dad happy?" Frankie turned the conversation again.

"Ecstatic," I mimicked her. "My dad's good. Franco looks even more like Caleb than usual right now." I quickly snapped a photo with my phone and texted it to her.

A few seconds went by. "Wow! No kidding! You look a lot like your dad, too, Darius."

"I thought I looked like Tommy Vext," I joked, slightly embarrassed.

"You do. But I can call Tommy Vext sexy and not feel weird about it because he's a famous musician and not my brother," she clarified.

"Go jump your man," I grumbled. "I need to get back inside before Franco comes looking for me."

"That was already my plan," Frankie laughed. "See you soon, Darius."

My heart felt lighter as I walked back in. My dad looked up and gave me a questioning glance as I slid back into the booth. I pulled my phone out and shot Amelia a text letting her know Frankie told me, and I was going to have Franco call her.

I handed the phone to Franco. "Call your mom."

"Is she okay?" Franco looked worriedly at the phone.

"She is. Just call her," I prodded Franco gently.

My dad and I stayed silent while we waited, and I put my arm around Franco, so he didn't feel isolated. He moved a few inches closer to me and held the phone to his ear.

"Hi, Mom," Franco spoke quietly. "Da-uh, Darius told me to call you."

My heart skipped a beat. It sounded like Franco was going to call me dad. I bit the inside of my cheek and kept my face neutral while Franco listened to whatever Amelia told him.

"We are out having a Chicago pizza," Franco answered. He fell silent and was listening again. "Really?" his little voice cracked. His head was nodding as if she could see him, and I smiled. "I love you, Mom. Okay, I'll tell him. Bye."

He handed me back my phone, rested his head against my side, and started crying. Worried, I hugged him tight and shot my dad a look. "Hey, little man, what's wrong?"

"Mom said she's getting better for real," Franco cried, hiccupping. "She said we were going to have an ice cream party and celebrate, and she wants you to call her after we get back to grandpa's house."

My dad teared up, and I kissed the top of Franco's head. "I have some other good news for you," I waited until he looked up at me. "You're going to have another cousin soon. Auntie Frankie is going to have another baby."

I grew a little concerned when he buried his face in my side again. My dad shook his head at me. "He's probably overwhelmed," my dad said quietly. "We can go home now. I'll go get a to-go box."

I shifted slightly, wrapped my arms around the

sobbing boy, and rested my cheek on his head. "We got this, Franco. Your mom is going to get better. We will get married and have our little family. Your cousins will all look up to you and follow you around like annoying little monkeys pulling at you all the time."

Franco nodded his head but didn't let me go. Having been in his position, I knew how hard it was to see your mom suffer the way they did. The good news was often followed by bad; it was a cycle Franco had been in for a while.

"We got this," I repeated, sliding out of the booth when my dad returned and boxed the leftover pizza. "You and me, little man. We are a team. Remember what my mom used to tell me?"

"We don't always win, but we always fight," Franco's muffled voice came from my side.

"That's right," I smiled. "But this time, we're gonna win. Know how I know that?"

He finally moved and brought his tear-soaked face up. "How?"

"Because I have you, and we are a family," I tapped his chin.

Chapter 46

The next three months went by in a blur of doctor's appointments, school projects, babysitting, and helping field the remodeling my dad was doing in the small house he bought. He'd be in the state in a week and hopefully moving in.

Amelia had one bad scare since we'd been back, and I damn near had a complete mental breakdown. Skull kept me in check by helping him find a location to open a small gym. He'd told me that Damien was going to do that too. Skull felt like he would be honoring him by following through with it.

He'd put the word out that he was looking to retire and set up a meeting for the club to propose replacements and hold a vote. A few of the guys he said felt betrayed by him leaving. As much as he wouldn't admit it, that had him on edge.

It had me worried too. More than once, I sat there and wondered how Skull had gotten involved in things like that. He had done so much when we were younger to make sure it didn't happen, and it still did. He'd been so concerned Trigger would go that route, and instead, he took Trigger's place.

Amelia and I had talked about it extensively, and we both believed it had something to do with Trigger's death. As much as I had sought help and talked through my past with counselors about PTSD, I thought Skull had it.

Amelia was out with Frankie today doing girl stuff, she told me. Franco was in school, Jake had the kids, and I was alone. It was winter, so riding wasn't an option. I had all this nervous energy building in me, and I'd already cleaned the house, did my school work, worked out, prepped dinner, and been to my dad's property to check on the job.

Still restless, I sat in the chair and looked back over my life. It wasn't the route I would have taken, yet despite that, I still ended up where I wanted to be. It all changed when my mom got sick. That one single thing had been what changed everything, possibly the worst thing and the best thing, as her sickness brought them back to me.

Here I was, facing that same sickness in Amelia. Almost like it came full circle to that. A loop through hell, but here I was. I'd survived when two of the most incredible men I'd ever known didn't. I was sitting here because of those men. Sacrifice. Was that what all of it boiled down to in the end?

What would I have become if I hadn't joined the Navy? Not here waiting for Amelia, that's for sure. My mom sacrificed her family to move across the country and get an education. Both my parents sacrificed time with me to make their way to success, only to realize it was a sacrifice they could have avoided.

Skull and Trigger sacrificed their pride to get the help they needed to change their future direction. Only their sacrifice didn't pay off, and we lost Trigger to that same lifestyle he'd been avoiding. Were some things unavoidable?

I disagreed with that. We made our own destiny by the choices we make. Yet, that didn't feel right either. Amelia didn't choose to get sick and have cancer. However, she decided to fight it and refused to believe it would take her. Frankie didn't decide to lose her entire family, and she got what she wanted.

Was it possible that I could get everything I wanted? Sure, I supposed anything is possible. Why was I so fixated on losing it now that it was changing for the better? Fear? Why now? I used my deductive reasoning skills and ability to gather intelligence and analyze, and I kept returning to fear.

Maybe I answered my own question. Things all pointed to changing for the better, and my fear that it would backslide as it had many times before. I had my future in the palm of my hand, and I kept looking for ways to postpone it because I wanted that guarantee that it wouldn't change, and there was never a guarantee. The SEALs taught me that; they drummed it into me until I wanted to choke the instructors.

Was I afraid to be happy? God, that sounded utterly stupid and ridiculous. I *was* happy. Skull was breaking free from criminal behavior, and my dad was moving here to be close to me. I had pieces of Caleb and Damien in my life; I had an entirely new family. I had the love of the woman of my dreams. I was fulfilling my dream of helping others; what the hell was wrong with me?

Fear. That's what was wrong with me. I stood up. I was thinking in circles, getting nowhere. It was irritating the hell out of me. I went to grab a piece of blank paper and sat at the kitchen table, and tried to apply math and logic to the issue as I would for making an explosive.

After five minutes of doodling, I threw the pen down in frustration. You can't apply logic to a fear. I grabbed my phone and went to lean against the wall, looking out the slider to the backyard.

"Hey, Dad," I said when he answered. "I need your help."

"You've got it, son. What's going on?" my dad's warm voice washed over me.

"My brain is a mess. I feel like I'm stuck in a muddy hole. Am I afraid to be happy?" I blurted out.

There was silence on the other end of the phone, and I looked at it to make sure I hadn't lost the call. It showed I was still connected, and I put the phone back to my ear in time to hear my dad say, "I think you need to back that up for me. Are you and Amelia okay?"

"Yeah, we are fine. Amelia's out with Frankie today, and my brain is in this weird state where I keep thinking about everything and the future, and I keep trying to rationalize holding off on doing what I want. I've tried applying logic to it and analyzing it, and I'm going in circles. I know how far I've come from when I got home from the war, and then I get stuck on who I used to be before joining and the completely different person I was when I came home, to the again stranger I seem to be now, and somewhere in the mix of all that, what if everything falls apart again?" I rushed out, understanding that it was a pandora's box I had dumped on my dad.

My dad let out a small chuckle and then sighed. "Darius, you aren't afraid to be happy. You are alone today and have downtime, right?"

"Yeah," I answered, confused.

"When was the last time you had real alone downtime?" His question made me stop and think.

"A long time," I replied slowly.

"I'd say it's all catching up to you. Your heart knows it has what it needs to thrive, and your brain is trying to reconcile that with everything else. It's like a fail-safe. Apply what you did when making explosives in a controlled situation where you weren't using it in combat. You built-in something to protect it from going off, right?" My dad's voice echoed in my mind.

Something he said clicked. "My brain is trying to protect me from being too comfortable with the good upswing?"

"Sort of; your makeup is to analyze, observe, and form plans. It's what is happening now that you don't have all kinds of other things pulling you and distracting you. The what-if game that people play, if you will," my dad supplied.

I laughed. "In other words, I'm overthinking."

"Basically," he laughed with me. "You can't foresee the future, and you are trying to. Understandable when your loved one's life is on the line. Instead of planning for eventualities that might never arise, live for today. Life is precious, and if something happens, you take it a day at a time. You would regret it for the rest of your life if you waited to grab something that meant as much to you as Amelia and Franco do."

My dad's words showed undeniable wisdom as he lived through losing my mom. "I know," I said on an exhale. "Does it matter that I miss that person I was before the war, before losing Trigger?"

"It matters because you rebuilt yourself into who you are now. Trauma shapes you, son. That person still exists in pieces inside you, and you are merging all the people you were into who you are becoming. It's an ongoing life process, Darius. Changing means we are growing and learning. Didn't you say that to me once?" My dad tossed it out there for consideration.

Had I? I couldn't remember. It was a sentiment I agreed with; the only change that scared me was loss. "The doctors told Amelia yesterday that cancer had shrunk to almost nothing after the surgery last month. They think one more round of chemo will kill it off."

"That scares you?" My dad sounded bewildered.

"No. I was only relaying the latest news. I think the part that scares me is the recurrence chances. Realistically, how much more of this can Amelia's body take? Amelia's spirit is a warrior queen; I don't think she's breakable. On the other hand, her body has a limit on how much it can endure," I paced a little, not entirely comfortable voicing those words.

"You'd be surprised what the human body is capable of, Darius. With a spirit as strong as Amelia's, I don't think you've seen everything she is capable of; don't doubt, son, just believe. Taking leaps of faith isn't easy, and I know the things you've lived through make that harder, but the payoff is more than worth it," my dad advised. "Amelia won't let you fall, you take that leap, and she will leap with you and sprout those wings you know she has. It's okay to soar."

Fuck, my dad had just nailed it on the head. That's what had me worried; my body had physically jolted with his words. "Holy shit, dad, you got it. That's my fear. Letting her carry me and my fears. I don't want to be a burden on her. Damn."

"Oh, son, you are looking at it wrong. Taking that leap of faith shows Amelia you have trust in her. Reverse the situation. Do you think she's afraid you won't catch her when she makes independent leaps? Even if you both fall, you fall together and rebuild together. You share the burdens. Marriage is a partnership, not one person carrying the weight for both of you," my dad's voice was soft but firm.

"Jesus, I'm an idiot." I smacked the heel of my hand on my forehead. "Amelia would kick my ass for thinking that way too. It should have been obvious to me. I saw how you and mom were together, and that's what I want. I think it's what I have unless I misread the relationship."

My dad laughed. "You aren't. Don't be so hard on yourself, Darius. Amelia is your first serious relationship, to the best of my knowledge. Am I correct in that?"

"Yes," I wasn't sure where he was heading. "I avoided relationships after that stunt in high school. I dated, but casually. Then Amelia showed up, and my entire mindset changed in about two seconds flat.”

"It was that way for me and your mom too. I knew the moment I laid eyes on her,” his voice turned nostalgic. “Not a day goes by that I don’t think about her.”

"Thanks, Dad. You helped me see what I needed to see. Can’t wait until you are here and you get to meet her face to face.” I caught him up on the remodeling, and then we hung up. I needed to get creative and think of a spectacular way to show this woman how much she meant to me.

Chapter 47

swear, you beautiful and crazy girl, you do this on purpose," I grinned at Izzy as I changed her clothes. "Couldn't wait to do this at home. No, you come here and dive into the muddiest hole there is. It's all gonna get used against you when you start dating. I'm keeping note of all the dastardly things you do."

"I hungwy," Izzy said as I toweled her hair dry.

"You're always hungry. How is it that DC missed the mud, and you didn't? Huh? Did you roll in it just to make me do this?" I grabbed her before she could run out of the bathroom. "Oh no, you don't. Socks, Izzy."

"No!" she pouted.

"Yes," I scolded, "it's not warm enough for bare feet."

Her little defiant face stared back at me, trying to gauge how far she could push me. It felt like hours we had a staredown, and she finally relented, plopping down on the ground and putting her feet in the air. It took all my willpower not to laugh.

"Thank you, now go find your brother and Franco. I'll get us a snack," I picked her up and put her on her feet.

She bolted out of the bathroom with a squeal. "Fwanco!" she screamed. I loved how her r's sounded like w's. That kid was the perfect mix of devious from Jake and Frankie. Their raucous laughter floated down the hallway.

I was rinsing Izzy's clothes when Amelia stepped into the bathroom, laughing. "Izzy's going to be a hellacious teenager."

"She's already got that trait down pat," I grumbled, standing up. "Terrible two's, DC wasn't this bad."

"He's making up for it now with Izzy as the ringleader," Amelia's peal of laughter made my heart skip a beat. "You don't fool me one little bit, Darius. You love it."

I grinned again because it was true. "Somewhere up there, Caleb and Damien are laughing their asses off at me."

"Was your dad upset that we had to postpone his party?" Amelia leaned against me, pressing me against the counter.

"Nah. Dad can't wait for another baby to play with." I slid my arms around her waist and leaned down to kiss her. "I can't either, honestly. Frankie makes cute babies."

"That she does. Come on. We can't leave them alone too long. Izzy might figure out how to turn the fireplace on or something else equally as dangerous," Amelia moved and tugged on me.

I groaned. "You shouldn't have put that out there. I swear that kid latches on to everything she shouldn't know and learns them only to spite us."

Amelia laughed again. "She's testing you. That girl knows she has you wrapped around her pinky. Nothing but putty."

Franco had them at the kitchen table playing with Play-Doh. Amelia sat down and started playing with them while I sliced up an apple, got some crackers, and cubed some cheese. That was a mess I could deal with cleaning.

It was still between lunch and dinner time. Izzy's birth wasn't as traumatic as DC's was. I hoped that this was even easier. Frankie had been calm when they dropped the kids off, and Jake was frazzled. My dad was on his way over, too.

I glanced at my watch. "You guys want pizza for dinner?"

"Macawoni and cheese," Izzy demanded with a pout. She was still irritated with me for bathing her, I saw.

"What does everyone else want? You can't always have everything you want, Izzy." I looked around the table. DC only stared back at me with Damien's eyes. Franco wasn't any better than me when it came to Izzy.

"Mac and cheese is okay with me," Franco shrugged.

Amelia hid her smile. "I'll cook us up some chicken; the adults can have a salad."

I narrowed my eyes at Izzy. "I've got my eyes on you." I pointed my fingers from my eyes to hers, and she giggled.

"Sucker," Amelia cheerily murmured as she walked by me to take the chicken out to prep it. I couldn't argue with her. DC went along with whatever Izzy wanted, and so did Franco.

"Devil child," I muttered and followed Amelia.

"Because she knows you all will cave," Amelia stated. "A pretty girl pouts, and men fall all over themselves to give her what she wants."

"You didn't pout," I snarked.

"Nope, I swung my hips because I'm not two," Amelia fired back. When she was right, she was right.

We seasoned the chicken Cajun style and left it to marinate in the fridge. My dad got there a few minutes later and dove headfirst into the Play-Doh mess while listening to Franco chatter about school.

"Paints a nice picture, doesn't it?" Amelia stood next to me in the doorway.

"Needs my obnoxious sister and her whipped husband to complete it." I put my arm around Amelia's shoulders and kissed her head.

"You aren't one to talk," Amelia joked quietly.

"Yeah, but I make it look good," I moved and struck a pose that made Izzy break into giggles, followed by DC.

"Silly Uncle D," DC told me with a heart-melting smile.

"Sucker," Amelia repeated affectionately.

The kids happily played with my father until dinner time, and he magically got them to clean up their mess, to the shock of Amelia and me. She made our salads while I used my extraordinary culinary skills to make a box of macaroni and cheese.

"Your dad has the magic grandpa touch," Amelia

remarked as we watched him herd the kids with their empty dishes into the kitchen and then lead them back to the living room to watch a movie.

"No joke." I peeked around the corner and saw Izzy and DC on his lap while Franco put a movie on to watch.

We had just finished up the dishes when we got the call. Frankie had the baby, and he was a boy. Thankfully smaller than DC, though not by much.

"It's a boy!" Amelia told my dad. "No name yet. Eight pounds, two ounces."

"I'll watch these guys if you want to go see him," my dad offered.

"Thanks, Dad. We'll wait until tomorrow morning and let Frankie rest." Amelia and I sat on the couch, and by the movie's end, both toddlers were asleep. I was setting DC down in his bed when my phone beeped.

I quickly silenced it, so it didn't wake up the kids and walked back out to the hallway and looked.

Frankie wants to know why you haven't come to see your nephew yet; Jake had texted.

I was going to be polite and let her rest for the night; I wrote back.

I quote, she said, get your ass to the hospital now, Jake replied.

I snorted and went to show Amelia the texts. "Looks like we are going after all," I told my dad. "You can stay?"

"Sure can. Franco and I will make some popcorn and watch another movie." My dad shooed me off. "Go on, get."

Amelia rolled her eyes but went to get her purse. "Be good," she told Franco and gave them kisses on the cheek.

Traffic was light, and we made good time. Jake met us in the hallway, looking as happy as could be. "She's been waiting impatiently. The birth was relatively easy, and she's doing great."

"Of course, she is. The woman has supernatural powers," Amelia grinned. "Show us number three."

Jake let us in, and Frankie beamed at us. "Here's our goblin," she told us.

"Please tell me you didn't name him that," I quipped and bent over to see the little guy.

"He has a squished-up face, and he looks like one." Frankie held him out to me. "Meet William Darius, your godson, and nephew."

"Are you joking right now?" I whispered and looked at the little bundle in my arms.

"Nope," Jake answered. "We'd like you both to be his godparents. Just like with Izzy."

Amelia tapped my arm, and I handed the baby over. "You gave him my name?" I looked between Jake and Frankie while Amelia whispered to the baby.

"Sure did. William's middle name, at least. That way, I am guaranteed a babysitter for life," Frankie smiled victoriously.

I quirked my lips up. "Your daughter took a mud bath after you dropped her off," I told Jake. "You sure you want me to babysit?"

He laughed. "Doesn't surprise me. You can handle it."

I leaned over and hugged Frankie. "Thank you. William is after your dad, isn't it?"

Jake nodded. "And my grandpa."

"Now, stay off your wife for a minute. Damn, you're gonna have a sports team," I reached over and fist-bumped Jake. "You did good, Frankie."

"I always do. We have some good guardian angels that make sure of that," Frankie took the baby back that Amelia handed her. "No complications. Dr. Waters is letting me go home tomorrow afternoon."

"So soon?" I was shocked by that. After Izzy, they kept her for a couple of days at least.

"It's not like Frankie gave them an option," Jake huffed out. "She'll be okay, Darius."

We talked for another half an hour, and then Jake walked us back out. We ended up on a route through the ER because we hadn't been paying attention to where we were going. Jake's arm flew out and slammed into my chest.

It halted me, and I glared at him until I saw he was looking at who was coming in the door. I didn't catch it at first because medics were blocking my view. Then I saw him. Skull covered in blood. My knees buckled as a flashback to Trigger hit my brain.

Chapter 48

Eyes on me, soldier!" Amelia's voice penetrated the fog, and my vision came back into focus. My eyes snapped to hers, and I took a slow breath in.

"It's happening again," I whispered. Jake steadied me.

"No, it's not," Amelia grabbed my hand and dragged me over to the counter, Jake on our heels. "That man that was brought in, this is his brother. What can you tell us about him?"

The nurse's eyes flashed to Jake, and recognition dawned. "Are you Francesca's husband?"

"Yes. Can you help us?" Jake asked.

"Hold on," she ran back behind the closed doors.

"No badge anymore, sorry, Darius. Hopefully, Francesca's admirers will work," Jake apologized and kept his hand on my back.

The nurse came hustling back. "Jamal Morrison, correct?"

A weird feeling washed over me, and all the hair on my body raised. It was that same feeling I got when overseas, and shit was about to go sideways. I nodded my response to the nurse and did my best not to crush Amelia's hand that was holding mine.

"Two gunshot wounds and a knife wound. They are prepping Mr. Morrison for surgery right now," she told us. "I let the doctors know that you are out here and family. From what I overheard, I don't think anything is fatal."

Yet, that feeling didn't abate at all. And when I turned around, I was face to face with a cop. It was an instant replay in my mind of Trigger once again. It didn't take me down this time. However, all my defenses closed around me.

"Hey, Jake." The cop looked at me. "The nurse told me you are the victim's family?"

"He is, and he's in shock. He was here visiting my wife and me to see our new baby," Jake stepped in, halfway standing in front of me. "We took a wrong turn because we were talking and ended up here when we saw Jamal getting brought in. Can you tell us anything?"

"I was hoping he could tell me more about Jamal," the cop's eyes flicked between Jake and me. "I don't have a lot of information to go on. I heard the shots fired, headed in that direction, then the call came in, and I responded."

"There were no people on the scene to question, Mark?" Jake asked skeptically.

"Not the honest type," Mark responded cautiously. "I'm not looking to cause trouble, and I'm not accusing you of anything, sir. I'm trying to understand what happened so I can go after who is responsible."

"Where did this happen?" I reached out and

pulled Jake back to stand even with me. In my mind, it presented a united front.

"First, you need to know Darius was on my squad with me," Jake told Mark.

His eyebrows raised slightly, and his entire demeanor changed. "You aren't part of the Prince's then?"

"Not anymore. When I returned from overseas, I was. Because Jamal wanted to take care of me. I was pretty fucked up," I told the cop.

"I can only imagine. This incident happened outside of the Prince's clubhouse. I was a block over when I heard the shots. By the time I got there, which was only minutes, I found Jamal on the ground and a few of the club members standing back near the door who claimed they were inside when it happened, and they saw nothing," Mark lowered his voice and gestured to some empty chairs with no people around them.

I took a step to follow him, and Jake held me back a moment. "Mark won't fuck you over. I don't believe it, anyway. When I worked with him, he was diligent and respectful. I've never seen him go after anyone because of their skin color. Tell me if you feel uncomfortable at any time, and I'll call in our lawyer."

"Skull was leaving them, Jake. This shit is them taking their revenge. It could have been me, and may still be, but Skull was protecting me. The same way he protected Damien, only more because we have history. There is not one shred of doubt in my mind that this is why he is in here right now," I whispered, furious.

"Do you know who?" Jake's gaze sharpened. "I'm

putting some of my club on watch duty at your house.”

“No, Skull never told me specific names. He’ll have to be the one to answer that, and I am sure he won’t unless they come after me. Skull is still loyal to these guys, and I’m betting that hasn’t changed, even after this,” I snapped and then tried to calm myself.

Amelia tugged me. “Don’t leave him sitting there; it looks suspicious. Go, tell Francesca what’s going on, Jake, so she doesn’t worry. I’ve got him.”

Jake glanced at Amelia and nodded. “I’ll be back in a few minutes.”

We went and sat down across from Mark. “Jake went to tell Francesca where he is,” Amelia filled him in when he glanced at Jake’s retreating form.

“They had another baby?” Mark smiled softly.

“A little boy,” Amelia couldn’t help but grin.

“Jake deserves it. I’m sorry if I came across as abrupt. That wasn’t my intention,” Mark apologized to me. “I’m not going to ask you what activities Jamal was involved in or anything like that. I want to find whoever did this. We clear?”

“Clear,” I responded. I didn’t feel like I could relax.

“Approximately eight twenty-three, I heard two gunshots. I served too, and I know what they sound like and where they were coming from direction-wise. Instinct had me headed there when the call came through, and I responded that I was en route. When I arrived, lights flashing, I saw a body lying on the ground and three men outside the door. I radioed for an ambulance immediately, then backup. The three men at the door claimed to know nothing and saw nothing.

Backup arrived and began questioning and processing the scene," Mark broke it down for us. "I followed the ambulance. Both to make sure whoever did this didn't come to finish it and question Jamal."

"He won't snitch, you know that, right?" I bluntly stated.

"Figured as much. I'm sure you are well aware that the club is on our radar, and Jamal is too. We know he's the club president and part of the reason for its growth and success. I'm not asking you to rat on him; I'm asking what would make members that report to Jamal turn on him. There's no one else it could be other than one of his," Mark supplied.

"Jamal was retiring," I answered after a pregnant silence. "I'm with you; it was an inside job. All I knew was that some members saw his leaving as a betrayal since they joined under him. They are loyal to a fault. Given what I know of them and my observation skills, there could be fear that his leaving is a sign of the club falling apart or a hostile takeover. Jamal leaving could be construed as him saving his ass or that he turned on them. He never gave me names and kept me well away from anything considered illegal."

"This was retaliation for him retiring?" Mark looked surprised by that.

"I'm almost one hundred percent positive about that. Jamal's doing it for me. I don't want to lose him the same way we lost our brother when we were teenagers. Well, I was a teenager. This club was never his path; I think he went this route to avenge our friend's murder. It made him feel like he wasn't weak in the face of it, and the next time someone came at him like that, he'd be able to stop it from happening. Jamal is complex, and he is not a bad person," I explained, feeling the need to defend him.

"Jamal was stepping down and out of the club for you?" Mark questioned, trying to understand the dynamics.

"Yeah." I didn't feel like Mark needed to know all of our histories."There's a lot of backstory there that isn't relevant to the situation," I scrubbed my hands over my face. "Me, my family, which includes him, he didn't want any of us to catch the fallout from that lifestyle."

"I'm not trying to pry. The information gives me a good read on who he is as a person, not someone we are trying to pin crimes on; that sounded wrong. Your friend didn't pull any weapon or retaliate, there were no signs of a fight, and I think that is what I am trying to understand," Mark frowned at his words.

Jake showed back up then and sat next to me. "Pick apart the club, man. Look to see who suddenly went out of town or is now lying low. Use the contacts you have to watch them and track movements. Listen for the leaks that will invariably happen. They'll want to discredit Jamal. Don't fall prey to the rumors. Some may be true, but these guys are slick."

Mark bristled subtly. "I know."

"Where was Jamal shot?" I changed the subject.

"Shoulder and chest, but it missed the heart, or I wouldn't be here," Mark said unapologetically. "It didn't look good, but in my opinion, nothing was fatal. A knife wound to the side."

Amelia stood, shaken. "I'll call Dad and let him know what's going on."

Six hours later, Skull was moved to a private room and put under guard. They wouldn't let me back to see him; however, the doctor came out to tell me that they replaced his shoulder, stitched him up, and pointed out that Skull was lucky. With a one-inch difference, he would either be dead or paralyzed.

I texted Jake to let him know, and we headed home with Amelia driving because my nerves got shot all to hell.

Chapter 49

They kept Skull in the hospital for a week. Then he spent forty-eight hours incarcerated because one of the brass was out for his blood. They couldn't hold him longer than that because they had nothing on him, and Skull wasn't happy about it.

They released him, and I brought Skull back to my house. Amelia and Franco fussed over him, and my dad came by to check on him and help with physical therapy. I was a tad worried it would bring trouble and texted Jake that Skull was at my house.

Jake told me his club was still monitoring us, and he pulled some strings on the police force to have a patrol come by every so often. Feeling slightly better, I relaxed. Skull was released, my dad's retirement/house warming party was the next day, and after that, I was proposing.

No one knew of my plan except Franco, and that kid was a master at keeping secrets. Jake knew I was proposing, and he would follow me to the site, but that was it. I'd called in some gigantic favors from General Allen, one of the brass we reported to overseas that took a particular interest in our squad.

It was an enlightening talk with the general. We talked about Caleb and Damien, and he asked about Jake. PTSD came up more than once, forcing me to think about the direction my life had taken me.

It wasn't until that conversation with him that it hit me. I didn't want to be the person I was before life knocked me over. I missed the simplicity and directed plans I had formed and often felt like I was waiting for the next ax to fall. Who I was now built off that foundation and shaped me with each event I saw, lived, and felt. My world wasn't insular anymore; it felt like I had no walls. Each of my scars was a battle won.

Some days, I thought I had come full circle, and on days like today, I realized I hadn't; I just changed the circle's shape to something else. Each moment spent with the people I loved solidified that. Maybe the mark I left on lives wouldn't be as large as the ones that Damien and Caleb left; I was okay with that now. My duty was to live my life and not try to live up to their shadows.

I was an adult; it shouldn't have taken me this long to figure it out. It wasn't anything my dad hadn't told me already. That kid that had aced all his classes still existed in me, I was doing the same thing now, and my support group cheering me on had grown.

"Hey, bookworm!" Skull said over my shoulder. "Make me a sandwich."

I laughed. "Make it yourself. You've still got one good arm."

"Just had to make sure you didn't lose yourself in your head, man. You had that distant look," Skull tapped me on the back of my head. "Now, you calculatin' again."

I smirked. "Maybe we should make a bet and arm wrestle to see who wins."

Skull laughed. "No bet. Not even if I had two good arms. I ain't stupid. The student surpassed the teacher some time ago." He sat down across from me and gave me his own calculating smile. "They accepted my offer."

I frowned for a moment. "What offer?" Then it hit me. "The building for the gym?"

"That's the one. Now I gotta keep my ass out of the clink to make it work. Going legit takes some serious work. That's what the shit that got me here started out as. I made a couple of business moves that put the club into a legitimate territory, genuine business. One of the guys got pissed that they'd have to pay taxes now," Skull shook his head.

"You got shot over taxes?" A deep belly laugh burst from my lips.

"And stabbed, don't forget that part." Skull's eyes crinkled at the corners with his wry smile. "I'm sure he's paying for it now. That move put them right into the spotlight."

"That would not have been the reason I would have thought," I chuckled. "You started legitimizing things back before I even left."

"Some of the guys aren't too smart. I think the guy they voted in as the new president understands." Skull one-shoulder shrugged. "If not, it's not my problem. I'm no longer attached to any of the paperwork for the shell company, the bar, or anything. I cut all the strings. Left a legacy to your boy in the process."

"What do you mean?" I sat back and crossed my arms over my chest.

"New bike shop opened last month. Other end of town from the club." Skull stared at me, waiting.

"Okay?" I didn't get it.

"Damien, Darius. I called it Demon Prince," he spelled out for me. "Couple of the new members can turn wrenches. They'll manage it."

I raised my eyebrows and whistled. "Nice. Bet that went over well."

"As I said, they ain't too smart." Skull shrugged again with one shoulder.

He stopped talking when Franco walked in, followed by Amelia. "When you getting' that bike, kid? I'll teach you to ride when this useless thing heals up," Skull nodded to his shoulder.

"Aren't you supposed to be moving it?" Franco frowned. "That's what the therapist said."

"See? Franco knows what's up." I stifled my laugh at Skull's expression.

"He'll get a bike when his mother decides she can live with the thought of him riding with you," Amelia fired off as she walked by. "I've heard the stories."

"I can help you do the exercises," Franco offered, setting his backpack down.

"Relentless," Skull sighed. "Come on. I'll let you torture me."

I grinned and followed Amelia. "What did the doctor say?"

"Scans look good," was all she said.

I didn't know how to take it, and I understood she

wouldn't lie, so I accepted her answer. "Caterers are all set for tomorrow, and I ordered an ice cream cake that we can pick up on the way. Dad's an ice cream fanatic."

"My mouth just watered. The cake is all mine and Dad's. We aren't sharing," Amelia stood on her toes and kissed me. "Maybe I'll share a little."

The next twenty-four hours passed in a blur of homework for Franco and me and then a lot of running around to get everything ready for the proposal and the party. Frankie had me invite their club since I was now a part of it, and I was glad I did.

My dad was the happiest I'd seen him since my mom died. He played with the kids, talked with the adults, ate a bunch of food, and didn't stop smiling. He was welcomed into the fold with no hesitation and looked like he'd been around the group for years.

Skull didn't engage much with the club members, and I couldn't tell if that was because of them, him, or both. He sat out of the way and remained quiet and content for the most part. Yet when the rumble of several motorcycles sounded in the distance, he snapped to attention, as did every club member.

Jake became the soldier he had been overseas in a flash. We were in the backyard. An alley ran along the back sides of the houses on this street. From the way the sound echoed, we couldn't tell if the bikes were coming down the alley or pulling up on the road.

Three of the club moved to block the alley, and three more went to the front. Jake and I stood in the middle, waiting to see which direction we needed to go. Frankie and Amelia herded the kids into the house. I glanced at Skull and faltered for a brief moment at the look on his face. He looked unsure.

To his credit, Jake didn't turn his fury on Skull. He'd seen how Skull hadn't shown an ounce of aggression, anger, or attitude towards anyone. Through the house's windows, I saw the guys out front signaling as the guys in the alley called out in incoming.

Jake cursed. "Stay with me. We are stronger together. Still got the moves?"

"Like I could forget," I bit out. "We can't let this go far."

"It won't," Jake promised. "I've been carrying since it went down. Too many years on the force and overseas to trust that they'd let it go with a couple of bullets."

"Three bikes in front," Jake's friend Mike called out.

My dad went to look. "Dad, get inside with the kids and Frankie."

"No, son. This is my house." My dad stood slightly behind Jake and me.

"If more than three show up back here, things will get ugly," Skull warned with a waver in his voice. "I'm not armed, Dar."

"You shouldn't be either," Jake snapped. "They're watching you. Misstep, and they'll bring you in again."

Skull closed his mouth and nodded. I knew that Jake wasn't saying it out of derision; his tone was because there was a danger to his family. The two were a lot alike in that way.

"Watch my six," I said softly to Jake and moved to

the alley. It struck me as odd that the bikes in front were already here, but whoever was coming around back wasn't. The Prince's weren't that disorganized.

"Go high," Jake told me, moving behind me.

I nodded and hopped, grabbing the low branch of the tree in the corner of the yard. Jake hadn't drawn his gun, and I wondered if he had realized the same thing as me. There had to be two different things going on right now.

I climbed a little higher in the tree until hidden from view but not so high I couldn't jump down fast without getting hurt. I looked back at the house and signaled to Jake that his friend was coming.

"They are there as a deterrent. It's not an act of aggression," Mike told Jake. He spoke softly but loud enough that I could hear him.

"From what?" Jake snapped again. "How the fuck do they even know he's here?"

"The shooter," Mike answered. "One of the guys out front said to check Skull's phone."

"The guy coming up the alley is the guy who shot and stabbed Skull?" I asked, wanting the confirmation.

"That's what they say," Mike told me.

"Get out of the alley," I barked to the club members that had taken up a position as a barrier. "I've got this."

"Do what he says." Jake reinforced me. "Don't cross any lines, Boomer."

"Hell no, I got way too much on the line for that shit. My aim is disabling. Nothing more." I saw the headlight glint and motioned to Jake. "Call it in."

Jake looked back at Skull, then at me, and nodded. He pulled out his phone, made a call, spoke softly, and shifted closer to me. We were both aware that Skull knew who the shooter was, and I was disadvantaged because I didn't. Loyalty ran deep with Skull, even for those that betrayed him.

My timing had to be perfect. I shifted my weight and made sure I was clear of the fence, crouched, and watched as the guy slowly made his way down the alley. He was peering into each backyard as he crept closer.

It was ridiculous to think that he was sneaking up on anyone. He was on a damn Harley; it's not like those are quiet. I dropped when he was right under me. He must have caught movement out of the corner of his eye because he looked up and planted an elbow in my gut right as mine slammed down on the spot between his neck and shoulder.

He crumbled, and Frankie came running out with a cable tie, making me laugh. Jake bound his wrists, used his shirt to pull the gun from the guy's pocket, and set it on the ground out of his reach.

"This guy won't be out long," Jake told me. "Mark is coming in from the north end of the alley. Skull, if you want this to end, you'll have to ID him as the one who shot you."

"Yep," Skull answered sourly, not looking happy at the prospect.

"No one got hurt, Skull," I reminded him.

"Can't believe you let that pussy get a shot in on you," Skull huffed derisively. "I taught you better than that."

Jake belted out a laugh at the statement. "Damien would've made you run laps for that. Give me your damn phone, Jamal, so I can delete whatever tracker is on there."

Chapter 50

Franco had loaded his backpack with the things we would need, I had the ring in my pocket, and we were all dressed up. Franco looked way more nervous than I did, and it was sweet. We both wanted it to be perfect, and neither complained that Amelia was taking longer to get ready.

Jake was five minutes out anyway, and Skull and my dad would ride with them. All anyone knew, except Jake, was that I had put together an unforgettable family date for all of us. Jake's friends Mike and Susie had their kids for a few hours, and I told Jake to have Frankie bring her camera.

I heard the footsteps in the hallway and turned to look, my breath catching in the back of my throat. Amelia was a vision in a sheer red silky-looking shirt and pair of black leather pants, complete with some sexy red half boot type shoes. She had knotted some type of wrap around her head, covering the hair that started to grow back in.

"Close your mouth, son," my dad joked. "Amelia, you look stunning."

I snapped my jaw closed and glared at my dad.

"Biggest understatement ever," I said, walking up to her. "I'm going to fantasize about you in this outfit," I whispered in Amelia's ear.

Her rich laughter filled the room. "Glad that it's a hit. Doesn't look like I am late, either."

"Worth it," I raked my gaze over Amelia again.

Skull sat on the couch with a smirk, shaking his head at me. I was sure he knew what I was up to; they probably all knew. Skull was lucky that Mark hadn't taken him into the station last night for more questioning after yesterday's incident, and I think Jake had something to do with that. Regardless, I was happy he'd be a part of this.

I turned to the window when I heard the crunch of tires on the driveway and felt a smile spread across my face. It was time; this was happening. My heart strummed out a strange rhythm for a moment and then settled.

Franco raced out the doorway pulling my dad behind him. "You're okay to ride with Jake, right?" I asked Skull, my hand low on Amelia's back.

"Yep, all cool, man. I got your pops, right?" Skull patted my shoulder.

"Yeah, Franco will ride with us," I reminded him, steering them both to the driveway after locking the house.

"So, any clue as to where we are going?" Amelia glanced at me as I walked her to the Jeep.

"You'll find out soon enough," I grinned, unable to hide my excitement.

"You look like a kid about to get caught sneaking

out of the house," Amelia laughed.

"Hey now, I never had to do that. I was the good kid," I scoffed, helping her in and closing the door. I rounded the car and motioned for Jake to follow me. I caught his grin and tried to school my face.

This little scheme of mine had taken a lot of coordination and several favors. It was rare I was able to surprise either Amelia or Frankie, and I had a feeling this would get both of them. I pulled out and headed to the joint base.

Amelia would know something was up when we pulled off on that exit, so I didn't have long to keep things a secret too much longer. Franco chattered about some game he was playing with Skull and how he thought Skull was letting him win, but he would get him in the end.

I got a raised eyebrow look when I took the exit that would lead us to what used to be the Air Force base. Amelia silently reached for her purse and pulled out her ID as we pulled up to the guard gate. I handed them over, saw the soldier look at a piece of paper and smile, handed us a day pass, and let us through. I waited for Jake to get through and then led them to the airfield.

"What are you up to?" Amelia turned in her seat to thoroughly look at me.

"I thought it would be fun for Franco to get to experience you in your element," I told her, quickly getting out of the Jeep and opening the door for Franco, who scooted out and was practically vibrating with excitement. I went to help Amelia out with a faint smile on my face.

"What exactly does that mean?" she asked me, with a slight look of happiness glinting in her eyes.

"Darius! What is going on?" Frankie called out.

Jake had a very amused look on his face. "I don't even want to know the favors you called in for this. Hell of a surprise date."

Skull and my dad were giving me considering looks. I led them to the designated hanger and held the door open for them to file in, Amelia hanging back to kiss me and grasp my hand. It felt like my heart was going to explode.

"Captain Wade!" a deep male voice called out excitedly.

Amelia stopped in her tracks and gaped at me. "Are you kidding me right now?"

Franco was bouncing on his toes, a grin splitting his face. "We wanted to surprise you, Mom!"

"You succeeded, you little rascal," she tousled his hair and returned her gaze to me for a moment before turning and holding open her arms to the waiting pilot that had flown with her on most of her missions overseas. "Scotty," Amelia said as he wrapped her in a bear hug.

"Are you ready to take her up?" Captain Scott asked her.

Amelia spun back to me, her eyes as wide as I've ever seen, and she whirled around to face the pilot. "Lead the way."

Frankie ran up to my side. "We get to go on a plane that Amelia is flying?"

"Sure do. The same plane Amelia flew while she

was in service. Cool, huh?" I waggled my eyebrows at Frankie.

Skull looked a little unsure, and my dad was about as excited as Franco was. We followed them out to the airfield where the cargo bay was open, and Franco squealed. Jake was still grinning and shaking his head at me.

"Give me the pack," I told Franco, then shooed him up to his mom. "Frankie, go with them. Sit up in the cockpit with Franco."

Frankie gave me an incredulous look and then shot forward to join them. I stifled my laugh at the exuberance the two were showing. I couldn't have hoped for a better reaction than I was receiving. Jake and I led the way up the cargo ramp, memories flooding my mind.

"Man, this brings back memories," Jake told me softly. "Never thought I would set foot on one of these again."

"You okay?" I checked him quickly for signs of something that would trigger one of the bad memories.

"Yeah, I'm good. Gotta hand it to you, and so are you. How the hell did you pull this off?" Jake motioned for my dad to sit on one of the jump seats. Skull gave them a cautious look but followed suit.

"General Allen," I told him. "You'll be helping me when we get up to altitude." I looked over the cargo area and smiled at the pre-loaded crates.

"Son, is this what you got transported on?" My dad leaned forward to look at me, past Jake.

"Sometimes," I told him. "It was even Amelia

flying for some of them. The pilot that greeted us is who she mostly flew with too."

"Man, you don't go halfway on anything, do you?" Skull shook his head again. "You know I've never flown, right?"

Jake laughed. "Hell of a way to start. Stay seated. This flight is nothing like a commercial plane."

I chuckled, pulled out earplugs for my dad and Skull, and handed them over. "You'll thank me."

Another fifteen minutes, while I was sure Amelia was doing a pre-flight checklist, the cargo door started to close. Skull looked like he wanted to bolt, and he sat utterly still. Only Jake and I were slightly relaxed.

I pulled Franco's backpack to sit between my feet. "Operation proposal about to commence," I grinned at Jake.

"You've got style," Jake laughed and clapped me on the back. "Frankie is never going to let me live this down. No date we've been on has been this elaborate."

"The crate is loaded with silk flowers." I went over the plan with Jake while we taxied to the airstrip. "Once we are airborne, I want to line the bay with a row of them. We'll use the night lights, the pilot knows."

"Whatever memories of being on this plane I had will get replaced with this," Jake smiled.

The takeoff was smooth though Skull looked like he wanted to leap out of his skin; my dad just looked thrilled to experience it. When we leveled out, Jake and I sprang into action. We opened the crate and got the bay lined with fake flowers.

From Franco's backpack, I pulled a framed photo

of Amelia in full gear, getting ready for a flight, and one of Damien, Jake, Caleb, and me out by a convoy. I even found rope lights in there, along with some battery-operated candles. Jake was beyond amused, and we got the plane strategically decorated.

I pulled out my dog tags, draped them over the frame, and stepped back to look at our scene. Jake ran his fingers over the photo, shadows dancing in his eyes. I took a knee before the picture, Jake joining me as we each said words silently to our lost brothers.

It wasn't the most conventional way to propose, but a C-17 had never looked so romantic. Skull got brave and unbuckled from the jump seat and came to stand beside me. "Someday, you'll have to tell me more about what it was like to be on one of these while you were over there."

I turned my eyes to his and nodded slowly. He moved to take a knee before the picture and pay his respects to Damien and the man he never knew before returning to sit by my dad. I motioned for my dad to get up, and I walked him up to the cockpit, opened the door, and let him see what it looked like up there.

Franco and Frankie were both enraptured, and Amelia had never looked more beautiful. The woman was born to fly, and it was evident how much she missed it. Frankie was snapping pictures of everything she could.

Franco looked at me and smiled. He knew that Frankie was supposed to be the first to come out once we were back on the ground. The pilot knew as well. We were heading toward Mt. Rainier, where they would do a fly-by purely for the scenery and then return. Flight time was about an hour, which was all I needed. My plan was working perfectly.

My dad and I returned to the cargo bay, and I asked if Skull wanted to see upfront, and he gave a slight nod and allowed Jake to lead him up this time.

"I'm so proud of you," my dad yelled.

I tugged his earplug out. "Thanks, Dad. It's not as bad when you are up here. It's louder at takeoff and landing."

A few minutes later, Jake and Skull came back, Skull immediately strapping in with a slight smile on his face. I felt the plane turning and went over what I was going to say when it came time. I still hadn't figured that part out yet.

Jake grabbed the pictures so they wouldn't slide off and break, and we held them. My dad stuffed his earplugs back in when we started to descend, and my heartbeat kicked up in speed. I know the length of time was probably fifteen minutes, but it felt like two seconds before the tires hit the runway.

The engines were screaming as we slowed down, and then the volume dropped as we taxied back to the hanger. I got up, set the pictures back in place, and stood there. Jake motioned for the others to unstrap and then had them line up behind me, our new squad.

I saw the cockpit door open and knew Amelia would be doing a post-flight check with Captain Scott. Frankie appeared, her face transforming to one of absolute disbelief, then changing to pure joy. She snapped a series of photos and then came flying down to us to take up a good position to get pictures.

Franco came down next. His face was beaming with a broad smile, and he came to stand next to me. We waited for another five minutes before Amelia appeared. She wasn't facing us yet; she still faced the cockpit.

The moment she turned, her entire body stopped its motion as she took it all in. I'd done it; she hadn't expected this at all. Every last damn thing I'd survived brought me to this moment, and I'd do it all again for this right here.

Amelia's fingers fluttered over her mouth as she tried to cover her surprise. Captain Scott helped her and moved off to the side as she slowly approached me. Her eyes fell on the two pictures and flew back to mine.

"Amelia, on one of these beasts, is where I first laid eyes on you, and I wasn't the same since then. You turned me down and haunted me. You were easily the most beautiful thing I ever saw over there, and I pined for you like a lost puppy. When you walked back into our lives, I vowed to myself not to lose my opportunity again. Do you know the reason I call you Wings? It's because you give my heart wings to soar, and when I falter, you swoop in and save me. You are a warrior and the wings that allow my heart to fly. We've come so far, endured so much, and somehow still managed to find the strength to love. Will you do me the honor of marrying me?" I got down on my knee and held out the ring.

"You know what?" She moved a few steps closer, and I saw the tears. "I think maybe this time I won't turn you down, Boomer."

"Is that a yes, Mom?" Franco asked, confused.

"Yes," Amelia's voice came out strong. "Now, it's

my turn. I'm fully in remission," she announced and held her hand out for me to slide the ring on her finger.

My heart stopped for a moment, and then I crushed her to me and swung her around, whooping like crazy. Only Frankie didn't look surprised by that news. Something I'd give her hell for later. I was too damn happy right now.

"Is it my turn now?" Franco looked at his mom.

She nodded at him and moved to stand next to me. I gave my attention to Franco, who stood before me looking unsure. "Speak from your heart," Amelia told him.

"Okay. Darius, I love you, and I want to call you Dad. Will you adopt me?" Franco turned his giant eyes that were all his dad on me.

I swallowed because if I didn't, I was going to sob. "Nothing would make me happier, Franco. If that's what you want, that's what we will do."

"You guys, I'm still full of pregnancy hormones. You're killing me!" Frankie cried as she snapped pictures. "You're in so much trouble for not telling me any of this, you boys."

Chapter 51

One year, two months, one week, and four hours after I proposed, I was getting married. Amelia had reconstructive surgery; that was her one wish for the wedding. She was still in remission, and the doctors told her she might not be able to have another child, but it was possible. I would have given her the moon if I could have.

She'd had them remove some eggs and requested me to donate sperm on the chance that she couldn't, and we would find a surrogate. She was adamant that she wanted a child with me, a brother or sister for Franco, and another cousin for Frankie's brood.

Frankie was about to pop with her fourth child. It wasn't a bad thing. My world was full of life and so much love that my past seemed far removed. Even if the memories surfaced at odd times, they didn't hold as much power over me as they used to.

Both Jake and I had taken significant steps in that regard. I attended PTSD meetings with him now, and on the rare occasions that something surfaced, we banded together and got through it. Each loss we survived, we voiced it, aired its horror, and what triggered us until those triggers became less potent.

I saw clearly how much our pasts define who we become in the future. I witnessed it with my parents and each person in my life. We weren't solving the world's problems, we were simply healing the world one person at a time, and I still believed that had a ripple effect.

Amelia and my dad wanted to see a traditional wedding, so we did that. And as I stood up at the altar waiting for the queen of my heart, I exhaled the lingering thoughts of wishing my mom, Caleb, Trigger, and Damien could be here with us.

Because they were, DC and Franco were evidence of that. With Jake and Skull standing up here with me, I felt settled. My dad walking Amelia down the aisle toward me was perfect. Franco and I sang Amazing Grace, and my dad cried with joy.

Later, when Frankie went into labor at the reception, I couldn't help but smile. I spun my wife around the dance floor, DC, Franco, Izzy, and William next to us, and my dad, the child whisperer watching over us for any mishaps.

Something good came out of that damn war; she was married to me now. That night, with our house full of kids, we came together as a married couple, trying to be as quiet as possible. It wasn't easy.

"I'm the happiest I have ever been in my life, Wings," I kissed Amelia's neck.

"Ditto, Boomer." Amelia's fingers traced the scars that remained. "It's everything I hoped for; I have to admit that. I knew you'd get around to it eventually, and it kept me going."

"Well, now we are going to keep practicing until we can add a kid to the team that Frankie's creating," I promised. "No matter what happens, what we have is all I will ever need. Everything else will be a bonus."

"I think after you graduate and join Skull in the clinic for troubled youth that he thinks should partner with the gym, *then* it will be perfect. You'll have accomplished what you set out to do all those years ago," Amelia amended. "I'm so proud of you."

There was that heart-exploding feeling again. I rolled over and lay on top of Amelia. "I love you."

Epilogue

On our second anniversary, we were at dinner when we received the call that our surrogate had confirmed that the pregnancy was viable. I burst into tears and said a silent prayer to all our guardian angels to watch over this baby. I was going to be a dad.

Amelia had opened a business flying small planes for people wanting to charter scenic flights, and I was working with the Knights of Dawn and Skull's gym counseling youth on the wrong path and those trying to stay off the wrong direction. Skull taught them self-defense, how to channel their anger, and instilled confidence in them. Together, we showed these kids that they didn't have to be victims of circumstance; they could find a way around it. The life I had thought was whole when I got married just blossomed into something more with a baby on the horizon.

Its creation might not have been traditional, but that created life would never lack love; I could hardly contain it all. We quickly spread the word and left the restaurant in a rush to join our family for an impromptu celebration.

Franco was over the top happy, and both he and my dad cried right along with me. Izzy wasn't sure what to do with my tears, and she curled up on my lap and hugged me while Scarlett patted my leg.

"These are happy tears, girls. I'm happy," I slid down to the floor to play with them.

Franco and Frankie smothered Amelia with hugs and kisses, and I looked around the room at something that caught my eye. I could swear that I saw my mom clapping her hands in joy, Damien and Caleb's arms around her, with Trigger next to Caleb.

It was a thought that brought peace to my heart. "I never stopped fighting," I whispered to the ghosts.

"And you won, baby," my mom whispered back in my head.

Resources for Veterans

DoD Safe Helpline
is the sole secure, confidential, and anonymous crisis support
service specially designed for members of the Department of
Defense community affected by sexual assault.

www.safehelpline.org

877-995-5247

SAMHSA: Substance Abuse and
Mental Health Services Administration

www.samhsa.gov

1-800-662-4357

www.988lifeline.org

Call or text 988

www.veterancrisisline.net

dial 988 and press 1

or text 838255

www.crisistextline.org

text HOME to 741741

www.ingramcontent.com/pod-product-compliance
Lightning Source LLC
Chambersburg PA
CBHW060306100726
47907CB00002B/302